DERAILED IN CHANCEY

3

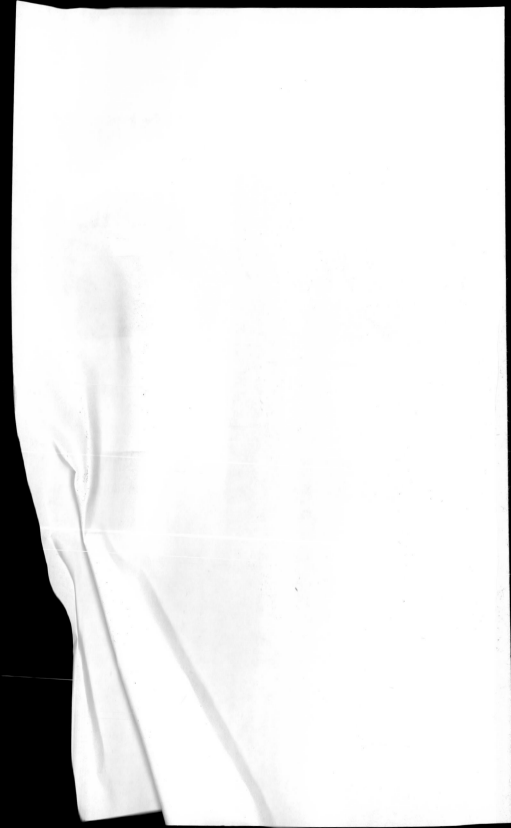

DERAILED IN CHANCEY

3

KAY DEW SHOSTAK

August South
PUBLISHING

ISBN: 978-0-9962430-4-9

Library of Congress Control Number: 2016902948

SOUTHERN FICTION: Women's Fiction / Small Town / Railroad / Bed & Breakfast / Mountains / Georgia / Family

Text Layout and Cover Design by Roseanna White Designs
Cover Images from www.Shutterstock.com

Published by August South Publishing. You may contact the publisher at:
AugustSouthPublisher@gmail.com

In Memory of Darla
I miss your laugh.

CHAPTER 1

"She's a skank." My teenage daughter, Savannah, throws her opinion into the back of the mini-van along with her pillow and purse. Early morning sunshine does nothing to warm the frigid air of North Georgia in January.

I'm dressed in a well-worn, Walmart special sweatshirt and pants, tennis shoes hastily laced, and an old jacket thrown over all that, so mixing with the other parents picking up the youth from their ski trip is not in my plan. After opening the back door of the van for Savannah, I step back beside the van and out of sight, I hope.

My eyes scan the church parking lot for my youngest child, Bryan. This was his first retreat, and he's so young, only eighth grade. However, only a wasteland of pillows and suitcases and barely ambulatory kids are spotted in my search.

"Some help here, Mom?"

"Oh, okay." Savannah is trying to make room for her huge bag, but there's a case of Coke and two bags for the church clothing bin that need to be moved. Head buried in the back of the van I ask, "So, who's a skank?"

"Bryan's girlfriend."

"Brian Cooper? But I thought he was going out with your

friend, that tall girl. Don't you like her anymore?"

"No, not Brian Cooper. Our Bryan."

"Our Bryan? Our Bryan doesn't have a girlfriend."

Then Savannah turns and points. I follow her lead, and there at the back of the bus are a girl and a boy leaning against the bus, no—correction—the boy is leaning against the bus and the girl is leaning on the boy. Body to body. The boy looks an awful lot like my son, but that's impossible. The girl has her forehead pressed against the boy's forehead, and the boy's arms are clasped behind the girl. The boy's arms are actually lying on the girl's hips. Then, because he probably feels the double-potent laser beam I'm shooting at him, the boy looks at me. Bryan looks at me.

He pushes the girl away and comes running across the parking lot—scared and confused. Okay, wait, that only happened in my mind. In reality, he looks away from me, back to that, that girl—and they laugh. You know, not a birthday party laugh, not a Saturday Night Live laugh, a secret, personal laugh. You know.

"Yeah, I wondered if I should call to warn you." Susan appears at my shoulder and my head rotates toward her. The only thing that could take my eyes off my son and his little friend is the person who assured me this ski trip was a good idea. My used-to-be-friend who is responsible for this freak of nature happening.

"I told Mom she's a skank," Savannah sighs, like the world-weary woman she is at sixteen, and sits on the edge of the van's back opening.

Susan pulls out her ponytail holder and then redoes her pony tail. "Brittani is not a skank."

"Brittani? Is that the name of that, that *girl* lying on my child over there?"

"Here they come," Savannah warns.

This time I have no trouble picking Bryan out of the crowd. When did he start walking like that? That rolling swagger kind of walk? It's probably because that girl is wrapped around one of his arms and he's off-balance.

"Hey, Mom."

What, no hug? And when did he learn to make his voice deep like that?

"This is Brittani. Brittani with an 'I.'" He looks at her, and his eyes dilate. You may say that's impossible for me to see, but I'm here to tell you his eyes dilated when he looked at her. Scratch looked—when he *gazed* at her.

"Hi Mrs. Jessup, I'm Brittani Bennett." She sticks her hand out, and her strawberry red fingernails catch my eye. My little boy has a girl laying all over him who paints her fingernails red? And she has eye makeup on, too. The skank.

Susan nudges my arm with her sharp, thin elbow. She thinks I'm going to touch this, this person? But what do I do about her hand out there in mid-air? Manners take over, and I reach out and shake her hand (which is really warm because it's been encased in my son's hand) with only the tips of my fingers.

"Where's your stuff, Bryan? I know y'all are tired. Let's get on the road."

"Sure. It's over here. Let me help Brittani with her stuff first."

"Bye, Mrs. Jessup, sure was nice to meet you." Brittani waves at me over her shoulder. Her jacket is lime green and her toboggan hat frames her tiny face. They walk away, and she wraps her arm around Bryan's again and lays her head on his shoulder. When did he get that tall? Red curls fall down her back and her jeans fit like a glove. Her hips, hips on which my child's arms rested only moments ago, sway like they know what they're doing. *Oh. My. God.*

Savannah stands up and walks around to the passenger door. "Told you" is her parting shot before she gets in and closes the door.

I gnaw my lip. "Susan? What happened on this nice, Christian retreat you forced me to let my little boy go on?"

"I didn't force you," Susan retorts. "I even invited you to go along as a chaperone. But, yeah, you know they have to grow up sometime."

"So, did your eighth grader, big ol' grown up Grant, find himself a skank on the trip, too?"

Susan sighs. "Brittani is not a skank, she's a sweet girl. Bryan is a good-looking boy. Of course girls are going to be attracted to him."

"Yeah, when he's older. Not when he's still in junior high. What happened to the giggling, embarrassed, do you like me, passing notes stage?"

"Well, sometimes they skip right over that. Hey, I have to go make sure the music stuff all gets back in the choir room right. You know how upset folks get about stuff like that. We'll talk later, okay?"

Susan hollers at Grant to put his bag in their car as she tosses him the keys. Grant and Bryan's other eighth grade friends are throwing a football at each other and acting goofy. Why isn't Bryan with them? Instead he's putting Brittani's bags into the trunk of a black car. He slams the trunk, and she walks to the passenger door. He follows her, and I watch as she slithers her hand inside the front of his jacket and rests her hand on his side, then she reaches up and kisses his cheek. Of course, he's taller than her so her breasts *accidentally* brush his chest.

I didn't learn that move until college.

He opens her door for her and then closes it once she's tucked inside. Curse the day I thought teaching my son manners was a good idea. He's a walking marshmallow headed straight for the fire.

As the car passes I watch Brittani and a girl who looks like an older sister chattering and laughing. Brittani sees me and waves like we're best buddies.

My mouth won't seem to close.

My teeth are cold.

He's humming. There was no fight about Savannah claiming the front seat. No complaining about lack of room for his stuff. Now he's sitting in the seat behind me, his head leaned back, his eyes closed, and he's humming.

Savannah snarls, "Shut up, Bryan. We all know you're in love, do we have to hear the soundtrack, too?"

"Sure, sorry."

Sure, sorry? Just last week he would've reached up and yanked her hair or at least stuck out his tongue in her direction.

And where did that stupid smile come from?

Chapter 2

"Do you realize how many bookings we have for January and February?" Laney calls from the B&B office off the kitchen as we push inside the front door, loaded down with suitcases and pillows.

"No, do not lie down on the couch," I direct to Bryan who dropped everything and is lumbering toward the couch. "Here, take your stuff upstairs. You can lay down up there."

Savannah is already trudging up the stairs. "I'm sleeping all day. Don't wake me up."

Bryan mumbles agreement, but I see him check his cell phone and smile. It's that girl. I know it is. Stupid Family Plan that made getting him a cell phone seem like a reasonable move.

"Did you make coffee?" I ask Laney. She doesn't answer, but the red light on the coffee maker and the rich aroma that welcomes me into the kitchen say she did. "So, what were you yelling about when we came in the door? And what in the world are you doing up so early? But mostly, why are you here?" With my cup of coffee, I lean against the door jamb in the B&B hall.

Laney is seated in the only chair in the tiny room that used to serve as the laundry room. However, as we discovered in our move last summer, our washer and dryer wouldn't fit in it, so our laundry room is in the basement. This worked out fine since we needed a place for the computer and bed and breakfast stuff. Still can't believe we moved and opened a B&B in the same few weeks. I hate small towns and the people that run them.

"I'm up so early because I was headed down to pick up the girls from the ski trip, but Susan called and said she'd drop them off at the house," Laney explains. "It sure is handy having her for a sister. And since I was already dressed, figured I'd come up here and take a look at things. Have you looked at how many bookings we have for the weekends in January and February?"

"Seriously?" Over her shoulder I see the color-coded calendar. "I know we took a bunch of calls over the holidays. Maybe they got the memo about us changing our name from Trackside Delight to The Crossings."

"I don't know, all these men coming up here to watch trains might've liked thinking there was a possibility of a little delight trackside. The Crossings sounds so hoity-toity."

"You mean, classy?" I say. "You know it's a better name. The Crossings, a Railfan B&B. I'm getting a cool sign painted up. And, before you think I forgot, I called the registrar's office and changed the name on the paperwork. You're not the only one who knows how to get things done." Laney is full of energy and ideas, which is great in a business partner, but I've discovered it has to be reined in or, well, or you're running a B&B with a bordello-sounding name.

Laney's mascara-laden eyelashes flit up and down, and she's chewing on her lips. Great, she's thinking. Last time she thought this much she ended up in a gambling scandal that almost put her in jail. Instead, she made a ton of money and gave loads to the town.

"You know, we're like a success." She swirls the chair around, and I step back just in time to miss getting hit by her knees. Laney's eyes are not only made-up, she has on pink lipstick, her mass of black hair is pulled back in antique-looking silver combs, and her gray sweater is nice enough to wear to church. How does she do that this early in the morning? Of course, maybe if I had that body I'd be inclined to dress it up.

"We're not exactly a success yet," I counter. "What if all these people come here and don't like it?"

She waves her hand at me and swivels back to the computer. "Now that I'm not the Chancey City Treasurer, I'm going to concentrate on our business. I bet some of my poker luck rubs off, don't you think?"

Laney no longer serving as the town treasurer is directly related to her poker scandal. Just my luck she's shifted her focus to The Crossings. "I've got *so* many ideas and can't wait to try them." She closes the calendar on the screen and pushes back her chair. "I'm starving. Let's go to Ruby's."

I sweep a hand down my sweat suit, Vanna White style. "Look at me. I can't go out in public."

"But you've already been out in public picking up the kids. Come on, we've only got two more days until we're back in the midst of high school drama. Do whatever you need to do to yourself, and let's go." Laney pushes past me and heads down the hall, away from the kitchen and dining room. "I'm going to pull the sheets off the beds in the Orange Blossom Special and the Chessie rooms. Those are where Hank and Shelby were supposedly sleeping, right?" She turns and nails me with wide eye innocence, "Only *you* would have your father-in-law and your husband's ex-wife hooking up under your roof. You are one to keep an eye on, dear Carolina."

"I had nothing to do with that." A shudder involuntarily expresses my disgust. "They're gone and Etta is off to her beach house. Believe me, I will never think of a good old-fashioned family Christmas the same. I'm going to get changed."

In the kitchen, my coffee mug finds a place in the sink full of dishes. Someone needs to unload that dishwasher. That was one good thing about Shelby and Hank's affair coming to light:

her guilt spurred her to clean. Jackson's mom, Etta, left the day after Christmas to go clean out what she wanted from the house where she had lived with Hank for forty-six years. With recently inherited money, she'd purchased a beach house on the Carolina coast, and without malice, she'd told Shelby she could have Hillbilly Hank. That's not a slam, that's his alter ego and star of his successful book series. Well, successful on the senior citizens tour. Hank seemed a little shell-shocked at first, but by time he and Shelby left they were planning on expanding out of the South with his talks. They had a whole itinerary of Midwest nursing homes and senior citizen groups to visit.

On the stairs, headed to my room, I pause, and my hands act as scales. "Let's see: beach house or nursing home tour? Couldn't happen to a nicer person, that Shelby." Literally, she was so nice I'd wanted to throw up for a solid month.

Talking from Bryan's room reaches me at my door. A step takes me to his closed door and although I can't hear words, I can hear his tone. Oh, yeah. That girl. Another involuntary shudder runs through me. Bet Laney knows who this Brittani girl is. What was her last name?

"Bennett, yeah, Beau's niece. Why?" Laney pushes the door to Ruby's Café, and the warm smell of baking and coffee washes over me. Two more days of Christmas vacation means two more days of empty seats at Ruby's. On Thursday everything will come back to life in the mornings. I haven't been here since before Christmas except to dash in to pick up muffins for home.

A couple farmers sit at a table, and Flora and Fauna, old maid sisters, are sharing a booth with a couple women their age. Other than that, the place is empty.

"No gamblin' allowed in here. Just think you ought to know." Ruby leans on the back counter and cocks her head in mock innocence at us. Well, not really at *me*.

"And here I was just betting Carolina you'd be sweet and welcoming this year." Laney flips her hair and juts her chin at me. "Ruby says there's no gambling here, so I'll have to pay you later cause you most definitely win. She's mean as ever. Let's sit up here by the window, too cold back there."

"Hey Ruby. Hey Libby," I call. "Looks empty without all the Christmas decorations, doesn't it?" Being new in town, avoiding decades-old feuds is essential, so being full of good-natured greetings comes in handy. Ruby and Laney haven't liked each other since Laney stole Ruby's daughter's boyfriend in high school. The fact that Laney married him and they now have two daughters in high school doesn't mean a thing. A feud is a feud is a feud.

Don't you just love small towns?

Libby Stone gets to our table just as we sit down. "Coffee?"

"Yes, please. So, how are things with the newlyweds?" I ask as we push our cups toward her.

"Forrest is beside himself having his momma and daddy together. You know they divorced when he was only a baby, so this is all new to him. Cathy and Stephen seem happy, but his mother is fit to be tied. She keeps making snide comments, and you know Cathy's mouth. I may be her mother, but that girl hadn't got a lick of sense when it comes to keeping her mouth shut. And Stephen... Well, never mind. What kind of muffins can I get you girls?"

Laney leans forward. "Oh come on. What about Stephen? You know neither one of us thinks he's half good enough for Cathy."

Libby's bones settle, her shoulders drop and after a long sigh she sets the coffee pot on the edge of the table. "He thinks he's way too good for her. He bosses her around and we all know he thinks he's God's Gift to Women. She says she can keep him happy. Lord knows, I don't even want to think about that." Libby's shoulders tense, and she shakes her short gray hair. "Muffins?"

Laney nods her head and smiles. "Well, us cheerleaders have our skills when it comes to keeping a man happy. I bet—"

"That one on the sign. The new one. Door County Cherry Chocolate." My apologetic grin does nothing to ease the transition in the conversation, but seriously? Who knew being a cheerleader in a small town was a lifelong calling?

"Laney?"

"Oh, I'll take one of those, too. Is Door County around here? It doesn't sound familiar."

Libby waves at some folks coming in the front door. "No, it's up in Michigan or Wisconsin. Ruby's daughter and her husband went up there for a couples retreat last week and brought back all this stuff made with Door County Cherries. They're real good, tart but sweet. I'll be right back." She scurries over to the new arrivals and begins pouring coffee.

The coffee is strong and hot and smells heavenly. "I almost forgot about Cathy and Stephen eloping, with everything else that was going on over the holidays. Maybe having a wife at home will keep him from eyeing our daughters at school." My lip curls, and my mouth sours. "The creep."

Laney raises an eyebrow. "Me and Jenna had a talk about that. I asked her if she and Savannah had really tried to lead him on to get him to leave the younger girls alone. You're going to love this. She said it was all Cathy's idea."

"What?"

"Yeah, he got Cathy pregnant their senior year of high school when she was the head cheerleader. The way I figure it, she decided being off at college and then coming back here to teach might stir up some old memories. So, I think she wanted our girls to get his motor running and then she'd offer him the real

17

deal—his very own cheerleader every night. I know she saved all her old uniforms and she does learn the cheers each year working with the team. You gotta admire her tactical planning skills."

"No, I don't! She used our daughters to, let me quote you, 'to get his motor running'? What is wrong with you?"

"Oh, it's all about getting the ring on the finger, and she did it. You know it's a practiced art." Laney's cynical look melts into a smile as Libby returns with plates for each of us. "Thanks, Libby. They look divine!"

Buttery yellow muffin surrounds jewels of deep red and chunks of melted chocolate on the cornflower blue plates. My mouth twists into a frown. *Seduction as a 'Practiced Art'? Just how early do they start practicing?* "So, you know this Brittani, with an 'I,' Bennett?"

Laney pauses with her knife almost to the bowl of creamy butter. "Wait, did Bryan get himself a girlfriend on the ski retreat?" She nods at my grimace. "Oh, that's what's got your panties in a wad." She sinks her knife in the bowl and lifts it out full. She places it inside her muffin, which she'd torn into, then pushes the sides back together. "Brittani is cute. But then, so is Bryan. I bet they are adorable together, aren't they?"

"No. They're too young. Well, he's too young." I pinch off a bite and hold it. My eyes bore into the piece of muffin, but what I'm really studying is the picture in my mind of them lying against the bus *and* each other.

When Laney opens her muffin the butter is melting. She lifts up half and takes a bite. "Ohh, wonderful. Dark chocolate and the tart berries. This may be my all-time favorite." She chews a minute and then swallows. "They're not too young. They're in high school."

"No, eighth grade. You know, like your nephew Grant. Remember him? *Little* Grant."

Her head tilts. "That's right. Bryan *is* Grant's age, isn't he?" She takes another bite and shrugs. "Okay, so she's in high school, but he's almost there."

Suddenly the dark chocolate is bitter and the cherries only tart. "She's in high school?"

"Yeah, I've seen her when I've worked there in the office." She sits her coffee cup down before it reaches her mouth. "Hey, wonder if they'll still let me volunteer there now that my gambling thing has come out? You know there will be somebody trying to get me out of there. People can be so judgmental."

"She's in high school? He's just a...a..." my brain screams "baby" but I know that's not what should come out my mouth.

Laney fills in the blank. "He's just a teenage boy with raging hormones who's been picked out of the crowd by a hot high school girl. Believe me, he's the idol of every boy at Chancey Middle School today. He's got it made."

After what came out of Laney's mouth, "baby" sounds way, *way* better.

CHAPTER 3

"Why would all these people be coming to the B&B in the winter? Wait a minute." My cell phone slides down under my chin as I try to count out money for the cashier at the Piggly Wiggly. "There." Bags gathered and phone secured, I check to make sure Jackson is still on the other end. "I'm back. Where are you anyway?"

"Up near Dalton. Remember me telling you all about it Sunday."

I ask about his work so he'll think I'm interested, but why would he think I actually listen? "Sure, that's right. Dalton. Okay, so about all these people coming to the B&B?"

"Some of them are just excited about a new railfan place. They try and patronize any new place and help it get on its feet. Then you gotta admit we got some great coverage with that story in *Trains and Travel* last fall. Our ghost story coming out in the October issue didn't hurt. But mainly, when there's no leaves on the trees you can see the trains better. Remember, it's all about the trains."

I turned the key in the ignition, and the van's engine roared to life. "Yeah. I guess I just, well, I just didn't think…"

"You didn't think it would work. You thought it would just

fade away unsuccessful and you'd get your way without lifting a finger. Right?"

Yes. "No. I'm just surprised. I'm going up the hill so I'll probably lose you. Will you be home—" I can't ask him if he's going to be home for dinner. He's probably already told me.

"No, I won't be home for dinner. I'm going straight over to Anniston, Alabama. Just like I told you. I'll be there through Thursday and home Thursday night late—"

My thumb mashes the appropriate button, and he's gone. He doesn't know I'm still sitting in the Piggly Wiggly parking lot and didn't lose him on the hill. It's the first time I've ever hung up on him. Stunned, I put the car in drive, pull onto the road and turn towards home.

We never fought until we moved to Chancey. Never. Now it's all we do. We can't have a civilized conversation because we're mad before we even get started. Last January, my world consisted of my wonderful job at the library in Marietta, and my modern and manageable home in the suburbs with a garage door and privacy fence to dissuade visitors. Jackson worked in downtown Atlanta and was home every night at the same time. The kids had well-staffed schools where professionals handled everything and volunteers were as efficient as the staff. No one bothered me about going to church, planting a garden, having parties, working at the school, carrying my weight in the historical society. Nobody bothered me about anything.

And here in Chancey? They won't leave me alone. Like that stupid retreat. I knew it wasn't a good idea for Bryan to go. And a B&B? Another bad idea I never wanted, but who's left to run it now that Jackson is off traveling with work all the time? Savannah and her acting would be handled by a qualified drama department back in Marietta. Back in civilization. But no. Here I'm forced to chair the Theater booster club. Me, of all people.

Cruising up the hill, I see what Jackson means about being able to see so much farther without all the leaves. Houses, surrounded by old trees now bare and see-through, appear massive with peaked roofs, third stories, and tall windows. After the Civil War, these houses watched over the town of Chancey. Comfortable monuments to the movers and shakers, but Chancey's heyday was just that—a heyday. Now the movers and the shakers are only Chancey royalty who are born here and stay here. No one moves to Chancey.

No one except us.

Brown weeds, which in the summer formed a green tunnel, lie in heaps beside the road leading across the railroad tracks and right up to our house. As I cross the tracks, my head just naturally swings to see if there's a train coming from either direction. Back when I liked Jackson, I enjoyed looking for trains to tell him about. He loved knowing that I shared his passion for trains. But really, all I was doing was trying to make him happy. Way off, an engine is coming out of the mountains on the other side of the river. Jackson sure has a point about the better view. Instead of pulling into the driveway, I turn into the little parking area in front of the house, get out of the car and walk toward the river.

Years ago when the train bridge over the river needed to be replaced, Chancey folk convinced the railroad to turn the old bridge into a walking bridge. Now it lies parallel to the new one with a paved surface, wrought iron fencing, and antique-looking lamps. This bridge is a destination for every railroad-obsessed fan across the country. Searching out this holy grail is what led us to discover Chancey the autumn before last. And then, like in a bad chick flick, the house sitting by the river and the tracks was for sale. One, just one, momentary lapse of my carefully controlled world, and here we are. Don't you hate it when that happens?

Gray-green water lies cold and flat beneath me. In a painting, today's sky would appear unfinished, as if the artist forgot to paint it. Groups of pine trees dot the hills like good patches on a moth-eaten blanket. Bare tree limbs reach and cross as threadbare places the moths have finished with. But in the stillness, there is movement. That black articulated ribbon, smoothly sliding through the brown and red of the Georgia hills. A light advances on the river, and behind it comes tons of steel and coal. It seems as big as the mountains it's leaving, and as it barrels onto the thin ribbons of gray, there's no way the bridge will hold it out of the still water below. Yet, here it comes. Loud, intense, in a hurry, bringing its own wind and heat. Flying past me is car after car full of black chunks of coal. Some of the cars are tagged by graffiti artists from across the nation, trying to tell their story to the world it passes through. And pass it does.

Turning to watch the final car as it crosses where my van drove over the tracks only moments ago, the one person I do not need to see after a fight with Jackson walks toward me.

Peter.

No, not Peter. Peter's mother. Missus. My tongue and mind collide, and my face flames.

"Morning, Missus."

"Carolina, is your middle name, 'Lollygag'? If not, it should be."

Why couldn't we move to a little town with a nice old lady? Surely they're out there, right? "No, ma'am. Lollygag is even worse than the one Mother and Daddy saddled me with. Do you need something?"

Missus wears a gray cape over a wine-colored pant suit. Her boots are gray and match her cape and gloves. Her lipstick is perfect, and the scarf wrapped around her head, both ends tucked in the neck of her cape, contains red, gray, and a touch of blue to add an element of surprise.

"I need to get to Beau's for my hair appointment, but the email from Laney with the update of B&B reservations made me rush out of the house to try and find you since you didn't answer your phones. Any of them." She stops next to the railing and pats her scarf. "Excuse me coming out looking like this, but you left me no choice."

Her eyes raking my jeans, knock-off Lands End shoes, bushy hair and bare lips beg me to apologize for my appearance. Ever notice how pretty people talk down about themselves only to make you feel bad? I won't apologize.

"Shoot, Missus, you look great. Having to get the kids from the ski trip this morning made me rush out like this." My smile is pure apology. Who am I trying to kid? Pretty people cause my tongue to scrape and bow on sight.

She nods her acceptance of my compliment—and my apology. "Now, you have seen the reservation schedule, correct?"

"Correct."

"We must not disappoint any of our guests. Word of mouth is extremely important in a venture such as ours."

"Jackson and I are well aware of that, since this is really *our* family venture."

A gloved hand brushes my words away. "Don't be silly, you are no more qualified to make a success of this than Laney was to be Chancey's treasurer. Everyone's gratitude in my uncovering that disaster has spurred me on to be even more on top of our town's future. You know now that my granddaughter is home in Chancey where she belongs, my interests can no longer wane and be half-hearted. So, don't consider yourselves alone in this venture. Besides, FM promised Jackson we'd be around even more as his schedule causes him to be out of town. His project over in Anniston sounds fascinating."

My brain is taking up all the energy my body is producing right now, filtering through the information in Missus's last paragraph. Words won't form, and my fingers can't move to pull my jacket closed. Only thing that is getting any leftover electrical impulses is my eyes. They blink rapidly.

"I have to get to Beau's for my appointment. Glad we could

talk and are on the same page. This month is critical." She folds her hands together, and her red wine lips move like they are trying to smile. "And speaking of Beau's, it's a shame how you refuse to maintain that delightful haircut and makeover she gave you before Christmas. You really aren't unattractive, and besides, most of our B&B guests are men. So, go fix yourself." She turns. "I'll be back later."

Her silver-blue Lexus crosses the railroad tracks before my muscles receive enough brain impulses to be able to move. My bones are frozen as if they are made of ice. The jog off the bridge and up the stairs doesn't warm me up, but at least the house will be heated.

And loud, apparently.

Even before my foot hits the porch steps, sounds from inside reach me. TV? Music? When the doorknob twists in my hand, and the door swings open, my first thought is that I locked that door when I left. Second thought, something's burning. Third thought – who are these kids?

Teenagers cover my furniture and living room floor. Some are familiar, now that I think about it. Bryan's friends Grant, Jacob, and R.E. are attached to the TV via cords, and apparently they don't like that arrangement because they are shouting at the TV screen. They don't seem to be in pain. Of course that might have to also do with the row of girls behind them, cheering them on. Music blares out of the tiny device sitting on the end table with a lime green ipod stuck in it. Over all, there is a haze of smoke coming from the kitchen. Aha, a direction in which to head.

"Hey, Mom. Why is this smoking?" Bryan stands over my electric griddle. That girl/woman, Brittani with an 'I,' stands next to him holding a dipper full of batter. Bryan nods at me and asks, "Does the smoke mean it's ready?"

"What is going on here?" I ask

Brittani's big blue eyes rake me over much like Missus's

did, but I will not apologize to a teenage prima donna.

My hands smooth down my hair. "Sorry I look so disheveled. It's just cold out there, and I had to run out quick." Shoot, who am I trying to kid? "Are you making pancakes?"

"And bacon. Brittani brought it all."

Oh no, something I hadn't even thought of. *"You drive?"*

Her eyes, skin, and lips all glisten as she laughs and lays a hand on my little boy's shoulder. "No, ma'am, Mama took us by the store, and then dropped us off with everything on her way to work."

For the record, I have never, ever hated the Southern accent more than coming out of that pink lip-glossed mouth.

Stepping to the griddle, just so happens the most direct path lay between the two cooks, I jerk the cord out of the wall. "Griddle needs to cool down a little. So, Bryan, what's going on?"

Love has made him blind, deaf, and really, really dumb. There is no trembling, no fear shows on his face, no regret springs up begging my forgiveness. Nope, he grins.

"We're having an after-retreat breakfast party. Everyone's parents said it was okay."

Brittani steps around me. "Mama says to tell you 'Hi' and she can't wait to meet you and see your lovely home. It sure is lovely, Mrs. Jessup."

"Do I smell bacon?"

"Oh, yeah. I bet it's ready. We've got two pans of it in the oven." Bryan reaches past me to plug the griddle back in. "I'm starving."

"Here." I brush some more oil on the pan and then shrug off my coat. "There's a couple bags of groceries in the car. Bryan, you go get them, and I'll get a batch of pancakes made. The bacon needs a couple more minutes."

Brittani takes my coat and follows Bryan out of the kitchen. She's here. In. My. Kitchen. She's definitely a skank with

26

evil intent. Any female that shows up at a guy's house with bacon has bad plans. Bacon is a smart woman's Trojan Horse. Lord knows, I've used it for years to keep Jackson happy.

Chapter 4

"Are they still there?" Savannah asks when I finally remember to turn on my cell phone. It rings almost immediately when I take it out of my pocket. "And why don't you ever answer your phone?"

"Because all the people that call me are bossy and mean."

"Like who?" she demands.

"Never mind." Rolling over I lay on my back, head resting on my magazine. "Yes, they are still here. They are watching back-to-back episodes of something I'm sure I shouldn't approve of, but I can't make myself care enough to interfere. So instead I'm hiding out in my bedroom making inspection tours every fifteen minutes. Where have you been all day?"

"Thanks for asking." Okay, here is a perfect example of why teenage daughters will drive you crazy. She's mad because I didn't check up on her. Last week I was, in her not so humble opinion, 'stalking' her. "I'm at Anna and Peter's house. Peter's invited us and his folks over for dinner tonight."

"I'm not sure I'm up for, well, for…" – shoot, I can't say "being around Peter," can I? – "…being around Missus."

"You know leaving is the only way to get rid of those brats taking over our living room, don't you? Bryan has put up an open invitation on Facebook. Dating that skank has turned him into Mr. Party. Wait."

Voices come through but no words. On the ceiling, orange tinges the purply-blue air. The window towards the river shows tree limbs touched with the winter sun hanging low in the sky. In the mountains, winter days start late and end early with dark gray mountains for bookends.

"Great news, not. Peter says he doesn't want to break up Bryan and Brittani's party so we'll come up there. Apparently he made a huge batch of chili for some other thing but now he's bringing it up there. With cornbread."

"No." I flip over and push my hair away from my face. "No, I—"

"Too late, Mom. Missus *concurs* as she needs to talk to you about B&B stuff. They are loading up things as we speak. See you in a bit, apparently."

My head falls onto the open pages of my *Southern Living* magazine. Why did I not appreciate the gift life had given me when Missus and Peter weren't speaking? Balance existed when they staked out polar opposite positions on most everything. Now they are about as reasonable and balanced as a bee swarm.

"Well, it's time for my next walk through the downstairs anyway," I mumble climbing off the bed. Bryan is our third child discovered to have hormones, and so this isn't my first time at this particular rodeo. However, it is my first tour as Rodeo Ringmaster.

Our oldest, Will, now safely ensconced at the University of Georgia, has only recently come into being the life of the party. Focused and serious, his hormones kept themselves busy with sports and homework in junior high and high school. Savannah was born a teenager, but in Marietta her friends had killer houses with pools and hot tubs and maids so we were relegated to sitting up and enforcing curfew when her hormones surfaced. Now, it seems Bryan wants to change that. Open invitation on

Facebook? Isn't that how serial killers find victims?

On the stairs, cold air rushes up to meet me, and the living room is empty. Well, empty of bodies. It's well over-quota in Coke cans, chip bags, plates of cookies, and socks.

Turning the corner, cold air steadily pushes in the open back door. Through it also comes whoops and hollers.

"Hey, Mom. It's snowing!" Bryan calls as I step onto the deck.

Sunlight shoots across the back yard and turns the snowflakes into glitter. The flakes swoop, dive, twist and twirl, preening in the spotlight. The dark clouds above us act as a ceiling and heighten the intensity of the light shooting from the narrow strip of sky the sun has found between the clouds and the mountains.

Stepping into the slanting light is like walking into a lit snow globe. Flakes the size of dimes cover the deck and railing so I gingerly walk to the edge where Bryan meets me. In the slice of brightness where the sun isn't blocked by the house or the trees, my youngest looks up with bright brown eyes and pink cheeks. "Isn't this great?" He turns and joins his friends even as the stage begins to dim with the disappearing sun.

They run and swirl and laugh and call to each other—in my yard. They've been here all day—in my house. My heart squeezes. All I've done is complained and sulked around carrying my burden. My burden of a child with friends. A child who wants his friends to come to his house. A child whose sweetness I don't deserve.

"How does a snow fire sound?" I ask.

They yell, and there's even a clap or two at my suggestion. Bryan runs straight for the shed where our wood is stored. Wait. Has he done this without Will or Jackson? He probably needs my help. My feet don't touch the grass before I stop. Brittani stands by the shed, holding the door open for him. Nope, he doesn't need me. Check that. He may need me, but he doesn't want me.

But then I guess that's when our kids end up learning the most.

"Anna, you haven't stopped smiling since Christmas." Across the table from me, the petite girl nods.

Newfound confidence fills her voice. "It's like a dream come true, seriously. The other night I was watching a Lifetime movie, and it didn't even compare to my story. Coming here to find my family and then not telling anyone who I was. And then, well, you know. The girls kidnapping Gramissus. Wasn't that just like something you'd see in a movie and say, 'That wouldn't happen'? And yet it did."

"Wait, what did you call Missus?"

Peter stops behind his niece and strokes her hair. "Granmissus. She kept saying either Grandmother or Missus, and that's what it led to."

With a look to my left, the softness settled on Missus' face catches my breath. The son she's idolized and the granddaughter she never knew fill her eyes.

Anna reaches a hand out and covers Missus' hand. "All's well that ends well, right? I know this is what Mama would've wanted."

Any mention of Anna's mother brings pain. Given away at birth when Missus found herself pregnant from a fling while her husband, FM, was in Korea, Anna's mother ended up with much older parents. A teen drug addiction, then the death of her parents when she was in her twenties left her on her own with her own baby daughter. Her heart, weakened from the years of drugs, led to complications and pneumonia and her death less than a year ago. Anna arranged to get to Chancey, one of the only clues she had about her mother's birth family.

Peter shakes his head and then turns to look out the back doors. "They've got a good fire going now."

"Thank goodness you showed up when you did. Bryan did not need his mother coming out to help him build a fire. Did you meet Brittani?"

"Oh, yes, I met Brittani. She's quite cute. Reminds me of her Aunt Beau." Peter grins and says, "You know Beau was a beauty queen back in the day, right?"

A picture Laney put in my head about Beau and her runner-up being found together, only in their sashes, makes me jump out of my seat. I lean my face forward to hide my red cheeks. "Yeah, I know."

Missus clicks her tongue against her teeth. "Of course you know. That Laney Connor can't keep her mouth shut. I'm sure she filled you in on all the sordid details."

FM comes down the hall where he'd been changing out a bad outlet in the Chessie room. He enters the kitchen with a whistle, twirling a screwdriver. "Let me tell you, that was quite the scandal, wasn't it?"

"What? What is it?" Anna and Savannah both pound us.

Missus glares at her husband while I begin bustling around the kitchen. "Is the chili ready? Peter, tell the kids we're eating soon. Savannah, where's your entourage tonight?"

Savannah pauses, then huffs at how childish she finds us all to be. "Okay, I'll just ask you about Miss Beau later. Uh, everyone's out at the Connor's watching movies."

All four heads turn to Savannah sitting at the far end of the table. Her dark hair is pulled up into a messy bun, tendrils fall around her face, but not enough to hide her downcast eyes. Although, now that I think about it, she doesn't look like she wants to hide, and after a moment looking down, she tosses her chin up and bats her eyes. "I'm playing hard to get."

Peter rolls his eyes for all men everywhere, and FM chuckles.

Missus asserts, "About time," with a little slap on the table for emphasis.

"You?" is the thought that materializes audibly from my mouth.

"Yes, *me*. Aren't we eating? I'm starving."

Anna shakes her head as she stands up. "I'd have given anything to have all the friends you have in high school. I wondered why you were hanging out with me all day."

"Anna!" Savannah squawks. "You're my friend. I'm not hanging out with you because…because…okay, maybe I am."

Now I'm rolling my eyes. Why does she have to be so honest? I set a tray of Styrofoam bowls on the table. "Savannah, that's not nice. Now take these out to the kids. Tell them they can come eat in here if they're cold. Anna, can you take these spoons? Here's some napkins and crackers."

"Mom, Anna and I are not wrapped up in all that 'just be a nice girl' stuff from your generation. We prefer the truth. Right, Anna?"

Anna escapes out the door, but Missus nails the tall, honest one related to me. "You can call it whatever you may choose, but it is plain old rudeness and lack of overall manners."

Savannah's shoulders jerk her back in the face of the stern-voiced older woman standing with hands on hips before her. And just like that Savannah realizes she's been kicked off Missus' throne. A true heir has shown up.

The queen is dead. Long live the queen.

Isn't this when all the bad stuff starts in the fairy tales?

Chapter 5

When the kids finally went back to school on Thursday, I tried to miss them. Really, I did. But sun broke through the clouds, filling the house with a blue winter light. No bass from an upstairs CD player vibrated through the living room so, with the kitchen window cracked, the mellow chimes hanging on the deck could be heard. My cup of coffee and I chose a seat in the rocking chair where the kitchen mess couldn't be seen.

Besides they'll be home this afternoon, right?

Sitting and drinking coffee can't last long. A full house of B&B guests arrive tomorrow. We don't know how they heard of us. Things were so hectic over the holidays that we didn't make the careful notes we'd decided we'd get when folks called. So, no chitchat based on prior knowledge, but it will be okay. Obviously, they're here for the trains, railfans they're called, and that's all we need to know. Jackson will be here tonight, and maybe he'll recognize their names if they're from one of the model rail clubs he's been involved with.

Jackson. We've not talked since Monday when I hung up on him. He's called, and the kids have answered. (Sometimes even without me telling them to answer, after a quick check of the caller id.) My cell phone died, and I haven't recharged it.

It's been busy here, you know. Thinking of him coming home tonight makes it kind of hard for me to breathe. The quiet finally allows my mind to go where I've managed to stay away from. He said the "D" word at Christmas. Divorce.

That's not even a possibility. At all. Probably he was just upset because of what all was going on with his mom and dad and Shelby. Probably. He's back on the road now, and I'm sure things look better for him. Taking all those days off at Christmas might not have been a good idea. Too much time for him to think. What is it about living here that makes us both *think* so much? Is it the space? The nosy people who ask nosy questions? Back in the suburbs we just didn't think this much. That doesn't sound like a good thing, but we were happy.

At least I think we were happy.

Cold coffee and a glance at the clock make me finally get up. Tightening the tie on my robe, I shiver at the cold air blowing in the window, but it feels so fresh I leave it open. Maybe being cold will make me clean faster. It's not a big mess since after the chili and cornbread evening, Peter and Anna gave it a thorough cleaning. One thing I have to say for these Chancey people, they like coming up here so much they always do more than their fair share. Most of the time they bring the food and do clean up. Guess they realize if I had to do it all, no one would ever get to come here. Not sure why they all want to come in the first place, though.

The B&B rooms are ready. Laney washed the linens the other day, and throughout the week, I've spruced them up from the full house we had of family and friends over Christmas. I only need to put the new air fresheners in each room. I pick them up off the kitchen table, and the kitchen is officially done.

Winter light brings out the blue in the gray, soft-knit throw in the Chessie room. Around the room, the prints of the Chessie kittens from early advertising by the Chesapeake and Ohio Railroad add a playful and happy feel. Lustrous cream walls also keep the room from being gloomy and gray. Yards and yards of unbleached muslin frame the window, pooling on the floor and even providing a home for a stuffed Chessie cat Susan found at an antique store around Thanksgiving. Vanilla is the scent for this room, obviously.

Just as obvious, the citrus freshener must go in the Orange Blossom Special room. Bright even in January, the room feels like that Florida vacation all those northerners were seeking with a ride on the Orange Blossom Special train. Leave behind snow and cold for bright light, green leaves, and orange sunsets. On the window seat we've added more kitschy pillows to go with the quilt featuring an old map of Florida: with bright colors and figures depicting all those Florida highlights—Southern belles, water skiers, palm trees, alligators, a sun with dark shades, and glasses of good old OJ.

My least favorite of our three rooms is the Southern Crescent room, but it's usually the men's first choice. Reminiscent of a smoking car on a passenger train where dark wood and emerald velvet reign, the feeling is private and classy. Dark wood shutters block the window seat from the outside. A wing chair, complete with a brass lamp and a stack of Trains magazines in a leather binder, beckons to a man's sensibilities. And since most of our customers are men, it works. The scent of bayberry matches this room perfectly—familiar, yet classy. With the freshener stuck behind the leg of the chair, it's out of sight, and the rooms are ready.

The phone rings, as if it picked up that I'm through with my cleaning.

"Hello, The Crossings, a Railfan B&B."

"Hi, this is Aaron Morse, and I made reservations for this weekend. We were wondering the earliest time we can check in tomorrow?"

"Oh, hello. We don't have any guests tonight so you can come as early as you like."

"Great. We'll be there around 10, if that's okay?"

"Perfect. I'll be sure and be here. Gives you almost another full day to watch trains, won't it?"

"Uh, trains? Sure. Okay, sounds good. Thanks. See you tomorrow."

While we are talking, I sit down in the little office and pull up our reservation page. So it's Mr. Reynolds, Aaron Morse, and Carter May Schuster. Hmm, that's an odd name. We must've left out a hyphen somewhere. But it would be weird for a man to have a hyphenated last name, wouldn't it? And with Carter for a first name, it's like he has three last names. What folks will name their kids never ceases to amaze.

Still holding the phone when it rings, I jump, then push the talk button out of reflex.

"Crossings."

"So you *do* still live there?"

Jackson.

"What do you mean? Of course I still live here."

"You've not been avoiding my calls?"

"What? No, the kids have been home, and it's been kind of crazy. I answered it just now, didn't I?" What he doesn't know won't hurt him.

"Yep, sorry. Anyway how are things? Kids went back to school today, didn't they?"

"Yeah, it's nice and quiet. Finished cleaning just now and took a call from our guests who are coming this weekend. They want to check in tomorrow morning."

"Good. I'll be home tonight, but it will be late. Like after ten. I'll just be in the office tomorrow so a normal day. Any plans for the weekend? You renting the house out to a passing carnival?"

"No. Are you?"

"No, of course *I'm* not. So, no high school theater fundraiser or pageant tea or any event where the entire town shows up?"

And what would be my cover for hanging up on him now?

37

"No."

He groans into the phone. "Okay, I'm sorry. I've made you mad again. It's just I am exhausted and really need to rest. I'd also like to spend some time with just you and the kids, okay? Does that make me a bad person?"

"No" jumps out, and then I clamp my lips together. Breathing through my nose allows my mouth to stay shut which prevents me from talking. However, I think he's getting the idea. My breathing fills the space in the conversation.

Finally he sighs. "Maybe you and I can go out Saturday night? Up to Dalton or even go back to Marietta. Dinner on the Square? They'll still have the luminaries up, right?"

When I open my mouth to speak, a big draw of air keeps me from hyperventilating. Breathing only through your nose is hard if your nose is a little stuffy. "Okay, sounds good. Unless a carnival comes knocking. You know I just couldn't refuse a carnival." Oops, maybe hyperventilating wouldn't have been that bad.

"Whatever. I gotta go. See you tonight."

Mashing the end button, I toss the phone onto the nearest stack of papers. Good talking to you, too.

Another quick scan of the upcoming reservations confirms that we didn't make any notes on any of our upcoming guests. We'll be winging it. Sure would be nice to know if they expected anything like a bonfire or how they found out about us. Maybe it's just my librarian habits that make me want to know what's going on. Or at least who's sleeping in our house. What if they're bad people? My kids sleep here. That's never even dawned on me. I bet Jackson hasn't thought of it either, and this was *all* his idea.

With another tug on my robe belt, my feet hit the floor, and I push back the desk chair. "Darn well guarantee he's going to think about it this weekend" is my promise directed at the computer, followed by a stern nod. "Time for a shower."

Chapter 6

"Mom? Where are you?" Savannah's call follows the slamming of the front door.

"Hey, I'm upstairs, but I'm coming down." Following sounds of cabinet opening and shutting, I find her in the kitchen. "Clean sheets on all the beds in the house, even upstairs. Some kind of record, I'm sure. How was your day? Good classes for the semester?"

"We don't have anything to eat," she says as she pulls a spoon out of the drawer and then shuts the drawer with her hip. She peels open the yogurt in her hand and sits at the kitchen table. "Spring play tryouts were announced."

"Already? So what's the play?" With a glass of ice water, I sit across from her.

"*Our Town*? I've never heard of it, but…" she drags out the last word, and her grin definitely comes from more than just the strawberry yogurt. "The lead role is a dream. Perfect for me. Her name is Emily, and she's a teenager at first, then a young married girl and she dies. And then she is even in the play after she's dead. There's like this cemetery scene and everything." Savannah's eyes glow. "It's like *Twilight*, you know, with the vampires or some horror thing, I think."

"Uh, I think you may be a little off. It's not really like that from what I remember."

She finishes her yogurt then gets up to rummage in the cabinets again. "So far I've only seen the scenes Stephen gave us to audition with. And there is definitely a cemetery scene after she's dead. Want some?" Sitting back down, she holds out the open top of the Cheetos bag.

"Sure." I dump a handful of puffy orange Cheetos on the table in front of me. "And, it's Mr. Cross. Not Stephen."

"Whatever. But this Emily part is all mine. Seriously, I'll be perfect in it."

"So, how do auditions work? Do you try for a particular character?"

"Yeah, we had a quick meeting after school. Oh, yeah. Bryan went over to that kid Homer's house after school today, so he didn't need a ride. He said he'll call you to pick him up later."

"Homer? Where does he live?"

"You know, that kid on his basketball team. You gave him a ride home after practice a couple times before Christmas. He lives over in those new houses on the other side of the high school."

"That's right. Wonder if there's a parent home? I don't trust eighth grade boys, even Bryan."

"So, auditions are going to be in two weeks and I'm going to nail Emily. Jenna says she's still going to audition for Emily, but figures she'll end up with something else. Although there really isn't anything else, just old women."

"So you're not trying out for anything but Emily?"

"Of course not. No need to distract me from the lead role. Seriously, Mom, after the pageant I realized acting is my calling. Emily *is* me." She lifts up orange coated fingers in a motion that the obvious conclusion has been reached and the decision made. "Want any more?" she offers before she closes up the Cheetos bag.

"No, but I do want to know what is going on with you saying last night that you're playing hard to get."

She throws the bag in the bottom cabinet and then leans against the counter. Her dark jeans make her legs look even longer and after wiping her hands on a paper towel she pulls the sleeves of her gray shirt down over her hands, then crosses her arms. "Just that everyone takes everyone else for granted here. Have you noticed that? They all know everything about each other. Everyone knows everyone else's parents and brothers and sisters and even grandparents. It's kind of creepy."

"Hand me a paper towel. Okay, but what does that have to do with you?" Using the condensation on my glass of water, I wash my fingers, then dry them on the paper towel Savannah gives me.

"Well, it's like the groups were set up even before they were born because most everyone is related and so there isn't any change or switching around." She pushes away from the counter and goes to look out the back door. "I don't know. It's just different from home. Like me and Ricky are supposed to be together and that's that. Back in Marietta there were so many people everyone didn't seem so stuck."

"Do you feel stuck with Ricky?"

"And Angie and Jenna and Susie Mae. I like all of them, but…" She shrugs and then turns back toward me. "Anna's nice, but she's so in love with the whole Chancey thing that I can't talk to her. She'd give anything to have been in high school here. Being Missus' granddaughter and Peter's niece is like her greatest dream come true."

"Well, she's just never felt like she belonged anywhere."

"I know, I get it. But this place just seems really small sometimes. Even if I don't want to date Ricky, I'm not sure that I won't always be his girlfriend. You know what I mean?"

My head nods slowly. "Yeah, I grew up in a small town. Daddy ran the big car dealership in town, and we owned a houseboat out at the marina where Mother threw parties that were the talk of the town. I never fulfilled everyone's expectations of who Jack and Goldie Butler's only child was supposed to be."

Savannah nods and I see her thinking through the past several weeks when her grandparents' RV was parked in our driveway. "Okay, I can see that. They are a little, uh…"

"Larger than life?" I supply the words.

"Yep. So, that's what I'm trying to do. Control everyone's expectations of me. Not be so predictable. At Chancey High, everything is supposed to be completely predictable."

"Okay, good luck with that, but you were rude to Anna last night. Just because she's nice and trying to fit in, don't abuse her."

"Right, abuse her. Mom, I'm not doing that. She knows I didn't mean it the way you and Missus took it. But I'll talk to her." Savannah picks up her purse and books from the table and starts toward the living room. "I've got to be at the school for the basketball game by 6:30."

"Of course, I've yet to see you cheer at the basketball games. Maybe I'll come tonight. You want some soup and a grilled cheese in a bit?"

"Okay, just holler when it's ready."

Picking up the phone, I dial Bryan's cell number.

"Hello."

"Hey there. Savannah says you walked over to Homer's?"

"Uh huh."

"Is a parent there?"

"Uh huh."

"What time do you want me to pick you up?"

Unlike the other questions this one apparently requires some conversation. Conversation I'm not privy to as the sound barrier implies his hand is over the speaker.

"Can I go to the basketball game tonight? We'll just walk

over there and then Savannah can give me a ride home, okay?"

"You don't have any homework?"

"Nah."

"I guess it's okay then, but you better not have any homework. And what about dinner?"

"Homer's mom said she had some frozen pizzas we can eat."

"Well, okay, I guess. See you at the game." My pause doesn't extract any more communication. "So, bye."

You gotta love conversations with a teen boy playing a video game. Short and to the point.

Chapter 7

Yep. Looks as empty as it does on TV.

One benefit of living in a small town—and believe me, I keep looking for benefits—is the local sports are televised on the local cable network, GTC. Which is why Savannah has been cheering for several weeks now, and neither Jackson nor I have seen her cheer in person. We saw the *real* cheering, you know, at the football games. But at the basketball games, they just do a lot of kneeling on the floor at the end of the court and pounding on it or running on and off the court to do some formation (which rarely works).

Wood polish, sweat, and popcorn bring depth to the scene as the smells mingle with the background noise of whistles, shoes pounding the court, and girls voices yelling about going and fighting and winning.

"Hey, Mrs. Jessup!" yells a girl at the table next to the popcorn machine.

"Oh, hey, Jules." I unwind my scarf as I walk across the half-dozen mats laying in the foyer to catch the slush and yuck from outside before it gets to the gym. "So you run the concession stand here?"

"Yeah, for the theater group." Her light brown eyes are

eager, which belies the disinterested slump of her shoulders. "Somebody's got to do it, and I'm not on the basketball team or a cheerleader." Her lips purse and she shrugs. "And who wants to sit in that crowded student section and get mashed?"

"True, true." My head nods, but my heart knows she'd love to be welcomed in the student section. Of course, being a student is far from the only qualification. "Well, on behalf of the theater club boosters, thank you for your help. Well, I better get on in and see how the game's going, but think I'll have a bag of popcorn first. How much?"

"A dollar. Thanks, Mrs. Jessup."

A tad stale, too salty, and a weird daffodil yellow, the popcorn is perfect. Exactly what it's supposed to be, a fundraiser that tugs at old memories and jaded taste buds. Always sold by a Jules-like boy or girl who sits out in the cold hallway raising money for the bright and beautiful to perform. Kids like Jules are way more in my comfort zone than the three children I birthed. How funny that someone who distrusts pretty, confident people would be mother to three of them. One day the king and queen of Pretty People Land will arrive to correct the mix up and give me the timid, awkward, backstage-working, popcorn-selling people who were switched at birth with Will, Savannah, and Bryan. Sure, I'll miss them, but the world will once again be set right. Right?

The lower bench is empty on this end so I set down my purse and scarf while trying to shake off my coat without spilling my popcorn. Finally I settle on the wooden bleacher and the warmth of the building envelopes me. At the sound of whistles, the players leave the court, and the cheerleaders run out. They turn to face us, and Savannah waves at me before she places her hands on her hips.

The cheerleaders nod their heads in unison. The cheer is good and coordinated right up until they have to move from one place to another. Then things look a little chaotic but eventually they are all in the right clumps, and they start jumping around and lifting the smaller girls up. And up. And, okay, kind of up. One by one the girls slide back to earth, and the crowd yells like it was supposed to look like that. Not a single smile is diminished. Hey, just thought of something—maybe it *is* supposed to look like that. Full of confidence and washed in success, the girls bound off the court to their kneeling positions at the ends, under the goals.

Pounding feet come down the stands behind me, and Bryan plops beside me. "Hey, Mom. Can I have some money to get a coke?"

"Where are you sitting?"

"Up there." He points up behind me to a group of kids pressed into the corner of the stands, against the painted concrete block wall. He grins, and he's not sophisticated enough to tamp his eye sparkle down. "It's the student section. For the high school."

"Let me guess, you're sitting with Brittani with an 'I'? Why are they so far away from the court? Shouldn't they be closer to the actual game?"

He shrugs 'cause he doesn't know or care. It's the Student Section, and he's been welcomed that's all he needs to know. He hands me my purse. "And Grant's mom is sitting over there waving at you. I think she wants you to come over there."

Squinting, I spot Susan, and we make eye contact. A quick nod tells her I'm coming. Grant takes the two dollars, says "thanks," and strides toward the doors. With my coat, scarf, purse and popcorn, I feel like a bag woman moving around the narrow strip of wood between the padded walls and the basketball court.

"You came!" Susan exclaims as she clears a spot next to her. "Put your stuff down there and then sit here."

Finally after all the hellos and arranging of my stuff, I take in my new view. "Ooohhh, we can see the student section from here."

"Tactical maneuvering on our part. Every week or so they move it trying to stay out of view of the TV camera and the Parents section." Susan says. "But we just move to another spot, too."

My eyes rake the moving pile of hair, jeans, and tight sweaters across the game floor. "Bryan is sitting with that—" A jab to my ribs makes me stop and turn to Susan who with expanded eyes is directing me to look behind us.

"Oh, hi, Beau. How are you?"

"Carolina, good to see you. What have you done to my beautiful hair cut?"

My hand flies to my head. "Well, I just don't remember to style it or use all those products. Sorry."

Beau leans over and pats my shoulder. "Sorry? Don't say sorry. I just should've given you a cut that was easier to maintain. You come by soon, and we'll get you fixed up. Okay?"

"Really? That's great…"

Beau cocks her head, and her smooth milky skin and happy red hair play up her deep green eyes. "No problem. Besides, I hear we're practically related what with Brittani and Bryan an item. Isn't that great?"

Susan taps my leg, "Turn around, the girls are back out on the floor."

My quick flash of an apologetic smile to Beau is very quick and accompanied by a "Thank you" as I direct my eyes to the floor. This time the girls do a dance to some hip hop song and they grind and gyrate around the floor to the point of being embarrassing, but when they finish the crowd cheers them again. The Atlanta Falcons cheerleaders doing that bit might be erotic or exciting. This group of girls managed to just make it embarrassing with their jerky moves and different body types. In our old 3,000 strong suburban high school, the cheerleaders all were ranked gymnasts, beauty queens, and dancers. Here they are just an assortment of high school girls, some underweight, some overweight, few coordinated or athletic, in non-risqué uniforms giggling through all the moves. But I know how they look to the other students. How perfect and talented they appear. How charming their lives. How glossy their hair and tanned their legs. Wow, what a delusion we can sell ourselves in high school. I know, because I would've sold my soul to be one of those out on the gym floor in my small-town high school. Where is the devil making offers when you need him?

Susan lifts her chin and voice, "Has any one heard if Ruby's is open tonight?"

She's answered with shakes of heads, and Beau finally responding, "I'll call and see."

"Ruby watches the girl's game on the TV and decides by half-time of that game if she feels like going down and putting on coffee for folks to come by after the boy's game," Susan explains. "But if you call and ask before the end of the girl's game, she gets mad and won't open. We're not allowed to call until the boy's game starts, and only one person is allowed to call."

"Business etiquette here needs its own instruction manual, I swear."

The lady on the bleacher below me snorts, "Part of owning a business in a small town like this is you get to call the shots. No competition means no competition."

Beau snaps her phone shut. "Yep, she's open. Says she heard big news about some power plant or something coming to Chancey and wants to get the skinny on what everyone else has heard."

"Really? A power plant? Chancey?" bounces back and forth in the crowd of women. A couple have tighter lips than normal, including Susan whose husband, Graham, is chairman of the city council. With a nudge of my shoulder, I lean closer to her. "So, what do you know?"

"Been waiting for it to hit. Looks like it's a done deal, and folks are going to have fits," she whispers.

"How can something like this be a 'done deal'?"

Beau leans over our shoulders. "What's Graham know?" And then the echo around us follows suit. "What does Graham say? What's going on?"

Susan presses her lips tight and smiles. "Hey, look, we scored. Way to go, Joe John!"

All eyes turn to the court and hands clap. Then, on the way back down the court, one of our players in his white uniform takes the ball away from the opposing team's player in his red uniform and starts dribbling to the basket, so now people are standing and clapping and yelling encouragement. However, I notice Susan beside me is pushing the buttons on her phone like she's calling in a scoop to the paper about the game. Cupping her hands around the speaker she talks only loud enough for someone paying close attention, like me, to hear.

"They know. It's going to hit the fan at Ruby's tonight." She shoves her phone in her jeans pocket, grimaces at me, and then joins the yelling as our team takes the lead.

So I told Jackson I'd be home when he got there tonight. But Ruby's is a must. Right?

Right.

CHAPTER 8

Poor Hank. He's taking note for the newspaper as fast as he can, but not one thing being said makes any sense. Well, at least the *Chancey Vedette* this week will actually represent what happened, 'cause none of this makes any sense.

Ruby has a coffee pot in one hand, her other hand planted on her hip, and her mouth wide open with lots of words coming out. Words forming threats, challenges, and swears. "If that power company thinks it's going to come in here with all its pollution and greed and ruin, I say ruin, into my home, it's got another think coming." Libby gets her hand slapped when she tries to take the pot of coffee from her boss. "Leave that alone. I'll get to it. More important things here than coffee."

"Not really," I murmur with a glance at my still empty cup. Looking around, it's easy to see who is not here—anyone who could tell us what's really going on. Thinking back, Susan never actually said she was coming to Ruby's. She correctly anticipated the red faces and upset folks that fill the chairs and booths around me. So, with a sigh and a scrape of my fork, I get the last bit of the Door County Cherry Pie. Looks like it's time to go home where Jackson arrived about half an hour ago.

Guess it's time to leave this scene of confusion and

consternation for the one waiting for me up on the hill.

Ruby's old glass door shuts behind me, and my ears fill with the silence of a January night. Clouds no longer trap the glow of the street lights in an orangey fog close to the ground like earlier this evening. Crisp blackness disperses all light so the stars stand out, close and yet so distant. Lack of cloud cover also means any heat left over from the sunny day is gone. Gone from the square are the Christmas decorations and lights. The bonfire circle from the fall is empty; abandoned until footballs fill the air again. Stepping off the path to cross to where my car is parked, my feet don't crunch in the leaves releasing that pungent autumn scent of spice and wood. No, the leaves mush beneath my boots, and the smell is old and muddy. January is to the senses like tofu is to a hungry person. Nothing.

February at least gets the title of cruelest month which works because it *is* cruel to be so close to spring and yet so far from it.

January? Nothing. Even the Super Bowl changed months a couple years ago.

My phone rings as I pull it out to call Susan. Ah, great minds think alike. Susan. "So where are you?" I open with.

"You still at Ruby's?"

"No, just left. Folks were pretty upset, but they really don't know at what. Where are you?"

"Home. Listen, it's not as bad as everyone is thinking. We'll talk later, okay? What I want to know is what's going on with you and Jackson?"

"What?" My purse lands in the passenger seat as I bend to settle in the driver's seat. "What about Jackson?"

"Bryan called here looking for you. He told Grant he needed

to find you 'cause his dad was home, and you were supposed to be there. What's going on?"

"Nothing. He's just been out of town this week and, well, I told him I'd be home when he got home. Nothing."

"Carolina, it doesn't sound like nothing to me. Sounds like Jackson and Bryan both think it's not 'nothing' and, wait, why didn't they call your cell?"

"I turned it off so I could hear...you know, the game and stuff."

A long pause allows us both to think about how lame that sounds.

"I'm going home right now. They can all talk to me as much as they want."

"Good." Another pause says that we have too much to talk about and not enough we want to talk about. At the same time we say, "Okay, talk to you later." With an even more awkward pause, we both hang up.

Most of the houses are dark, and the moonless night makes it feel later than the ten o'clock my phone says it is. Even our house, which usually appears to be a beacon leading planes toward Atlanta's Hartsfield Airport, is dark. On the porch I see a blue reflection that says the TV is on. Good. No big scene to walk in on.

"Hey," I whisper into the dark room, but it gets lost in laughter from the couch. That movie, about the delinquent kid, Ferris Bueler, is on. Again. Jackson and the kids could watch it every day, and I regret I ever wasted two hours on it. Unwinding my scarf and unbuttoning my coat, I watch the kid in the leopard print vest run around stupidly on the screen. At the end of the couch, a quick survey shows a perfect family scene. Jackson sits in the middle with a bowl of popcorn, Savannah sits on one side, and Bryan on the other. None of them acknowledge my arrival. This is not good.

"Hey." This time a wave is added.

"Hey, Mom." Bryan breaks the ice, and Savannah flashes a smile/grimace at me. Jackson just stares at the TV.

After a minute, they laugh again at that idiotic movie, so I step back toward the door to hang my coat and scarf on the coat rack. Then at the door of the kitchen I try again. "Anyone want anything?"

No answer except for Jackson saying, "I love this part."

I review my options as I fill a glass of water from the tap and lean against the sink. Join in and suffer through the rest of the movie about the juvenile delinquent they've seen, and I've endured, about a million times? Join in, but take my book with me and read while they watch the movie? But I'd have to turn on a light, and they'd probably complain. Go to bed and claim the bedroom for myself, stake out territory so Jackson has to decide where he wants to sleep tonight? My heart hurts, and I turn to look out the window at the darkness.

This strategizing silence is something friends have described and we saw with Jackson's folks, but it's never been part of my day-to-day existence. My parents really like each other, and if they fight it happens, ends, and all is well. This, this cold war freezes me on the inside. Everything feels alien and strange. If a way could be found to go upstairs without going through the living room, I know I'd take it. What a coward.

I step from the dimly lit kitchen into the dark warmth of the living room and stand behind the couch. With just a step, my hand could settle on Jackson's shoulder. With just a few words, this ice could be broken. With just a short walk to the chair, I could join in.

"Night, all. I'm going upstairs."

Savannah's head raises, and she turns to look at me, but it's too late to change my mind, so avoiding her look, I head up the stairs.

Tomorrow. We'll deal with all this tomorrow.

Chapter 9

"Hello? Thought I'd stop in and see how things are up here on the hill?"

"Susan?" Laney and I both come out of the kitchen to see Susan popping her head around the front door.

"Sure, come on in. Why aren't you at work?"

Laney echoes me, "Sure everything won't just go to hell without you down there running things?"

Susan smirks at her sister but doesn't come all the way in. "Well, we were just around."

Her "we" makes my eyebrows climb and pulls me on into the living room as Susan moves aside for Graham to also come through the door.

Laney's cocked head speaks as loud as her tight lips and crossed arms.

"Morning, y'all." Graham has on his business clothes like he's supposed to be welcoming us into his office over in Dalton instead of out gallivanting around making drop-in visits.

"What's up? Is everything okay? The kids?"

"Oh, yes, everything's fine. We just, well, Graham just..." Susan steps aside again as if to push her husband forward.

"I just wanted to say 'hi' and, uh, well, that's about it. I had some business here in town this morning, and I mentioned I hadn't seen the B&B, well, The Crossings, for a while. Susan says y'all have a full house this weekend?"

A quick glance at Laney shows she's not moved a bit and doesn't look like she's going to, so with a nod I answer. And wait.

"Okay, well, things look good. What time are your guests going to get here?"

Laney answers, "Supposed to have been here at 10, but they called a bit ago and said they were running a bit late. Why?"

Susan pulls on her ponytail and looks at the floor. Graham shrugs and grins. "Just wondering. Hope it all, the weekend, and stuff goes well. I think we'll drop in and have coffee at Ruby's, okay, hon? I haven't been there on a weekday in forever." One hand on the door and the other on the small of his wife's back, Graham nods goodbye and closes the door behind them.

Through the front window we watch them get in their car, turn around, and cross back over the railroad tracks.

"Did you see what that sister of mine had on?"

"I guess. That was weird, wasn't it? Where'd I leave my coffee?" Back in the kitchen, coffee cup found, I retake my seat. "So, you honestly have never gone to bed angry with Shaw?"

"Susan had on her councilmember wife's outfit. I was with her when she bought it last spring after Graham was named chair, and they had to go to the groundbreaking for the remodeling of the laundromat." Laney, with arms still crossed, joins me in the kitchen.

"Now that you mention it, I haven't ever seen her wearing it. It is kind of formal. So I guess they have a function to go to." I brush off Laney's conversation. "Anyway, Jackson slept upstairs last night, but we ignored each other. Honestly, I don't know when the last time was we went to bed *not* angry at each other."

"What function could they possibly have? Nothing is going on in Chancey. For goodness' sake, it's January." Laney pours the remains of her coffee down the drain. "Nothing happens in these hills in January. I think there's still some caveman hibernation instinct left over up here. I'd call Susan on her cell, but she won't talk with Graham there." She leans back against the counter. "You know, something is going on. I feel it. Damn, being city treasurer was a pain, but at least I always knew what was going on."

My fingers stretch against the table top. Laney wouldn't stop until I told her what was bothering me this morning, now she's got a new mystery to tangle with and mine is old hat. And it really is just that—same ol', same ol'. Husband and wife fighting, not talking. What's new or interesting about that?

The doorbell rings. We both jump and move into the living room. "Must be the guests," Laney says. "Nobody else here rings the bell. Nobody here even knocks."

"Hello, welcome to The Crossings. I'm Carolina, and this is Laney." Trying to keep the frown out of my voice is as hard as not looking the people at the door up and down.

"Hello, Frank Reynolds," the first man says as he thrusts his hand forward. In his other hand is a briefcase, a real briefcase, not a carry-all stuffed with train magazines and timetables. His suit—yes, *suit*—is dark brown, and all this is capped by a very nice tie. Not jerked loose, but tightly in place. One look at Mr. Reynolds, and it's obvious he's use to being in charge. The next person also wears brown, but it's a skirt.

"Hello Carolina, Laney. I'm Carter May Schuster, and this is such a lovely home." She also carries a briefcase, and her brown skirt has a matching tweed blazer. Over her arm is a tailored, deep burgundy coat. "And this is Aaron Morse," she says as she moves away from the open door. "He's the one who made the reservation."

"Hello, I believe I made the reservations with a Mrs. Butler?" His light green eyes fall first on me, then on Laney as he shakes our hands.

"That would be my mother," I explain. "She was here for the holidays. Come in, please. It was me you talked to yesterday."

"Thank you. I'll get our bags after you show us to our rooms." Aaron's blue blazer and khaki pants identifies his role as assistant as much as his kind of shaggy blond curls and lack of briefcase.

His words cause Laney to nod. "Of course. Mr. Morse, Mr. Reynolds, and Ms. May-Schuster, if you'll follow me this way." She leads us through the living room into the dining room and then down the hall. Something is strange about the way she's walking though. Not the direction, but her actual walking, very tight or something.

"Mr. Reynolds, here is the Southern Crescent room for you." He steps out of the hall and into his room, saying, "Thank you. The room is very nice." He quickly shuts the door, but Laney doesn't miss a beat. "Ms. May-Schuster, here you are. The Orange Blossom Special room."

"Oh, just, Carter May. My last name is Schuster. This room is just lovely. I do have some calls to make. I'll leave everything up to Aaron. Thank you, ladies." She shuts her door, and we three remaining turn toward the last open door.

"And for you, Mr. Morse, the Chessie room."

"Please, call me Aaron. That door at the end is the bathroom, I'm assuming?"

"Yes, it is, Aaron." Laney pauses and steps into the Chessie room. "Let me fix this window blind."

I can't see anything wrong with the blind, but Aaron and I follow her into the room anyway.

"So, Aaron." Laney turns, and I see what was wrong earlier, now that she's got her sexy back. Her eyes dip and flutter, and her body dips and flutters as well. Poor little Aaron just swallows and takes a step back. "I take it y'all aren't here to look at silly old trains, right?"

"No, um, no, ma'am." Aaron's earlier energy melts around

us and he tries to regain his footing by looking down at the bed. Then his eyes spring away from there. It would be funny to watch if I wasn't so interested in his answers.

"Well, that's not really, um, ma'am, I'm not sure what all…" Then as he thinks of a lifeline he straightens his back. "I have some calls to make, if you don't mind." He fumbles in his pocket and brings out his phone as proof.

Reminds me of the sweet little blond virgin holding up a crucifix at the grinning vampire.

Chapter 10

"Well, I guess we know why Graham and Susan were out canvassing the neighborhood so early this morning." Laney says this without looking at me because she's busy tapping on her phone. She barely lets the person she's called say hello. "Hey, the folks you and Graham were looking for are here." She hangs up and lays her phone on the kitchen counter.

"Okay, that makes sense, but who are these folks?"

Then my eyes widen and I whisper, "Power plant? No! Here? I mean, at Crossings? I don't want to get mixed up in all that. Everyone at Ruby's last night was fit to be tied. Susan wouldn't do that to us. Would she?"

"Where else would they stay?" We lean toward each other over the corner of the kitchen counter, and the whispering is fast and furious. I guess that explains the awkward look on Aaron's face when he clears his throat.

"I'm just going to get our bags."

Big smiles bounce forward as we straighten up and say, "Sure."

We follow him to the door and offer to help, but he assures us he can handle it.

"Carolina? Laney?" Carter May comes up behind us as we

resume whispering and watching Aaron like a hawk as he gets the three small bags.

"Yes?" We turn, separate, and hide again behind big smiles. "How's your room?"

"It's lovely. You have a beautiful place here. Can you give me directions to a restaurant called Ruby's?"

"Oh, it's easy." I point out the window, "Follow the road down the hill that you came on. At the bottom-"

Laney pushes my hand down. "Silly girl, they can just follow us." She turns to Ms. Schuster. "We were heading down there just now. Are y'all leaving soon?"

"Yes, that's perfect, if you can wait just one minute. Mr. Reynolds is finishing up a phone call while Aaron gets the bags."

"Of course, just let us know." Laney grabbed my hand when she pushed it down, now she pulls on it to lead me to the kitchen.

Back to whispers. "She called Graham, and he told them to come to Ruby's. My brother-in-law may think he can keep all this hush-hush, but not unless he lets me in on it. Get your purse. I'll drive."

In the car, Laney puts on lipstick while she waits for an answer from whomever she called while I was looking for my seatbelt.

"Missus? Meet us at Ruby's in about five minutes. Okay, bye."

"What? Missus? No, you are just stirring things up."

Laney grins a big, shiny pink grin at me. "Hey, it's Friday, and this will be better than happy hour." She watches our guests get in their car and back around to let her out. "They need to hurry. I don't want to miss Graham's face when Missus walks in."

As for Graham's face when Missus walked in, it probably wasn't much better than his look when Laney sashayed (and we know Laney can do some sashaying) in with Mr. Reynolds' arm tucked in hers. I can't say what Graham did when he saw Missus, due to a trip to the ladies' room. (Laney said I didn't have time to go at the house.)

Laney and Missus have a table as near as possible to the movers and shakers table with my spot, the empty one, faced away.

"Thanks for saving me a seat."

"Shhh" seeps from them both.

Libby glides by, pours me some coffee, sits down a muffin I didn't order, and then silently slips to another table.

Dinner theater. That's what I'm reminded of. Might as well have a spotlight on the table with our guests, our co-owner/ sister, and her husband. They are all dressed for their parts, costumed, if you will. They are animated, verbal. No one else in Ruby's is saying a word. Ruby is sitting on one of her own stools staring at Mr. Reynolds. Her face is screwed up like one of those shrunken apple dolls at the county fair. Her sweatshirt is new, bright green, with only one word appliquéd in blue and white stripes, "NO". Must've been all she had time for last night.

Talk at the table flows easily, but nothing important is said. Susan is the only one at the table who looks uncomfortable. When she gets up to go to the bathroom, she gains an immediate entourage.

She turns at the small plywood counter. "What are you all doing here?"

Missus frowns. "We have to go to the bathroom. Now who are those people?"

Laney is next to her sister at the sink and Missus hasn't moved much past the door, which means I've staked out the territory straddling the toilet bowl. Ruby doesn't believe in creature comforts. She'd have an outhouse if the town would let her.

Susan reaches for her ponytail, to pull, but there's not room to raise her arm. "They're business folks who want to meet with Graham."

"It's the power plant, isn't it?" Laney asks.

"If Graham Lyles has sold out Chancey, I'll see him strung up!" Missus threatens.

"Lynching? Really, Missus?" I don't have room to throw my hands up in disgust, so I'm stuck with just rolling my eyes. "You people here take things way too seriously. But, Susan, did you have to tell them to stay at Crossings? You know how this town is."

"I didn't tell them to stay there. Laney's the one that always wants us to advertise. Let everyone know we're here."

"Term limits," Laney mutters. "If it weren't for term limits, Graham wouldn't have gotten my seat on the council, and then none of this would've happened. Of course I say we need to advertise, doesn't mean we want every Tom, Dick and Harry who wants to rip up the town and put in a power plant."

A knock on the door stops us all mid-sentence. At the same time, in those high-octave, Southern belle voices, we all say, "Just a minute."

Then a laugh leaps out of my mouth. "I bet the whole place is just sitting there staring at this door."

Susan bites her bottom lip, then giggles. "Graham probably had a heart attack when y'all followed me in here."

"Look at us," Laney says, pointing at the mirror and then we all start laughing. Four grown women crowded in a cheap, faux wood-paneled bathroom that barely allows one person to turn around.

Missus claps her hand over her mouth, then trying to catch her breath, says, "And everyone from Chancey knows how little this bathroom is. We're going to look like one of the clown cars at the circus when we come out."

Another knock sends us off laughing again. Missus opens the door. There stands Mr. Reynolds and the laughing stops.

"I thought, well, there's only…never mind. Ladies." He backs off and waves us past him. Everyone stares at us as we proceed past the tall, distinguished gentleman in the dark suit. Everyone, that is, but Graham. For some reason his elbows are propped on the table so his hands can cradle his hidden face. Susan slides in beside him, and we return to our table.

Missus turns to find Ruby and points at her coffee cup. "Ruby, my coffee is cold. A warm-up, please." Ruby scowls at Missus and flags Libby to our table and Missus' cup. In mid-stream, the bathroom door opens, and all eyes watch Mr. Reynolds walk to his table.

"So, Graham, let's get on with our tour, shall we?" As his tablemates gather their things and rise, he steps toward Ruby, causing the crevices in her face to deepen.

"What a wonderful place you have here. Have you ever considered publishing a cookbook? The muffins at our table were unlike any I've ever had. If you think you might be interested, please let me know. My wife knows some folks in the publishing business." He hands Ruby a business card, and her mouth drops open.

Words fall out of her mouth like dribbles of water after a trip to the dentist. "Well, now. A cookbook." Her face slackens and her pinched-up, defiant look is gone. Carter May and Aaron both come over to tell her "Thanks," and by time the door closes behind Graham, Ruby is actually smiling.

She hops down from her stool, takes off her apron, and yells. "Closing, folks. Finish up and out with ya. Changed my mind about lunch. I got…stuff to do." She bustles through the kitchen to her office in the back while we all take last swigs of coffee and either stuff our muffins in our mouths or wrap them in napkins to take with us. When Ruby says she's closing, she means it.

Besides, show's over.

Chapter 11

Out on the sidewalk we loosen the scarves we just tightened and slip off gloves we just slipped on. Missus unbuttons the toggles on the front of her evergreen wool cape. "Oh, feel that sun. Makes me itch to get in my garden, and it's only January."

Laney lays her head back. "Makes me want to go to the Friday wine tasting over at Fox Mountain." She flips her head, and hair, back in place. "Why not? You said Jackson is in town, right?"

"Yeah," I say, "but I don't know if he could get off early. Would Shaw be coming?"

"Sure. Missus you want to go? FM around?"

"We can't just go flitting off on a Friday afternoon lark, Laney. Besides, I need to get to the bottom of this mess with this potential power plant. Those mountain wineries are just tourist traps."

Laney laughs, "That's only because you couldn't get one to settle in Chancey."

"Not that she didn't try! Hey, y'all." Peter walks up behind us and puts a hand on his mother's shoulder. "Who's going to the winery?"

"Us," Laney says. "Not your mother. She's busy. You wanna

go?"

"Absolutely. Mother had me looking into all the wineries when she was trying to get one started here, but I haven't been to any of them as a real customer. Where are you going?"

Time for me to bow out. "I'm not going to be able to go. Jackson is in town, and he can't get off early enough, I'm sure."

"So, if we go now we'll be back before he gets home, right?" Laney looks at her phone. "Shoot, we'll be back before the kids even are home from school. Besides," she waggles her eyebrows at me like a challenge. "I drove you down here, so you don't have a way home."

What in the world am I doing, sitting here in the sunshine on a deck overlooking a mountain range, half tipsy—with Peter. Of course, Shaw ended up meeting us here. One of the perks of owning a car dealership, I guess, is no time clock to punch. Laney and Shaw are huddled in one corner of the tasting room at a table for two. From the looks of it, they're tasting more than the wine.

"The walk around the vineyard was nice. We'll have to come back sometime when there are actually leaves, and grapes, on the vines." Peter jerks his head up from where it was resting on the wall behind us. "I mean, we as in a group. You know."

The sun flushes my face. (It is the sun, don't you think?) Him using the word "we" hadn't even caught on my conscience, at least not until it caught on his. "Of course. Jackson would love this place."

Peter smiles and nods, "Absolutely. So Jackson likes wine?"

"No, not really...but, well, the view is so nice."

"Yes, it is."

I will not look to see if he's looking at me. My life is already feeling like a cliché chick-flick. "So Missus had you looking for a winery for Chancey?"

"Yeah, but there wasn't a good location there, so they all settled over in the direction of Dahlonega. Hard to believe these are the same mountains I was raised in. Wineries, tourist trains, whole towns making believe they are in the Alps. Things do change, don't they?"

My nod echoes his, and his words fade in the bright sunshine. Quiet settles over the hazy, blue mountains, and there's not even the usual bugs to challenge it. How peaceful.

Laney's voice registers as she and Shaw join us out on the deck. "Y'all dozing out here?"

"No, not at all," we protest, but the way we both jumped belies our words.

"Did y'all get some of that Riesling? It was okay, kind of sweet." She pulls the arms of her sweater down. "It's a little chilly when the sun goes behind a cloud. 'Bout ready to go?"

"Sure am." My behind is numb from sitting. It feels good to stand up.

"Shaw's in buying us a couple bottles of the red one, can't remember the name, but it was the second red one. If y'all want to buy any, get it, and let's go."

Blinking-eyed, foggy-brained, and numbed-butted, we follow Laney back into the tasting room, then up the stone stairs, and out to the front patio. Before us, hills of bare vines undulate, broken up by gravel roads and patches of grass. It's been so relaxing. Jackson and I have to come up here sometime. Shaw has his arm around his wife, and over his shoulder he asks, "Peter, would you or Carolina drive Laney's car back? She's going to ride with me."

What? No way. "Peter can, I'll ride with you two. You can drop me off at my house."

Laney hands her keys to Peter as we cross the pavers leading to the parking lot. "Uh-uh. Just me and Shaw on this ride." She winks and laughs. "No passengers allowed."

My face flames. We are in the shadows, so no blaming the sun this time.

Peter clears his throat. "I'll drive and take Carolina home."

Staring holes in the back of Laney's light blue sweater doesn't work. She doesn't turn around or even acknowledge the spot she's put me in. Maybe she doesn't even know she's put me in a spot? This is all in my mind, this thing with Peter, right? Right. Silly me.

Laney and Shaw continue down the hill to Shaw's car, and Peter opens the passenger door of Laney's car for me.

Why are there butterflies in my stomach?

Hope Jackson doesn't come home early.

How do these things happen to me?

Of course, Jackson is sitting on the front porch when we pull up.

"Thanks for driving, Peter. Guess you better get Laney's car back to her. So I'll just say 'goodbye' now, and you can drop me off." Laney's dark windows, and the bright sunshine will keep Jackson from seeing inside the car, I hope. My purse is sitting in my lap, and before we cross the tracks, my seatbelt is off.

"Yeah, you're right." Peter takes his right hand off the steering wheel and lays it on the edge of my seat. "I've enjoyed today. Hope you did?"

Staring at his hand, I nod.

The car stops and I grab the door handle, but not before he adds, "Reminds me of when we used to meet under the willow."

A gasp catches me. "But we, that wasn't, it wasn't you. Not really…"

His hand moves back to the steering wheel, and he laughs. "You're right. Never mind. Sorry. Tell Jackson I said 'hello.'"

Chancing a look at him, his dark beard and hair hide most of his face, then he turns away from me completely. What is this aching in my chest to see him so sad? This was such a mistake.

He puts the car in reverse before the door is even closed, and I step away.

"Hey, welcome home," Jackson says from the porch. "How was the wine tasting?"

"Good. You're home early."

"Yeah. Was that Laney's car?"

"Uh huh. So when did you get home?" He's stretched out in the rocker, and there's a beer on the table beside him. "I left you a message about the wine tasting. You know, if you wanted to join us."

He nods and lifts his beer for a drink. "Didn't say which winery, though, and then you didn't answer your phone."

"Oh, it was in my purse, and I left that in the car since we walked around the vineyard a bit."

He sits his beer down and stands up, one hand shifts to rest in his jean pocket and with the other he reaches out to me. "Well, you're home now. Sit down, and I'll get you a glass of wine. We've got a little bit more sun until it goes behind the mountain." He pulls me to him, and when we kiss, it's sweet and warm. My heart and lips smile. I've missed him. I've really missed him. Relief makes my smile even bigger.

He pulls the other rocker closer to his, and when I sit down he leans over me for another kiss, sweet as before and even warmer. He winks at me as he goes inside to get my wine.

Snuggled in my coat, sun bathing my face, remembering Jackson's kiss, my chest lifts and falls in a deep breath. Everything is fine.

"Here you go." He hands me my glass and then drapes a throw from the couch over my legs. "It's a tad chilly when you sit for long out here." He sits and pulls another throw over his legs.

I reach out and lay my hand over his on the arm of his rocker. "I'm glad you're home. We need some time, just us. You're right that there's been too much going on. Spending tomorrow down at Marietta Square is a great idea." Suddenly I see our life like he sees it. "You're right, I have let things get way out of control here. Honey, you are so right."

"Naw, it's not you. It's just how it is here…"

"But not anymore. We come first, from now on, I promise." With a toast of my wine glass toward the sky, I seal the decision.

"Well…" Jackson takes a deep breath.

"I'm so sorry things got out of whack. Oh, and things aren't getting any less crazy here." I lean up in my rocker and set my glass down. "Our guests? They aren't here for the trains. They are here about some power plant. Susan and Graham are all in on it. Folks are all riled up about it, and we don't even know what it is yet."

Jackson shrugs, "It's a power plant. Down on the river. Mountain Electric already owns the property, and it's a pretty sweet deal for Chancey."

"What? How do you know all about it?"

"Well, that's what I came home early to tell you about. We're putting in a bit of new rail for the plant. Mostly it's rehabbing the rail that's already there, but there is some new tracks to lay. I was made manager of the project today."

"Really? But why doesn't anyone know anything about all this?"

He lifts his beer and takes a swallow. "It's really just a revival of a plan that got mothballed back twenty years ago. And, honestly, sometimes it's easier if folks don't know about it until it's kind of a done deal. It's pretty straightforward, and they've got lots of great plans laid out for Chancey. Wait until you see the waterfront plans, really nice."

My legs start bouncing, and the throw falls to the porch floor. No matter, I'm not really cold anymore. "But this can't be a 'done deal.' When were you going to mention it to me?"

"I'm 'mentioning' it now, aren't I? And tomorrow there's going to be a reception for Mr. Reynolds to present it all to the complete town council."

"A reception? We'll be in Marietta."

"No, that's what I wanted to talk to you about. They want to hold the reception here, so I told them sure."

Now I'm no longer not cold; I'm hot. "Are you kidding me? After all the grief you've given me about planning stuff every weekend. You know if we hold this reception here everyone is going to think we're on the side of the power plant."

"We *are* on the side of the power plant," he says. "It's not some big, obtrusive, smoke-producing plant. It's tiny and will be out in the woods. It means some jobs for Chancey and a state-of-the-art waterfront park. Even an amphitheater! Wait until you see the plans. Everybody will be excited about it."

Standing, I shake my head at him. "You're delusional. Folks are not going to be excited, they're going to be torn apart. This place had a knock-down-drag-out over the blinker being changed to a real stoplight. A power plant?" I kick the throw and head for the door. "No way is that reception going to be here tomorrow."

"Carolina."

Jackson has stood, and his voice is low. Matter of fact, I don't think I've ever heard it that low. "The reception is tomorrow afternoon at 2 p.m. It's important for my job that it go well. My boss will be here as well as other people from the railroad. Susan is going to call you to talk about it, and I'd appreciate your help."

My hand grips the door handle, and I turn to tell my husband he can go jump in the river.

His blue eyes are sad, not defiant when I turn around, and that throws me. "Jackson…I don't think…"

"Did you and Peter have a good time today at the winery?"

My mouth hangs open. Jackson shakes his head at me and with a couple steps is off the porch and headed around the house.

Managing to close my mouth, my lips press together. *Good thing he decided to run away,* I think with a shake of my head and a lift of my chin, but then my chin starts quivering.

Very, very good thing.

CHAPTER 12

"The way I see it, it's an answer to prayer." Laney points at me with the end of the lemon she's getting ready to slice. "Now that Chancey doesn't have my gambling revenue, the money has to come from somewhere. By the way, the house looks great."

My eyes won't roll because they're too tired. "Thanks. Couldn't sleep." The real problem was I couldn't sleep next to Jackson. So I didn't. And there's only so many hours the couch is comfortable. By 4:30 this morning, the air was scented with Lemon Pledge. Besides, cleaning in the wee hours insures no worries with the sun streaking the windows or anyone walking on my clean kitchen floor.

"Mom, you ready to go?" Savannah slumps in the kitchen doorway. "Hey, Miss Laney."

"Where y'all going?"

"Haircuts at Beulah Land." Savannah snags a slice of lemon and puts it in her mouth.

Laney dumps the rest of the slices in the glass jug of water in the sink. "You're both getting haircuts? You both were able to get in?"

"Yep," I say. "Really just trims. I called Beau first thing this morning, and she said she could fit us in." I throw the dishtowel in my hands onto the counter, and take my coat off the back of the kitchen chair. "As far as I'm concerned, things are done here. Susan is bringing up the cookies and finger foods later. You've got the lemon water, ice tea, and coffee all set." My smile, however, doesn't mask my low growl. "I've got to get out of *this* place."

"What?" Laney turns to me and cocks her head. "What was that last part? You have to get out of *this* place?"

"Never mind." Didn't mean to say that out loud, I've got to wake up.

Outside the morning is gray, and the warmth from yesterday's sun is all memory.

"Savannah, this car is a wreck. Do all these water bottles still have water in them? And why is your good coat crumpled on the back floorboard?"

"Its fine, Mom," she says in that flat voice which tells me that in her opinion, and the opinion of all reasonable people everywhere, I'm overreacting. But in an insincere gesture, she dumps an armload of junk out of the passenger seat and into the back. "We're just going down the hill."

"What's with this seat?" My legs stretch out in front of me like I'm laying down. Which, now that I think about it, I am. "How do I make it sit up straight?"

"You don't. It's fine. Dad keeps trying to fix it, but it just falls back again. Why do you think no one ever wants to ride with me?"

We cross the tracks. At least they felt like the tracks. I can't exactly see out to the ground. I do, however, have a nice view of the sky. "How are things with Ricky?"

"Fine. He asked me to the senior formal. Can I get a dress?"

"What's a senior formal? How expensive of a dress?"

"It's dinner and a dance for the seniors."

"You're not a senior."

"And their dates."

"Oh. So when is it?" We stop, so I assume we're at the stop sign at the bottom of the hill.

"End of March."

"So you're good with Ricky again."

"Yeah. We're fine." She sighs. "There is this other guy I want to go out with, but he'd never ask me because everyone thinks I'm Ricky's girlfriend."

"Well, aren't you? You're already talking about buying a dress for a dance you're going with him to that's two months away."

"I'd need a dress whether I go with him or someone else."

"But how could someone else ask you if you're already going with Ricky?"

"Exactly."

We turn left, so Beulah Land Beauty Salon should be coming up soon. "Who's the other guy? He's a senior, I suppose."

"No, he's a junior."

Okay, I know I'm sleepy, but… "So he couldn't ask you to the formal anyway. Right?"

"Yeah, and I really want to go to the formal. Guess I can deal with Ricky until formal's over."

Luckily we pull into the white gravel lot of the beauty shop so I don't have to answer. As the mother of two boys, sometimes I really can't stand teenage girls. Even my own.

Savannah bounds out of her car seat. I roll out of mine. "I'm driving on the way home. This seat is ridiculous."

The white gravel sparkles, even without any sunshine. One of Beau's cousins owns a quarry over in Jasper and gets the shop a good deal on their highest quality white stone. Its part of the theme of the Beulah Land—you know. Like Heaven. The house is painted Sky Blue, and the front door is gold. Shiny, metallic-looking gold. However, the inside is all sleek wood, black paint, and burnished aluminum. A waterfall and live palms set a mood of relaxation and elegance. Apparently Beau's aunts won't let her redo the outside as it's a "Chancey Landmark".

The door opens with a chime, and Beau waves at us from her station. "Sit over there at the sinks, and we'll get your hair washed."

Our coats on the rack by the door and our purses on the shelf, we settle ourselves in the two reclining black chairs and lay our heads in our respective neck rests on the sinks. That coat rack seemed awfully full, now that I think about it. And how can every seat be taken except these two...

"Hey, Mrs. Jessup. Hey, Savannah."

My eyes pop open. Brittani stares down at us from right between our chairs. "I wash hair here on Saturdays for Aunt Beau. I'm really good at it, but since we're kind of like family you don't have to tip me." Her giggle is accented by a squeeze on my arm.

"Oh, yeah, hi, Brittani." So much for relaxing. I can't believe my son's girlfriend is going to wash my hair.

"Savannah, I'm going to do your mom's first, okay? That way Aunt Beau can get started on her. Aunt Pearl's going to trim your hair, and she's not ready yet, okay? Mrs. Jessup, you have to relax! Just lay back, and let me get my hands in your hair. Don't you just love getting your hair washed by someone else? I told Bryan I'd wash his hair for him sometime just so he could see how good it feels."

And she wants me to relax? She strokes my hair, and the warm water flows over my scalp. Oh, yeah, who needs sexy videos on MTV when your girlfriend will wash your hair? For crying out loud. Not to mention the whole draping her short self over me as she reaches in the sink. She ever gets Bryan in this chair, just go ahead and order the peanuts for the wedding reception.

My shoulders and neck muscles are hard as the white stones in the parking lot by time Brittani sets me up in the chair. She pats my hair and wraps the towel around my head. Wow, every chair in the place *is* taken. Scissors are flying, curlers are being wrapped and unwrapped, and little squares of tin foil are shining all over a couple heads. Over the dryers the talk buzzes loud.

"Okay, Mrs. Jessup, just sit here for a minute until Aunt Beau is done." She pauses beside me, tilting her head. "Sure is good to see you."

A little smile leaks out, along with a tiny nod, then I motion with my hand around me at the shop. "I figured when we got two appointments at the last minute it was because it wasn't busy."

Brittani laughs and reaches out to lay her hand on my arm. "Not at all. Saturday is always full, but Aunt Beau said she wanted squeeze y'all in." She scrunches down to look in my face and wrinkles her little nose, "Guess it's because of me and Bryan she got ya in, don't ya think?"

Savannah coughs, or gags, and thankfully Brittani feels the need to watch out for her new sister and offers to get her a drink of water.

"Right here, Carolina," Beau hollers across the room as she pats the back of the chair in front of her. "So, you got a shindig going on up at your house this afternoon?"

Did even the dryers get quieter? Okay, I see now. I like that it's not due to Brittani and Bryan's new relationship that we got appointments, but now that I know the real reason, I'm not much happier. I sit in her chair and stare down at my clasped hands. "It's something Jackson's boss planned, I guess." Mumbling doesn't work because Beau just repeated what I said for those with towels wrapped over their ears.

"Jackson's boss planned it, you say? So it's official. Hmmm, who does Jackson work for again?" she asks as she unwinds the towel on my head.

A mumbled answer causes the hairdresser next to us, Aunt Pearl, to stop working, "Speak up, Carolina. We can't hear. Did you say 'The Railroad'?"

"I really don't know anything about anything." This time

said loud enough for everyone to hear.

Beau throws her mass of short, shiny red hair back and laughs. "Baloney! Why else would you make a last minute appointment for Saturday morning unless you have news to share? Good one, girl. Half the people here, including Hank sitting back in the break room with his note pad, didn't even bother trying to get appointments but showed just up when they heard you made an appointment. You know, kind of like when the mayor of Atlanta calls a press conference."

"You suggested I stop in for a haircut. That's the only reason I'm here. And Savannah needed a trim." A deep breath does nothing to slow down my heart beat, but when I close my eyes and sit back a calmness causes my chest to relax a bit, until... "Wait, how would everyone even know I made an appointment?"

Beau's deep brown eyes are completely untroubled as she smiles at me before whirling me around to face the rest of the room. "Twitter, of course," she says as she makes the first cut of a dark brown curl. "You want an easy style, right? Short is okay?"

"Twitter?" Nods around the room from people I can't even believe own a computer cause me to shake my head. "Y'all do Twitter? No way."

"No to short?" Beau asks.

"What? No. I mean, Twitter, really?"

"Seriously, Carolina. I run a beauty shop in the mountains of North Georgia. What else am I going to tweet if not when someone of note is coming to the shop? I mean, really. And everyone doesn't do Twitter, but ya only need a couple and then the rest get the story out by conventional means."

Aunt Pearl sweeps up the hair from around her chair. "So what does the railroad have to do with this power plant? They going to help try and get it approved? Good luck with that."

"Hold still," Beau tells me when I shrug. "Just answer Aunt

Pearl, you know she's going to keep asking. But hold still while you do it."

"Okay, okay. Honestly, I don't think approval is needed."

Pearl's broom stops in place, a woman by the front windows stops crocheting, and Hank comes to the door of the break room. Savannah moans, and a large hunk of hair falls on my right side.

Hank blinks at me and points with the end of his pen. "What do you mean approval isn't needed?"

"What are you doing to my hair?" I plunk my foot off the chair rail and touch the floor to turn me to the mirror.

"You said short. I asked you." An ear that hasn't been out from under hair cover since my mother gave me pixie haircuts in elementary sticks out for God and everybody to see. My hand darts out from under the black plastic cape and reaches for my bare ear. "Beau, my hair is gone."

"Well, not all of it, yet. But enough so as to make it imprudent to stop now. You said easy to take care of and short. What did you expect?"

"Carolina?"

"What?" I squawk with a jump. Hank is standing at my side with his pad of paper right next to the side of my head still covered in hair. "Hank, you scared me to death."

"You know, what do you mean it doesn't need approval?"

"I don't know, something that was approved years ago and put on the shelf. I did not say to cut it short."

Beau sighs, "It's going to be fine. You'll love it. Hank, move. I'm working here." She spins me away from the mirror.

Hank turns to the ladies under the dryers, but doesn't move far. "Who remembers talk of a power plant back some years ago?"

"Oh, Lord, I do. They bought all that land from Helen Boyd's son who wanted to move out to California in the sixties." An old woman covered in her own black hairdresser's cape with her turquoise turtle neck sticking out of the top pushes back the dryer hood, and a blast of hot air hits us all. Her curlers have little drying hairs sticking out of them, and they wave in the hot breeze. "Remember, way out north of town on the river."

"Yes, now that you mention it, that's right!" A woman in the waiting area stands up. "My Charley was on the council, and they passed it 'cause the power company was going to build us a new high school. That's right."

"Well, what happened to it?" Hank asks.

Around the room the nods slow and then become hesitant head shakes. "I don't rightly remember," the lady under the dryer hood shouts to be heard over the wind tunnel behind her. "It just kind of went away."

"It was hectic times, you gotta remember," Pearl says with a sigh, but then thinks better of identifying herself as one who remembers the sixties. "'Course I was just a kid way back then."

Several heads, many there to get their gray covered, nod in agreement.

Hank, risking Beau's wrath, steps back toward me. "Did Jackson mention anything about a new high school?"

Beau elbows him out of her space. "Shoot, Hank, we don't need no high school now. Big one is practically new and not near full. Besides, nowadays big companies don't give nothing away. They just take and bulldoze."

As hair falls from the previously still covered side, I shudder and spit out. "Not always, like maybe they'll do something good for Chancey." My lips clamp shut, I close my eyes and shake my head. Nobody is fooled into thinking I don't know something.

The guesses come from all sides.

"An airport."

"Could be a new courthouse or library."

"We sure could use a new library."

"Or sidewalks, sidewalks would help everyone."

"Sidewalks, library, whatever—if it means a power plant taking over Chancey, then I'm against it!" As she shouts, the old woman standing in the waiting room pounds her hand on the table next to her, and the young woman on the other side of her jumps up to meet the challenge.

"My kids are young and need some advantages. Time this town stopped living in the past. A new library would benefit us all. I say we should do it!"

Another woman under the dryer yells, "Our property butts up against the old Boyd land, and the only way a power plant will be built out there is over our dead bodies."

Hank scribbles and wanders around the room as the shouts grow louder, and the necks grow stiffer. Savannah has picked up a hair dryer and is drying her own hair. Pearl is so engrossed in the arguing she hasn't noticed she didn't even trim Savannah's hair.

And it all fades to a buzz in my head when Beau whips the chair around and pulls off the cape from my shoulders. My ears, neck and face are completely uncovered. A few curls hang at the nape of my neck, but they are going to be lonesome. There's not another curl in sight, my hair is short all over with the curls reduced to spikes. It's horrible. Just horrible. A catch in my throat warns me what's going to happen, but I can't get up fast enough. Tears begin running down my face. Savannah steps up to me, and her open mouth tells me even more than the mirror. She shuts her mouth and swallows.

"Oh, Mom."

I grab my purse from the counter and shove it at her. "Pay. I'm going to the car."

"Really Carolina, you're going to love it." Beau calls this to me, but I notice she doesn't follow me out the door to expound on her assurances. I jerk open the passenger's side door and fall in.

Laying down when we drive back through town sounds like a great idea now.

CHAPTER 13

"So, reckon there was a war party at Beulah Land?" Laney drawls as she meets us in the driveway. After rolling out of the car, I had pulled up my coat collar and hunkered down into it. We were on opposite sides of the car as we passed so surely she didn't see my hair.

"Law, Laney, you should've seen them fighting. This is a real mess. Where are you going?"

"Home to change. I'll be back for the reception thingy. And who was fighting?"

"Everyone..." My foot pauses on the first step of the porch. "I guess your informant didn't give you the details." I turn to face her and smirk because she's always acting like she knows everything that goes on in Chancey.

She leans one hip against her car door and folds her arms. "Well, a fight could just be assumed when you said you got appointments at Beulah Land this morning. No one gets appointments on Saturday mornings, those slots are handed down in wills. But when I mentioned a war party, it wasn't due to there being arguing." She steps away from her car and opens the door, then laying one arm on top of the open door, she lays her chin on her coat sleeve and bats her eyes. "No, honey, it's because you done been scalped." She winks and gets in her car. "See ya later. Let me know how Jackson likes your new look."

Savannah is waiting behind me on the front porch. "Mom, it is really short."

I resist the urge to reach up and pull the little plugs of hair like I did the entire ride home. Savannah said it was only making them stand up straighter.

"What is your dad going to say? Especially with his boss coming this afternoon and everything?"

She strokes her long hair and shivers. "I don't know, but it's too cold to stay out here."

We open the door, and she peeks around it. "Nobody in the living room. I'd say let's go upstairs and I'll see what I can do with it, but there's not much left to do anything with." Her smile is pure sympathy, and while I'm heartened she can feel compassion (I have doubted it from time to time), it is painful to know she feels I deserve that much of her limited supply.

"Aw, it's okay. Wonder where your dad is?" We pull off our coats and leave them on the rack by the door. Without the big warm collar, my neck feels especially bare, but the strangest sensation was bending over to set my purse on the floor and nothing falling around my face. Nothing moves at all, no bangs, no side hair, nothing moves at all. As I straighten back up, nothing moves again. The back door opens, and I start to run up the stairs.

"Hey, you're back. Good, we need to—what did you do to your hair?" Jackson stands in the opening to the kitchen. Behind him comes Bryan and our three guests. Jackson slowly moves into the living room so everyone can stand below staring up at me.

Bryan weaves around his father. "Wow, Mom, it's really short. It's shorter than my hair." He looks around. "It's shorter than Dad's."

Jackson just stares as he walks toward the stairs and comes

up behind me. Our three guests say stuff like how much they like it, but I notice they quickly all have things in their rooms to see, too. Bryan adds a couple more "wows" until Savannah hits him and snarls, "Shut up."

"Let's talk in our room," Jackson says.

In our room, the mirror affirms Bryan's wows, and tears gather to blur my shocking view.

"You did this to get back at me, didn't you?"

"What?" The anger in Jackson's voice dries my tears quicker than a Kleenex. "You think I did this on purpose?"

"And you're telling me it was, what, an accident?"

"No, but I didn't do it to spite you."

"So why did you do it? You like it this way? I just find it hard to believe you would do this the very day my boss and important people are coming to our house. It just doesn't sound like an accident to me."

"I wanted to look good so I went to the beauty shop." Finally, I turn towards him. "It's your fault that I even got an appointment."

"My fault?"

"If everyone in town didn't want to know about this stupid meeting today and what's going on with the power plant, I wouldn't have been able to get an appointment." I collapse to sit on the foot of the bed and gaze at my awfulness.

"Well, you didn't say anything about anything, did you?"

Why does that person in the mirror staring at me look so guilty? "I don't know." But the guilt oozes out of the mirror and into my lowered, halting voice.

"What did you say? What did you tell all the *ladies* at the beauty shop? This information needs to be handled carefully. This type of thing can blow up, and if the information comes from my family? What did you say?"

"I don't know. I don't remember. It was fairly traumatic for me, seeing my hair massacred like this, you know." My voice raises with forced innocence as I wholeheartedly choose victim over villain.

Jackson steps closer to the bed so he can see me. Our eyes meet, and he shakes his head. "Of course. It is all about you, isn't it?" He drops his gaze and strides to the door. With his hand on the knob, he pauses. "Don't you ever get tired of feeling sorry for yourself?"

He leaves the room before I can answer. Or at least before I could think of something to say other than the word bouncing around in my head.

No.

Yes.

CHAPTER 14

"It's kind of all the rage with the celebrities, so maybe you're just on the cutting edge." Susan grimaces. "Pun not intended."

"And did you happen to notice how young and how thin all those celebrities are that have opted for super short hair?" My words are mumbled around the peanut butter cookie that wouldn't quite fit on the tray.

Laney takes a cookie from the center of my carefully arranged spiral of treats. "Yeah, and they tend to have really high cheekbones and big eyes." She bites her cookie, looks at me, and shrugs. "It's not that bad, it's just hair."

Not much comfort from someone whose hair has been named as a global coolant 'cause it blocks the sun. "Thanks, Laney, not for reminding me I have jowls instead of cheek bones and that my eyes are puffy instead of big, but for ruining my cookie platter. Jackson wants everything *perfect*." Susan and Laney's heads snap towards me. Oops, just a tad too much sarcasm?

Laney's eyes grow large, and her smile looks like the Grinch's when he's got a "perfectly awful idea." "You did that to your hair on purpose."

"No, she wouldn't do that." Susan chews on her lip. "Would you?"

"First Jackson and now you two! I don't care enough about all this to ruin my hair."

Laney picks up the platter of cookies. "Well, you can be pretty passive-aggressive. That's all I'm thinking. C'mon, let's join the party."

Susan hands me a plate of cheese straws. "Whatever. It's not that bad."

She follows me with a tray of homemade pimento cheese-filled celery bites, and when we get to the door, I turn over my shoulder. "You know, everything you say about my hair would have a lot more validity if you'd quite stroking that security blanket you call a ponytail."

"Honey, here's Mr. Arther and Mr. Stokesbary from the railroad." Jackson gets my attention to shift forward where he stands slightly behind two men in dark suits.

Laney reaches for the plate in my hands. "Here let me put this on the table so you can say, 'hello.'"

We all shake hands as the doorbell rings and the guests staying with us enter from the other side of the living room. "Frank. Carter May. Good to see you," Mr. Arther says as I wave him past me.

The room fills with the other Chancey council members, and soon, a hum permeates the room, which I survey from beside the staircase and near the front door.

Savannah tiptoes down the stairs behind me. "Do I have to say anything to anyone? Can I just leave? I'm going to Angie's."

A puff of air, which used to fluff my bangs, shows that I'm thinking, but really what's to think about? "You don't think it would be nice for Daddy to get to introduce you to his boss?"

She rolls her eyes but comes the rest of the way down the stairs. She passes me then turns, "Don't you think it would be nice if you actually came and talked to people instead of hiding beside the coat rack?" A toss of her head, and she walks into the group surrounding her father like she's running for office.

Maybe I should check out the food and drinks, see if anything needs replenishing. The morning's gray skies have lightened to blue, covered by a spider web of clouds. The dining room windows provide a view of the backyard, sloping down to the ring of bare trees on the bank of the river. Muddy yellow grass slopes away from the house, and the only real color in sight is a couple cardinals enjoying the hunk of suet we hung off the back deck at Christmas.

"You ladies outdid yourselves on the food." Carter May holds a piece of the celery stuffed with pimento cheese. "Is this homemade? It tastes just like the pimento cheese my mother makes."

"Yes, Susan makes it, Graham's wife? She's the one in the navy skirt and jacket."

"I did meet her. Seems awfully nice. Everyone seems nice."

A burp of laughter catches me off-guard. "Excuse me. Sorry about that."

Carter May pops the rest of the celery piece into her mouth. She wipes her fingers on her napkin and nods. "Yeah, I know. Everyone seems so nice because we've only met the people who want the power plant, or who don't know about it. Right?"

"That's about it."

She leans to pick up a cookie. Holding it aloft, she turns her back on the living room. "So was there really a scene at the beauty shop this morning?"

I shrug, then nod. "Yeah, there was." Reaching to straighten an already-straight table cloth, my eyes shift down. "Jackson's worried I might've said some things I shouldn't have."

Carter Lee crosses her arms and huffs. "Men. They think they can control talk. Believe me, that can't be done. Especially in a small town like this. Frank thought we could just sneak in here and have a 'look-see,' as he called it. I told him we might as well enter a float in the Christmas parade. Men."

I nod. "Yeah, Jackson jumped all over me. He doesn't

understand small towns either. He doesn't get that if you don't tell them what to talk about they are going to make up much worse stuff."

"I hate small towns," we say at the same time, and when our eyes meet, laughter bursts out. We quickly cover our mouths and busy ourselves filling glasses with sweet tea. We sip our tea for a moment, and Carter May sighs.

"Well, guess I better get back out there and be charming." She straightens her short tweed jacket and shakes her head back. Her thick, shiny, auburn hair falls into place, but as she pushes it behind her she looks at me. "If I had any guts at all, I'd cut my hair off like yours. It's got to be so freeing, and don't you feel like you've lost 10 pounds? I enjoy my hair sometimes, but most of the time it's just a pain in the butt. You know?"

My head nods, but not in agreement. Mostly out of habit of being agreeable and to give me something to do while I think. My hair has always been a pain. Thick, uncontrollable. I don't like fixing it *or* playing with it. Wait, maybe I do agree?

Carter Lee reaches up and tugs at one of the short curls at the back of my neck. "Very cute. You are just so brave." She leaves me still nodding, still thinking.

Wow, brave.

"Okay, Mom, I'm leaving now." Savannah picks over the table, putting assorted food into a napkin cupped in her hand. "I told Aston I'd bring him something to eat. He worked all morning and didn't get to eat lunch."

"Aston? Do I know him?"

"Probably not. He's just a friend."

"Just a friend who is a junior and can't go to the Senior Formal?"

"Maybe. He's a nice guy. Angie knows him pretty good from some language club they're in, and he's over at her house." She tucks another napkin around the stash in her hand. "So, I'm leaving. Are y'all doing anything tonight?"

"We were supposed to have a date night, but I don't think that's happening. Probably just hanging out here, or maybe we're expected to go out with our guests. Who knows?"

Savannah scowls, "This is all about some power plant or something?"

"Yeah, and your Dad is going to manage the railroad work for it, so it's a big deal for him."

Her head tips, and her light gray eyes lock onto mine, "And you, too, right?"

"Of course. Yeah." My assurance followed only a small hesitation, but I can see she's concerned at this divided front we're presenting, so I smile. "Honestly, I don't know enough about it, but if your dad says it's a good idea, then I'm sure it's a good idea."

She sees through me and shakes her head. "Okay. Whatever." She places her napkin bundle carefully in her big coat pocket and moves into the kitchen. From there she takes a head-down, straight-through approach to the front door. However, just as I look away from the closing door, it opens again, and she scurries back through it. She closes it firmly behind her and looks for me. "Kitchen," she mouths.

I meet her at the kitchen table. "What? I thought you were leaving."

"You're not going to believe what's happening outside." Her eyes are huge. "Ruby is out there, and she's got a bunch of people with her. They have signs and stuff." Her eyes narrow, and her lips thin. "How am I supposed to get to Angie's now? They have me blocked in."

"Uh oh." Laney comes scooting into the kitchen. "Libby just texted me that Ruby and a bunch of people are headed here from the cafe. They're going to picket."

Savannah snarls. "They're here. And blocking me in."

I push Savannah towards the kitchen door. "Get your dad in here. Laney, go outside and make them go home."

"Dad, Mom wants you," Savannah nearly shouts from the kitchen door.

"I meant go get him! Quietly, you know. Laney, go stop them."

"Get serious. Ruby has hated me for twenty years. You think she's going to do anything I ask her? We're just lucky we didn't remember to open the front curtains or everyone would know what's going on."

Jackson enters the kitchen. "Know what? What's going on?"

Savannah crosses her arms and tosses her hair over her shoulder. "Some of Mom's friends are out there picketing."

Laney reads from her phone. "Libby says Beau and some of the ladies from the beauty shop were at the cafe talking about, well, about stuff they heard this morning."

"So it *is* your friends," Jackson accuses.

"No! I mean they're my friends, but not, well, not…"

Susan sticks her head in the doorway and hisses, "Jackson, Carolina, y'all need to come see what's going on."

The wooden front door is open and crowded around the glass door are most of the people who were just moments ago eating cheese straws and drinking sweet tea. Graham stands at the front of the group, and as I watch his face, it goes from angry to surprised. He abruptly moves back and pulls the wood door closed. "Nothing to see out there," he laughs. "Just some folks wanting to know what's going on. Let's all have something more to eat, and Susan and Carolina will go talk to their friends." He says our names a little louder than necessary and motions at us over the heads of those around him. "Let the ladies through."

Susan grabs my hand and pulls me behind her toward the door. Jackson follows us, but at the door Graham pushes Jackson back toward the living room. "Go talk to them," he says, indicating the men from Georgia Electric and the Railroad. He grips Susan's upper arm. "Get out there, and get your son out of here," he growls through clinched teeth.

Susan and I both inhale, "Grant?"

Graham grits his teeth. "Bryan, too."

Sure enough. There they are. Front and center. Well, not quite center as there is a petite redhead in the middle of the two boys. Of course.

Ruby has on her green "NO" sweatshirt, and that's what the signs all say. "NO." Ruby is marching in a circle on my front lawn and alongside her are the ancient sisters, Flora and Fauna, a younger man and woman I don't know, and the three juvenile delinquents.

Susan and I march straight for the two boys who think we're going to pay for their college.

"Bryan, put down that sign and go to the backyard. You can go in the house through the basement door. And don't you *dare* show your face in the living room."

The boys lower their signs, but from the row of cars near the tracks comes a shout. "Don't infringe on their rights to protest."

We both squint at the half-lowered window. "Beau?"

Bryan lays his sign on his shoulder and shifts his shoulders like he's in authority. "Miss Beau has a business to protect, so she can't protest. That's why protesting is a thing for young people."

"Not young people that live in my house," Susan says as she grabs the sign from Grant. "Get home right now, and don't you even think about stepping foot out of your bedroom until your dad and I get there." Susan says this with one hand wrapped around the sign's post and the other wrapped around her son's upper arm. He can barely keep his feet moving as his mother drags him toward the road.

As Grant trots across the driveway and toward his house, he rubs his arm. After Susan's display, all I have to do it look at Bryan, and he drops his sign. With a quick wave at Brittani, he darts through the cars parked in the drive and heads to the backyard.

Brittani quickly fades toward her aunt's car, and Ruby steps forward. "I'm not worried about my business and neither of you is my mother, so what do you say to that?"

"Come on in." I wave my arm toward the house. "There's homemade pimento cheese, peanut butter cookies, sweet tea, lemon water, and coffee. So, come on." With one arm around Ruby's shoulder and another on Fauna's elbow, or Flora's—I can't tell them apart, we walk to the porch. "It's just too cold to have y'all out here, and everyone would love to meet you."

Susan takes my cue and steps over to the others and draws them into our group. She and I smile wide, as Jackson opens the door, to assure him it's all okay. He and Graham meet our smiles with deep frowns, but Mr. Reynolds gets the idea.

He pushes past our husbands and steps onto the porch, "Ruby! Wonderful to see you again. So glad you and your friends could be here." He reaches out his hand and as he shakes their cold ones, he pulls them toward the front door, and they flow through it.

Soon the porch is empty except for Susan and me. We cock our heads and motion for Beau to roll down her window. "Are you coming in?"

"No, I have a perm to put in at 3, and I'm running late for it. Carolina, Brittani wants to know if she can come in and hang out with Bryan?"

My tongue is glued to the back of my teeth, but my eyes are bugging out of my skull. I can feel them, plus I see the alarm in Susan's eyes. She hurriedly answers, "Not a good idea today. Maybe some other time, okay?"

Beau waves and starts up her car.

Susan waves at her and turns to me. "Okay, maybe a little bit of a skank."

CHAPTER 15

"If I had known all I had to do was be some kind of loud-mouthed rabble-rouser to get an invite to your little party, I would have been up there with a sign and an idiotic sweatshirt."

"Missus, do you even own a sweatshirt?" Laney shouts from the kitchen.

"Carolina, am I on speaker phone? Did you put me on speaker phone? I do not talk on speaker phone. Goodbye." The clunk of her hanging up makes me jump.

"Shoot. Who knew that's all it would take to get rid of her? Carolina, when are the power plant people leaving?" Laney asks from beside the suds-filled sink, from which she just pulled her hands.

Leaving the tiny office space, I stop to lean on the door jamb. "They are supposed to be leaving this evening, but Ruby invited them to her church tomorrow, and they're thinking about staying another night. And then they'll be back in a week for some community meeting."

"Excuse me?" Carter May's voice from down the B&B hall behind me causes me to turn.

"Oh, hi. You didn't go out to look at the property?" I pull out a kitchen chair for her to sit on.

"No, we'd have needed to take another car, and I was just there this morning." Carter May pulls her jean-clad legs and bare feet up in the seat with her. "Besides, too many engineers talking makes my ears bleed. I'm purely marketing."

Laney sets a glass of iced tea in front of her and *tsks*. "Lord, yes, some of the talk this afternoon got all technical and boring." She puts another glass down for me and then turns to bring her half-empty glass to the table. "Best part was watching Ruby act like she knew what they were saying, and then Flora, or Fauna, whichever, falling asleep with her head reared back on the sofa."

We all start giggling. "Her snoring was louder than the talking and then when my pretentious brother-in-law started trying to wake her up it got louder." Laney fans herself with a napkin.

My laughing doesn't keep me from defending my friend's husband. "I don't think Graham is pretentious. He just wants everything to be done right."

Laney waves her napkin my direction. "Yeah, because he's pretentious. He and Missus may fight like cats and dogs, but at heart they're the same. They have great and glorious plans for this town. In its current state, Chancey can't earn them the due they are, well, due."

Tea threatens to snort out my nose when I think about Graham looking out the front door and seeing his son leading the protest. "Grant protesting" is all that comes out around my laughing and choking, but it's enough. Laney and Carter May get tickled, and with the laughing, we don't notice Bryan until he's standing at the refrigerator.

Laney can't resist. "Bryan, honey, don't you know better than to let some girl talk you into embarrassing yourself like that?"

And why should I resist piling on? "Not to mention your dad. You knew his boss was here."

"Mom? A power plant?" He pulls out a carton of ice cream from the freezer, and as he turns to put it on the counter, he shakes his head. "Do you know what that will do to our town?

Pollution. Big trucks." Between dips he waves the spoon in our direction. "It's nothing to laugh about."

"Sweetie, we don't really know any of the details yet." Carter May nods at me, but I can tell she's not getting into the conversation. "When your dad gets back, I think you ought to sit down with him and see what he has to say."

He licks the dipping spoon before tossing it in the sink and then with the closed carton in one hand and his full bowl in his other hand he turns back to open the freezer. When he closes it, he mumbles under his breath, "Brittani was right."

"What was Brittani right about?" I ask.

"That y'all would try to change my mind."

"It's not changing your mind to just give you the facts."

"But they're her facts," he says, tilting his bowl toward Carter May. "And she works for the power plant, right?"

"Well, yes, but that doesn't mean they're not right." Now I'm the one mumbling. He's standing in my kitchen holding a bowl of chocolate ice cream, but he's doesn't look like my little boy. This is the young man from the church parking lot, the one with a deep voice and a swagger. This fellow is looking at me like I might not hold all the answers. Like maybe Santa Claus and the Easter Bunny were just the beginnings of my lies.

With a slow head shake, he moves toward the living room and then, just like he's been taking lessons from his older sister, he sighs.

Who gave him permission to grow up?

Laney draws my attention away from the living room door as she sits down at the kitchen table. "So, where are you from, Carter May? Are you married?"

You can tell our guest is from the South the way she doesn't even hesitate at a stranger asking personal questions.

"Alabama. Went to Tuscaloosa. Roll Tide and all that. My husband and I moved to Atlanta right out of school, but he just couldn't stay away from Bama, so we've been divorced now for about ten years. Just long enough for him to have his own litter of kids to dress in crimson. Roll Tide."

Southerners not only don't hesitate at the questions, they answer in detail.

"You don't have any kids?" Laney carries on.

"No." Carter May lets her legs down from where she had them in the chair with her. "Think I kind of always knew we wouldn't work out. Being a couple on campus is a totally different thing than being a couple out in the world. His biggest goal was getting back across the stateline, and I liked Atlanta more every year."

"Where do you live in Atlanta?" I ask. "We lived in Marietta until we moved here last summer."

"Really? You've not even lived here a year?" Carter May shakes her head and smiles at my grimace. "Let me guess. You didn't move out here willingly."

Before I can wholeheartedly validate her statement, Laney waves her hand across the table. "Baloney. Carolina just likes to act like she's miserable. She loves it here."

"How do you know what I love?"

"I just know. You love being the queen bee up here on the hill." When Laney's left eyebrow arches and her smile turns wicked, I try to interrupt whatever it is she's going to say, because obviously it's going to be evil, but I'm not fast enough.

"You especially like being the queen when dashing Prince Peter comes to call. Did you have fun yesterday at the winery?"

"Laney," I growl under my breath. "Stop it."

Carter May draws her legs back up to her chest and leans back with a growing smile. "Who's Prince Peter?"

Laney purrs. "Ummm, just a good-looking local hero who used to have eyes for me, but now finds himself fascinated with our friend here."

Suddenly, I'm burning up. My sweater is damp with sweat, and my face is melting. "He is not. Stop it, Laney."

"Yeah, Carter May, most of the fall he played like he was a ghost just to hang out up here and moon over Carolina."

"Really? Was he the ghost I read about in that article? I read everything I could find about Chancey, but that was the best." When she tilts her head, Carter May's auburn hair falls across the side of her face. "What does Jackson think of all this?"

Remembering Jackson's hurt eyes yesterday causes a blanket of cold to drop over me.

Laney again waves her hand of dismissal. "Oh, it's all good. She and Jackson are crazy about each other, and a little harmless flirting can stoke the fire, if you know what I mean. Right, Carolina?"

"Sure. It's all harmless, but I'd appreciate you not bringing it up."

Laney leans over and pats my arm. "Whatever. Enjoy it while you can. Once he realizes he can't compete with Jackson, he'll move on. Why, he might even take a shine to Carter May when he meets her. She's younger and actually available."

Carter May laughs and stands up. "Oh, I don't think so. Guess I better check my phone and see how the guys' trip out to the site is going." She scoots her chair in and excuses herself down the hall.

"And I reckon I should go on home," Laney says as she stands. "Conner bought steaks for the indoor grill tonight, and then he and I have a date to watch that new Hugh Grant movie. I love Hugh Grant, and Conner loves what watching what Hugh Grant does to me." She winks as she puts her purse over her shoulder. "What about you? Y'all going out with the power plant people?"

"I don't know. Jackson may be, but I'm not. I feel like Carter May about all the engineering talk. Maybe she and I will share a pizza and watch a movie. And I need to see if Bryan is talking to me. I'm sure Savannah is going out somewhere. Hey, do you know this new boy she's interested in. Um, his name is Ashville, or Ashton, or A…"

"Aston? Aston Roberts?"

"Yeah, that sounds right. He's a junior."

"How can she be interested in him? She's dating Ricky."

The woman dismissing "harmless flirting" of married folks a minute ago has turned to ice.

"Oh, she's not interested like that, she just mentioned him. You know, in passing."

Laney knows I'm trying to cover myself, and she nods. "Sure. He's a good kid, I guess. Folks are kind of snobby. They live up in Laurel Cove in one of the houses that overlooks the bluff. Snooty. They're not really *from* here."

"Okay. Doesn't really matter." I stand up. "Enjoy your steaks and your movie."

Nothing more is said about the kids, but as I watch her turn her car around and cross the tracks, I face-palm in my head. "Great. She's probably on the phone to Susan by now, and the Trout family is circling their wagons around poor little nephew Ricky who's getting ready to be dumped by the big, bad girl that's not *from* here."

Savannah is going to kill me.

Chapter 16

"So? You and Jackson get things worked out?" Susan asks as she pulls on the heavy side door at the high school.

Of course, I couldn't wait to put on my navy turtleneck shirt until *after* I ate leftover lemon bars for breakfast. Now powdered sugar sprinkled on my breasts looks like fabric paint adding a touch of winter to a model train layout. "Where's the nearest bathroom? This stuff won't brush off."

Susan again pushes a door open for me as I'm occupied trying to fluff the white powder off my front, and we enter the high school bathroom. "I know better than to eat anything with powdered sugar on it in the morning," I mumble while yanking off a piece of brown paper towel. Susan leans against the sink next to the one I choose.

"Did you and Jackson get things worked out?"

"About what? There, how does that look?"

"Fine, if instead of a dusting of white you wanted your shirt wet with little balls of paper towel on it."

"Shoot." The mirror validates Susan's point so I move to the air dryer on the wall. However, just before its roar begins, Susan repeats herself and moves closer to me. I move closer to the dryer. "Can't hear you."

Susan is not going to want to hear that Jackson and I never said a civil word to each other all weekend. She is not going to like that I don't know where he's working this week, and don't care. She is going to tell me what she and Grant have learned in marriage counseling, and how not talking is *never* the answer. Susan will express her sorrow with her sad, brown eyes, little shakes of the head, and a gentle pat on my upper arm. She might then say, horror of horrors, that she will "keep us in her prayers."

And this stupid dryer isn't giving me any ideas about how to keep all this from happening.

"There! That's better. We better hurry, don't want to be late."

"Do we have an appointment?" Susan asks.

This time I'm opening the door. "Umm, maybe, I don't know." Just keep pushing forward, don't slow down. At the principal's office, with my hand on another door, Susan catches up with me as I pull on the shiny brass handle.

"Okay, I get it. You don't want to talk about you and Jackson. Got it. What you need to know is I'm not asking for me. I'm asking for Bryan."

The door slides closed again. "What? Why would you be asking for Bryan?"

"Because he's talking to Grant about it."

"Bryan is talking about us to Grant? I don't think so." With a shake of my head, I jerk open the door. "Hey Eileen, we're here to get the costumes Steven, Mr. Cross, wants fixed. I think he was going to leave them in the library."

"Yep, he left you a note." Eileen, a heavyset woman with a penchant for big earrings made of feathers, leaves her chair, peels a yellow sticky note off her desktop, and brings it to the counter Susan and I are standing behind. "Hey, cute haircut. Now you need some killer earrings since you can see your ears. You wouldn't believe how cheap you can make them." She turns her head for me to get a full look at the turquoise beads and feathers cascading down the side of her head. "These only cost me about three dollars since I buy everything in large quantities. Oh, they would be stunning with that dark blue turtleneck."

"Oh, they would, wouldn't they? I love feathers." "On ducks," I squeeze out of the corner of my mouth towards Susan. Susan puts her elbow on the counter and hides her smile in her cupped hand.

"Then they're yours!" Eileen sticks the sticky note on the counter in front of me and starts taking off her earrings. "I made two pairs last night, one for me and one for Juanita, but Juanita forgot and wore red today." Eileen points out Juanita sitting at the attendance desk. Juanita tries to look sorry, but it doesn't fool me. That's pure mirth in those bright blue eyes.

Juanita shrugs. "Silly me, completely forgot." She stands and comes to the counter wearing her red sweater and black slacks and tiny diamond studs. Susan has to turn away and dig in her purse to hide her laughing now.

"Here. Good thing you came in here instead of going straight to the library isn't it? I have the other pair in my desk, and I'll put them on in a minute, but I want to see how you look right now." Eileen reaches out a handful of feathers and beads and actually shimmies in her delight at sharing the wealth. "Just put 'em on."

"Yeah, just put them on," echoes from somewhere deep in Susan's purse.

So I do.

Juanita's short stature is more than made up for in enthusiasm. "Look at you!" she squeals with her scrunched-up nose and tasteful diamond studs.

My peripheral vision tells me I'm being attacked by blue-tinted birds from both sides.

"Move your head back and forth so you can see how light they are and how they move," Eileen instructs.

So I do. And the attack intensifies. Eileen beams and hands me the sticky note. She then leans across the counter and whispers, "And they'll distract from the white stuff on your shirt."

Back in the hallway, Susan darts away from the windows of the administrative offices and collapses against the brick wall. "Oh my. This is a whole new look for you."

"I feel like Cher..." but before I can finish, a bell rings and doors begin smacking open all around us. Students pour out and fill the hall.

"Mom? What are you wearing?" Savannah stares at me from one of the doorways. Then her stunned look turns to anger. In about three strides of her long legs she's in front of me. "And how do certain people know certain things about me?"

Oops, Aston. "Huh? Look at my earrings. What do you think?"

She rolls her eyes, flips her hair, and walks away.

I'm going to pretend I don't know what that means.

"C'mon." Susan pulls my arm in the opposite direction of Savannah and we jump in the current of bodies. At the door to the library we peel off and dive into the quiet. Taking a deep breath I remember why I became a librarian. Books. The smell of books. Deep hits pull the aroma into my lungs and brain. Better than drugs any day.

"Cool earrings. Very sexy." Stephen Cross interrupts my fix and gets a scowl for his trouble. Not that he notices. "Haircut is good, too. Whole new look for your man, I take it? Lucky Jackson." He comes from between the bookcases to our right and walks toward us. When he stops he puts out his hand and tugs at a curl at the back of my neck. "I assume Jackson is the lucky man. Or is there someone else?"

"No. Stop that. Don't touch me." Why do some men think they can just reach out and touch you? With a step back I try to not act flustered, but too late. Now he's got that look that says, "I know I got to you."

Susan's lips are pressed tight, and she stares daggers at

our daughters' English and drama teacher. "We just want the costumes." Susan seems to be unmoved by the good-looking teacher while the rest of us who talk smack about him when he's not there, find our tongues numb and our words slow in his presence.

"Sure. I'm putting them in your very lovely hands, Madam President," he says as he reaches out and grasps my hands. My sweaty hands. He drops them before I can even begin to recoil, and he turns to point. "There they are. All in bags and separated as to which ones need just cleaning and which ones need repair. You ladies are so wonderful to help me out like this."

Susan pushes past him and grabs two of the bags. "We're doing it for the kids. Not for you."

"Of course, of course. Well, I better get to class. Have a beautiful day, ladies. And, Carolina?"

My head lifts at my name just in time to see him wink. "I meant what I said about your hair. Whomever he is, he's a lucky man."

He's already turned and gone by time my dry throat gets out the word, "Jackson."

Susan does an impression of Savannah, complete with rolling eyes, ponytail flip, and a shake of her head. To all this she hefts her bags off the floor and adds, "Let's go."

I'll get the door.

CHAPTER 17

"Of course. At the funeral home. Why would anyone find that strange?" My monologue ends with me staring out my windshield at the line on the sign I'd never noticed. The big letters professionally painted in shiny black with a sophisticated outline of gold couldn't be missed, seeing as they are painted on both sides of the four-foot-by-four-foot sign beside the road. "Carr's Funeral Home." It was the equally shiny, equally lined in gold words below those words I'd never noticed—

"and Dry Cleaners."

Old blacktop forms the center of the mostly gravel parking lot and leads directly to the front double doors. Red velvet drapes hide the interior space and keep the funeral home from being on display to my searching eyes. The drapes are needed because Carr's Funeral Home claims the prime location in an ancient strip mall with wall-to-wall windows and glass doors. I creep my van past all the red velvet and bounce off the black top onto the gravel part of the parking lot. Please let there be another entrance to the dry cleaner's.

At the end of the building, I park in front of a door with a hand-lettered sign taped to it. The writing isn't legible from the van, so out I go.

"Carr's Dry Cleaners. If door is locked, come to the front entrance of the funeral home. If a funeral is in process, go around to the back doors of the funeral home and ring the bell marked for morgue deliveries only."

With only one eye open, I raise my hands to the door handle…and pull. Awesome. It's not locked.

"Hello?"

"Hey, you just caught me. What can I do you for?"

The overcast day outside shouldn't have blinded me, but the space I step into is solid darkness. The man's voice comes from straight ahead of me, but I can't see anyone. "Hello?"

"Sorry about that, sugar." Suddenly bright light floods the room. "I'd just turned off the lights and was fixin' to lock the door. So, now, what can I do you for?"

Blinking, I take the two steps between me and the counter and the old man standing behind it. "Hi, I'm Carolina Jessup, and I have some costumes from the high school drama club we need to get cleaned."

"Well, howdy do, Miss Jessup. Glad to help you out. Costumes in your car? I'm Alfred Carr and this here's my establishment. Let's get your things in, okay?" In his torrent of folksy words, he'd bounded out from behind the counter and pulled the door open behind me.

"In the back here?" Mr. Carr was already at the back of the van, opening the door. "There they are."

"Here let me help." I offer but he's already scooped up the bags and is swooping towards me. I have to dash, but I'm able to get to the door and hold it open for him.

His big grin greets me from behind the counter by time I get inside. "Any special cleaning instructions, Miss Jessup? You say this is for the high school?"

"No, I mean, yes, it's for the high school. No, no special cleaning instructions. Just after countless nervous teenagers wearing them over the years, they have a certain aroma."

The tall skinny man with his close-cut white hair drops his hands to the counter in exclamation. "Lord, I just love teenagers! Don't you? All that energy, all that potential."

"Well, I uh, have three, so I might be a tad biased."

He nods his head wildly at me. "Oh, absolutely, those of us with teenagers *are* biased in their favor, I find." He claps his hands and his white, long-sleeved dress shirt barely rustles due to its being heavily starched. The stiff collar is buttoned up to his chin, like he was getting ready to put on a tie.

I blurt out, "You have teenagers?"

His laugh rears his head back and makes his dentures jump around in his mouth. "Lord, no! I'm too old for that. Seventy-nine last May. But I got a passel of teenaged grandkids I keep around here to liven things up. Family business, you know."

"Seventy-nine! Oh, Mr. Carr, you don't look that old."

"Thankee, sugar. Now, speaking of teenagers, I'm going to grab Debra out here to write up your ticket. I got a body just been delivered from the hospital, and I need to get to it." He shakes his head and purses his lips. "'Nother one of those meth cases. Young woman, well, young to me. Poor thing. That's why I keep any kids around me busy. Work 'em hard, I say, is the best way to show you love 'em and need 'em. Everybody wants to be needed. Don't you think?"

"Yeah, Mr. Carr, I think you're right. It was good to meet you, but don't let me hold you up."

He reaches across the counter and meets my outstretched hand with both of his. "Sugar, the pleasure is all mine. Jessup, I'll remember that name, and keep you in my prayers." He drops my hand and steps back. "Debra'll be right here."

Leaning on the counter, it hits me that I didn't flinch at all when he said he'd keep me in his prayers. No guilt, no nothing.

"Hello Mrs. Jessup. I'm Debra Carr Boling. Paw says you have some cleaning?"

The "teenager" is all of forty years old. She pulls the

costumes from the bags and lays them across the counter. "There's thirteen pieces, right?"

"Sounds good to me. Is Mr. Carr your father?"

"Yes, ma'am. Do you want to pay now?"

"Yes, but can you also write out a bill for me? It's for the school, so I want a record of what we got cleaned and when."

"Sure thing." She writes on a pad she pulled to her. "You new to town?"

"Yeah, since last summer. Are you from here?"

She shakes her head and sighs. "No, Paw doesn't like living in the middle of everything. We live out in Nine Mile."

"I've not heard of that. Where is it?"

Debra tears off my receipt and hands it to me with another sigh. "Nine Miles down the river from the railroad crossing."

Of course it is.

"Your stuff should be ready to pick up next week sometime."

"Okay, nice to meet you, Debra." I say to the back of her head when she turns around to flip the light switch. She follows me to the door, and as I scoot across the threshold, I barely beat the door. The lock twists behind me. Gray skies meet the gravel lot. A chilled wind carrying bits of freezing rain and snow greet me, so I hurry to my car and switch the heater to high. A shiver moves down my arms, and I look for my gloves, but the receipt in my hand stops me. "Put this where you can find it," I implore. Before I put it in the zippered pocket of my purse I look at it, and another shiver is greeted with a laugh. Across the top of the receipt is stamped "Carr's Funeral Home." Below that Debra had written, "13 delivered."

Sounds like I'm a delivery guy for the mafia.

CHAPTER 18

"I'm home brewing another pot of coffee 'cause you can't even go into Ruby's without a scene anymore." Arms crossed and leaning against the counter, I look out my kitchen window while keeping my phone tucked between my ear and shoulder. "Oh, yeah, and why didn't you mention that the dry cleaner's was in the funeral home?

Susan's laugh just makes me shake my head. "So, you got to meet the Carrs?"

"Yes, I got to meet some of the Carrs. Seem like nice people. I'd never heard of Nine Mile before. Guess it's out in the sticks?" *Even more than Chancey?*

"Way out. Come to think of it, it's out in the direction of where the power plant would be. Whew, wonder if anyone's thought of that. Carrs are tight people. Nobody goes on, or even near, their property."

"Really? Seemed pretty nice to me, especially Mr. Carr."

"Oh, they can be real nice when they've got something to sell you. And they sell a lot of stuff."

"Really?" My attention focuses on the bottom of our yard where the low-hanging sky and the wet tree limbs meet. Through them the choppy river moves past. Here and there bits of sunlight break through and cast a pewter glint on the snow-covered patches of ground. "Hope this weather breaks soon. I can't take so much gray."

"Supposed to by later today. Hey, I've got to go. Is the bed and breakfast booked this weekend?"

"Yes. Only it was under Carter May's name this time so we didn't know it was the same group renting two weekends back to back. There's some kind of public meeting isn't there?"

"Yeah, Thursday night. You going?"

I turn from the window and rinse out my coffee cup from earlier. "Probably not. I'm sure it's just the first of many, and you know these big projects usually take forever to actually get going. Everybody's all excited right now, but by time they actually get started, no one will care."

Busy pouring my coffee, I don't even notice Susan's silence for a bit. "Susan. Are you there?"

"Yeah." She pauses again. "I've got to go. Talk to you later." She hangs up, and so do I. "I don't need Ruby's to have coffee and relax." Settled into an end of the couch, I pick up my January issue of *Southern Living*, which I never finished, and congratulate myself on avoiding the drama always found in Ruby's.

Missus is probably laying out plans for getting back on the town council, or Peter is there working up ways to involve me further in Chancey. Or Laney and Ruby are sparring over old beaux, or the real Beau is there instigating another protest.

Wonder how Cathy and Steven are getting along now? Libby sure seemed worried about them. I guess with his parents getting involved it would be hard to not get involved. Also, I never did find out more about Brittani's parents. She's Beau's niece, but is it through Beau's brother or sister? I don't think Beau has a brother, does she? And then this Aston kid, what is it Laney said about his folks? Rich or something? Hope Ricky doesn't get mad and disinvite Savannah to that senior dance thing.

What exactly is that thing, Senior Formal? Do many juniors go with seniors? Is Jenna going, I wonder? Angie's not dating anyone, so she's probably not going. Although she was laughing with that boy she works with at the Pig the other day.

Bet the owners of the Piggly Wiggly are hoping the power plant gets built. You know, Ruby's head was quite turned with Mr. Reynolds talking about her writing a cookbook. Maybe all the business folks will be behind it. Even the Carrs. Susan said they sell a lot of stuff. Wonder what else they own? Why stop at just a dry cleaner's and a funeral home? Carr? Have the kids mentioned any kids with that name?

Cold coffee and an unopened magazine greet me when I come to from my congratulatory ruminations of why I was glad I hadn't gone to Ruby's. I get up and take my cup to the kitchen. "At least at Ruby's I remember to drink my coffee." The cold coffee disappears down the drain, and with a start I realize that I miss the diner, drama and all. Matter of fact, the drama might be what I miss most.

Okay. Nobody can know that. Nobody.

Savannah comes in the door just as I'm walking down the stairs. Afternoon sunshine, portended earlier by Susan, comes in with my daughter. She raises her eyes to me, her eyebrows follow, and then her arms and hands. "Don't blame me," she says. Everything drops—eyes, arms, eyebrows—and she walks to the kitchen.

"Hey, Mrs. Jessup!" Brittani calls, crossing the threshold. Bryan is busy holding the door for her while also carrying two bookbags.

"Mom, Brittani is going to study here, okay? Her mom said

it was okay."

"Thanks so much, Mrs. Jessup. Bryan is just so smart about science, and I have a huge, huge, huge test tomorrow." Brittani stands at the foot of the stairs, taking off her coat and generally being adorable. Her smile is fixed on me, until she turns and reaches up to kiss Bryan's cheek. "I'm so lucky to have such a smart boyfriend."

I forget to breathe for a minute, watching them.

The two of them turn to the couch to unload their bookbags, and Savannah comes out of the kitchen. "No way. I'm watching Dr. Phil in here. Go study somewhere else." She plops down in the chair, kicks off her shoes, and opens a Little Debbie Swiss Roll cake.

I've managed to come off the stairs. "You can use the dining room—"

"Come on. We'll go up to my room," Bryan says, hefting the bookbags back onto his shoulder. "Let's get something to eat." They brush past me and into the kitchen.

Savannah turns up the volume. Dr. Phil starts talking, but she talks over him. "This is an update on that fourteen-year-old girl that was on the show a couple years ago pregnant. Remember her whole family was on here?"

"Yeah, I remember," I say. "Oh, is that her son?"

"Yep. And look. She's pregnant again."

Sure enough, the girl, now all of 16, is big as a barn again. Her parents look as if they've aged a couple decades since I saw them last. Savannah pulls her feet up under her in the chair and turns to look at me. "So. What are you going to do about those two in the kitchen? You going to let them study in his *bed*room?"

Hmmm. I could send Savannah up to my bedroom to watch TV. Or I could enforce my suggestion of studying at the dining room table. Making sure they leave the bedroom door open when they're up there could work. Or...

While I stare at the TV, chew the inside of my lip, and go

over my myriad of options, they leave the kitchen, walk behind me, and walk up the stairs. Savannah actually turns in her chair to look at me, but I'm not going to notice her accusing look. Why is my face so hot? They're just kids. Just last week a bunch of his friends were in his room burning CDs, and there were girls there. How can I now all of a sudden say Brittani can't be there? It's like there's something special with her. What would that imply? What ideas would I put in their heads?

"Just leave the door open," I squeak. They probably heard me, right?

Savannah shifts back to watching TV and turns up the volume. She sighs, but I'm not noticing that either.

CHAPTER 19

"Wait, why is she getting help from him? Isn't she a year ahead of him?" Susan whispers as she winds the cord up on the vacuum cleaner.

With a shrug, I go to shut the church hallway door. Voices of the other clean-up volunteers can be heard at the end of the hall.

"Hey, wait a minute." Laney pushes the door open as I push it closed. "Thought I'd find you two back down here by yourselves so you could gossip." She closes the door behind her and walks into the room, looking from side to side. "Oh, darn, you've finished in here. I was so hoping I'd get here in time to help."

"Sure you did," her sister says. "You've probably been sitting across the street in your car waiting until you figured the work was about done. Looks pretty good, doesn't it?"

A ceiling leak right after Christmas had flooded the youth room at the church. Once the leak was repaired, the clean-up and restoration of the furniture had been needed. Of course, seeing as the furniture was all hand-me-downs, too worn out for our homes, the room never would look good. But clean and dry was something.

Laney flops down on the red and black plaid couch (not to be confused with the burgundy and navy plaid couch across from it). She pats the armrest. "I think this one was here when I was in youth group. So, what were we talking about?"

Susan rolls the vacuum in the corner and moves about the room straightening, picking up pieces of lint, doing whatever it is busy people always find to do. I sit on the other end of the red and black couch. "Brittani and Bryan. They're studying together every afternoon." My lips tighten, then I add what I hadn't told Susan. "In his bedroom."

Susan stops doing whatever she was doing and puts her hands on her hips. "What? You let them study in his room?"

"But he's just in junior high. They keep the door open, or I open it when I go by."

"Not a good idea." Susan picks up the window cleaner and moves to the door and the window in it. "In my opinion, that is. But, Lord knows, I didn't let any boys up to study in Susie Mae's room, and she found ways to get alone with 'em."

"I didn't let boys in Savannah's room either, but with a boy it's different. Will never had girls around in high school, but when it's keeping a boy out of a girl's room, it feels right, honorable. Most girls don't want boys in their rooms because they're so messy. But with a girl going into a boy's room, it's like…well, I don't know."

Laney tilts her head. "I never thought about that. Telling a girl she can't go into a boy's room is as good as saying she's wild or something."

Susan rips off another paper towel. "So, Sis, how many moms had to bar you from their sweet little boys' rooms?"

"I'm thinking." She nods. "You know, it did happen a couple times. I didn't take it personally at the time, but I am now."

"See?" I hit the couch cushion and a cloud of dust lifts. "Oops, sorry. But see, it is weird. Can't you see me saying to sweet little Brittani with an 'I', 'No Girls Allowed up there. Little Bryan is too innocent for your evil ways.'"

Susan and Laney laugh, and Susan turns to me. "Okay, gotta

admit that does sound like Norman Bate's mom in *Psycho*, 'None of you teenage witches allowed up there to defile my sweet baby!'"

Laney smooths down her winter white wool jacket, pulls a dark red lipstick from her pocket, and takes off the lid. Before she gets it to her lips, she points it at me. Then at Susan. "If I had a son, I'd buy a case of condoms, and they'd be everywhere he turned. In the cereal box, his night table, his gym bag, everywhere." She finally points the lipstick at herself and begins applying it.

Susan and I are left with upraised eyebrows and downturned mouths.

After rubbing her newly colored lips together, Laney asks, "What does Jackson think? He was a teenage boy once."

"Jackson? Well, he's been gone…"

Susan turns on me. "Have you still not talked to him? Carolina, you've got to cut this out." She sits across from me on the navy and burgundy couch. "You have to talk to him."

Laney crosses her arms, "Are you two still not talking? I thought I fixed that. You know, don't go to bed angry and all that."

"Maybe that's easy for you and Shaw," then I look at Susan, "and maybe since you and Graham are in intensive therapy talking is easy for you, but that's just not how it works with me and Jackson."

Winter light fading outside intensifies the glare of the florescent bulbs. My voice had raised at the end and now my last words hung in the air. How did we go from talking about Bryan and Brittani to me and Jackson?

Finally Susan stands back up (she had been sitting all of two minutes). "I've got to go if we're going to have any supper before the meeting tonight." She puts the window cleaner and roll of paper towels in her bag of cleaning supplies. "Y'all coming tonight?"

Laney stretches and struggles off the low couch. "Of course. Wouldn't miss it."

They both look at me. "Me? No. Seriously these kind of things like power plants take forever. I'll get involved at the end when it really matters. If it ever even gets that far."

Laney walks to the light switch and raises her hand to it. "From what I hear it might not take all that long. Right, Susan?"

Susan shrugs and lifts her bag. "Jackson will be there, right? And the others, Frank and Aaron and Carter May?"

"I guess. How would I know? Remember, we're not talking." I push myself off the couch and wave my hand in the air. "I'm sure I'll hear everything that happens when they all get back to the house."

Laney smirks at me. "So, you and Jackson talk as long as there are other people there? That sounds perfectly healthy to me." She flips off the lights and adds, "Not." She opens the door, and as I walk through it, she puts an arm around my shoulders. "Honey, we're on your side and just want to see you smiling again. You aren't smiling these days, and it's not just because of Brittani with an 'I.'"

"I know. Maybe we'll get it straightened out this weekend."

Susan, arms full, bumps my hip with hers. "We're here for you." She winks, and we all laugh a bit.

Laney tightens her grip on my shoulders in a quick hug and then lets her arm drop as we turn the corner toward the end of the hall. "So, let's all go buy some condoms."

Poor Mr. Williams. The old janitor probably thought working in a church he wouldn't have to hear such things.

Oh well.

CHAPTER 20

"I can't help it that you thought we'd all rush right up here to tell you what happened! You should've come to the meeting," Jackson hisses at me as he throws his suit coat across our bed.

My hissing matches his for the low volume, but is sharper. He may be annoyed, but I'm mad. "You asked me to make a dessert, so I made dessert, made coffee, didn't go to the meeting. It's been hours since you left and no phone call? Nothing to let me know you weren't coming back up here for dessert?"

"Oh, grow up, Carolina. Ruby invited everyone there for dessert. Community goodwill is key for Frank and Carter May." He throws his dress shoes in the closet one after the other. "It was a good meeting, a good night. Can't you just lay off?"

Our bathroom mirror shows my hair is sticking out from all the static electricity built up from my frenetic brushing. I've already changed into my nightgown and robe. "Well, a call would've been thoughtful."

Jackson unbuttons his shirt as he walks to the bathroom door. "Yeah, well you actually showing up at the meeting like you said you were going to would've been thoughtful, too. Why didn't you show up?"

"I was never coming. I just said I was for Carter May and

Mr. Reynolds. You know I don't do things like community meetings. Especially when everyone is fighting."

Jackson takes off his shirt, wads it into a ball, and throws it towards our dirty clothes hamper. "So, I'm supposed to know when you are just telling people what they want to hear? It would help if we actually talked. You know I have to travel, and you not taking my calls makes it impossible to communicate."

I lay down my hairbrush and go to my side of the bed. As I take off my robe, I realize Jackson is putting on a sweatshirt and jeans. "Aren't you going to bed?"

"Not yet. There's a practically full moon out tonight, and I'm going to chill a bit on the deck. Open some wine and relax. It's been a full week." He sits down on the bed and slips on a pair of old loafers he uses as house slippers.

"Won't it be cold out there?"

"Might be. Just want to take a look around and wind down."

At the door, he hesitates with his hand on the knob. "Sorry I didn't call, and thanks for making a dessert. I might have a piece of it now."

"Okay." *Maybe I should go down with him.* The thought flashes through my mind, and I reach for my robe.

Jackson pulls open the door, then looks over his shoulder at me. "I'll try not to wake you when I come up." Turning away and stepping into the hall, he adds, "Or I might just sleep in Will's room." The door shuts quietly behind him.

Jackson acted all concerned about waking me up, but I doubt I've even entered his thoughts since he closed our bedroom door. Hours. Hours have passed since he went downstairs. A couple of those hours, I huddled at the back door of our room. The back door that goes out onto a dilapidated walkway down to the big deck outside the kitchen. It's double-locked because we don't think it's safe, so it took some searching to find the key for the deadbolt. By time I found it, cracked open the door—very quietly—there were voices on the deck. Jackson enjoying the moonlight with Carter May.

I couldn't hear what they were saying, but they didn't sound cold.

They left the deck a while ago. Sounds of the cabinet doors in the kitchen opening and closing and drawers being pulled open then shut reached me for a bit. Then nothing. Nothing at all. A peek down the hall shows no lights in the living room. No lights anywhere.

Except the lights on my clock. 4:10 am.

Lights on a clock suck as company.

"Of course they didn't leave any coffee," I point out to my righteous self when only the dregs of the pot empty into my cup. But it's the only complaint I can scrounge up. Counters are clean, dishwasher loaded with saucers and coffee cups, kids out of the house on time, two wine glasses washed and left drying upside down. Dismissing those glasses, I put on more coffee.

Silky black liquid pressing into the glass carafe adds its addictive aroma, and as bits of sunlight push their way into the kitchen, I wrinkle my nose in disgust, but then shake my head. Too little sleep makes everything bad this morning. Clean and empty kitchen. Winter sunshine. Fresh coffee smell. It's all stupid. Or at least that's what I keep thinking.

As I wait for the brewing to finish, I wander over to the door to the deck. There, beside the table are two chairs pulled close together. No one remembered to separate them. Of course, guess since they left the wine glasses they'll say everything is all innocent. I turn, lift my head, and stride down the hallway of the B&B rooms. At Carter's door, I stand still for just a moment before I grab the knob and turn it slowly.

"Carolina?" A voice behind me startles me, and I pull shut the door with a bang.

"Carter May, you're here." I fall back against the door to her room. "I thought everyone was gone."

Carter May steps around me and reaches for the knob of her door, where my hand just rested. "Were you looking for me?"

With the center of the hall empty, I push past our only female guest who must've been in the bathroom. "Coffee should be done. Can I get you some? That's what I came to ask."

She shakes her head and her auburn hair falls across one of her eyes and part of her mouth. "No, I had coffee with the rest of your family this morning. Savannah and Bryan are just delightful young people. Jackson really enjoyed getting to sit down with them this morning. We all enjoyed it." She swings her hair off her face and opens her door. "Wish you could've joined us." Inside her room she waves her toothbrush at me. "Just going to put this away and then I have to head out to the site. Everyone else is already out there, but I had some phone calls to make."

I march back down the hall, pour a cup of coffee, and head upstairs as fast as possible so when she comes back through the kitchen in her perfect fitting navy slacks, navy and cream sweater, and shiny, swinging hair I won't be anywhere around. Not that my robe can't stand up to scrutiny.

I'm betting it, and all its stains, could stand up on its own just fine.

CHAPTER 21

What I want to do is wrap my robe tighter around myself, go down to the basement, bring up a half-dozen of my old paperback books, lock the doors so no one can enter the house, and sit, read, drink coffee, and eat Oreos all day.

Instead I have on my olive green cords, oatmeal beige sweater with the thick cowl neck, and some earrings I found in Savannah's room. My hair is clean, styled, and make-up is my friend. The cute boots Laney made me buy last fall, when I was going to try and look stylish, are on my feet, and my feet are in my car. I'm going to walk into Ruby's like I know what I'm doing. Like I am in control of my life, my marriage, and my hair.

"Well, look who's come down off the hill," Missus greets me with one of her traditionally caustic welcomes, but then her eyes squint and her head tilts. "Carolina, you look well this morning. Very well. Sit here. Peter can sit over there when he gets here."

Missus pats the seat beside her, and suddenly my cute boots feel like cute clown shoes. I tug at the curls at the back on my neck. Peter. Oh yeah. I slide in the booth.

"I'd heard you got a new fashionable hair style. It's awfully short, but maybe you can manage it that way. You've done a quite acceptable job this morning. Ah, Peter, there you are."

"Mother. Carolina." Peter takes his place on the other side of the booth.

Peter seems like someone that would like fashionable, new things but then you know how men are about long hair. Demurely I look up to see if he's noticing my hair. His gray eyes are cold, and he stares at me. "So was it your idea for that silly woman with all the last names to hire Anna?"

Missus stops her cup on the way to her mouth and sits it back down, hard. "Who's hired Anna?" She turns to me. "Carolina?"

"Wait, I don't know," I say. "I don't have any idea what you're talking about."

"This morning. First thing. Anna gets a call from that woman working for the power plant that's staying at your house. Carter Lou or Taylor Jo, something stupid, you know."

"Carter May?"

"Yeah, her. Oh, thanks, Libby." He turns over his cup to have it filled. "And I'll take a bran muffin when you get back over this way." We wait for Libby to fill mine and Missus' cups. "Her. Carter May. Apparently Anna talked to her last night after the meeting because that woman talked about opening an office here."

"What would my granddaughter be doing in that woman's office? Surely Anna's not going to quit school."

"Oh, yes, she is most definitely going to quit school. Says she wants to work a bit and then take some night classes. Possibly. We know how that'll turn out."

"Wait," I say holding out my hand and pushing it down as if I can calm these two down with just soothing words and hand motions. "What would Carter May even want with an office here? She's from Atlanta. Isn't she?"

Peter scoffs, "You moved here, right? After that debacle of a meeting last night we might as well call ourselves Atlanta North."

"But Jackson said the meeting went great."

Missus sniffs. "Great for him. Great for you. Great for Carter May."

Ruby plops her hand and the wash rag it's holding on the table and sits on the edge of Peter's seat. "Scooch over." She motions at me with the dingy gray rag. "All dolled up with the money you plan on making from the power plant, I see. Try and tell us you want to just fit in here all these months. Should've known it was all a ploy. Win our hearts and get into our good graces with that stand-offish, suburban attitude of yours. And the worst part, you used your kids. Got us to like your kids." She folds her arms on the table and looks between Missus and Peter. "What are we going to do now? There's no hope, is there?"

Neither Ruby nor Missus are known for being reasonable, so I appeal to Peter. My good friend who has a crush on me, Peter. "Peter, c'mon. You know these things take forever. It'll never get approved, and even if it does it will take years to be built. You all are acting like it's all over before it even gets started."

"Your 'oh so out of touch,' passive act is old now," Peter sighs. "You know as well as we do that a year from now that power plant will be up and operating."

"What? That's not possible."

Missus huffs and tightens her lips before turning toward me. "Permits were granted years ago. They own the land, and with some new pre-fabricated plant they have, they can be up and running by next spring." She huffs again. "At least that's what they say."

Ruby, Peter, and Missus all stare at the table.

I don't know where to begin. "Honestly, I didn't know. How could I have known…"

Three sets of eyes find me. I back pedal as fast as I can. "Oh, yeah, but well, me and Jackson, we…you know he travels so much, and we have Crossings to run."

Silence, uncomfortable and uninterrupted, makes me feel I should get up and go home. Laughter from across the dining room catches all of our attention. "I guess not everyone got the bad news, huh?" My smile tries to lighten the mood.

"Oh, they got it." Ruby watches the group as she gets up from her place in the booth. "That's some of the business folks who are excited about more customers and the whole lake park thing has people all atwitter. And not the Twitter on the computer thing."

"What lake park?" I ask.

Ruby shakes her head at me. "Law, I hope that cluelessness of yours is just an act. If not, I just feel sorry for you."

Missus pushes against my leg. "Let me out. I have an appointment to talk to the mayor this morning. See what he thinks is going to happen."

I move out of my seat and let her pass. As I sit back down, she stands at the end of the table and arranges her shawl over her shoulders. "Peter, we will talk later about this supposed job Anna thinks she is going to take."

"Okay, although she seemed surprisingly stubborn this morning when we talked. She's always seemed so eager to get along, but she was fierce this morning. We'll talk later." Peter's eyes slide across toward me and then he moves towards the end of his bench. "Should I come with you to see the mayor? I'm free."

Missus shakes her head. "Not this time." She looks at me, but just presses her lips together and leaves.

"Bye, Missus." I say to her back before turning to Peter. "She sure is a downer this morning."

"You should've been there. We went in with all our arguments ready and then we find out it's all grandfathered in from when the power company put forward their plan twenty years back. Some special arrangement put in place at the time because everyone was vying for the plant. Everyone wanted the money and jobs. Apparently we, Chancey, put together a contract that allowed the company to come in and put up their plant with no problems in the future. Guess the future is here."

"And Missus didn't know anything about it?" My incredulousness must've come through on my face because I see Peter mirror it back right before he drops his face to stare at his coffee cup.

He squints one eye and looks up at me from a tilt. "Yeah, that's what she says. Says she was busy with the historical society or something. It doesn't ring true, but…" He shrugs and drains his coffee cup. He turns in his seat to look for Libby and her refill pot. "Honestly, I'm not sure it's such a bad idea. It was just a bit disconcerting that it was all figured out with no input from us. Hey, Libby." He smiles at Libby, making sure she's seen his empty cup, then turns back to me.

"Input from 'us' you said."

Peter's dark hair flops on his forehead as he nods yes. "Uh-huh. Oh, thanks, Libby."

I wait for Libby to leave then ask. "Who is 'us'?"

"Us, you know, Chancey."

"Peter Tecumseh Bedwell. You don't mean Chancey. You mean you and your mother."

His eyes go wide, and while he's saying "No, no" with his mouth, his eyes say I'm right.

"Well," he caves. "After all we've given to the town to show up last night and be humiliated?"

"How were you humiliated? Just because you weren't in on the ground floor? No one consulted you? There won't be a Bedwell Pavillion at the new park? Oh, I really do hate small towns." I push out of my seat. "I may be clueless, but at least I don't think the world revolves around me." I take a five dollar bill out of my pocket and lay it on the table.

"You think that's what I think? C'mon Carolina, you know I'm not like that. I'm not like my… my…"

"Your mother?"

Peter picks up his hot mug and leans against the side wall

of the booth. "Right. I'm not like my mother." He cocks one eye at me. "I do find that woman, Carter May, um, interesting, I guess. She's not married, is she?"

I wrap my brown scarf around my neck. "No, I don't believe so." My stomach turns at the jealousy I will not, *will not*, acknowledge. While tamping down my jealousy, the conversation lags. So Peter likes Carter May. Good. My focus needs to be on my marriage. My family.

"Okay, bye, Peter. Uh, good luck with your mixed feelings about Carter May. I'll put in a good word for you when I see her tonight." I turn but only get half a step when I feel a tug on my sweater.

Peter has leaned out of the booth and has hold of the hem of my bulky sweater. His face is that of my friend again, and his eyes are full of worry. "Carolina, she's, uh, she's not interested in me."

"Who, Carter May?"

He drops my sweater and looks down at the table. "You need to know. She's after Jackson."

And all the sounds of Ruby's fade while my mind is filled with two laughing voices in the cold and the dark last night. But I laugh and turn. "Don't be silly."

Chapter 22

"Hey, look at you." Susan gets up from her desk and starts clearing out the only other chair in her tiny church office. "Love that sweater and earrings. Laney up at your house this morning, making you play Dress Up?"

Waving my hand at the emptying chair, I say, "Don't do that; I'm not staying. And, no, I don't need Laney to dress me. I know how to dress up, I just don't see the point in it, living up here in the mountains."

She wipes off the dust on the back of the metal folding chair, pauses, and tries to get her eyebrows to come back down to a normal level. "Here, have a seat. Sorry it's just an old folding chair, but then we are *way up in the mountains.* Practically hanging out in caves."

"Okay, I didn't mean that exactly, but after living in East Cobb—which rhymes with snob, remember?—things are definitely more relaxed up here." I lower myself to the cold metal chair.

Susan sits back down behind her desk. "I know, I know. Sometimes it just comes off so, so snobby, when you folks from the big city start talking about the mountains like we're a bunch of hicks. Another family moved into one of the so-called cabins over in Laurel Cove, and the mom was here this morning telling us how we can be just like the youth group they left in Decatur."

"I've never been up to Laurel Cove. I hear it's nice."

"Nice doesn't even begin to describe it. The homes are mansions, although we're supposed to call them 'cabins,' and the lots are wooded and huge. Most sit along the river and the bluff or on one of the lakes. Their clubhouse is built in and around an old mill with all this stonework and natural light. They have every amenity they had in Atlanta, except us backwards hicks in the neighboring towns don't keep up. The woman this morning actually said the church was so 'authentic.' She should've just said 'cute' or 'sweet' or 'traditional' 'cause all of that means backward, hick, and "Thank God we've arrived now to fix it!'"

"Well, she sure got you stirred up. And I bet last night's meeting didn't help either. A year? The plant can be up in a year?"

Susan stares at me, then jerks the elastic holder off her ponytail. "Still not talking to Jackson?"

"You are obsessed with me and Jackson. He was gone by time I got up this morning. Why can't I come talk things over with you, my friend?"

Running her fingers through her hair making a new ponytail, she sighs. "Okay, whatever. Yes, a year. The plans last night went over pretty well. The lake park will be amazing, and Mountain Power is footing the whole bill. Putting in an amphitheater, docks, boat ramp, a sand beach. The whole nine yards. The lady from Laurel Cove was practically in tears of ecstasy talking about it this morning."

"Missus and Ruby were up in arms talking about it this morning." Okay, so I leave Peter out. Sue me.

"Same as my mom and aunts. Mama won't even talk to Graham right now. She says it's going to change everything here. The old folks think they see forbidding writing on the wall. I'm torn. It means change, but maybe the change will be for good." She pushes up the arms of her brown sweater. "Maybe there will be things to make the kids want to stay in the area."

"Maybe. It's just hard to know, isn't it?"

We sit in silence for a bit, and then I stand. "Well, I'll let you get back to work, and I need to get back up to the house and see what's on schedule for the weekend."

"Tomorrow is supposed to be sunny and warmer. Graham is smoking ribs. Y'all want to come over for dinner?"

At her door, I pause. "Sounds great to me. I'll check with Jackson and let you know."

She grins. "I don't know, you might actually have to talk to him."

I stick my tongue out at her and leave her doorway, mumbling under my breath, "Believe me, I know. That's the problem."

Almost to the outside door, my name comes echoing down the walls of concrete block. "Carolina. Are you still here?"

Susan darts around the corner I'd just turned. "Good you're here. These costumes are done. Clean and repaired." Draped across her arms are three long dresses. "Stephen called and wanted to see if he can use them in the new play. Would you run them by the high school?"

"Sure. That reminds me: the cleaners called, and some of the stuff I'd dropped off there is ready. Guess they send it all out, and it comes back at different times." Shifting my purse and keys, I drape the costumes over my left arm.

"Don't even try to figure out any kind of schedule if the Carrs are involved. They work hard, and they're good, but very elusive on where they'll be and when they'll be there. Just kind of who they are." Susan pushes the door open for me and holds it. "Everyone knows it. Here, let me get your car door."

Cold air blows against my neck, and I miss my thick mane of hair. A shiver down my back makes me jog to my van. Susan yanks on the back door's handle, and the door slides out of the way. "Thanks. These dresses do look perfect for *Our Town*, from what I remember."

"See this green one? How amazing will that look on Savannah?" Susan holds out an emerald green dress with shiny black buttons down the front. The white pressed collar is sweet, and with Savannah's black hair and blue eyes, the collar will frame her face perfectly. It looks made for my daughter.

"Oh, it does look just right for her, but who knows what part she'll get. Or even if she'll get a part."

Pushing the bottoms of the dresses into the van, Susan laughs. "Right. The role of Emily is perfect for Savannah, especially in that dress. The big puff sleeves and the full bow in the back will set off her figure too."

"Well, Savannah agrees with you. Not about the dress, yet, but she says the role is perfect and the only one she's going for. Although she's a little off on the cemetery scene."

Susan pulls the sleeves of her thin sweater down to cover her hands. "It's cold out here. Thanks again for taking those over, but I also wanted you to see that dress. I'm freezing, so I'm going to run in. Bye! See you tomorrow for dinner!"

I hold one hand over my cold nose while the other is turning the key in the ignition. I always dart out without a coat, and then I'm freezing half way through my errands. With the heater on full blast, I turn left out of the church parking lot and start up the hill towards the Carrs' strip mall empire.

"Please, please let there not be a funeral and let someone be in the dry cleaners. I do not want to go around to the back door where the bodies are delivered."

Several cars line the sidewalk in front of the funeral home, but there's no hearse or people walking around in black suits. Matter of fact there is no one in sight. Past the funeral home windows I pull my van into the gravel parking at the end and see that the "open" sign is in the cleaner's window.

Only takes a minute to get the five costumes that are ready, but Debra, who's behind the counter, has no answers on when the others will be done. Again she rushes me out the door. I push a button on my keychain, which causes the sliding door on the passenger side to open. I hang the costumes on the empty hook above the seat. Tucking in the bottoms of the plastic bags, I look up and across the interior of the van.

Out the other side's windows, I see Carter May and a man come out of the funeral home's main entrance and stand beside one of the cars parked there. They bend their heads into their coats and scarves, but stay close enough to talk. However, as I get ready to dismiss them, the man pushes her against the car and starts kissing her. She pushes him away, but he leans back towards her.

Then another man comes fast out of the funeral home doors, and as he leaves the shadows of the overhang I realize it's Jackson. As he strides up to them, the other man holds his hands up like he's innocent and walks back to the front doors. Jackson takes Carter May's arm, and they both lean on the car.

By now, my knee is resting on the floor of my van, and the side of my head is leaning on the back of the front seat. They stand by the car, Jackson still with his hand wrapped around her upper arm. Then he releases his grip and reaches up to brush her auburn hair away from her face. My mouth is dry from hanging open, so I close it and swallow.

Suddenly as they stand there I'm taken back to the day I watched Bryan kissing Brittani after the ski trip, leaning against the bus. Granted they were leaning on each other, but still, the déjà vu is making my stomach turn. Carter May leans toward him, toward my husband, and then lays her face against his shoulder. Apparently my mouth has dropped open again as it's dry. Another swallow, and Jackson puts his arm around her and they walk away from the car to a car I hadn't noticed at the other end. Jackson's car.

He puts her in the front seat, then goes around the back of

the car. I lose sight of him until he opens his door and gets in. They pull out and head down the road away from town.

I, uh, I need to go.

CHAPTER 23

"Did you get those earrings out of my room?" Savannah holds the front door of the high school open for me, and I glance at my reflection in the glass. Hammered silver ovals cascade past the ends of my short hair and meet the cowl neck of my sweater. Look how good I look. I should've gone right over there and given Jackson a piece of my mind.

"Are you coming in, or what?" she asks. "Those earrings, weren't they in my room?"

"Oh, yeah. Hey, thanks for meeting me at the doors. No way I could've gotten in with all this. Wait until you see this one dress, perfect for Emily to wear." I grin and whisper, "Perfect for you to wear."

Savannah starts digging through the layers of clothes in my arms. "Wait," I say. "You're going to make me drop..."

"Oh, this *is* perfect." She jerks on the hanger and pull it out of my arms. She holds it up to the big circular mirror on the ceiling that shows who's coming and going to the front office staff. She presses it to her, sways, then turns around to face me. "Mr. Cross said we can put them in the drama closet for now and he'll look at them after his next class. Why are you dressed up?" She leaves me to carry the other seven garments and sashays down the empty hall.

"I'm not dressed up." For crying out loud, I must've let things go if it's this big a deal.

"You went all the way up to my room to find earrings, didn't you?"

"Okay, so I did try a little harder this morning. Do you even wear these earrings? I haven't see you wearing them since Grandma got them for you for Christmas."

"Still doesn't mean you couldn't have asked me to borrow them."

"Really? The person whose room is the center of some kind of mystical vortex in the universe where all my scissors disappear to? Where my shampoo and hairbrush spend more time than in my own custody? Where every pair of boots I own gets kicked to the back of your closet? Where your daddy's flannel shirts end up smelling like Bath and Bodyworks Mango Summer? You're not exactly someone to whom I feel property rights really matter."

"Whatever." She pulls open the door to the storage room beside the gym and holds it for me. "I'll get the lights."

"The musty room slowly lights up, and we pick our way across to another door marked "Drama Closet" in black electrical tape. Inside, metal clothing racks on wheels line one wall, and we make room for the cleaned items to hang together. Savannah goes through them, ignoring the men's outfits and the period costumes from some play set in ancient Rome or Greece.

"Look, these other two dresses. Yuck, looks like old ladies, so that's good. I'm the only young woman in the play."

I rest against a free corner of a prop table. "Yep, I know. But should you be so sure?"

"Now that I've seen the green dress, how can it not be me? Besides, Mr. Cross has been so sweet all week." Savannah holds the dress up to herself again and watches herself in the large mirror on the back wall.

"I know he's married and all now, but I still don't trust him."
I look around the windowless room. "Don't ever come in here
with him alone."

"Mom. You are so weird. He's my teacher. Besides, Cathy
says she's keeping him busy at home, so we don't have to worry.
We stopped the flirting with him before Christmas." She pulls
her dark hair up in a ponytail and looks at a side view. "And
he seems pretty tired so guess they're still in that honeymoon
stage. At least that what we all think."

"You all discuss your teachers like that?" Seems my teachers
were all old, and the thought of them having sex was almost as
bad as thinking about my parents doing it. Wait, though, there
was Mr. Bonner who taught literature, and we all had a crush
on. But sex? No way.

She drops her hand from holding her ponytail and it hits her
hip at the same time her left eyebrow jumps. "Mom, they're
married. They better be having sex or they'll go find someone
else to have it with. It's how things are." Her certainty fades
a bit, and she looks down at the dress she holds. "It's hard to
stay married, I bet."

There is way too much of a question in her last statement and
in the way she leaves it hanging as she hangs the green dress
on the rack. She's asking about me and her dad, just like Susan
keeps doing. No, it's none of their business. Jackson and I will
work things out without all this interference.

"Well," I change subjects, stay away from Mr. Cross anyway.
You need to get back to class, and I have things to do." We part
ways in the hall. I leave through the front doors and go to find
my van where I left it in drop-off parking.

Waiting for the car to warm up, I let the scene at the funeral
home replay. Who was that guy? The one that kissed Carter May.
Maybe if I drive back over by there, he'll still be there. Maybe
he's one of the Carrs. Yeah, he's one of the ones everyone talks
about being from back in the woods, and he got carried away,

and Jackson was just protecting his friend. His co-worker.

It takes all of three minutes to get to the entrance of the funeral parlor. There are still several cars out front so I decide to stop in and just see…just see…whatever.

Tinted glass keeps me from seeing inside, and when I pull open the door, harsh lighting gives me a view of a very small beige reception area. Beige walls, beige linoleum, beige trim around two beige doors. The door straight ahead of me is open, so I walk on through. Here dark red velvet begins its reign. Curtains cover what must be fake windows, as this room doesn't have any outside walls. Chairs face away from me in three separate areas, all divided by, let's say it together, dark red velvet. The chair cushions are the same color, but I doubt the fabric is velvet. In two of the areas, the chairs face a coffin sitting on a table covered in dark red velvet. There's a small pulpit at the front of each area.

"May I help you?"

I jump, but turn to find an older man watching me and trying not to scowl. He works his mouth to not frown, and his eyebrows to stay calm and relaxed.

"No, I'm just looking," pops out of my mouth in a reflex I've used with shopping clerks down through the years.

His scowl wins. "Just looking? At a funeral home?"

"Oh, silly me. No, I'm looking for a friend of mine. I thought I saw her here earlier? Carter May Schuster?"

His scowl only deepens, and he tugs on the cuffs of his black suit. "Let me get Mr. Carr."

Good. Maybe this is the guy I saw with Carter May. But hurrying out of the office he walked into is the older Mr. Carr I already met.

"Why hello, Mrs. Jessup. Alfred Carr, you remember me from the cleaners last week."

"Yes, I do. I was…"

"Your husband was here earlier. He's mixed up in all that

power company baloney I hear."

"Ah, I guess so." He has my hand grasped in both of his, and his smile is as practiced as his grip. He leads me to a couple of the dark red cushioned chairs in one of the areas with a casket. He walks us right up to the front, ignoring my legs dragging. Once we are at the front row, he sits us both down and rests our hands on his bony knee. "There is some mistaken thought that the power company can just move out to our neck of the woods and open up shop. I hope you will impress on Mr. Jessup that we just can't allow that. You understand, don't you?"

All I want now is to get out of here. The smell of old flowers, the wood polish of the shiny casket, and his aftershave have my stomach in motion. My hand inside his is warm, too warm and way too moist. "I do understand, but I think it's pretty much a done deal."

He suddenly drops my hand, places his elbows on his knees, and clasps his long, sweaty hands together. "That's what that woman said. Carter something and that man who came with her."

Halfway up, I fall back down on the dark red cushion. "Who was she with?"

He waves an arm in front of him. "Your husband, right? And another man, her husband or ex or something. Mrs. Jessup, you have to make sure they understand we're not giving up our privacy. It's our land, and being bordered right up to some park where all the teenagers will be hanging out and making a racket is not going to happen. Not at all. We'll buy all the land back there ourselves if we have to." He sits back, and his face has lost its animation. His eyes are sad and a bit shiny as he shakes his head. "It's our way of life. It's for our kids." It's as if he's a balloon slowly deflating. I reach out my hand and pat his shoulder then I turn to get out of there. Gloom, despair, and agony on me. Yeah, that old Hee Haw song could be the advertising jingle for this place.

So, I think as I put my van in Drive, Carter May has a husband? A current husband? Another ex-husband in addition to the one in Alabama? Wonder what Google has to say about all this?

CHAPTER 24

"Because I haven't had time to check. Besides, you're better on the computer than I am. Wait a minute, Laney, I'm going down the hill." Clutching my cell phone between my shoulder and ear, we wait out the interrupted reception that happens whenever I drive down the hill from my house. You know, much like that communications blackout when a spacecraft is on the dark side of the moon.

"You there? Okay, it's been Grand Central Station in that zoo I call a house all weekend, and now Carter May is staying through the week. She's looking for office space here in Chancey."

"So, she was here with this husband? Who told you he was her husband? Where are you going now?"

"Piggly Wiggly," I say. "Can you believe I'm going grocery shopping on Sunday night? There won't be one fresh, decent-looking vegetable in the whole place, the bread will all be picked over, and forget getting lunch meat for lunches since the deli is already closed."

"Hey, just swing by my house and pick me up. We'll drive out to the interstate and go to Wally World."

"Walmart?" I squint. "Seems a long way just for groceries."

"Quit whining and come get me. We'll go to Starbuck's first and then shop. Kids are at church, right? Where's Jackson?"

Jackson? "Okay, I'll be there in a minute. Talk to you then." I press the red button on my phone. Jackson. Well, Jackson is on a little hike with Carter May up at Ander's Lake. Of course, I said "no" when she asked me to go first. It's cold and dark. I thought maybe a bear would eat her, but just then Jackson came back from taking the kids to youth group and when she asked him to go? Let's just say he didn't answer wisely or correctly.

The only lights as I drive through downtown Chancey are at the churches. How a town this small keeps three churches running beats me, but there really isn't anything else for folks to do. Well, until the stuff out at the lake gets built. Carter May hired a firm to flesh out the plans for the park and make a number of computer models. The graphic artist doing that will be coming to stay at the B&B tomorrow and a real estate developer she's also hired as PR for Mountain Power is also coming. Forget that supposed downtime between weekend guests. This new plant has the house overrun with people. Not to mention Jackson just informed me this is now his number one priority at work and he won't be traveling for a while.

With all that in mind, Starbucks and Walmart beside the interstate sound restful and pleasant.

Out on the winding road to Laney and Shaw's home, the light of a nearly full moon plays with the curves in the road. The tall pine trees let it shine through their dark green shadows. The sharp cold of last week eased up over the weekend, and now a softness fills the air. No spring thaw yet, but the softness speaks of warmth to come.

Laney is waiting for me on her big porch and walks out to the drive when I pull up. She opens her door, waves at me, and then motions toward the sky. "Hey there! It's such a beautiful night I thought I'd just wait for you out here. When I came out and saw that moon I almost called you to cancel." Settling into her seat, she sighs. "It's a perfect night for a romantic walk."

Without even getting the car in reverse, I turn and stare at her. "Why did you say that?"

She hesitates in pulling off her gloves. "Because it's true? But Shaw is deep into our taxes and filling out Leslie's student aid paperwork for college. You don't think it's a beautiful night?"

I back down the driveway and head off toward the interstate. "Jackson and Carter May are out walking at Ander's Lake."

"And you're going to Walmart with me?" She sighs and lays her head back. "Lord have mercy on honest women. Why won't women like you ever get it through your heads that other women cannot be trusted with your man? So, your wanting info on Carter May is about Jackson, isn't it?"

"That, and I just want to know more about her. It's not like I sent them off on their little jaunt on purpose. She asked me first and I said no. I thought Jackson and I could have some alone time tonight."

"Well, that's a good sign that you wanted to be with Jackson. Did you tell him that?"

"What? That I thought we'd do something together? No. I mean, well, no."

Laney looks at me. "Wait a minute, he wasn't even supposed to be home tonight, was he? He was signed up to help with the youth outing, but they had to cancel it when the bus wouldn't start. Angie came home 'cause she didn't want to just hang out there and play games, and she told us what was going on. No notice. You couldn't have been planning for some alone time, could you?"

"Maybe."

She shifts in her seat and stares at me. (I can't return her stare because I'm driving, you know.) "Carolina, listen to me. You are lying to yourself because there is something you don't want to look at. Worse than that though, you're lying to me. You're actually putting the words together and saying them out loud. Lying in your head is way easier, and mostly has fewer consequences, than when you start saying it out loud."

I try to focus on the curves in the road. I try to focus on the moon lighting the bare fields on either side of us. I try not to think about how I actually did just lie to Laney. A real, honest-to-goodness lie.

"Susan's right, isn't she?" Laney continued. "She thinks you and Jackson are having trouble, and I keep telling her she doesn't know what she's talking about. But she does, doesn't she?"

As the country road widens for turn lanes and ends with a lonely traffic signal, I slow down to stop. In the turn lane, the van suffused with the glare of the red light overhead, I nod. "Yes. Susan's right, but I don't want her to be. I want things to be like they used to be. Before he changed jobs, before we moved up here, before I became this mess."

Laney reaches over and pats my hand gripping the steering wheel, and I wait for some comfort now that I've told my friend the truth.

"Honey, you are a mess."

Shoot. Forgot who I was talking to.

"Excuse me. That's mine," the young man says as he stops Laney's shopping cart from running over the box of macaroni in the middle of the aisle.

She snorts at me. "Used to think all these men dropping things in my path were flirting with me. Now I see it's just because they are too vain to push a buggy."

She's right. There are several men around us with arms full of groceries, no buggy in sight. I shake my head. "Wonder what the deal is?"

Laney opens the end freezer unit and grabs a box of waffles. "Their wives have sent them to the store to pick up a few items for the week. As long as they don't get a shopping cart they can tell themselves they aren't grocery shopping." She tosses the waffles in her cart and lets the freezer door close behind her. "Besides, they tell themselves this way is faster."

Another man walks out in front of my buggy with his arms full and his eyes studying his list, and I come to an abrupt stop. He looks up and smiles and continues on his quest. Laney rolls her eyes and sniffs. "Amateurs."

"It's gone, all gone," I whimper after draining the last bit of vanilla cappuccino and setting the empty cup in the seat of my buggy. Then to Laney, I say, "We missed you up at Susan and Graham's yesterday. He smoked ribs, a pork roast, and sausages. Susan always makes entertaining look so easy. I host something like that, and the entire community has to help out."

"Well, Shaw and I really wanted to watch the Falcons' playoff game and not be distracted with lots of people. Did y'all watch the game?"

"Yeah, it was on. Mostly the guys and, well, Carter May, watched it."

"And you hung out in the kitchen with the 'girls', right?" Laney stops beside the display of grapes and chooses a bag. "Honey, you don't want Jackson to come home because he's married to you and you have children together, you want him to come home because you are the most fun person he's ever been around. When he thinks of being with you, you want him to think of good things like food, laughing, and sex. And if you can throw in sports, it doesn't hurt."

"Oh, Laney, you are just too much. Real life and real marriage aren't like that." I push my cart on to the mounds of potatoes and onions.

"Of course not." She follows me. "There's real life, and there's perception." She holds up a bag of potatoes. "Look at this. This is real. Potatoes are brown, lumpy, and dirty. But a bowl of mashed potatoes, steaming hot with a pat of butter melting in the middle of them? No self-respecting potato wants to be thought of as brown and lumpy, when it can be remembered as hot, delicious, and beautiful."

I'm not sure how I feel being compared to a potato. "I can't control how he remembers me. You can choose how you think of potatoes. He chooses how he thinks of me."

She puts the bag of potatoes in her cart. "Sure he does, but think about it. In his recent file labeled 'Carolina,' what have you deposited there? Fun moments? Sweet moments? Things that make him feel good about himself and his family?"

"Well, he doesn't seem too concerned about what he's putting in my file folder. He's gone all the time, and he's more excited about this stupid power plant than me or his family." I grab a head of lettuce and head for the checkout lanes.

Laney pulls up in the lane next to mine. While we empty our carts and pay, I revel in the fact that I sure put that stupid Southern Girl baloney back in her face. Potatoes. Sure, mashed potatoes are great, but that's not how they come out of the ground. They're all fixed up and prettied up so someone will want to eat them, not live with them. I'd rather be real any day than just look good.

At the entrance of the optical center, I stop to wait for Laney and study the poster of glasses, but all I see are potatoes. Potatoes in their raw, sturdy, natural way. Potatoes un-gussied-up, unembellished, the way they were meant to be by God.

"You ready to go, or are you buying glasses?" Laney pushes her buggy past me.

Outside we walk side by side under the tall, bright lights. The parking lot is full, and people walk in both directions, toward the store and away from it.

At my van we park both carts up to the rear door and begin unloading.

"You're right." Laney says. (And lightning doesn't strike or anything.) "You are right, Jackson has sure not given you anything good to fill your folder on him with lately. Makes it kind of hard to want to be around him, I'm sure."

"Oh, it sure does." I wait for her to pull her cart back, and then I lower the hatch and shut it. She takes both buggies to the corral, and I get in the driver's seat and start the car.

She opens her door. "It's almost nice out there. Maybe spring actually will come again." Laney unwraps her purple scarf from around her neck after she's seated. "You know auditions for the Spring Play are this week. Is Savannah excited?"

"She sure is. I think Emily auditions are Tuesday, and the cast list will be up by Friday. Your girls trying out?"

"Angie would rather die, but of course Jenna knows the school would fall down if they had an event and she wasn't up on the stage. She's not even trying out for Emily. She says it's perfect for Savannah, and they all say they aren't even going to try out for it." Adjusting the heater vents, she adds, "Susan told me about the green dress."

"It is perfect, for the part and for Savannah."

The moon is higher as we make our way back through the foothills. The landscape is almost surreal. Barns, cars, trees all reflect a blue glow. The shadows are the blue of shadows in the comics. We ride and look and listen to country music on the radio. It's low, but adds such a peaceful feeling to the drive.

As we turn onto Laney's road, she says, "You are right, you know, about what Jackson has put into your recent memory. Your file folder labeled 'Jackson.' What do you think you should do about that?"

"What do you mean? How can I change what he puts out there for me to remember? I can't."

As we near her house, she puts her scarf back around her neck. "So, you can't do anything about that. Yeah, I agree." (Again, no lightning, and I'm getting used to being right.)

147

We get out of the car and in just one trip, we manage to get all her things up the few steps of the porch and into her kitchen. She walks me back to the half-glass porch door. "You can't do anything about what Jackson does. The only thing you can control is what you give him to put in your folder. That's all."

"But…" I don't know what I want to say. This being right thing is harder than it looks.

We step out onto the porch. "There is no 'but,' Carolina. You can't control what Jackson does. Realize this: the only memories you can change are the ones you participate in." She leans on the porch railing, and I walk down the steps. The blue glow and midnight shadows fill the yard. Up in the sky, the moon hangs like a huge, luminescent pearl.

I turn back towards the porch. "So, tonight?"

Laney's face is blue, and the moonlight strikes silver lakes in her black hair. "Jackson's memories of tonight do not include you. Your choice. He'll appreciate you went to the grocery store, but it won't make him smile the next time he sees a full moon."

On the short walk to my van I take a look at what is in Jackson's recent Carolina file.

I need to get home.

CHAPTER 25

"Mom, can we have a Super Bowl party here?" Bryan asks before he gets fully in the front door Thursday afternoon.

"No. You can't." Savannah answers him before I have seen either of them. However, they find me in the kitchen. (Not a real good hiding place.) "Mom, tell him 'no.'"

"Mom, pleeeaaassseee. It might be cancelled if we don't find a place to have it. Shira's mom and dad won a cruise vacation and so they can't have it at their house."

"Why here?" I ask. "We don't even have a big TV. Doesn't someone in the youth group? This is for the youth group, right? Don't some of them have big TVs?" I reach up and pat Bryan's shoulder. "I'm sure someone else will volunteer, honey." When it hits me that I really do have to reach *up* to pat my youngest child's shoulder, I step back and stare at him.

His blue eyes are not intense like Savannah's; they are soft and touched with grey. "No, Miss Susan says no one else has volunteered. She didn't want to ask you because she said you're busy with Crossings and stuff, but I told her you're not busy. And Brittani's mom said she'll help you."

Oh, Brittani. "Well, why not have it at Brittani's house and I'll help her mom?"

His eyes might not be as intense as his sister's, but they do a pretty good imitation of their signature roll. "Yeah. No, they don't do things like that."

I turn my back on both of them as they root around in the refrigerator. "Really? That's all I have to do is say that we don't do things like that?" Over my shoulder I check out Bryan's reaction.

Bryan smiles at me as he throws a flour tortilla Frisbee-style onto the counter. "Mom. They already know you do. That we do. Parties and stuff, you know." He sprinkles shredded cheddar cheese onto the tortilla. "It's real easy. Everyone brings stuff for sandwiches, and most of the kids get picked up at half-time since their folks have to work the next day."

Savannah licks down the edge of an ice cream sandwich. "Yeah, why is there school the next day? Shouldn't the Super Bowl be like on Saturday or something? Or shouldn't we get the next day off?" She bites into the sandwich but keeps on talking. "If you do have the party here, I'm not going to be here. I have my own party to go to."

"Close your mouth when it's full. That's gross," I say. "We're not doing the party here, and I don't remember you asking permission to go to any party on a school night."

"See? That's why it's so lame that it's on Sunday. It's at Aston's, and I'm helping him put it together."

Bryan is pulling his tortilla with melted cheese out of the microwave, so I sidle closer to Savannah and whisper. "And Ricky is okay with that?"

She pops the last bite of ice cream sandwich in her mouth and purposely keeping her mouth shut, shrugs.

Bryan, now talking around a mouthful of cheese and tortilla, answers, "He doesn't yet but he will when he shows up here and you're not here, won't he? Brittani says everyone is talking about how you are two-timing Ricky with a junior who's not even on the football team."

"Bryan, don't talk with your mouth full," I admonish.

His sister helps me out with my parenting. "Yeah, especially when you are just saying what your gossipy girlfriend tells you is going on at the high school. You're still in junior high, remember?" She licks her fingers and picks up her books off the table. "I'm going up to study."

I yell at her back as she passes into the living room. "Savannah, I'll need to talk to his mom before I say okay to you going to Aston's. You hear me?" The only sound is Bryan closing up the cheese after making himself another cheese tortilla. "Do you think she heard me?"

Bryan shrugs. He doesn't care. "So, we can have the party here? I'll call Miss Susan, okay?" he says as he dials a number on his phone. "You just need to let Brittani's mom know what she can do to help. Okay?"

"Wait, did I say…"

He hands me his phone. "Here, Mom. You should probably talk to Miss Susan." The ringing stops before I fully have his phone in hand.

"Hey Bryan, so she said 'Yes'?"

"Susan, it's me on Bryan's phone. So the youth need a place to have the Super Bowl party?"

"Oh, Carolina, that's great. Thanks so much. You just need to provide the paper plates and napkins and cups. I have folks bringing all the food and drinks. It was supposed to be at Shira's, but they won some cruise or something. Why does that never happen to us?"

"Really. But, seriously? We don't even have a large TV. Doesn't someone have a big TV that wants to host it?" Okay, whining is not going to get me out of this, but it does make me feel a little better.

"The people with big TVs are having their own Super Bowl parties. It'll be a snap, I promise. I'll be there to help you, and Brittani said her mom would help, too. It'll be fun, you'll see."

"Okay. When is the Super Bowl?"

The pause seems a bit long and causes me to stop wiping out the melted cheese in the microwave. "Susan?"

"Oh, I figured everyone knew when the Super Bowl is. It's Sunday. This Sunday."

I slam the microwave door. "Well, of course it is."

"Boy, we really appreciate you helping out like this at the last minute. Really do."

"Whatever. I've got to go. Apparently we're having a party here in only a couple days."

Closing Bryan's phone, I open the refrigerator, then let it close. I open the freezer and pull out an ice cream sandwich to take with me to the living room window. Late afternoon sun fades into the stripped limbs of the maples beside the house and causes long, skinny shadows to fall through the living room. Across the tracks, the pine trees soften the hillside with their dark green clouds, but on this side there are only bare limbs and a windswept yard. Sitting on the sofa, I tear open the white paper on my treat and then holding the flat sides between my finger and thumb, I lick at the softening ice cream squeezed in between the dark cookie rectangles.

I can't believe it's already Thursday. The week has flown by and I've not only not breathed, I've not talked to Jackson (definitely haven't put anything worthwhile in his Carolina file), and I've apparently missed any Super Bowl hubbub. I had a drama club meeting, a women's historical group meeting at Missus' house, then I oversaw the boys' auditions for *Our Town* yesterday, which mainly meant making them behave while each one went in to their audition. Savannah just shrugged about her audition and told me the green dress might be a little short for her. Last night we all went to the dinner at church so we could hear about the summer mission trip. I only went for the free meal. After what happened on the ski retreat, there is no way Bryan is going on another trip with that group. And here is it Thursday, and we are now hosting a Super Bowl party on Sunday.

All the ice cream I can reach with my tongue is gone so I munch on the outside cookies while I realize what bothers me even more than hosting the party. Apparently there are all these parties around town in the houses with big TVs and we've not been invited to a single one?

What's the good of being social butterflies if no one ever invites you to their garden?

Chapter 26

"I can't stay here. You are the one that wants to have the kids' party. I'm going to Shaw's." Jackson pours another cup of coffee and leans against the counter. His tie lays across his shoulder, and he smells of freshly applied aftershave. His shirt is crisp for meetings in Atlanta today. Low kitchen lighting and dove gray skies outside make the room feel intimate, and I'm reminded of the mornings we shared coffee when the kids were little.

At this table. Every morning. Staring at the scratched maple table worn to a soft glow through the years, I try, but can't remember when we stopped having coffee together before work. "When did we stop having coffee together in the mornings?"

He sits down across from me. "When Bryan finished elementary school, you didn't have to get up so early and you started working some evenings at the library. I told you to stay in bed one morning, and you did." He sighs and smiles. "I've been on my own in the mornings since then. It's not bad, kind of peaceful."

He's lying. I'm not sure what he's lying about, but he's not looking at me and he's rubbing his finger and thumb together. He isn't good at lying. "Really? I don't think I realized it had ended." And I picture him here, and back in Marietta, in the semi-darkness of a sleeping house alone. "We used to talk a lot when we had coffee, didn't we?" Matter of fact, that's why I'm up this morning, to catch him to talk about the Super Bowl party.

"Yeah, I guess we did." He stands and sets his cup in the sink.

"Do you want a refill?" he asks as he points at the coffee pot.

"No, but really, back to Sunday. Why didn't you tell me we were invited to Laney and Shaw's party?"

"I didn't *not* tell you on purpose. Figured Laney would tell you about it. Shaw told me to invite Mr. Reynolds and Carter May and whoever else was here."

"So, Carter May's going?"

"Of course. I better get going." He gathers his briefcase and laptop and walks around the table. I lift my head for a goodbye kiss that doesn't come.

He strides into the living room, and I see how far we've drifted from not only each other, but who we used to be. Softly he opens and then closes the front door behind him, and now I'm the one alone in the early morning quiet.

Funny, my coffee doesn't usually taste this bitter.

By the time Savannah comes downstairs, I've accomplished a lot in the Crossings office—and I've drunk two pots of coffee. My foot jittering on the floor while I wait for the toaster to pop up a bagel is going ninety, as Daddy used to say. A headache is building in my neck, and it hurts to turn and greet my daughter as I push the toaster lever down. "Good morning. Can I put a bagel in for you?"

"No, some of us from drama are meeting at Ruby's, then we'll all be together to see the cast list when Stephen puts it up."

"Mr. Cross."

"Whatever." She pours a glass of orange juice and looks out the windows of the back door. Her hair is in a sleek pony tail, and she's wearing a dark red sweater over skinny jeans and black boots. The lightweight sweater is belted with black cords wrapped several times around her waist. Despite the pain in my neck, I twist to see her reflection in the window. Full make-up and earrings say she's decked out.

"Well, good luck on getting Emily."

"Sure. I'm mostly worried about Aston not getting the part of George. The leads usually go to the senior boys to encourage them to stay in drama, but there's not a senior that will look good with me. They're too short." She turns to face me. "So. Aston's party?"

"I told you I need to talk to his mother." My bagel pops up. I carefully fling it out onto the counter and lick my burning thumb while I look up at her.

Outlined in a thin black line, her eyeroll seems even more dramatic. *It's kind of early for eye rolling, isn't it?* "Mom. Why? She's going to think that is so lame."

"I don't know Aston. If you'd bring him over here so I knew him it might be different."

"Mom. Really. He's fine. His family is fine. You don't need to talk to them." She sets her still half-full glass down hard. "I don't know why you have to be so difficult."

"Just taking after my daughter," I mumble under my breath as I smooth cream cheese on my bagel. Louder, so she can hear me as she's putting on her coat in the living room, I say, "I'm sure Susan or Laney can get me Aston's folk's number. I'll just give them a call today." I chew and wait.

Bryan comes clomping down the stairs. "Hey, get out of the way."

"Don't step on my purse, stupid."

"You want me to let you go to a party on a school night and

you're calling your brother 'stupid'?" I carry my breakfast to the doorway. "Not a good way to get me on your side, you know."

Savannah pulls her ponytail out of the neck of her coat. "Okay. Sorry, Bryan, you're not stupid for stepping on my purse and breaking my stuff." She leans her head and looks at me. "Is that better?"

"I didn't step on your purse, and if I did, why is it laying in the middle of the stairs?" He switches tacks. "You're leaving now? Are you going to Ruby's?" Then he asks me, "I don't want to go early, so how am I supposed to get to school, Mom?"

"The school bus?" When did kids start deciding riding the school bus wasn't an option?

He elbows past his sister, and I let him pass into the kitchen. He yells behind himself, "Nope, too late. Budget cuts. Remember, they don't have separate buses now so I would have had to catch the elementary bus fifteen minutes ago and go to early study hour."

Savannah's loud "Bye" is punctuated with her slamming the door. Luckily, I've already heard our guests up using the B&B bathroom because the whole house reverberates.

"Okay, I'll get dressed and take you." I pull up the hem of my robe and go upstairs. Now I'm remembering why I don't get up with Jackson in the morning. It's not even 7:30 am and I feel like I've put in a full day. And just wait until my coffee wears off.

CHAPTER 27

Jeans and a long-sleeved T-shirt are enough this morning as the sun spills over the mountains making promises it can't possibly fulfill yet, but let's us keep lying to ourselves. Bryan even has on his long cargo shorts and a tee shirt with no jacket as he comes loping down the front steps to meet me in the van. "Feels good out here," he says as he swings into the passenger seat.

He punches the buttons on the radio until his music comes pouring out, but I don't let that punch *my* buttons. Sunshine, tennis shoes, the smell of thawing ground, and all on a Friday morning. Besides, he's getting out of the car soon; then the radio is all mine.

"Look," I say at the bottom of the hill near town. I point past Bryan out his window. "See all those green shoots, you know, plants?" The whole area at the bottom of the hill is covered in daffodil sprouts. "Oh, Bryan, I love daffodils. This will be all yellow."

A tap of a horn behind us makes me move on. "Wonder if we have any daffodils up at the house? I should've planted some last fall."

"Um, hello? Winter?"

"No, you plant bulbs and they need the winter cold to, well, to get them started or something and then they come up every spring. They smell delicious."

Last summer is just a blur to me, and I can't remember any flowers around here at all. Wait, the park. Around the gazebo. Yeah. And Missus' front porch and walk. Okay, that's right. Flowers, I need to think about what flowers to plant.

"Here you go. Have a good day." A grunt is all I get in response as he spills out of the door while swinging his backpack across his shoulder.

He pushes his door shut while I push the buttons on the radio to my classic rock station. "Sweet Home Alabama" is playing and everything lifts. My spirits, my smile, my voice. Singing and tapping on the steering wheel, I turn towards the town. A cup of coffee from Ruby's and afterwards, a walk in the little park to see if anything is coming up there. Doubtful if anything will be green yet, but the camellias are blooming so I can take a look at them.

Back in the suburbs everything is so landscaped. Even the gas stations and convenient stores have their seasonal flowers taken out at the first sign of too much heat or too much cold. Beds of pansies become beds of begonias in a matter of minutes. Fresh pine straw is thrown around like confetti at New Year's. The subdivision entrances alone keep dozens of nurseries and landscapers in gas and groceries. Front yards compete with their manicured lawns, sculpted crepe myrtles, and azaleas arranged by color. Tastefully arranged pots of trailing leaves and flowers guide visitors to shiny front doors. Except, few visitors walk up those sidewalks as everyone is too busy running. Running to work, to school, running to baseball, tennis, or ballet, or just plain old running. Perfect homes with perfect lawns…and I loved it. Loved never having a neighbor park their old cars on their front lawn. Loved having a uniform way to plant and decorate and act. Lack of a cohesive plan leads to…that.

Pulling my car into a parking place facing the gazebo I gaze at the row of old Southern beauty homes on the other side of the square. Missus' and FM's house sits right in the middle. The salmon and gray paint scheme outlines the dignity of a home that has survived much and loved many. Cared-for flower beds heaped with pine straw for wintering say how much it is loved, and the shiny brass wall sconces and door kick-plate welcome one to sit in the swing and have a glass of sweet tea. All that guides your eye to the next beauty.

A beauty which looks to be home to a family of raccoons. I don't think anyone lives there. A truckload of pine straw couldn't hide the mess in the yard. Maybe a truckload of pine logs? But lest I fail to mention the plusses, a small decorative bush grows out of the front corner gutter, and the porch does have furniture on it. Of course, it would be hard to sit on the furniture as it's stacked to the ceiling of the porch and is home to a passel of wild cats.

Passels of wild cats do not live on front porches in the northern suburbs of Atlanta.

Like the good Chancey-ite I have become, I get out of the car, focus on the pretty houses, and ignore the eyesore on the corner. Looks like the warmer weather has brought out more than just me, and when I pull open the door, I greet folks with a big smile and "hello."

I'm greeted with a quick silence that rises and then falls into quick whispers.

"There you are. Gallivanting around again, I suppose." Missus rises from her table and marches toward me. She grabs my purse and chunks it onto the nearest table. Then she starts going through it.

Susan scurries up to me and whispers, "Your phone?"

"Oh, I don't think I have it."

Missus turns and sighs in disgust and shoves my purse away. "Oh, of course you don't." She points to the stuff she's taken out of my purse and left surrounding it on the table. "Pick that up and come sit down."

"I'm not staying." Jamming everything back in my purse I look up at the counter. "Ruby, can I get a coffee to go? Just this one time?"

Susan grimaces. "No, you're not going to want to go right now. You're not going to believe what's happened."

"What's happened? Is everyone okay? Savannah? Jackson?"

"Nothing that bad, just...well. Here sit down." She pushes me to the booth Missus has settled in.

Libby sets a cup in front of me and begins pouring. "I'm so sorry, Carolyn. I don't know what he's thinking. Just don't know at all."

"Someone paid him." Missus nods at her own words. "Money. The only explanation."

"What? First you scared me, now you're just confusing me. Not unusual here, but what is going on?" What in the world are they all worked up about now? Taking a sip of coffee, I breathe deep. Probably found out the cheese at the grocery deli is imitation.

"The casting list. Jenna called. Laney headed right over there to see what she can find out." Susan pats my hand.

"Stop that." I pull my hand away. "What, Jenna didn't get a part?"

"No, she got what she thought she would. One of the moms, the older women." Susan sits back and looks across the table at Missus.

Missus sighs. "Savannah got the part of the other mom."

"Savannah? My Savannah? But I thought she was going to be Emily. She, I mean, everyone was sure about it." Poor Savannah. "But, well, she'll have to deal with it. Disappointment is part of growing up." My stomach rejects the just-swallowed sip of coffee as my own disappointment settles in. Wow, is she going to be hard to live with. So much for daffodils and sunshine.

Libby still stands over me. "I am so sorry, Carolina. Stephen must've, well, I don't know what he's thinking."

"Libby, he's just your son-in-law; it's not your responsibility," I say. "Besides, he doesn't have to give anyone any part. He just thought someone would make a better Emily than Savannah. Who did get the part of Emily?" And just like that, no one is looking at me.

"Susan?"

She mumbles and so I lean closer. "I didn't understand you. Who?"

Susan lifts her head, squeezes her eyes tight, and says it. "Brittani."

Brittani got Savannah's role? Brittani with an "I"? Bryan's Brittani?

Well. Isn't this going to be interesting?

CHAPTER 28

"This freshman class is one of *those* classes." Laney flings the corner of her winter cape off her shoulder. "See? Just look down there." From our perch high in the stands, we stare toward the basketball court and an animated group of students with their instruments. "Mr. Watkins, the band director, changed the rules this year to let freshmen try out for the Pep Band, and so many ninth graders tried out to cheer for the freshman football team, their squad was bigger than the varsity squad. Cathy says the freshman cheer stunts are better than varsity's." The set of her mouth and hardness in her eyes tell all that there is not only ice skating in hell, but ski slopes are soon to open.

Nods around us say we're all on the same page. Except I'm not. "What do you mean, 'one of those classes'?"

Laney's mother, Gladys Troutman, answers. "Every so often a class comes along that is just superior. Better athletes, better students, big personalities, and they take over a school. Janice from the front office told us at the circle Christmas dinner that this class' scores are the best in the county. Math, especially."

Susan groans, "Oh no. Poor Grant."

Gladys agrees. "He already has enough trouble with math, and now to be right behind this class? The comparisons will be brutal. I remember Scott's class; it was one of these special groups. They took over Chancey High when they walked in the front doors as freshman. All the other grades just paled in comparison."

"And we knew it," says a woman from the bleacher above Gladys. "I was the grade ahead of Scott. They were all gods. Whatever they competed in they won. Rather quickly we just bowed out of their way."

"Are they bullies?" I ask.

Susan shakes her head. "No, they just shine. Most of the time, a class has maybe one set of gifts, like a whole class of athletes, and the school excels in sports until they leave. Or they stand out academically, and they all get into great colleges. And it works in the opposite way, too, sometimes you get a class that is mean or lazy or bored, and the teachers hate those years. Then one like this comes along. They seem to cheer each other on to greatness in every area."

"So, Brittani, is that good?" I ask, although it sounds like I don't want the answer. "Savannah refused to talk about it. She changed into her cheerleader outfit and left within minutes of getting home from school. Bryan beamed all afternoon, but didn't have any details. He hadn't even known Brittani was trying out, apparently no one knew except Mr. Cross."

Libby, still with her hangdog look from this morning, sighs. "Yes, usually freshmen only try out for practice and the bit parts, but Stephen says she just *is* Emily. The costume fit like it was made for her, and with all that red hair will be stunning up on stage. He said her poise was amazing, and she looked fresh and young after watching the older girls try out. I'm sorry, Carolina."

Being the final game of the season, the gym is packed. My purse takes up space beside me for Jackson when he gets here. He's promised to be here to see Savannah cheer, and I keep scanning the main doors to catch a glimpse of him. I have on the outfit that everyone commented on the other day, and I'm dying in it. The warm day outside didn't clue in the janitor to not turn the heat up high. Sweat swaths my scalp, and my hair is flat and damp. Smart people who wore layers have stripped them off, and everyone is fanning themselves. However, the arms of my sweater are tight and glued to my arms, and my boots may be cute, but they sure don't breathe.

"Carolina, aren't you burning up?" Laney practically yells. "Why did you wear that sweater?"

There. That's why. In the doors comes Jackson with that sexy, rumpled-look of a neck-loosed dress shirt and right beside him is Carter May. Her hair is back in a thick pony-tail and as they walk she takes off her navy suit coat. Her pink silk shell is simple and neat. It tucks in the waist of her straight navy skirt, and when they start up the bleacher steps, Jackson has to hold her arm to give her balance in her stiletto pumps.

"Got room for us?" Jackson asks down the row.

Laney growls low into my ear. "Hell to the no," then adds loud and syrupy, "Really just one here, Jackson."

Susan stands up. "Carter May, why don't I introduce you to some folks? Just wait there for me."

My friends. I feel cooler already, then Libby stands up right behind me. "Oh no, here's my seat. I can't stay anyway. Ruby just texted me she wants to open tonight so I'm headed down to put on some blackberry cobbler for y'all after the game." She climbs over folks in her row and pushes Carter May towards her place. Jackson arrives in his seat, and when we are all ready for the game I turn partially around. "Carter May, I hear you hired Anna for your new office?"

Jackson turns backwards, too, and we're met with her legs. Right in our faces. The tight skirt has a slit on the side and that darn expensive fabric just won't stay in place.

It's getting hotter in here.

"Yes, she is just a doll. So helpful and so quick. I'm encouraging her to take more courses in marketing. Everyone here is so helpful."

"I hear you've met the Carrs?" Laney asks.

"Yes, they really aren't very helpful, though, are they? They think they own that whole side of the river. Maybe now that I'm paying them rent they'll be nicer."

Can't help it. I turn around again. "You're renting from them?"

"Yes, on the other end of their strip mall from the dry cleaner's. Good office space in Chancey is not easy to come by, and they had two spaces, which is just what we need. Right, Jackson?"

My husband nods, and his gray eyes dart to me. "Railroad's decided to open a temporary office here while the project is ongoing."

Damp from sweat and now burning up on the inside, I stand up and start climbing over Jackson's legs. On the other side of him, I stop and seethe. "How great. You two get to live in the same house and now work in the same offices. How great is that? I'm getting a Coke." The rest of the people in the row had decided not to wait for me to barrel them over like I did Jackson and have cleared out to wait at the end. So, with all the dignity one can muster on shaky stands drenched in sweat, I head for the concession stand.

After all, isn't that where I really belong? Out in the dingy entrance making it possible for the pretty people to be in the bright lights?

Dark coolness greets me outside the side doors, and I pull my sweater away from my body to try and let some of the heat evaporate.

"Carolyn Jessup, you have got to get a hold on yourself." Laney rushes up behind me. "You can't just keep causing scenes like that. I don't care how much your mama and daddy raised you on *Gone with the Wind*, people don't react well to temper tantrums and storming around.

"Laney, he likes her." That's all I get out before the tears begin. "I saw them. Together. Like, hugging. I saw them." Gulping for air, the words come haltingly. "And then they left together."

She pulls me around the corner of the building. "Here, sit here."

The cool stones feel good through my olive cords, but I can't keep from rubbing my arms. The heat has activated every itchy fiber knitted up in the beautiful sweater. Laney stand in front of me, pulls me up to stand, and reaches down for the lower edge of my sweater. Then she pulls up. Surprise allows her to get my sweater up to my head and my arms in the air. One more jerk and it's in her hands, and I'm standing outside my daughter's high school in nothing but my bra.

Lord, does it ever feel good.

Instinctively my hands reach around me to cover myself, and I hiss at my friend. "Give that back." She waves it just out of my reach, and then I realize she's not just waving it, she's fanning me.

"Calm down, there's no one here but us."

A shiver goes over me and releases much of my heat and steam.

Laney tosses my inside-out sweater on the wall beside me and then unwraps her cape. "Here, drape it this way." Then she takes off the woolen scarf wrapped around her neck. It unwinds into a long scarf of tweed and dark plaid. She reaches around me and ties the cape in place. "Now, just keep your arms down and you're fine. Honey, women of our age cannot afford to wear just one layer, especially if that layer is..." she pulls at the sweater she is turning right side out, "... 60% wool. We don't live in Antarctica."

She sits down on the wall and folds my sweater onto her lap. "Sit down."

The evaporation of my heat also took my anger. Limp, still

damp, and depressed, I sink onto the stones again. "I've lost him, haven't I?"

"Lost Jackson? I don't think so." She shrugs. "But maybe."

"But, we're married. He can't. He won't..." I realize what she's said, and I turn on her. "How dare you..."

"What? Say the truth? He's not bound to you with chains and handcuffs. It is possible for a spouse to walk away, despite what you do or don't do. That's just the simple truth."

"But we promised each other. We are so good together."

Laney laughs, "Oh, that's right. All those other marriages were just play acting, no broken promises. No good beginnings. I'm sorry, you're right. Your marriage is *special*."

"It was until we moved here."

"Yep, your marriage would've been spectacular, something angels themselves sang about unless, unless, oh no! The dreaded move to Chancey! Drat that dastardly town and those dastardly people, kryptonite to the holy, promise-filled marriage of Carolina and Jackson." She leans back and sticks her legs out in front of her. "Grow up."

Channeling my inner teenager, I stomp my booted foot. "It's true. We were fine before we moved here."

"Then you're fine now. Except you're not."

"You don't think a situation, a move, a big change can affect a relationship?"

"Affect it? Sure. Kill it in six months? No."

From around the building, I hear Jackson calling me.

Laney yells, "We're over here." She stands up and whispers to me. "Apologize. Be honest. Get on solid ground again. You have to do that first." As she straightens her black sweater she looks down at the ground. "We'll talk later, and I'll tell you a story that might help. Hey, Jackson, how's the game going?"

He stops and shoves his hands in the pockets of his dress pants. "Good, almost halftime and figured y'all would want to see the girls' performance."

"Oh, yes. Thanks." I stand up and hold my hand out to Laney for my sweater. "It was just so hot in there. Laney, well, traded with me."

"See y'all inside," Laney says as she hands me my sweater and then scurries toward the front of the gym.

Jackson doesn't move, just stands with his legs apart and his hands dug into his pockets. He looks up sideways at me.

Okay, here goes, let's see if Laney is right. "I'm sorry about that in there. I was just so hot and, well, so I don't know…"

He looks back down at his shoes, "Jealous?"

The heat floods back. "Jealous? I'm not jealous. Why would I…" Then flashing across my mind is Carter May's smooth pink shirt and the way it tucked so neatly into her skirt. And her heels. And her legs. "Okay, yes, maybe some."

"Maybe Carter May staying at the house isn't a good idea." Jackson's low voice causes my stomach to churn.

"Okay" is all that leaks out of me. He doesn't look up, but I can't move my eyes off him.

He clears his throat. "Can you tell her she needs to leave? We can make a reservation for her somewhere else."

Ice grows over me inch by inch. He won't look up, and I can't look away. All I want is to be in the gym or at home or at Ruby's. Anywhere but here. "Okay. Should I ask why you want her to leave?"

He bites his upper lip and rocks on his heels, but when his head jerks up it's because Bryan is running around the corner hollering for us.

"Mom. Dad. Savannah fell, and she's hurt."

We both dash toward Bryan, and I'm surprised how quickly the ice melted and released me when I heard my son's voice. His urgency and the picture in my mind of Savannah lying unconscious on the gym floor reminds me who I am. Not a woman in the midst of a romantic drama, I'm a mom. How silly the scene already feels.

Susan greets us at the doors. "She's fine. Just twisted her ankle. We've already got an ice bag on it."

We see our daughter seated on the first row of bleachers. "Did she fall during the routine?" Jackson asks.

"No," Susan says.

When we get to Savannah, fury rolls off her like hot fudge over soft ice cream. "She tripped me. Intentionally."

But when I look around, I don't see a guilty party. "Who?"

"That freshman." She presses her lips together then growls. "They're all evil." She stands part way up, but before her daddy can help her she drops back down. "Get me out of here."

We help her stand, and Cathy rushes up with Savannah's black and gold gym pants. "She didn't wear a coat today. You know it was so nice out. Sorry, but I have to go, half-time and all, you know."

As we get to the gym entrance, me carrying our things and Jackson helping Savannah limp out, we hear Savannah's name being called.

"Don't stop," Savannah warns, but the voice catches up with us. With a flip of red hair, Brittani with an "i" is at our side.

"Oh, Savannah. I'm so sorry. I should've gotten out of your way, but don't worry about halftime. We'll find someone to take your place. Bye."

Another flip of hair, and she's gone, but Bryan is right on her heels. "I'll get a ride home with Grant, okay? Savannah, hope you feel better." He runs off after the flying red hair. Wouldn't want him to miss halftime.

Jackson meets my eyes over our daughter's head, and then we both close our eyes as she declares. "I hate her. I completely hate her."

We get to the front doors, and they are held open by the concession kids like Savannah is a fallen queen. Well wishes and sincere concern is no match for her fury, though, and I get close to her ear to demand she say thank you. I add, "Or they'll think bad of you."

"Are you kidding?" She rolls her eyes, but then shouts in a lilting voice full of sarcasm, "Thanks, everyone. See you tomorrow." She then peers at me. "You forget, I'm not the beauty queen. I don't *care* what people think of me."

"Jackson," Carter May calls from behind us. She's running in her heels, and when she reaches out and grabs his arm, we all stop. "Do you want me to drive your car home?"

Anger at Savannah not caring what people think about her morphs into anger at myself and my lack of action, and I step toward the woman holding my husband's arm. "I'll drive the car. Jackson, you take the van and help Savannah. Carter May, you can ride with me."

CHAPTER 29

Carter May is packing her bags and hitting the road, and she also has been put on notice to keep her hands off my husband.

Gold has once again been found in Dahlonega, Georgia, and I'm selling tracts of land which will make you a millionaire.

Believe one line, you gotta believe both.

I did manage to ask her about the man I saw her with at Carr's the other day. She confessed he is her husband and that she's working to get back together with him and there will never be any other man for her.

There are also diamonds on those land tracts.

Honestly, she said doesn't remember which man I might be referring to. Probably a contractor or salesman. That's the truth. Well, that's the truth of what she said but of course she's lying about it. It was her husband, Mr. Carr told me, and we all know old moonshiners are notorious for telling the truth.

Staring into our freezer, I play out what I should've said. What she should've said. What am I looking for?

Over my shoulder, Jackson whispers, "Did you tell Carter May?"

"Move, you're in my light." Oh, yeah, something cold for Savannah's foot. "Surely we have a bag of vegetables in here, right?" Shuffling things around in the freezer, a solid block of hamburger slides onto the floor and the box of ice cream sandwiches spills its contents across my feet. "Here. Peas, perfect." With a dish towel wrapped around the bag, I take it to Savannah seated on the living room couch, leaving Jackson to shove everything back into the freezer.

"This will help the swelling," I say as I place the bag around her ankle then head around the couch and back toward the kitchen. "Do you want anything? Hot chocolate? Or a snack?" I reach for the blanket behind her. "Are you cold?"

"I'm fine, Mom. Fine. I just need some space. It's been a horrible day."

"Okay, okay." Dismissed, I head for the kitchen and turn to motion Jackson to just leave her alone, but he moves to stand in front of her. His hands resting in his pants pockets and his head dropped toward her, his gray eyes are focused his daughter.

His voice is low, in volume and timbre. "So someone tripped you?"

"No, not someone. Brittani. Stupid freshmen do not belong with the varsity cheerleaders. She's so clumsy and doesn't look where she's going." Held-back tears mix with her anger, making her words sharp. Time for us to give her some room. I motion at Jackson to come with me, we still have some talking to do about our troublesome guest. But he never even looks up.

Jackson sits on the coffee table next to Savannah's foot. "I hear she got the lead in the play."

Really? He wants to bring that up? Now? My eyes bulge at him, but he's arranging the bag of peas better on her foot. He thinks he can just waltz in here and—

"Everyone thought it should be my part. Everyone," she whimpers, much of the spark gone. Savannah pulls the blanket off the back of the couch and covers her lap. "There aren't any seniors in drama, so the big parts are supposed to go to us, the juniors." She snuggles under the blanket. "Daddy, I'm so glad you're home."

From behind the couch, I watch him smile at his girl and see her become the little girl I never get to see. This is so not fair. Tears begin to roll down her cheeks, and Jackson moves to sit next to her. When he puts his arm around her, she lays her head on his shoulder. He mutters, "I know, I know," and she cries.

I cry, too. But no one says, "I know" and then lets me lay my head on their shoulder.

A soft voice behind me saying, "Oh, how sweet. He's such a good father" stops my tears. They dry up right off my cheeks. Evaporate, just like that.

"Carter May. Here, let's go, uh, let's go out on the deck." I grab a bottle of white wine out of the refrigerator and two wine glasses from the dishwasher and sit them on the outside table. The night is still mild, but chilly. "Wait, I'll get us a couple quilts."

Out of the basket by the back door, I grab a couple old quilts and by time I hand her one, she has each of us a glass of wine poured.

"Oh, thanks, the blanket feels good," she says. "You know this weather won't last, but it's nice as a reminder of what's coming. This was your first winter in the mountains, wasn't it?"

"Yeah, I was raised in East Tennessee, but you know as a kid you just don't pay attention to the weather." We are seriously talking about the weather! A quick gulp of wine, and my mouth opens, and I decide to just let things fall out of it. "Mr. Carr told me the man I saw you with was your husband."

"Oh, yeah. I did tell him that."

Okay… "So was it true?"

"Kind of."

Hot dog! She is married. "You're married?"

"Not exactly."

"Not exactly?"

Now she's crying. Maybe I should go get Jackson.

"He, my husband, won't let me go. Everything is settled, he just needs to sign the papers."

"What do you mean? You're a grown woman."

"He won't let go of our relationship, and now he's followed me here. It's so great to have you and your family around so he can't get to me."

"What? Is he…"

She sits up and reaches her hand towards me. "No, he's not dangerous. He just thinks we shouldn't break up."

"So he's, like, stalking you?"

"Something like that. But he and I are over. He doesn't work, just wants to backpack around and be a river guide in the summer. He spent the fall out in Colorado, and now he's back here." She takes a drink and shudders a little. Pulling the blanket up around her neck she shakes her head. "No. No more losers for me. I'm looking for a different kind of man this time. Totally different."

The memory of how her eyes glowed watching Jackson with Savannah gives a clue to what she's looking for. "So, you two never had kids?"

"Oh, goodness, no. He thought he was too young, and he is young. Younger than me. After my first husband, remember Roll Tide and all that, I wanted someone more exciting, not tied down. So I can't say having kids was on either of our radar. But I grew up. You know there comes a point when you know you're ready." She sits down her glass after another drink. "And I'm ready. Just need a man."

I lift my glass to my lips for a little more encouragement and ready myself to tell her she has to leave.

"So, Carolina, are you happy here?"

Me? We're going to talk about me? The sip increases, and I drain my glass. "Sure. Yeah, I'm happy."

She nods as she pours more wine in our glasses. "You don't seem very happy. Do you miss the city? Your job?"

"Well, sometimes. Of course, but this is where my family is, so of course I'm happy here."

"But is that really fair to you? Jackson runs around with his job and then shows up for the weekends? You're left to handle Crossings, and let's be honest, I don't think this is exactly *your* dream, is it? A B&B for railfans?"

"But it's okay, we're making friends, and the kids like it."

"Really? Savannah doesn't seem that happy. Bryan, of course, is young. He's adaptable."

"Jackson really likes it here, and I'm learning to like things." How could my glass already be empty again?

"Didn't you get your Master's in Library Science a couple years ago? Went back to school at night?"

"I did. I thought I'd be working at the library."

"Yeah, I bet Jackson feels bad about you not being able to use your degree you worked so hard for."

I mumble, "I bet he does" as I pour myself some more wine. She only gave me a little bit last time.

"But at least up here you have lots of time to read. That's nice, I'm sure."

"Read? Yeah, right. These people think I'm at their beck and call. There's always a meeting of the Historic Women or the Dramatic Teenagers."

She laughs and leans forward to cough. "You almost made me snort wine up my nose! That's funny."

"Just my little names for the Historical Society and the drama club." A laugh blurts out of me. "And don't get me started on the B&B Ball Busters. Clean this, record that, paint this. They may call themselves Partners, I just call them Pains."

"Carolina, you are too funny." Warmed by laughter and wine, our blankets slip to our laps, and more witticism slips from my lips until we are hooting louder than the large, old barn owl on the riverbank.

The door to our bedroom balcony creaks open. "Honey?

Y'all are kind of loud down there."

Jackson's head sticks out the opening; the unsafe condition of the decking keeps him from stepping out. "Savannah went up to bed. You coming up soon?"

I laugh and wave a hand towards him. "Sure, sure." My left eyebrow lifts at my drinking buddy. "I guess he's in a hurry for me to come up so he can go sleep again in the spare room." And then I remember that my drinking buddy is Carter May.

Her eyes widen. "The spare bedroom?"

Above us the door shuts, and I laugh a little. "Sometimes, you know how hard marriage can be."

"I sure do. Sometimes things just don't work out like we planned." She drinks the last bit of wine in her glass and smiles at me. "Well, I better let you go so everyone can get a good night's sleep." We stand and gather our glasses, the bottle, and our blankets.

Sobriety falls over me like a cooler of iced Gatorade on a winning football coach. When the window above our heads, the spare bedroom window, lights up, a smile deepens across Carter May's face. Her lowered eyes seem to gleam beneath and through her lashes, and the glistening of her lips says she just licked them.

I follow her into my house, with the light from the spare bedroom window saying Jackson is still awake. With a small twist, I lock the back door.

Why do I feel as if I only locked the trouble inside?

Chapter 30

"No, I didn't tell her she has to leave," I hiss at Jackson from behind my coffee cup. "You tell her."

"She's a client and, well, I just can't." He jerks on his heavy winter coat, and then, shoving his hands in the pockets, he pulls out his black suede gloves. "Hope they got the heat turned on over there. It's 20 degrees outside."

"Why do you two have to go over to the new offices anyway? It's Saturday." I pull my robe closer around my neck. "Can't believe it's cold again. Last night it was downright comfortable sitting out on the deck."

Jackson stretches his neck to look down the B&B hall. Coast must be clear because he leans towards me. "What were y'all laughing at so much? I thought you were going to get her to leave and y'all are out there like reunited sorority sisters."

"I know. We just got to talking." A flash of headache greets me when I stand. "And drinking. Maybe just tell her we're full the next few weekends."

He shakes his head and pours his cup of coffee into a thermos cup. "Naw, I can't lie to her. She's a client and, well, a little burnt over her ex following her here."

The flash of a headache becomes more regular. "So you do

know about her ex?"

"Yeah." His head jerks to the side. "Here she comes."

Her hair and eyes shine. Her jeans ride low and tight, while her sky blue turtleneck covers everything but hides nothing.

"Hey y'all. Carolina, you taking it easy this morning? I so enjoyed talking last night." Carter May leans into Jackson and says out of the side of her mouth, "Your wife sure has one wicked sense of humor. She really has some zingers stored up in her. I guess it just takes a little wine to get them spilling out."

My words from last night jump right at the edge of my memory and my headache. She steps to the coffee pot, and as she concentrates on pouring a thermos cup for herself, she asks, "How did everyone sleep?"

Something about how she says that line causes me and Jackson to look down at the floor.

Jackson answers but moves toward the kitchen door. "Okay, I guess. So, we can go now. I'll drive myself, okay? Couple places I need to stop by."

In a line, we walk to the front door. Carter May moves through the door Jackson has opened. As Jackson pulls the wooden door closed, I jerk it back open. He comes along with it and questions me with his surprised look, then asks, "What? You need something?"

I grab a handful of his coat front and pull him to me. My cup gets sat on the table beside the door and that hand grabs the other side of his coat, and I pull him to me for a kiss. Quick, but thorough.

His eyes actually sparkle a bit, and he clears his throat, "Wow. Okay."

"Just a goodbye kiss. I've been neglecting that lately," I whisper as I let my robe accidentally drop open and my burgundy satin, spaghetti strap gown peeks through.

His eyes dart down to the opening and he smiles.

"I like that. Maybe I can see more of it tonight?"

"Maybe." Our eyes meet in a smile, and I push him out the door. He jogs across the porch and at the steps turns and winks at me. I know him so well, know just what he likes and how to get his attention. Satisfaction in the form of a little smile grows as I close the door. First step if I want to win him back is getting him out of the spare room and into our room.

Wait - *If?* Of course I want to win him back. Of course I do. *Don't I?* A frown reflects my jumbled thoughts. Probably just need more coffee.

My cup and the coffee in it are cold, so after pouring it out, I fill it with fresh, hot coffee and lean on the counter to stare out the kitchen window. Everything is still, frozen during the night. Yesterday the branches stretched and the grass softened. Birds ventured from the woods and darted to and fro celebrating an early, if only temporary, release. Humidity, the scourge of living in the South, added depth to yesterday's breezes much like a good dose of fabric softener takes towels from abrasive to embraceable. A hard frost covers every surface, every branch, and looks like snow.

With a bit of a neck stretch, the stiff curtain of the weeping willow comes into view. Today a steel curtain, yesterday wild whipping branches dancing with abandon and calling me to visit.

But I didn't. To the cup in my hand, I vow, "Next time we get a reprieve in winter I will walk down there." However, even my coffee cup can't hear my next vow, so I only think it. And I will talk with Tommy, or whoever is listening down there. Figure things out.

You know, that's probably the real problem. No one to talk to. No one to sort things out for me. Wine glasses in the sink smell of last night's wine, so after draining my coffee, I run some water in the glasses. How did Carter May know about my Master's degree? Jackson had to have told her. No one else here knows but the kids, and I'm not even sure if they know. All they cared about was that I wasn't there every night to drive them around. Since moving to Chancey I've tried to forget all the work I did for that stupid degree. It means nothing here. If, there's that word again, if I stay here, my degree is virtually useless. Ida May isn't letting go of her control over the library anytime soon and besides…this is my job. Turning around to dry my hands on the dishtowel, I survey the kitchen, living room, and the hall to the B&B rooms. How did I end up here? I have a Master's degree in Library Science. I love books, not guests. Libraries mean order, exactly the opposite of this place.

Maybe I don't belong here. I carry the dishtowel to the nearest kitchen chair. I've always assumed I belonged here because I knew I belonged with Jackson. But, well, what if I don't belong with Jackson? What if we no longer work as a couple? The kids? Maybe we could offer them more separately.

Thoughts swirl, new thoughts, never-before-thought-of thoughts whip around like yesterday's weeping willow branches. When the doorbell rings, all the thoughts stop and settle neatly to the floor of my brain. Who could be here this early on a Saturday?

"Hello," I say, opening the door.

"Hey there. Is this the Bed & Breakfast?"

"Yes. Can I help you?"

"Do you have any rooms for tonight?" The woman at the door is younger than me, but she looks tired. Her tiny nose is red with cold, but her eyes are bright and she rubs her mitten-clad hands like a little kid.

"We do have a room, a couple of them actually. We had a late cancellation."

"Wonderful. My husband is out on the bridge, and so I thought I'd check. He'll be so surprised." She holds out a mitten-covered hand. "Hi, I'm Wendy. Chuck is my husband."

After shaking her hand, we both move into the living room.

"It's cold out there," Wendy says as she pulls off her stocking cap. "Being bald sure doesn't help."

Her bald head surprises me, and I take a step back. "Oh, I bet it doesn't."

"Chemo. But it's already starting to grow back. See?" She bends toward me and when I look, a dark fuzz is evident.

"Oh, yes. Congratu-, wait, that's not…"

She grins at me and reaches out a hand, now free of its mitten, to grab my forearm. "Don't worry. No one knows what to say. Congratulations works for me." Out of her fanny pack she takes a wallet. "Cash okay?"

"Sure, but don't you want to see the room?"

"Naw, we spent last night freezing to death in our camper. We're not real picky at this point."

"You're camping in this weather?"

Wendy unbuttons her coat as she looks through the front window. "Yeah," she says as she points. "It's really comfortable and the heater keeps it warm usually, but we're not used to this kind of cold. We've been camping along the Gulf Coast, but then the nice weather lured us up here to the mountains. Camping's not much fun if it's too cold to even go outside. Oh, here comes Chuck." She moves to the door, opens it, and then shouts at her husband. "I'm in here."

Chuck turns toward the house. His slight build and long hair makes me think he's young, but as he comes up the stairs his worn face belies his youthful appearance.

"Hi, I'm Chuck Wilson."

"Carolina Jessup."

"Hon, I've got us a room here for tonight. Isn't this nice?"

He looks down at his wife, and his eyebrows dip. "You were really cold, weren't you? I'm sorry."

Wendy smiles and rolls her eyes. "Stop it. I was fine, but won't this be fun? Especially since it's too cold to sit around the fire."

Chuck responds to her words with a nod, but even as he looks around the worry never leaves his face. "This is really nice. Can't believe you have a room open, I mean with the train bridge right there and all. Where should I park the camper?"

"Oh, it's fine where it is. Can I get y'all some coffee? Sorry I'm not really dressed and ready for you. Usually folks don't arrive so early."

Chuck's lines deepen between his eyes and he starts saying he's sorry, but Wendy breaks in. "Oh, we're easy. You go back to enjoying your Saturday morning, and we're going to go find some breakfast. That Ruby's Cafe serves breakfast, I bet."

"Her muffins are wonderful. Do you want to bring anything in now? The room is ready."

"Honey, maybe you should lay down a bit. I can bring in your things."

She hits him with her empty mitten and then starts pulling her mittens on her hands. "Miss muffins at Ruby's Cafe? Not a chance. I'm not tired yet." She turns to me while she pulls her hat on. "Can we come back in a couple hours?"

"Sure. Front door will be open, and if no one is here your room is the one on the right. The Chessie Room. You sure you don't want to take a look?"

Wendy lifts her chin and shakes her head as she pulls on her gray and white knit hat. "Nope, I don't want to waste any of my feeling-good time. I'm sure I'll spend lots of time in the room later."

Chuck shrugs and turns to follow his wife outside.

Standing in the doorway with only a thin pane of glass between me and the cold, I watch the two of them leave. Wendy bouncing along in front of her burdened husband.

Our first walk-up guests, Wendy and Chuck Wilson. Campers dealing with chemo. You'd think meeting them would feel heavy, but my spirits lift and a surge of energy fills me. I shut the wooden door and lean against it.

All I'm doing is wrestling with my own fears, and in the light of day they really aren't worth wasting another day on, right?

Who wants pancakes?

CHAPTER 31

"You have your own drama unfolding in your home, don't you?" Unnaturally arched eyebrows rise to emphasize the question Aston's mother asks. The eyebrows keep their unnatural curve, but now her head tilts on her graceful neck. "Your daughter hating your son's girlfriend, and your daughter's boyfriend playing the love of that girlfriend on stage must make for some rather Shakespearean evenings at your little inn on the hill."

I sit across from Claire Roberts in a booth at Ruby's. Claire sits her cup back in the saucer, licks her frown, and shudders. "Monday morning. What wouldn't I give for a Starbucks up here? Or at the very least, unchipped cups."

"I'm sure we can get you another cup." I look around for Libby, but Claire dismisses that idea.

"Never mind. It really doesn't matter, does it?"

I shake my head no. Nothing really matters; I stumble around like I can do something right but nothing ever works for me. Right up to about five minutes ago I felt like such a good mother. Calling Aston's mother and asking to meet for coffee seemed so adult, so proactive, so un-me. She granted me fifteen minutes, and now I'm realizing that is just too long.

The perfect eyebrows raise again and the perfectly colored lips open. "The Super Bowl party at our house went wonderfully last night. How was yours?"

"It went fine, no broken bones!" I laugh, but I'm alone. Manicured nails, manicured hair, manicured eyebrows all stare at me. Claire Roberts is a CEO of something to do with healthcare in Atlanta. She is important, rich, and not impressed by quaint Chancey or my storytelling. Her sigh telegraphs her disappointment. "Who catered your event? It's sad how little choice one has up here."

"Yeah, um, the kids just brought lunch meat and we made sandwiches." I try to drink my coffee without showing my chipped nails and rough hands. "Savannah told me the food at your party was wonderful."

Claire nods. "Yes, it was. I don't know if I would use the same people for a dinner party or a real event, but for the Super Bowl, it was definitely adequate."

Adequate? Shrimp and grits, grilled vegetable kabobs, designer cupcakes in the team colors. Savannah had raved about the food. "Well, Savannah loved it. And sounds like she got to tell you about everything going on at our house."

"Yes. Yes, she did. Your daughter is quite attractive. However, that's not unusual; Aston only dates attractive girls." Claire looks at her phone, lying on the table only inches from her hand. She's willing it to ring. So am I.

Okay, I called this meeting. "You work in Atlanta?"

"Really Roswell. My husband, Aston's step-father, is a writer. We always agreed when he turned sixty, we'd move away from town. Who could've imagined it would happen so soon and I'd be so young and doing so well in my career. Now he has his peace and quiet and a lake to fish in and write beside, and I have this." Palm up, she glides her hand in my general direction. "Not just this kind of establishment, but this whole small town thing. You know what I'm talking about, right? Savannah says you moved from Marietta. That you got your Master's degree just in time to move to the sticks and run a motel?" She closes her eyes and takes a deep breath. "At least I still have my life back there. We bought a condo after we sold our house, and I live there during the week. Thank goodness."

I change the subject. "Is Aston your only child? I guess he gets along well with his step-father."

"We have Bill's children, but they are grown and live away. Aston's sister, my daughter Porsche, lives with her and Aston's father in California. That's where we're from. I'm sure you wondered about my accent." Her large blue eyes stare at me in thought, and then she leans closer. "If Aston picks up a hillbilly accent living here, I will kill my husband."

She may have leaned closer to me, but her voice carried and a gasp behind me told me Ruby had heard. "Um, I've never met Aston, but I'm sure he has a lovely, uh, non-accent."

Claire smiles and then lays a manicured hand on my arm. "I know you'll be happy to hear I've talked to Savannah about her diction and her working on losing her accent if she's serious about a career in the theatre."

She actually grasps my arm through my green, long-sleeved tee shirt, and her talons are sharp.

"Don't tell Savannah, but Bill is contacting some of his connections in the theatre world to come stay with us in the future. They can help Savannah get into a good school. You know, something not around here." She bites her lip, scrunches her shoulders, and squeezes my arm again.

I think she thinks we're friends.

"Oh, thanks, but Savannah is going in-state. We already have one son in college and another one at home so out-of-state is out-of-mind." Again, I laugh alone.

Her claw unclenches, and she pats my arm in sympathy. "Oh, well, maybe we can get her a scholarship. To be limited to in-state, well, that's not really acceptable, is it?"

Ruby grunts behind me, and that's about as articulate as I feel. I try not to be too noticeable shaking off Claire's hand, but in an exaggerated motion I pick up my coffee and take a long drink. Ruby's noises of disapproval are all I can hear now, she's hovering over us pretending to clean an already-clean table behind Claire. Our silence stretches.

Her phone, lying on the table buzzes, and we both sigh in relief. She picks it up and if possible looks even more composed and in charge. Across the way, Libby waves at me from her post behind the counter. Her smile is lopsided, and she adds a little shrug. No one thinks I'm having fun.

"Can you hold on?" she asks into her phone, then pulls it away. "Excuse me, but I'm going to have to leave." Claire's lips curl into what she must think is a smile. "I'm so glad you called and we got a chance to meet," she purrs/hisses as she stands and lifts her briefcase to her shoulder. She nods toward her phone. "Sorry, but I need to finish this conversation on my way. Next time we'll get together at our house. I promise better coffee."

I grin and nod, but she's already turned toward the door, talking into her phone.

My head collapses onto the table. Libby and Ruby are at my elbow before I can lift my head.

"Better coffee? She promises better coffee?" Ruby is sputtering, then she finishes with a roar, "Who was that? Is she one of your *old* friends from the city?" Ruby sneers and dismisses Claire with a shake of a dishtowel. "I don't like her. I gave her a chipped cup, maybe she won't come back."

"She lives here. Her son, Aston, and Savannah are friends," I explain as I lift my head.

Ruby plants both hands on her hips. "She lives in Chancey?" Ruby's whole face puckers in thinking mode, then smoothes--as much as that is possible. "Oh, Laurel Cove, right?"

"Yeah, they have a huge house sitting on the lake. Savannah says it's amazing."

Libby pats my back and pours more coffee in my cup. "Honey, how is Savannah doing with the whole play thing? I know it about broke her heart not getting the part she wanted."

"Yes ..." My words fade as our eyes all are drawn to swinging open of the front door. Missus blows in and demands. "Who here talked to Claire Roberts? I just saw her leave."

"You can't come into my place of business like it's your own personal school bus to bully," Ruby shouts louder than Missus and causes me to jump, but does nothing to slow Missus down until she is nose to nose with Ruby. You know, she does remind me of Mildred Buckwell, the terror of my junior high. Missus is tiny, like Mildred was, but she makes herself large with her spread-leg stance, extended elbows, and piercing eyes. Yeah, I'm even smelling that sawdust stuff they put down in the school hallways when someone got sick.

"Claire Roberts. The lady in the red wool suit, short blond hair, leather bag. She just left."

Before we can say anything she moves to the booths along the wall. "Were any of you folks with Claire Roberts? She just left." She whirls around to the other wall and the few people sitting there. She dismisses them with just a look, even before she asks them her question. Then turns back to Ruby. Libby scuttles out of her path.

Ruby lifts her chin. "Shermania, you do not scare me. I have client-customer secrecy, just like a priest."

Missus crosses her arms and taps her foot. "You do not. You just made that up. I find it hard to believe Claire Roberts actually drank your coffee or ate one of your muffins, but I just saw her leaving." Then she looks down at my table and sees the two cups.

"You? You know Claire Roberts?" She drops into Claire's empty seat and without taking her eyes off me says to Ruby. "Bring me coffee, and the cup better not be chipped. Okay, Carolina, spill."

What a delightful morning this has developed into.

"Her son, Aston, and Savannah are friends. Savannah went to a party at their house last night, so I thought it would be good for us mothers to meet."

"Oh, good lord, Carolina. You called Claire Roberts to Ruby's to check her out?" Missus scoots her chair closer to the table, and she folds her arms, covered in a very nice peach and cream sweater. "Savannah dating Claire's son?"

"Uh, well, I think she's officially still with Ricky."

Missus leans back and crosses her legs. Her winter-white wool pants are spotless and smooth. "Everyone knows Savannah is too good for a Troutman." She chews on the inside of her mouth for a moment, and I try to drain my coffee cup so I can leave.

When she leans forward, she whispers, "So, what did she say? What's he like?"

"Aston? He's nice, she says. He's a junior and—"

Missus closes her eyes and sighs. "Not the boy. Claire's husband, Bill Weatherman."

"Wait, Bill Weatherman the author? THE Bill Weatherman?"

Missus' head drops slack-jawed. "Honestly? How do you stay so uninformed?"

I ignore the insult, I'm so excited. "That is crazy. He's like one of my favorite all-time authors! Savannah was at Bill Weatherman's Super Bowl party? How cool is that?"

"Carolina, quit grinning. We have to get him involved in Chancey. Maybe we'll start a writer's conference or something." She pats her hand on the table. "Yes siree, this is our ticket."

Ruby rushes to our table and sits down one of her nicest cups, one Missus has never been given. Following it is a dark red saucer with a warm lemon muffin, sliced open with a butter pat melting on each half. After setting her load down, Ruby slides into the side chair. "Bill Weatherman lives in Chancey? That beautiful woman is married to Bill Weatherman?" Ruby extends her neck and tips her head in a mimic of Grace Kelly doing a photo shoot. "She did seem to have uncommon grace." I manage to swallow my mouthful of coffee before a laugh blurts out. "What? You hated her. She was rude and downright mean."

Ruby's mouth drops open. "Carolina, whatever are you talking about?"

"For crying out loud, you gave her a chipped cup and never even changed it out."

Missus picks up half of her moist, yellow muffin and smoothes the melted pool of butter around with her knife. "You gave her a chipped cup? I am trying to hold up this town all by myself while surrounded by rednecks and hicks."

"You seem to like my muffin," Ruby retorts.

Missus swallows and lays the bitten half-muffin down. "Being uncouth and a blithering idiot do not seem to hinder your cooking skills." She sips her coffee. "God is apparently still in the miracle business."

"You old..."

"Stop it," I say. "This feud makes both of you look bad, and does not let me focus on the wonderful news I just heard. This is about Bill Weatherman living in Chancey, not about you two. Missus, how do you know all this?"

"FM's cousin is the realtor for Laurel Cove. He told his wife, who is the secretary over at the Baptist church. You know the churches all try and get the rich folks to join their congregations. Even if they don't attend, they usually contribute a nice, little Christmas donation. But when she called to welcome them she found out they're not Baptist and so the church secretaries all got to talking to try and figure out which pastor should visit them."

Ruby nods. "You just can't leave things like this to work themselves out. Got to be proactive."

As high and unnatural as Claire's eyebrows were earlier, mine are barely scrunched above my eyelids and they look as natural as a caveman's. "What? That's disgusting. They'll go to whichever church they want. If any."

For once, Ruby and Missus are in agreement, and they roll their eyes at me.

"So naive." Ruby opines.

"So non-denominational," Missus agrees.

I stand up. "So out of here. All I had was coffee. Here." As the dollar floats to the table in front of Ruby, I grab my big coat. Then I struggle to put it on and maneuver around the table.

"Wait, Carolina," Missus shouts as I open the door.

Holding the door in one hand and my hat in the other, I stop. They were probably just pulling my leg with all that church talk. "Yes, Missus?"

"Ask Savannah to ask the boy. He'll tell her what she wants to know. She's good at getting what she wants."

Angry, I yank open the door. "I will not get Savannah involved in your scheming."

"Oh, okay. I'll ask her." Missus turns back to her table.

Outside, the wind smacks me in the face. Cold and raw was the forecast for the week, with spitting rain and snow thrown in to keep us tied to our radios and televisions. Usually any mention of snow sends Southerners to the grocery store, but due to hyped-up weather forecasts since October most of us have been stocked up all winter. Folks keep saying it's too cold to snow, but I've seen pictures of Fargo, Minnesota, and I don't think they say it's too cold to snow there. However, with unexpected guests, our stocks would be soon depleted if we really did get snow, so I don't wait for the car to warm up to head to Piggly Wiggly.

Everything is blue and cold outside my windows. Old asphalt roads no longer resemble strong, black ribbons; they are potholed and crumbling along the edges, almost white. Bare bushes spread like veins on the back of an old woman's hand and chunks of cheap gravel scatter along the roadside and look like the discards of someone's cup of ice. There is no sky, only thin, blue air that captures no heat and reveals no sun. The wind can find nothing to shake as everything is frozen in place.

The gravel in the grocery store lot doesn't crunch when I walk across it. Maybe it's too cold for sound. Or maybe it's Bryan's Spiderman toboggan pulled over my ears. Once inside, I jerk off the covering and shove it into my purse. Static electricity crackles, and I don't even try to smooth down my spiky hair.

I hate how this store smells. Not really how this store smells, I hate that it doesn't smell like my stores in Marietta. You know, artificial, but really good. This smells too…too real.

"Hey, Mrs. Jessup."

"Hey, Angie. You working Monday mornings now?"

"No, just here shopping for home ec. We're making banana pudding, and I knew we had some really ripe bananas here. Mrs. Frazier sent me over to get some." Angie lifts her full bag up.

"How much pudding are you making? That's a lot of bananas."

"Oh, I took all the ones we were going to throw away." She shrugs with her shoulders, her face, and the parade of metal attached to her.

As we pass, the door swings open at her approach. I rush to get away from the blast of cold air, but she stops me with a shout.

"And tell Savannah I hope she gets better. Somebody will bring her work over if she wants." Spurred on by the cold, she turns and runs through the door, and I watch her cross to her car. My hands tighten on the grocery cart I was pulling out and I shove it back in place. The loud clang hides the ugly words I spit. So, Savannah is playing hooky? I jerk the Spiderman toboggan out of my purse and jam it, two-fisted, back onto my head.

Okay, let's go find the girl.

CHAPTER 32

Before I can scream "Savannah," I see Wendy and Chuck sitting on the couch enjoying the coffee and pumpkin muffins I'd left for them to heat up. They were already staring at me as I barreled through the front door.

"Oh, sorry, guys. Um, ignore me. Just looking for, uh, something." I pull off my hat and drop it along with my purse on the stair landing. "Just going up to the top floor, Savannah's room."

By time I get to the third floor, I'm sweating. Her room is empty, and I sit down on her unmade bed to catch my breath and unbutton my coat. Looking around, there is chaos from one dormer window to the other. The door to her bathroom stands open. The lights are on, and I hear a radio or CD playing somewhere in this mess. There is no clear path across the room, so I pick my way between books, dishes, underwear, socks, and all manner of clothes to the bathroom where I turn off the lights. The music is coming from an iPod lying beside her sink, so I turn that off, too, and pocket it. I'll make her come ask me for it.

I consider looking for clues in her room, but decide it's not worth it.

She's didn't answer my calls or texts, so I kind of assumed

she was here asleep. Hate to have to call the school and admit I don't know where she is. I close her door behind me and start down the stairs. Wait. Laney is working in the school's front office this week. Down the stairs I trot, saying "hello" again to Chuck and Wendy as I grab my purse and go into the kitchen.

"Is Laney there?" Grabbing the dishcloth, I wipe up crumbs from around the microwave and then lean on the counter to wait. "Laney. I need to know who beside Savannah isn't at school today."

Laney laughs. "Already looked for you. When I saw she wasn't here, I checked to make sure both my girls were here and then ran down the other leads. Ricky is here, so are the other cheerleaders. Except Amy Walton, but her mother picked her up for an orthodontist appointment."

"Hmmm, so she's the only absentee of interest?" My anger starts sliding into worry.

"Did I say that?"

"What? No, I guess not. So what's the deal?"

"That Aston boy. He's not here either." Laney takes a deep breath. "Everyone thinks it's the Troutmans who cause all the trouble. But not today."

"Aston. Of course. Thanks."

Laney's voice is quieter and muffled like she has her hand around her mouth. "Now, Carolina, from one who has played a bit of hooky in her time, it's just too cold to be messing around outside. They're holed up somewhere nice and warm and cozy. Have you checked her bedroom?"

"Laney!" However, my outrage fades quickly. My daughter is skipping school with a boy, so Laney is just who I should be talking to. "Yes, I've checked her bedroom." My eyes close, and my lips have to be pried apart. "Any other suggestions?"

"His house?"

"Yeah, I'll check. Thanks." My eyes slide to the refrigerator. There on the white board is Aston's address. I didn't talk to his parents before the party, but I did force Savannah to write down his address before she left. 19870 Parsons Lake Road.

So I get to barge into one of my idol's homes and see if my wayward daughter is holed up with his stepson.

Should I take a book to be autographed?

Laurel Cove winds around the top of Kings Mountain, on land always thought too rough and too steep for homes. Until the luxury home market took off in North Georgia, that is. If all you care about is a view, don't have to get back and forth to a job, and don't want enough flat land to plant a garden, then Laurel Cove is for you. Oh, and I forgot to add, if you can afford a heated driveway to melt any ice, *then* have I got the house for you. Along the newly paved road lined with fieldstone walkways, small brass and black signs state the house number that goes with each driveway. No houses can be seen from the street as all the driveways go up. Straight up and then over a hill, which even as I drive up the one corresponding to the address from the refrigerator to the top of the hill, I can't see anything but more road going up.

Then, just as it looks as if the driveway disappears, the car levels out. The hood points down, and at the same time, weak lavender sunlight hits my windshield. Purple-white light fills this side of the mountain, and below me the house of stone and wood and glass looks like it's from a dream. The car rolls toward the stone-paved circle in front of the covered walkway of wooden pillars. I stop the car, turn it off, and get out.

Quiet envelopes me and makes me shut the car door respectfully. Wrapped in lavender light and mist, my eyes widen, and I forget to feel cold. This must be how it feels to stumble upon an enchanted castle in a fairytale. The house is notched into the side of the mountain. Trees lean into and caress the stone walls, and the timber corners mix naturally with the tree trunks. Then flung out, off the cliff and into the purple air is glass and wood and stone, but it must no longer be wood and stone because it floats there. I can't help myself as I walk around the car. I bend to look where it appears the house floats.

"Marvelous, isn't it?"

"Yes, it is." Oops, I straighten up and turn behind me where a man with a mass of white hair stands.

"Hello, can I help you?"

"Hi, I'm Carolina Jessup. Savannah's mom." It truly is Bill Weatherman. The face I've held in my hand as I've cradled his books stares back at me.

"Oh, wonderful. They are in the main house." He takes my elbow and steers me through the wooden pillars and up the walk toward the front door. "I was out in my studio working but was headed in just now to see if they are ready for breakfast. That's how I saw your car pull up."

"So, you know they are here?"

"Of course. What with school being off today and you having your home fumigated, where else would they be on such a cold day? Here we are." He throws open the front door with his right hand, while his left arm leaves my elbow and curves around my back. "Come in. Come in."

Dark brown leather furniture gathers around two fireplaces, which both feature flames and a seductive warmth. The ceiling is high and crossed with honey-colored beams. Again, the lavender air fills the space due to huge expanses of windows. Mountains meet me across floors of polished wood. Appearing to hang out in space, but leaning against a cleverly disguised railing, are Savannah and Aston. They are wrapped up in a fur blanket and kissing.

Mr. Weatherman smiles and drops his arm from my back.

"Ah, young love. I'll go let them know you're joining us for breakfast."

He strides across the floor, and I decide to just watch.

God, I hope they have clothes on under that blanket.

When he opens the door they turn (and they do have clothes on). When he tells them I'm here, there's only a grimace on Savannah's face, but one she clears up quickly.

"Mom," she says with a huge smile. "Isn't this place amazing?" She leaves Aston holding the blanket and darts to greet me near the fire on the right side of the room.

"Aren't you supposed to be at school?"

"Well, maybe, but really it's just so cold."

"Sorry, Mrs. Jessup, it's my fault. But how could we sit in those boring classrooms when all this would just be sitting up here empty? Hello, I'm Aston Roberts." The young man holding out his hand doesn't look like a junior in high school. He looks like that vampire guy in the *Twilight* movies. I don't exactly believe in vampires, but it would explain some things.

"Hello, Aston. Um, I don't think that's exactly a reason for skipping school."

"Oh. You lied to me? Ahh, beginnings of a fiction writer. You make me proud, Aston. My own children were so bogged down with the truth all the time." Mr. Weatherman steps over to us and dips his head toward me with a wide smile. "However, skipping is hardly the issue, true? We know these two are way ahead of their classmates in this little village, correct? Why should a day like today not be celebrated? Come, take a look at the view." He pulls me to the windows, and as hard as it is to imagine, the view is more stunning than the words that just came out of his mouth. Bogged down with the truth?

The fog and mists which entrapped downtown and even our house on the bluff this morning cause a blanket of white cotton below us. It's like standing on Mount Olympus looking down on earth.

"Feels rather god-like, doesn't it?"

My eyes dart up to his reflection. He just read my mind. Then a glance at my reflection reminds me I spent the morning putting on, then pulling off a knit stocking hat. Bill—*I mean, he just read my mind, so I don't have to keep thinking of him as Mr. Weatherman, right?*—has on a flannel shirt of a muted plaid, corduroy slacks, and a turtleneck. Yes, exactly what you'd expect. Aston, well, he looks like that vampire guy, and Savannah is Savannah. Me, yes, I'm the item that does not fit.

"Well, this is beautiful, but Savannah, you do need to get back to class. So let's go."

Then Bill touches my arm again. "But I hear you are a reader. A serious reader and I've so longed to talk to you. We wanted to invite you to the Super Bowl party last night, but your lovely daughter told us you were hosting a party for the town's youth. So admirable. So very Dickensian. Can't you stay and have breakfast? I'm making French toast with pecan topping and peach syrup."

He takes my hand and starts toward the kitchen, which I can now see as I turn away from the windows. Glass cabinet fronts and steel appliances gleam. Bills hand is soft and warm and then he draws it up to tuck my forearm under his.

He drops my hand as he opens the cabinet above the coffee pot. "Please stay and be our guests for breakfast."

And then, because obviously I've fallen into a lair of vampires who can bend my mind and my will, I say, "Okay. Why not?"

Savannah laughs. "I told you she would do anything you asked, Mr. Weatherman. She's, like, obsessed with you."

"With his books, honey. There's a difference."

Isn't there?

CHAPTER 33

"He's a little out there." I tuck my cell phone between my ear and shoulder while my hands are holding up two bottles of syrup to compare labels. I've got to make that French toast for Jackson. "And, Missus, he most definitely isn't contributing to any of the churches. Matter of fact, he may be starting his own. Wait, a minute, I'm at the Pig. Let me put you on speaker phone…"

"Carolina, people do not just start their own church. And do not put me on speaker phone."

"Okay, but seriously, you've not met Bill Weatherman. He may belong in a nuthouse. Instead he's in the most beautiful home I've ever seen, and his picture is all over *my* home because I have all his books. You know, I'm a librarian, but there are some books I have to just own, not borrow. That's how much I love, wait, *loved* his writing. Maybe he should start his own church. I could probably get out of bed on Sunday for that. Especially if he made his French toast. Missus, it was amazing."

"Let me guess, he served you real syrup? I can hear the sugar in your blood through the phone. So, I'm assuming Savannah has been properly placed back in school?"

I place one syrup in my buggy and sit the other back on the

shelf. "Why is that any of your concern? What were you doing down at the school checking on her in the first place?" I miss half of her reply when I turn off the speaker phone. No sense in discussing my daughter's truancy with the three people left in Chancey who aren't already talking about it.

Missus explains, "You told me you weren't going to talk to her about getting Bill Weatherman involved in helping Chancey and asked me to do it, as I recall."

At the end of the aisle, I stop the cart and shake my head. "You recall wrong, but never mind. You went to the school to talk to her? Missus, you can't do that."

"Obviously, I can't. She wasn't there. She was playing hooky."

"Missus, I'm going back by the meat case, and so I'm going to lose my signal. Leave Savannah alone. Bye."

Mapping out cell service is an acquired, but necessary, skill. The life it saves may be your own.

We didn't have sausage this morning up at Bill's, but to Jackson, any breakfast without meat might as well be a bowl of cereal. Besides, the idea of running a sausage link through that peach syrup has my stomach growling—almost. Picking my way along the meat case and then down the dairy aisle, the morning rolls through my head. It could've been a show on that Home and Gardening channel. Bill believes he knows what every person wants and then gives it to them. We ate, drank coffee, and talked about books.

Hey, maybe he's right.

Savannah and Aston sat with us the whole time, laughing and talking. If not for my bushy hat-head hair, it was perfect. Crazy, but perfect.

And now here I am in the Piggly Wiggly buying eggs, the thickest whole grain bread I can find in Chancey's limited selection, hazelnut coffee, peaches (canned, fresh are just too expensive and too much work, I don't care what Bill says), and pecans. A quick turn down a center aisle directs me to the magazines and paperback books, and I'm sure I'll find what I'm looking for. Yep, I knew there would be at least one Bill Weatherman book. The familiar picture of him in a white sweater, jeans, and loafers looks back at me. That's the man who cooked me breakfast this morning. Leaving the picture, I turn into the middle of the book. The scene is a picnic beside a moss-hung river in Louisiana and while I don't remember the story exactly, I do remember how the book made me feel.

Like I wanted to live in Louisiana, have picnics by the river, hold parties in the family home, drink chicory coffee, and eat beignets. Of course, he's also made me want to move to Montana and raise cattle. Shoot commercials in Manhattan. Drink moonshine and practice law in Kentucky. Own a restaurant in Seattle. Be surrounded by bluebonnets in Texas in an ancient stone house. Reading one of his books isn't like reading, it's like falling. Falling into whatever world he is gifting you with.

As I place the book back on the shelf, I realize I know all about the setting, but nothing about the story. Same for his other books now that I think about it. Hmmm, makes me feel kind of shallow. Then a look at the awards listed on the front cover reminds me that I'm not alone. No wonder he set such an amazing scene this morning, it's what he does all day, every day. And folks like me have made it possible for him to live in a scene straight out his mind.

You're welcome, Mr. Weatherman.

"How nice it is to have some help carrying in the groceries, Chuck, but you really shouldn't. You're a guest here."

"Oh, no problem. I'm just glad I hadn't left yet. I'm going

to take the camper over to Amicalola Falls and do some hiking. Wendy is going to stay here and relax. She's pretty worn out. Finding your place really was a godsend. I shouldn't have dragged her around for so long in that old camper. Here, just loop that bag over my hand and we'll have it all."

We shuffle up the sidewalk with our loads, but I move ahead of him at the porch. "Let me get the door. My hand is kind of free. It's going to be cold hiking, so be sure to dress warm. And don't worry about Wendy. We'll be here if she needs anything. I'm chilled to the bone, so once I get in this house I might not leave 'til spring."

As he pushes into the living room, a wonderful smell greets us. "Wendy must be cooking something," I say.

Chuck looks over his shoulder at me. "No, it's that partner lady of yours. Laney? She's making something."

I grumble behind him, "Not the Laney I know."

"Hey, guess what I'm doing?" Laney greets us in the kitchen.

"Cooking something?" I guess as we load the table down with our bags.

"Yep. A Dump Cake. Just took it out, and we're going to make some coffee and then visit."

"We're going to visit? What's up, Laney?" I'm trying to keep the suspicion out of my voice but it just won't behave.

"Don't be so suspicious."

See, told you.

"I'll have you know that Dump Cake is one of my specialties. I make chili, Dump Cake, and deviled eggs with paprika. I don't believe it's truly a deviled egg without paprika sprinkled on it. So see," she swats at me with the oven mitt, still warm from taking my 9x13 glass pan out of the oven, "my specialties represent all three food groups - Spicy, Sweet, and Southern."

Wendy laughs from the corner of the table beside the back French doors. She's cuddled up in a comforter from her and Chuck's room and only her head is visible. Covering it is another toboggan hat, this one hand crocheted with an owl's face on the front of it.

"Wendy, are you cold? I can turn up the thermostat." I turn toward the hall where the thermostat is, even though the house feels toasty already.

"No, I'm just cold sometimes. Being bald doesn't help, but then neither do some of the drugs I'm on. Besides, I've always been cold-natured."

Chuck comes back into the kitchen with a loaded backpack. "Honey, you sure you'll be okay here? You're going to take a nap, right? Want me to help you get settled in bed before I leave?"

"No, silly. I'm fine. Laney is making me laugh, and I can't wait to taste her Dump Cake." She leans up. "So come give me a kiss and enjoy yourself. I'm in good hands here." She winks at us as Chuck kisses her, then scoots out of the kitchen.

When the front door closes behind us, Wendy sighs and leans back in her chair. She lays her head back against the wall and closes her eyes.

Laney sits down across from her. "It's hard being okay all the time, isn't it?"

Wendy nods a bit. "We talked about this trip so much when I was sick that we took off as soon as we could. Worst part about it is without any friends or family around, he's on duty all the time. He hates to leave me alone in the camper, and I kind of hate it, too. I nap so much, and he's such an active guy, there's only so many books he can read waiting for me to wake up."

I put groceries away while the two of them talk.

Laney takes things out of the bags and sits them on the table for me. "Well, honey, you just sit there and take it easy. You were right. You are in good hands. Besides, I have stuff to talk to Carolina about that won't hurt for you to hear, and it might help you relax to just listen to other folks' troubles. You know, I think that's why soap operas and reality TV are so popular:

other folks' troubles make ours seem not so bad. Or they at least distract us."

Wendy laughs again and nods. "Deal. I'll sit and listen, eat cake, and probably doze. This feels so cozy."

"Carolina, hurry up. We can't have the cake until this table is cleaned off." Laney pushes all the cans and boxes toward me. "I'll go ahead and get the coffee started so it'll be ready by the time you're through."

"This place does smell amazing." I put away things in the cabinet above the stove. "I remember my mother making something called a Dump Cake. I wouldn't eat it because it had fruit in it. Once I had a flat out hissy fit when Mother made a cherry cake for Daddy's birthday about why anyone would make a cake out of anything but chocolate. Mother didn't even get mad at me because she couldn't stop laughing. Of course, that only made me madder."

"Oh, it has fruit in it. But it's nowhere near being healthy." Laney scoops coffee into the filter. "You dump a can of crushed pineapple into a pan, then a can of cherry pie filling. On top of that you sprinkle a box of yellow cake mix and a cup or so of chopped pecans. Over all that you pour a stick of melted butter and put it in the oven. And it tastes even better than it smells."

Wendy mumbles from her cocoon. "Reckon it's called Dump Cake because you dump it all in and cook it?"

"Yep, not an attractive name and ever so often through the years some uppity church ladies try to call it something else. But folks just look at 'em real questioning and say, 'Ya mean Dump Cake?'"

Wendy burrows her nose down in her blanket, and her laugh is muffled. Laney and I work in silence for a while. The heat kicks off and on, but other than the homey sounds we make, all is quiet. As the coffee pot gurgles to let us know it's done, I take down bowls to serve the cake.

Laney and I look over at Wendy. "Think she's asleep," I ask.

"Nope, just resting my eyes. I doze off and on sitting up, but don't really sleep until I'm in bed." She lowers her feet to the floor from being tucked up beside her. The blanket falls off her shoulders as she stretches. "This reminds me of being at my grandmother's house when I was growing up."

"Where did you grow up?" I ask as I dip a spoonful into the first bowl.

"All over. Daddy was in the army, but Momma wasn't well, so we stayed with my grandparents some. Then when they died and Momma and Daddy divorced, well, there just wasn't any home anymore. Me and my sisters aren't close and until Chuck, I didn't really have a family. Chuck's parents are wonderful to us, though. Real salt of the earth people."

I put a bowl of cake in front of her and hand her a spoon. "Mine and Jackson's families were both here over the holidays. They are all more like the cayenne pepper of the earth."

Laney raises her spoon and points it at Wendy. "Don't doubt her. I thought she was exaggerating until they were all here. Whew."

"So, Laney, what did you need to talk to me about so badly you came and made a cake?"

"Well, you know I was working at the high school this morning, right?"

"Yes, I called you there. Remember?" I dipped my fork into my bowl. "This cake is delicious. Can you believe I wouldn't taste it growing up? Now that I think of it, I should've known something was up when my parents didn't make me try it like they did with Brussels sprouts."

"It is so yummy. I'm so glad we decided to stay a couple extra days," Wendy says as she takes of sip of her coffee. "A couple more bites, and I'll have to say good night and get to that nap."

"Thank you, ladies. Glad you like it," Laney says, then she turns to me. "I wanted to talk to you, Carolina, but also Shaw is on a diet and thinks I should be too. So, figured I'd just have

Dump Cake up here. His loss. Anyway, something is going on with those Carr kids. You know, the ones from the funeral home and dry cleaners?"

"What do you mean? Are they misbehaving or something?"

"No, not exactly. They're all upset about the power plant. Unexpectedly so. No one can figure it out. There's kind of a panic with them."

I blow on the spoonful of glistening red and yellow sweetness before putting it in my mouth. Still hot, so I try and talk around it. "How many Carr kids?"

Laney digs in her pants pocket. "I wrote them down and talked to my friend, Jean. She's been there forever. Teaches science and is the assistant principal." She unfolds the piece of paper she'd pulled out. "There's six all told, but two of 'em live over cross town and not with the rest of the family. Jean says they live with the youth minister and his wife at that Baptist church out near the highway. The big one."

"They don't live with their folks? That is odd. Jean know why?"

Laney shakes her head as she sips her coffee. "The family has always just been so strange and so isolated, no one thought to ask. Plus, they don't really like people asking anything."

Seeing Wendy is dozing, I lower my voice. "You know I actually talked to the grandad twice. Second time I'd popped into the funeral home after I saw Carter May and Jackson hugging, and he told me—"

"What?" Laney's squawk makes me jump and Wendy almost fall out of her seat. "You saw them hugging?"

"I told you, didn't I? You know, that guy kissed her and then Jackson kind of rescued her. It was the day of the basketball game, and they were over at the funeral home renting office space."

Laney's head shakes back and forth in little quick shakes. "No, you didn't tell me. Okay, well, now we do have to put a stop to this. Has to stop right now. Well, not right this second now. We have cake to eat." She lifts up her loaded fork and tips it toward Wendy. "Sorry, didn't mean to yell like that." She pushes the fork into her mouth. "So, what were you saying about Mr. Carr?"

Wendy leans forward and concentrates on cleaning her plate, but still doesn't look awake. Wonder if she heard that about Carter May and Jackson. She hit it off with both of them over the weekend. Maybe she's not surprised.

Okay, now I'm depressed. A little more cake would probably help that. "I'm getting some more. Can I get either of you some?" I ask as I stand and walk to the counter.

Wendy shakes her head as she finishes off her cup of coffee. Laney gets up and joins me at the counter. "Give me just a tad."

We pick at our new helpings and lean against the counter. Wendy has closed her eyes again.

"So, Mr. Carr?"

I lick my fork. "He was just really upset about the power plant, well, not so much the plant, like pollution or the community or things like that. More he was talking about how they weren't going to live next to some busy thing like the waterfront. Sounded more like he didn't want company down in their neck of the woods. Real protective of their privacy."

"Yeah, the kids were like that too, now that I think about it," Laney says. "Struck me and Jean as strange that when we pointed out they'd have the waterfront park right near their homes they didn't want any part of it. I can see adults not wanting it, but kids? Just didn't seem right. And they were downright panicked about it. Bobby and Barbie, that's the twins who are juniors, said they were taking care of themselves just fine and didn't need interfering people down there poking around. They sounded like a couple of old codgers. However, it wasn't just something they had heard and were repeating. Jean thinks, and I agree, they sound petrified."

"Girls, I have to go to bed." Wendy bundles up from her chair, wrapped in the comforter. Laney grabs her dishes as she tries to pick them up and stay wrapped. "Thank you for the cake and the coffee and the chatting." Her lips form a weak smile, and her eyes look just as weak. "This afternoon made it into my good things about being sick list, because you know, without cancer, we wouldn't have met. But now I have to lay down."

At the door to the hall, a pale hand reaches out of her wrappings and holds onto the door jamb. Wendy turns to us and a troubled look etches her face. "I can't remember, but there was something I wanted to say about your conversation just now." She waves her hand towards the table. "While I was sitting there. My eyes would not stay open and my mouth wouldn't cooperate, now it's gone." She shrugs and says, "Maybe I'll remember later, ask me when I wake up."

So she did hear what I said about Jackson and Carter May. Well, maybe it will disappear with her nap. Laney looks at me and smiles, then both of us look to the darkening hallway Wendy shuffles down.

There's really nothing for us to say.

Chapter 34

"We get off Thursday night because it's Valentine's Day, but every other night I have rehearsal." Savannah hurls her bookbag towards the couch and her body into the chair by the window, where the afternoon light slants in.

Bryan passes me on his way to the kitchen. I reach to hug him, but settle for patting his shoulder. Who imagined he wouldn't always throw himself into my arms? Oh, well, the girl-child wants my attention, gotta take what I can get. "Isn't that what you expected?" I ask with a push on her bookbag to make a place to sit on the end of the couch nearest where she's fallen.

She stretches her legs across the arm of the chair, and her brown suede boots dangle in the air. "Bryan, bring me a Little Debbie. Now that I'm playing an old lady I don't have to make sure I can fit in that stupid green dress. And, no, this isn't what we expected. Play was supposed to be in May, but the renovations on the auditorium have to start in late April. Now the play is the first week of April. So Stephen, I know, Mr. Cross, squeezed them all together. No excuses for anything. Usually he works around our other activities like cheering and sports, but not now."

"Here." Bryan throws a cellophane wrapped pink heart cake

at his sister on his way to lay in the floor in front of the TV. "Brittani says it's going to be impossible to learn all the lines." He breaks apart his heart cake to get at the white filling. "She has a ton of lines. How many do you have?"

"No, dear brother, I don't have that many lines. Remember, your sweetheart stole my part so she has all the lines. I am an old woman. A mom. Why would I have any good lines? My stuff is easy to memorize. 'Get ready for school. Supper is ready. Blah, blah, blah,' like a mom. Brittani just won't have much of a social life, so get used to not getting any sugar for a while."

"Savannah!" I swipe at her swinging boot.

"What? They make out every chance they get. Not that they have to look hard for a place to make out, usually it's up in his bedroom."

Oh, yeah, I never did deal with that. "Okay, Bryan, no more studying in your room. Your room is off-limits to Brittani. Got it?"

Bryan nods and stands up. "Okay."

Savannah and I watch as he goes back into the kitchen. I look back at her. "That was too easy. What's up?"

She shrugs and frowns. "I don't know. They were still together today. They were making out at the end of the band building when I got out to my car. He hustles over from the junior high to get a few minutes of tongue before we leave. It really is kind of embarrassing, Mom."

Ewww. "You and her getting along any better?"

"She's a skank. She's a skank who made me trip and miss the last home half-time performance of the season, stole my part in the play, and thinks she is Stephen's favorite...Mr. Cross' favorite. Bryan's an idiot."

"No, I'm not. You're an idiot for two-timing Ricky." Bryan passes behind the couch. "Mom, Brittani's sister is picking me up. We're going to study at her house, okay? They'll bring me back home before supper. Unless they invite me to eat there."

He collects his coat and bookbag, then opens the wooden door so he can see outside. "And for Valentine's, her mom is taking us up to this Italian restaurant in Dalton. We'll have our own table, and it's her mom's treat since they want us to have a nice time, okay? There she is. See ya later." He steps out the door and then sticks his head back in. "Oh, Savannah, guess you have two dates on Thursday. Good luck with that."

Savannah growls, and wadding her cellophane wrapper in her fist, she leaps from the chair. "He's so stupid." She stomps into the kitchen, and I lean back on the couch.

Shadows creep across the room as the sun quickly loses its battle with February, and I'm still trying to match the taunting male teenager that just left my house with my youngest and sweetest child. He didn't even pretend to ask permission for going to her house now or going out with her parents on a school night to Dalton. For Valentine's. Who is this girl and why would her parents think she needs a date on Valentines? Can't they just buy her a box of candy? Last week I went out to coffee with Aston's mom because I was worried. Now it's obvious, the parents I need to worry about is Brittani's. It's impossible to keep my kids living like kids, when these other parents want their kids to have all the benefits of being adults. Aston's dad thinks he can choose when he will or won't go to school. Brittani's parents want her to have a real date on Valentine's.

For crying out loud, *I* want a real date on Valentine's!

"Whew, somebody got under Savannah's skin," Wendy exclaims as she comes into the living room from the kitchen. "She just blew out the back door mumbling under her breath about Valentine's."

Wendy sits on the other end of the couch as I turn on the lamp beside me and say, "I don't remember celebrating Valentine's Day in high school. Of course, I never had a boyfriend in high school."

Wendy smiles her lopsided grin. "Me either, but speaking

of Valentine's, I think that's the day we'll be hitting the road. Weekend is supposed to be warmer, so we'll head south and get back to the coast. Then home from there. We sure have enjoyed these two weeks with you. Thanks for the break on the charges."

"Shoot, y'all have been more like family than guests. Chuck is such a great cook; I'm going to miss him, and you are just way too easy to have around."

"You're sweet. We will definitely be back in the summer. We want to see this waterfront park everyone is so excited about."

"Sounds like it's going to be something, all right. Well, I better get in there and see about supper. Chuck put together a meatloaf, which I so appreciate, and I've got to get some potatoes boiling to mash. Jackson should be home soon. Chuck out for a walk?"

Wendy nods, "Yeah, he headed out when I laid down to nap. Is there anything I can do to help?"

"Don't think so. Maybe when it's time to set the table."

"Okay. Think I'll go out on the front porch for a bit and get some fresh air. Chuck should be back soon."

In the kitchen the room has darkened enough to need the lights turned on, but before turning them on I walk to the glass doors. Savannah's pink leggings stand out in the remaining beams of light coming through the trees as the sun sinks lower in front of the house. She's down near the weeping willow and its bare branches. They barely sway in the mild breeze and only when she turns do I realize she's not talking on her phone. She talking to herself. Or, maybe… That is where I talk to Tommy, or well, someone. Could she be…naw… Probably not…

But…no. I have potatoes to peel.

CHAPTER 35

"Ruby is using the last of her Door County cherries to make a batch of those Chocolate Cherry muffins since today is Valentine's Day." Laney breathlessly explains over the phone. "Even better, she's making the muffins chocolate, too. We just have to be there before they're gone. I'll save you a place."

She hangs up before I can say anything like where I am.

Or who I'm with.

Or what we're doing.

Thank God.

Peter walks out of the woods first and stands beside his car. Him out here in the middle of nowhere could be better explained than me by myself in the woods. However, us together out here? No one would wait for an explanation before hightailing it to Ruby's for coffee, chocolate, and tattling. He gets into his car, while looking around. Closing his door means it's okay for me to scurry to my van. I waste no time looking around, just dart into the driver's seat, start the car and leave.

Wendy finally remembered what she wanted to tell me about Laney and my talk in my kitchen that Monday afternoon when she was so sleepy. Yesterday she cornered me down in the basement while I was doing laundry. Her light blue eyes were stretched wide and she was strung tighter than a Real Housewife of Beverly Hills' forehead.

"Carolina, I remember."

I turned my back on her by pulling more clothes out of the washer, sure she was going to tell me something about Jackson and Carter May that I did not want to hear. Of course, since it was left to me to get rid of Carter May, she was still living in our house. When your husband asks you to get rid of a woman and you don't, you deserve whatever bad news you get, right? So I braced myself.

"Those kids. The kids Laney was talking about?"

Okay, we can talk about that. I turn around. "The Carr kids?"

"Yes, that's it." She suddenly comes unwound and sinks to the old chair sitting beside my makeshift bookshelf. "The way she said they were acting reminded me of how I used to be."

Perched on a box still full of books, I touched her knee. She seemed to need some energy or assurance. "It's okay. Relax and just tell me."

She worried her hands over and over and then laid them on her knees and looked up at me. "I told you my mom wasn't well. She wasn't well because she was an alcoholic. My whole life. It wasn't only due to Dad being in military that we moved so much, but also because she would ruin us in a town due to bounced checks or being out of control at the grocery store. She was brought home by the police many times. One time I found her half-naked on the front lawn when I was leaving for school. Anyway, my first and wildly crazy impulse was to always protect her. Every new place I didn't want anyone near us. I lied to so many police officers or school officials at our front door. When Laney said a couple times that the kids seemed almost panicked, it struck a chord with me. I don't know why I'm so sure, but I just feel they are protecting the adults. I feel that to the very core of my being. It's been driving me crazy that I had something to tell you, but I just couldn't figure out why you would need to know about my mother. I'd finally decided it was just strange mental gymnastics due to the medicines I'm on. Then I saw the dry cleaners ticket on the refrigerator and the name Carr's. It all connected suddenly." She slumped in the chair. "I don't know what it's all about, but it sure feels good to get that out of my mind."

I finished that load of laundry, helped Wendy back upstairs, and called Peter.

I pull my phone out of the pocket of my red sweater and dial. The empty gravel road stretches wide open, with only the dust kicked up from Peter's truck in the distance ahead of me.

"Peter? What do you think? What should we do?"

"Not sure. I'm going to stop in and see Graham first off. I think I know who that car out there belongs to and that makes things tricky."

"The blue car? Who?"

Nothing. "Peter? Are you there? Shoot, I've lost you out here in the sticks."

"No. I'm here. Carolina, you need to just never mind about all this. I'll take over from here. But, well, I'm glad you called me."

Another silence and then before I can get "goodbye" he blurts out, "Why didn't you tell Jackson?"

"Jackson?" *Jackson?* First time I've thought of him all morning. But I saw him last night and never even considered talking to him about it. "Um, Jackson is real busy, and he doesn't know this area, the people, like you do."

"Makes sense. But, he wouldn't like you out here running around in the woods looking for trouble."

The *"with me"* was only implied, but we both heard it.

With a turn onto the county blacktop, I exhale. "Well, like you said, my part in things is over so no harm, no foul. Jackson can read about it in the paper. I'm going to Ruby's to meet Laney. I have enough to think about right now, so you go handle things."

With a quick mash of a button, Peter is gone. I do wonder who the blue car belongs to, but I'm sure I'll read about it in the paper.

In the movies, the actress would be getting her tail into a real knot right now about the man telling her to just never mind. However, that's exactly why I called a man. I don't want to be involved in whatever the Carr family is up to out there in the woods. I only went with Peter this morning so we could get an idea if there is anything up at all. Now, it is in Peter's lap, and I'm going to have a Chocolate Chocolate Cherry muffin.

I am gifted at never-minding.

Chapter 36

"I don't know if it's more beautiful up here in the mountains in the spring or in the fall. Look!" I point but then grab back at the steering wheel so I can make the sharp turn at the top of the hill. In the month since Valentine's Day, color has exploded all over our hills.

"Okay, trees. Trees with flowers on them." Savannah doesn't even look up from her phone. "When will my car be fixed?"

"Not soon enough," I mumble, then add, louder, "This taking you to play practice every day for the last week hasn't been fun for me either."

"Then just let me drive myself. Give me the van."

"Every afternoon and evening? I don't think so. Besides, your car should be ready by Saturday. Bob at the garage is heading to Savannah for St. Patrick's Day and says he can't leave until everything is done. Thank goodness for the St. Patrick's Day celebration in Savannah or you may never get it back. Susan warned us Bob would give us a good price, but wouldn't be in any hurry."

"Yeah, back in Marietta we just went to a real garage where you don't know the people and they just do the work. Remember how nice that was?"

My lips press together hard. Yeah, I remember. Valentine Day's cold had me thinking warm weather would never show up. However, in the past month spring rolled into the mountains early on a wave of purple and white. Redbud trees (Buds are red, but the flowers are intense purple) fill the woods with splashes of color and the many cherry trees and pear trees swathed in white blossoms along the roads and in yards remind me of mornings waking up to snow cover. Pansies and forsythias provide bursts of yellow and the green of the trees and grass is that new green of supple, innocent blades and leaves. Tiny, almost translucent leaves, decorate their branches like delicate necklaces and bracelets. Sun pours through them, lighting them and promising warmth to aid their growth.

However, all's not been flowers and sunshine in the weeks leading from February to March.

Savannah wants to move back to Marietta for her senior year.

Matter of fact, it's all set. Her friend Marnie's mother has called me and says the house is just too empty since Marnie's twin brothers left for college and they would love to have Savannah move in with them next year.

Savannah is *over* Chancey. So over.

Do not say it. Do not say it. Do not say it. Do not say it rolls over and over in my head. So, of course, I say it.

"If you hadn't made two dates for Valentine's weekend, maybe your life here wouldn't be so miserable."

"Again? You're going to bring this up again?" She tilts her head at me. "I was breaking up with Ricky on Friday night, and so by Saturday night going out with Aston would've been fine. It's all that skanky redhead's fault." She throws her phone into her purse on the floorboard. "Today's the fourteenth of March, so it's been a month and still everyone acts like I killed someone."

"Honey, he was in a gazebo with a hundred candles and a cello player and in a rented tux. Taping it was a mistake, but he thought it would be a good night. A night he'd want to remember."

"He knew I couldn't stand Brittani and yet that's who he asks to video it? Why am I even talking about this again?"

"Because you could help fix this if you would just ask him to forgive you. Admit you were wrong. Do something besides mope around planning to move. You can't move from every bad situation in your life."

We stop in front of the entrance to the high school auditorium, and she slides out of her door. My sigh is audible. "Well, have a good rehearsal anyway. Think about what I said."

She leans back in the door. "Mom, no way do I belong here, and I don't plan on staying here. Why should I ask someone to forgive me that I plan to never see again in my life?" She closes the door and walks up the sidewalk.

The first star of the evening hangs in the softening sky. Pink and yellow tinge the light blue, and I roll my window down before I pull away from the curb. Since the weekend of Valentine's Day, Savannah has spent every spare minute burning bridges here. And building bridges back to Marietta, back to her old life.

Didn't help that the video of Ricky's rejection went viral. Standing there in a tux with a hundred lit candles and cello music in the background, his Georgia accent thickening with his tears, Savannah called him a hillbilly and informed him, and accidentally the world, that she had a date with someone who talked normal the next night. She did not know Brittani had been recruited to video the Special Moment from the bushes. Ricky did not know the flowers he was holding behind him had caught on fire. I did not know how sensitive people up in the mountains are to the term "hillbilly." Oh, yeah, and to their brand new gazebo catching fire.

They say what you don't know, can't kill you. They would be wrong.

Bryan (of course) says he knows Brittani is innocent in it

all, and since they are still dating I'm not going to argue. I do know that much. Honestly? He seems to have the most mature relationship going of all of us this past month. He and Brittani actually talk to each other, they had a civilized Valentines date, without setting anything on fire, and haven't gone viral on YouTube.

But doesn't her name seem to turn up when Savannah is crying too often for comfort?

Hesitating before pulling out of the school parking lot costs me when I realize the vehicle now too close to cut off is a huge combine, tall and wide and green, with a line of cars behind it to prove just how slow it is. My still-open window allows me to smell the fresh soil clinging to its front blades, the fumes of machine oil and gas tell of work done and to be done. Living in a farming community is a daily reminder that some folks still rely on the swing of the seasons, the rain, the warmth, bags of seeds, and acres of dirt. It's not only the birds and the bees that get excited as the air moves and the days lengthen. Farmers start showing up at ball practice with fresh mud on their boots, tractors foray onto the highways, youngsters brag about getting to drive the combine this year. Kids, who in the suburbs would be thought too undependable to feed the family dog, are anticipating their own calf to raise. Fields are not the only things lying dormant in winter in a farming town.

In no hurry to get in the line behind the combine, I put my van in park and enjoy the birds making the most of the lingering light. Darting to and fro between the woods beside the school and the field in front of the school, they are finding nesting material in the stubble from a recent mowing of the roadside weeds. Fresh linings for their homes, preparations for eggs and another crop of little ones. They are so busy and focused on the importance of their task. I feel I'm just as busy, but my activities don't seem important at all. Driving kids around takes up much of each day, and then the rest of the time I'm tearing off sheets and cleaning up the B&B rooms to get ready for more people coming to dirty the sheets and the rooms. Making nests for strangers to use a day or two.

Carter May still is staying with us, and every morning she and Jackson go off to work.

The power company is making great strides, and my refusal to be involved has made me suspect in both camps.

I've practically stopped talking to Peter because all I hear is, "Don't worry about it" when I ask him about the Carr family.

Much of my time and thinking went to the viral video episode, and by the time that settled down things in town had kind of passed me by.

Bryan has entered the phase I remember from when Will was leaving middle school. "Mom" is now a four-letter word, although many days he doesn't even say that many letters to me. He grunts a lot, and there is the mumbled thanks for food. He only has so many words and emotions, and those apparently must be reserved for that girl. Hearing his laughter and chatter through his bedroom door when they are on the phone stabs my heart. Things like this are what makes letting go of them easier. Problem is, I have to live with him for at least four more years. Hopefully, like with Will, somewhere around tenth grade he'll start talking to me again. Of course, that's just in time for real problems. My time for being able to fix things for my children is over. Gone. And I didn't even get to enjoy the last fixed boo-boo, the last make-it-better ice cream cone, the last head nod and look of wonder at my wisdom. Nope, the last time is always lost in the motion of life. Besides, at the time, how can you think it's the last time? It's so much of the day to day it seems it will last forever.

But it doesn't.

CHAPTER 37

In the early morning chill, covered by a light frost, the field of yellow daffodils at the bottom of the hill have bowed their bright heads. At the stop sign, I look at them and resist telling the silent occupants of my car, the semi-adults who let me drive them, feed them, and birth them, to look at the golden sparkle as the sun peeks through the trees. They no longer even roll their eyes at me; why waste such effort on the driver, feeder, birther?

So I look once more for traffic and pull onto the main road. At the school, where I picked up Savannah after play practice only nine hours ago, I pull to the second row of parked cars and stop. "Your car will be ready this afternoon. I'll go pay Bob later, and you can walk over to his shop and drive you both home, okay? You have your keys, right?"

"Yes, Mom. I know." Sounds like I actually got an eye roll.

Bryan mumbles "Bye," and it's just me again. In the school parking lot, again. I'd sigh, but what's the use? Not too long ago I would have headed straight to Ruby's ready for a morning gabfest. Now no one calls to tell me they are going there. Missus no longer calls me and instructs me to go there. Susan and Laney are busy, too busy for coffee. Too busy to drop in at Crossings. Probably too busy wondering if I think they are hillbillies and talk funny. Even Bill Weatherman and Aston's mom, Claire, are more welcomed in town than I am, and they're the ones who gave Savannah the idea of people here talking funny.

Across from the field of daffodils, with their heads still bowed, I pause at the four-way stop. Straight and I'm going to Ruby's. Turn left up the hill and I'm going home. But there's nothing I need to do at home, the B&B is ready for the weekend. The van idles as I think it over. I could start another book. I'm re-reading the ones in the basement, and I'm finishing one every couple days. They aren't holding my attention like they used to. Matter of fact, they are kind of sounding the same. Just a different location and a different set of names. But time does pass nicely and I don't—I nearly jump out of my skin when a car honks behind me. I put my foot to the gas and dart through the intersection straight ahead.

Maybe I'll just drive around the square and see how things are going. As I cross the railroad tracks, I look to the left and see that the gazebo repairs are almost finished. They only had to replace one side, but the paper said it was a real pain because the roof had to be jacked up and held in place and some of the floor had to be matched and replaced. Looks like they are about ready to paint it. A quick look to my right tells me that Ruby's is as inviting as always. Oh, she's added flower boxes to the front window, and they are stuffed with purple, yellow, and white pansies. Did she have flower boxes last summer? I can't remember. Last summer was such a blur. I stop at the end of the block and put on my left turn signal. Just as I turn, Missus' front door opens on my right and Bill Weatherman and his wife step onto Missus' porch. Right behind them are Missus, Laney, Susan, and FM. I push the accelerator and jerk to look straight ahead. Out of the corner of my eye, I see FM lift his hand in a wave at me, the others don't even see me go by. At the library I turn to the right and prepare to only go back through town on my way to my house on the hill and my books.

I'm no longer the flavor of the month in Chancey. Of course not, Missus has a successful couple who won't embarrass her and can actually do something for the town. Who needs a broken-down, old B&B? Who needs a newcomer who calls you names and burns down your gazebo? Who needs someone whose kids don't even want to talk to her?

This time I don't look to either side as I drive down Main Street and pause at the stop sign. There's no hesitation when I turn up the hill. Only when I get to the top of the hill do I realize I forgot to even look at the daffodils. And a tear leaks out. My throat burns, and by time I bump across the tracks in front of our house, I can barely see. Used to be I needed to be able to see approaching our house to figure out who all had dropped in. Now, I only have to look for trains.

No one drops in any more.

Over the tracks and into my spot closest to the sidewalk, Jackson's car causes me to tilt my head. It's parked in his usual spot at the corner of the house. Was it here when I left? Are he and Carter May driving to work together now? Probably. My Valentine's-induced seduction didn't exactly work. Let's just say he came down pretty hard on Ricky's side in the whole gazebo incident and left me to defend our daughter. I might have even said something about him choosing Chancey over his family. Of course this was all when I thought my daughter would do the right thing and apologize.

Apparently he knows her better than I do. Everybody probably knows my kids better than I do.

So, now he's ensconced in the spare room, and the whole town knows it. Whether Carter May leaked it first, or Bryan to the redhead, I'm not sure. Most likely it was when Ricky declared amidst the flames and cello music that he knew Savannah was confused, with her parents' relationship in shambles, and she retorted that just because her parents no longer shared a bed didn't mean it was a shambles.

Have I already pointed out she didn't know she was being videotaped?

The front door is unlocked, but I shake my keys anyway. No need to walk in on something I'd rather not know about.

"Hello? Jackson?"

He steps to the kitchen door. "There you are. Want some coffee?"

He moves back into the kitchen. I shrug off my jacket and hang it and my purse on the coat rack on the landing. Stepping back down the couple steps, I duck to look into the kitchen and see muffins, butter, and saucers. Two saucers and both unused. Looks like this is for me and him? Some part of me thinks finding him upstairs with Carter May would've been better.

I'm joking.

Probably.

"Hey there. Muffins? For us?" I take the cup of coffee he holds out to me.

"Yep. We don't seem to get a chance to talk so I decided to be proactive."

"Proactive? You been watching *Dr. Phil* at the office?"

I sit in the chair facing the backyard and watch as he smiles, sets his full cup on the table, and then sits across from me.

A light breeze blows in the window over the sink. It carries the freshness of the leaves and soil and a bit of the mustiness of the river. And daffodils. Then I see the bouquet of big yellow daffodils sitting beside the coffee maker. My lips pop open in surprise, and Jackson jumps up.

"These are for you." He sets them on the table. Daffodils are my favorite. The earthy smell takes me back to walking home from school through a field of daffodils and to how each spring Jackson tries to find me some at the local florist.

Burying my face in the bright yellow trumpets, I breathe deep. "Oh, I love that. I love these. Thank you." I set the vase in the middle of the table. "This is so thoughtful."

"Have a muffin. Ruby said they are lemon and chocolate, white chocolate, I think. Something new for spring she said."

Sure enough, when I break open the warm muffin, the hit of lemon is held up by a sweet, rich aroma. One bite tells me Ruby has another success on her hands.

"We have an offer on the B&B."

What? The lemon chocolate muffin clumps up in my mouth. While I finish chewing the lump and swallowing, my mind plays through what that statement could possibly mean. Finally I ask, "What?"

Jackson looks stunned, he waves his coffee cup around. "A great offer. Almost twice what we paid. And it's serious, there's even a contract. But we have time. The realtor that contacted me this morning says there's no hurry on making a decision as the buyer doesn't need an answer until the end of April. However, there is bonus money for signing the contract earlier than that. "

An offer? On the B&B? On our home? We both take bites of muffin like we aren't sure what to say now.

Does he want to take it? Do I want to take it? We could move back to Marietta, and Savannah wouldn't have to live with Marnie's family. She could live with her own family. And Bryan's relationship with Brittani would take care of itself since neither one can drive yet. My library science degree would once again have meaning. No more cleaning sheets for strangers or having strangers sleep in our house. Savannah's right, no apology would be needed. It would be like this all never happened. Like Chancey never happened. When I pop the last of my muffin in my mouth, chewing is hard because my smile is so big. Everything will go back to normal. Better than normal because we'll have more money to buy an even nicer house back in the suburbs.

Looking at Jackson I see him attempting to mirror my smile and he asks, "So, this makes you happy? Are you as done with Chancey as Savannah is?"

A deep breath draws in the scent of the daffodils again. "You know, maybe I am. Everyone here is mad at us, so maybe this is an answer to prayer."

He raises an eyebrow. "You've been praying?"

"Well, maybe not *my* praying. But you're still going down to church. Maybe it's an answer to your prayers. Right?"

He nods and then stands up. With his hands in his pockets he turns to look out the back doors. "Yeah, maybe it's the answer," he says.

I pour another cup of coffee, but it only makes it into my hand, my mouth is too busy talking to drink as I sit back down. "Reckon they want all the stuff in the B&B rooms? Probably that's why they are paying so much. I can't believe this has all worked out so well. And the housing market in Marietta is so depressed we'll get a great deal. Let's look in Forrest Chase Hills. I always wanted to live there, and that would keep us in the same school district as before. Plus, being so close to Roswell and Marietta and Atlanta, I'm sure I'll find a job." He stares out the back doors, and I stare at his back as I drink my coffee.

Standing, I pick up our saucers and then place them in the sink. After a deep breath, I go to him. We've not really touched in a while, but this is a whole new beginning. It's time for us to get back to who we truly are, as individuals, and as a couple. As a family.

With both hands on his shoulders, I lay my cheek against his upper back. His dress shirt feels smoothly starched, and I realize he must be taking his shirts to the dry cleaners. Guess I hadn't thought about it, but they've not been in the laundry lately. Of course. He works next to the dry cleaners now. Makes sense. "Jackson, I'm sorry for being such a pain at times about everything. You were right about Savannah apologizing. You were right about this place being a success. Things are going to get better now, and we'll get back to how we used to be." Funny how easy apologizing is when I'm getting my way. I wrap my arms around him and squeeze before letting go. "I'm going upstairs and if you've got time you could come help me..." I giggle and step toward the living room. "You could help me, well, get comfortable and then we can move you back into *our* room."

At the foot of the stairs, I look back to see if he's gotten my meaning and am delighted to see him at the kitchen door. He meets my eyes, and I notice him chewing the inside of his cheek. My eyes drop. Maybe I'm moving too quick. Maybe I'm...

"Carolina, I'm not moving back to Marietta. I'm thinking about staying here. In Chancey."

And I see that I have been right all along. This place has killed us. This place has ravaged my family and left us unfixable.

I nod at him and go upstairs.

Alone.

CHAPTER 38

"Will, when did you get home?" Like one of those sappy coffee commercials, I come down the stairs Saturday morning to the smell of coffee and my oldest child sitting at the kitchen table.

He turns, stands, and opens his arms. We hug and then I push him back down in his seat before I walk to the coffeemaker. "Did you just get here?"

"Here? Yeah."

I pull my robe out of my way and sit down. "What's that mean? Did you go somewhere else first? Last I heard, you weren't sure if you'd get home at all over spring break."

He shoves his sleeves up past his elbows and folds his arms on the table. "Well, I took off work. I'm graduating in May, if they want to fire me, they can. Mom, you sure don't look like you slept too well. Is everything okay?"

Smothering a yawn in my sleeve, I nod. "It's fine. Just everything is kind of crazy with stuff in town, Savannah, Bryan, your dad." The last couple words get buried in another yawn.

"Boy, that video of Savannah and Ricky sure was something. How did folks around here react?"

"Like hillbillies. Oops, that slipped out." We both grin.

"Seriously, I think I've about had it with Chancey. We don't fit in here."

"Really?" He picks up his coffee and takes a drink. "I thought things were going good with Crossings. Every time I call, y'all have guests. And with the stuff they've planned at the waterfront with the power plant and all, figured there'd be more business than ever."

"Well, you figure right. But just because Crossings is successful doesn't mean this is the right place for us. Savannah has already lined up a place to live in Marietta for her senior year."

Will's eyes bug open at me. "And you'd let her do that? Let her just decide she wants to move?" He coughs and shakes his head. "Her senior year? There's no way you'd have let me get away with that."

"Yeah, but you were our first one to leave, and we were fine in Marietta. You don't know what it's like here. Besides, Savannah won't apologize to Ricky, and the whole town is ostracizing her."

He leans back and rests his half-full cup on his chest. With the hand not wrapped around his mug he brushes his shaggy blond hair back from his face. "That's not what I hear."

"What do you hear? About Savannah?"

"Hey, Will!" Bryan runs down the stairs. "I thought that was you I heard."

"Sorry, buddy, didn't mean to wake you up."

Bryan grabs Will's neck and then steps back to punch at his arm. "When'd you get here?"

So this is the Bryan reserved for Brittani. Smiles, enthusiasm, actual words. Seeing the boys together helps soothe the weariness from the long, gloomy day yesterday after Jackson went back to work and the long, sleepless night that followed. Movement in the door to the dining room catches my attention, and I see that I'm not the only audience for the brotherly affection. Carter

May smiles at them and then looks at me and winks.

She winks at me? We are not in cahoots. We are not friends. We don't share winks over my sons. A little snort, shake of my head, and a turning away from her informs her of her dismissal. Not even dismissal, her nonexistence.

Out of the corner of my eye, I see she's recognized that she doesn't belong and has left the doorway. And then she's back.

"Warm muffins straight from Ruby's. Will, is there still plenty of coffee?" Carter May sets a huge basket on the table and then turns to the refrigerator. "And bacon. Bryan, you get everyone's egg order, and we'll get breakfast underway." She takes from the fridge a cookie sheet with strips of bacon already laid out and slides it into the oven which lets out a blast of hot air when she opens the door.

Will is digging in the basket and pulls out a dark brown muffin with a dollop of icing on top. "Let's just make a mess of scrambled eggs, okay? I'm starving."

Carter May leans back against the counter and smiles at me. "Scrambled okay for you, Carolina?"

How did she know Will was home? Why is it like I'm the guest and not her? My questions are good ones, but they make me look like an idiot as they go around and around in my head while my mouth is hanging open, nothing coming out of it. "Sure. Scrambled. Umm, you've already been out to Ruby's?"

Carter May laughs and wipes her hands on the dishtowel lying by the sink. *My* dishtowel. *My* sink. "Yes, figured I'd take that off your hands. I laid the bacon out last night because I know how the kids and Jackson are about bacon."

Bryan pushes around me to set the table. "Here, Mom." He hands me my silverware and a cloth napkin. He stops abruptly. "Or do we want to eat in the dining room, CM?"

"In here is fine, I think. Don't you?"

"CM?"

Carter May, CM, laughs again. "Oh, that's what some of the

kids started calling me. Cute, isn't it?"

Cute? He doesn't even speak to me but she gets a nickname? "I've got to get dressed." I stand up and hurry past Bryan and Will. Savannah steps off the last stair and tries to see around me into the kitchen.

"Will's still here, isn't he?"

"Of course. He just got here. They're doing breakfast. Why are you up so early?"

"Play practice at 10." She tries to step around me. "Is there bacon? CM said she'd get bacon."

"Wait." I move into her path again. "You're calling her CM, too?"

Savannah stops looking beyond me and looks into my face. Her black hair hangs thick and unbrushed around her face and makes her eyes look huge. "Mom."

And that's all she says. Am I supposed to get something from that? She stares at me like there is something I should be reading in her wide and darkened blue eyes. But there's nothing. So I step out of the way and let her pass. At the top of the stairs, I turn to look down when I hear my name. There leaning through the door and looking up at me is CM in my Christmas apron I forgot to pack away with the other holiday things.

"Carolina? Could you go by Jackson's room and knock on the door? I told him we wouldn't let him miss breakfast. Thanks!" Before I can answer, she swings back to the kitchen.

I knock on his door and wait to hear if he answers. Just as my knuckles touch the door a second time, he shouts his thanks and that he'll be right down.

In my room I sit on the bed. *Did I miss a day?* Yesterday was kind of an extended mope fest, but everyone seems to have moved on, and I missed out on, well, everything. Or at least something. Anxiety stirs my stomach, and I leap from the bed, throwing on jeans and the first shirt I grab from the closet. A quick wash of my face and brush of my hair, and I'm back in the hall. Just in time to run into Jackson.

"Hey."

"Hey."

I tug the pink oxford button-up down to smooth out the wrinkles. "So, Will is home."

Jackson sticks his hands in the front pockets of his jeans and rocks a bit, then nods. "Yep. He was down at Peter's last night."

"You were down at Peter's? All of you?"

"We just kind of ended up there." He leans toward me. "I didn't tell the kids anything about the house offer. Or anything."

"Are you involved with Carter May? Or should I say 'CM'?"

He leans back, jerks his hands out of his pockets and crosses them, pressed, to his chest. "Involved? Am I sleeping with her? No. We work together and are just friends." Then he whispers, "I told you to get rid of her."

My whisper back is sharp. "You get rid of her!"

"I told you, we work together, and I can't and…" his voice calms down and uncrossing his arms he shrugs. "… and maybe I don't want to." His mouth barely moves as he continues. "Look at the mess my mom and dad made of everything by forcing themselves to stay married, when they clearly should've ended it a long time ago. What if that's what we're doing now?" Pressing his hands against his head, he stretches his neck. "I can't think. I just can't think."

A sigh releases my anger, and I lean against the wall. My eyes close, and my body falls into the lean. "Jackson, what are we doing? This all feels so wrong, so off-kilter and yet I can't seem to find my footing here. Chancey has ruined us, can't you see that?"

"Couldn't be anything you've done, right? No," he says as he straightens up, and drops his hands by his side. "Chancey hasn't ruined us. Your attitude about Chancey has ruined us. Every time you start to lighten up and I think you might enjoy things here, you go all crazy and hole up here like some martyr."

"Martyr? You're the one that's crazy. I'm going down to spend some time with my children and let your *co-worker* fix me breakfast." I shove against him as I push away from the wall and stomp down the stairs.

At the bottom, I pause to straighten my shirt again and to glance upstairs to see what he's doing. He's still there, so I take a longer look and we meet eyes. He shakes his head, and his lips press tighter into a straight line. His lips then part, and he starts to say something when Will steps out of the kitchen.

"Oh, there you are. It's ready." He looks up and sees his father. "Breakfast is ready, Dad."

In a handful of steps I am in the midst of a happy scene. Delicious smells, noisy kids, country music on the radio, and somehow the woman at the center of it all isn't me. Will points me to my seat, which is no longer the closest one to the stove, but the one farthest away.

The guest seat.

Chapter 39

Breakfast was enlightening.

Will is courting Anna. Literally, she doesn't want to get involved, and he can't get her out of his mind, so he's courting her. Trying to win her over. Anna works for Carter May, so CM has become Will's big ally in love.

Bryan's decided to try out for the high school football team, and the first step is to participate in spring drills for the eighth graders. CM's brother played college football and would be thrilled to give him some tips when he comes to visit.

Savannah is potent as an enemy. That's not an enlightenment on my part, but I believe CM may be just figuring it out. With her light blue eyes shrouded in her dark hair, it was like having a witch at the table. Her eyes softened as Will talked about Anna. Bryan and football made her eyes smile, then they turned to ice when he mentioned Brittani being a cheerleader and cheering just for him. The adoring little girl she showed to her father on one side of her morphed into the mean girl from high school hell when she turned to CM on her other side. Me, she ignored; I didn't seem to warrant any of her favor or condemnation.

For the mother of a teenage girl, that's the honey spot.

Cleaning the kitchen, after I shooed all of them on to their

Saturday activities, all these thoughts swirl in my head. Just as I wipe down the table one last time, Bryan comes into the kitchen.

"Here, Mom, your phone keeps ringing upstairs."

"Okay, thanks. So football, huh?"

He looks at me like I'm a homeless person asking for money. There's pity, politeness, and a shrug. "Sure. Yeah." He turns and lopes out of the kitchen.

"Sure. Yeah." I mumble and walk to the French doors. Late morning sunshine has the back deck warmed nicely, and the doors are open. I pull out a chair at the table and sit down to see who's been calling me.

Whoa. Guess Susan and Laney are making up for not calling me in the last couple weeks all in one morning. Three calls from Susan and two from Laney. Each only left me one message. Susan's is the normal "Call me back as soon as you can." Laney however, sounds apoplectic.

"Carolina! It's awful. You have to call me. We have to do something. Call me ASAP. You can't ignore me anymore, if I don't hear from you before 11:30, I am coming up there to get you!"

Barely beating the time limit, I call Laney back first.

"Hey, I got your message. What's going on?"

"Finally! We need to talk. You are not going to believe what Missus has done. I'm at Susan's, and we're headed to the farmers market over in Jasper. We'll swing by and pick you up in about five minutes."

She doesn't wait for an answer but hangs up. Before I can call her back and say, "No," I realize I don't have anything else to do. Might as well go to the farmers market; I've been meaning to anyway. I jump up from the deck chair and dash to get my tennis shoes on, grab a jacket, and pour some coffee in a travel mug. There's no one left around to tell where I'm going, and as I step out on the front porch, Laney tears across the railroad tracks and into my driveway. Her big black SUV shudders to a stop, and before I close the front door, I lean back inside and holler, "I'm going to the farmers market with Laney and Susan. I have my phone."

Skipping down the porch steps, there is absolutely no reason I should feel this good. But the sky is the color of the Sky Blue crayon (my favorite one), and the breeze whispers by with a hint of warmth, sunshine, and new things. On the sidewalk I slow my pace and try frowning, try thinking about all the things going wrong. Then I hear a bird singing right over my head in the tiniest reaches of the maple tree, where leaves appear to be unfurling right before my eyes. It's a known fact I'm gifted at being delusional, so I guess I'll just go with it. By the time I reach for the SUV door handle, all frowns—both inside and out—are gone.

"Hey ladies!" I almost leap into the back seat. Like the good wife of a car dealer, Laney's made sure her car is spotless. The new car smell is as thick as the leather seats. "Nice car. I may just lay down here and take a nap."

"Thanks! Spring always means a new car. Law, I love that man of mine." Laney does a three-point turn and then checks before we pull across the railroad crossing.

"Hey, Carolina," Susan mumbles. She's busy reading something on her phone.

Leaning forward, I ask, "You bedazzled your phone?"

"Naw, it's Laney's. I'm reading the minutes from the council meeting."

I lean back and buckle my seat belt as we tear around the curves heading off the mountain. "Laney, you're no longer on the council. Why do you have the minutes?"

Our eyes meet in the rearview mirror, and she shrugs. "Sometimes one of the council members uses an old list of email addresses, and I get sent things." She shrugs again, and though her eyes are huge, wide open with wonder in the mirror, they are not innocent.

"Sure. Okay, so what's going on with Missus? Why the panic?"

One would think that driving might lessen the hand movements during a Laney diatribe. One would be wrong. So hands flying, mouth going 90 along with the car, we wind our way to Jasper.

"The Weathermans. Well, I guess Claire doesn't call herself Weatherman. Roberts, right? Well, they are now Missus' best friends. *Best friends.* And let me tell you, they are evil. Evil city people. I can see you rolling your eyes in the mirror. Quit rolling your eyes at me. I get enough of that at home with two daughters, thank you very much! They are truly evil. Tell her Susan. Tell her how evil they are."

Susan holds up her hand to indicate she's still reading and then she drops her hand and takes a deep breath. "Oh my goodness. Graham didn't mention a bit of this. What is wrong with him? He can't think this is good?"

"Told you, evil."

Susan reaches out and smacks Laney's shoulder. "You told me after Thursday morning's meeting this is what was happening." She turns around in her seat toward me. "We had breakfast over at Missus and FM's Thursday with Claire and Bill Weatherman. Very, very impressive people." With her smooth brown hair framing her sweet face where no makeup resides, she looks like a little girl. Sincerity wraps her every word and action. Still blows my mind that the two women in the front seats are sisters.

"I know," I say. "I was driving by and saw y'all on Missus' front porch. Looked like you were all leaving and were very friendly."

Laney slaps the steering wheel. "Why didn't you stop? You'd have given me the courage to ask what all I want to know. And quit rolling your eyes! What are you rolling your eyes at anyway?"

"Just stop? Just barge on in where I'm obviously not welcome. I've not heard from either of you in weeks, and you think I should've just stopped and made myself a part of your little party?"

Now they do kind of look like sisters. Both mouths hang open, and wide eyes stare at me. In between those wide eyes there is the same three vertical lines. And at the same time they say, "What?"

"The whole hillbilly comment and burning down the gazebo and embarrassing Ricky all over the internet. I know everyone is mad at Savannah." My voice lowers. "And me."

They turn from me to look at each other and start laughing.

Susan reaches back across the middle console; her open hand bounces in front of me. "Oh, honey, you thought we gave all that a second thought? Don't be crazy. Its kid stuff, and well, it was hilarious. You're the one that went into hiding. Grant said Bryan told him you were sitting in the basement reading all the time, so we figured you were just taking a break from things."

Laney smirks in the mirror. "Or off running around with Peter."

"What? Peter?"

"Well, you *were* seen out on one of the back roads. Driving separate cars, but still together, if you know what I mean."

"Oh, that was something else. Something I wanted him to check out for me."

Laney's reflection winks. "Oh, he's been wanting to check things out for you for a while now."

"Never mind." I shake my head. "Now what about Missus and the Weathermans?"

Susan folds her leg underneath her in the seat and turns even more towards me. "Chanceyland."

Laney lifts both hands off the wheel and lifts them to the roof of the car. "God help us. Chanceyland."

Susan nods. "Or there's Hillbilly Haven, Mountain

Memories, or any number of nauseating alliterations to say Redneck theme park. It started off small and tasteful. A little area where folks make and sell things like jam and hand-carved canes and whatever, but now that is just the start." She looks out the window. "This works, just pull in here."

Stretching to look in each direction, I see nothing that looks like a farmers market. "Where is it?"

Laney turns off the car and lets her seatbelt go. "Oh, the farmers market doesn't open for another couple weeks. Sometime early April."

Susan grimaces. "We just needed an excuse to get out of town without the kids and husbands and Missus. Well-known fact they *all* hate farmer markets and will not ask to tag along. None of them know it's not open yet. We act like its open year-round."

I slide out my door, and Laney laughs. "Your face! You look so surprised. I thought we'd brought you with us before. I thought you understood."

"No, I've never been invited to the farmers market before." We meet Susan at the front of the car. "What I can't believe is Susan lying like that. To your family? Laney lies all the time—we all know that."

Laney wraps Susan in a one-armed hug. "Shoot, that's why my big sis is so good at lying. No one expects it."

"So, what are we going to do?"

"We're going to walk through a couple shops and then get some lunch."

"Food? I'm still stuffed from Carter May's breakfast."

"She made you breakfast? Just you?" Susan's eyebrows aren't nicely shaped like her sister's, but they can climb up her face just as well.

"No, for everyone. Will's home."

They both nod. "How's it going with Anna?" Laney asks.

I shrug. Obviously there is nothing I can tell them that they don't already know.

"You have to watch that woman, Carolina. Everyone thinks she wants what you have." Laney steps to the wide open door of the first shop and lowers her voice. "Why you are still letting her live in your house is beyond me. Absolutely beyond me!" Then, in a more public voice, "I love the jewelry in this place."

We walk into an adorable shop with a young girl behind the counter. Laney heads for a counter of rhinestones and flash, Susan stops at a shelf of books, and I wander to the back where stuffed animals cover the wall. Looking at woodpeckers, foxes, rabbits, and every other mountain animal, I try to see myself as others do. As my—okay, I admit it—friends do. Why do I work so hard to convince myself I don't have friends here? Why do I spiral off the charts when I think they are mad at me? Staring into the big green eyes of a stuffed owl, it hits me. I've pushed away the people who like me and kept the one who is a threat in my very own home.

Susan walks up beside me. "Look at all these. Can you believe in only a few years we'll probably have grandkids to give them to?"

I push a finger in her face. My babies are growing up too fast as it is. "Hush your mouth. So, Chanceyland? What has Graham said about all this?"

Susan sighs, and her mouth tightens. "Not much. He thinks it's a big joke, and with the power plant and the park facilities, in addition to his full-time job and coaching Grant's baseball team, he's just overwhelmed. Plus, there is some other stuff going on that has him worried." She leans close to me and whispers, "Meth. In Chancey. Not just in Chancey, we're apparently supplying half of North Georgia. It's a mess because some law folks are apparently involved and no one knows who to trust." Her eyes dart to where her sister stands at the front counter. "Laney doesn't know all that. Graham says she's the type to go in with guns blazing, and no one can chance scaring the people in charge." She bumps her shoulder into mine. "One thing I know about you, you don't ever go off half-cocked. You never move too fast or talk too much."

She leaves me to see what Laney is looking at, and I look at my owl friend again. "That's me. Slow to act. Slow to talk. Almost like being called a sloth."

None of us make any purchases, and as we leave, Laney stops on the sidewalk and points next door. "This is a new place. It's tiny." She pushes open the door while reading the script painted on it. "Vicki Makes It Hot."

"Hello, come in," are the warm words which greet us. Hearing the words is followed by a swift intake of breath by each of us. Aromas pull us into the small store with soft lighting and the owner of the warm greeting. "Doesn't it smell delicious? I'm Vicki Mattle."

"The Vicki that 'makes it hot'?" I ask.

"Absolutely!" she says with a laugh. Bottles and bags, wooden crates and small bowls fill every table and shelf. Handwritten signs identify more kinds of pepper than I knew existed. And in every form imaginable. Ground, chopped, fresh, dried, and so many more.

"A pepper store?" Laney wonders. "I love spicy things."

"Me too," the owner says. "Here, smell this." She holds out a small, mustard-colored ceramic bowl.

"Um, is that cinnamon?"

"Spicy cinnamon. Amazing in a hot cup of coffee."

Susan wrinkles her nose. "Pepper in coffee? I don't really like spicy food."

"Look at this," I say. "It's for rimming margarita glasses. Spiced Salt."

"Here's a basket," Vickie says noticing the collection of bottles I have in my hand. "I also have a sugar for when you want drinks rimmed with something sweet, but with a pop of heat."

"You weren't here last time we were in Jasper. When did you open?" Laney asks.

"Just before Christmas. We'd had the idea for a long time and everything fell in place this past fall. Our house in Marietta sold overnight, and here we are."

All three of us stop and look at her. (Which isn't difficult, as the store's not much more than a large closet.) I place my collection of bottles and packets in the basket and ask, "Marietta? We moved from Marietta last summer over to Chancey." I hold my hand out. "Carolina Jessup."

"No way!" She takes my hand in hers. "Don't you just love living up here? Marietta was perfect for raising our son, Alex, but Karl and I were ready for adventure when Alex went off to Tech." She looks around her. "Happened a little faster than we thought, but it sure has been an adventure!"

Laney and Susan suddenly seem focused on their shopping as they look down and turn away from me. I ignore them and agree with her, "Know what you mean. Our move happened faster than I ever imagined, too. It's been really hard."

Vicki grins and steps back behind the counter as I sit my basket on it. "Yeah, but then it wouldn't be an adventure, if there weren't hard parts."

My sigh is heavy as she begins writing down my purchases. "Maybe everyone isn't cut out for adventure," I say.

She nods and gives me a compassionate smile. "I guess that's true. But I've sure learned a lot about peppers and opening a business, so nothing's gone to waste. Plus, it's made me and my husband closer."

"Oh. Well. Well, that's good." Maybe it's the aggressive aromas, or the low lighting, or the small space, but I need to get out of here. "I'll wait outside," I say as I take my debit card and bag. "Nice to meet you, Vicki."

On the sidewalk, I wait and think about adventures. Not sure I've ever actually gone looking for an adventure. Even when I was young. That could be one way to look at our move to Chancey, I guess. I mean, if you like adventures and all that.

Susan comes out the door first. "She seemed nice. Did you know her back in Marietta?"

I just say, "No." Not wasting my breath explaining there are over 50,000 people in Marietta. Folks in small towns think you should know everyone.

"This place is my favorite," Susan says as we meander to the next store full of jams, crackers, pasta, and assorted pottery.

Susan and Laney both pick up a wicker basket at the door, so I follow suit. Susan stops at the first rack of jam. "Stuff here is pretty good, plus it looks like what you'd buy at a farmers market."

"And they give samples," Laney explains as she heads to a tasting table in the middle of the shop.

An older gentleman with a flannel shirt and red suspenders says, "Good morning." Then adds, "My wife and daughters make most of the things here." He rubs his round, little belly. "So I can attest to how good everything is."

"Wow, they make all this?" As I look around I realize all the labels do look alike. Christa's Creations in slightly curvy script surrounded by purple mountain asters, as the back label identifies them.

"Yep, every bit. Christa started selling jam out of our house twenty years ago. We opened up this shop ten years ago, and we hire pretty much everybody in the family to do their part. Son-in-law dabbles in pottery. We ship, too." He hands me a napkin. "Help yourself. Where you ladies from?"

"Chancey," I respond while spreading raspberry-lime jam on a small cracker.

"Chancey? My, oh my, don't y'all have stuff a-jumpin' over there. My other son-in-law, not the pottery one, is on the board for our Chamber of Commerce, and they are keepin' a close eye on you folks."

Laney sticks her head from around a shelf of honey. "What do you mean?"

The old man's eyes pop, and he takes a deep breath, shaking his head all the while. "An amusement park? Some folks saying it could be something like a Dollywood or even bigger."

Laney's head tilts, and she comes around to the tasting table. "Dollywood has done wonders for that area of Tennessee. Dolly Parton started it to keep alive many of the crafts of her ancestors, you know. Woodworking, blacksmithing, basket weaving."

He rubs the back of his neck. "Sure, sure, and some are saying it's just what these hills need. Other' not so much."

Laney's bravado falls. "I know. I'm just sick about it. If I knew it would be done tastefully and let true crafts like your families get a foothold and do well, then I could be all for it."

Susan steps forward, agreeing with her sister. "But we're just afraid it will turn into a joke."

We all four drown our sorrows in some slivers of turtle fudge and bits of fresh peanut brittle. The sugar helps our moods lighten, that and a little more shopping, and by time we leave, Mr. Christa's Creations has to restock his shelves.

Laney pulls out her car keys. "Here, let's put this stuff in the car and then we'll decide about lunch."

"Decide my foot," Susan says, walking across the street. "We always eat at the same place, and you always get the same thing."

Laney presses the unlock button on her keys. "You know I love somebody else cooking for me, but I really love it when they cook me some marvelous grits. This place makes the grits so creamy it's like eating warm ice cream."

"Sounds good to me," I say.

Susan laughs. "Thought you were too full from Carter May's breakfast."

"Now that I think about it, I didn't really eat too much. Y'all she's liking my family a bit too much. You know?"

"Yes," they say in tandem, and Laney slams the car door for emphasis.

"But, I just don't get how a woman could go after a man

who's married. And has children."

They both stare at me, and Susan sighs. "That's not how it works in a small town. Pickings are lean. There's always a woman around looking to see if a good guy looks unhappy."

I almost stop in the middle of the street, but scurry on when a car turns toward us. "Graham?"

Laney huffs. "Of course, Graham. He's successful, charming, and a good provider. Women been flirting with him since the day he and Susan got married. Isn't that right?"

Susan shrugs. "Yep. Luckily he doesn't seem to really notice it. A lot like Jackson. Some men never realize they could stray, just doesn't enter their minds."

"And then there are men like my Shaw. He has to be reminded what he would lose if he so much as dared to follow one of these floozies up on their not-so-subtle hints. When a new single woman hits town, whether she moves here, is widowed, or splits from her husband, Shaw knows he's in for some good lovin' cause I need him to remember there ain't nothing worth losing this over." Her "this" is emphasized with a sweep of her arm down her curvaceous body.

My mouth is dry, and my mind spins. "Really? Women think like this?"

Susan shrugs again. "The ones raised by our mama do."

We stop at a small brick building. Laney opens the door for me and Susan to walk in. Sunlight on the dark wood floors spreads a welcoming carpet of light in front of us. Brick walls are offset by bouquets of fresh flowers and white tablecloths on the square tables. A smiling girl with a blonde ponytail leads us to a table beside the sunny front windows, and for a moment, we relax and look at the menu.

"I'm having a Bloody Mary. You too, Susan?" Laney asks.

"Sure. How about you, Carolina?"

We decide on a pitcher of Bloody Marys. We also decide to wait a bit before ordering since they serve brunch until two.

Bright green stalks of celery and a fat pickle welcome the spicy Bloody Mary into each glass. After a long sip, my thoughts come tumbling out whether fully formed or not. "But that holding on to your man thing, isn't that awfully old-fashioned?"

Laney leans over her glass to take a bite of pickle. "Maybe it is in the suburbs where if someone steals your husband you just go down to the corner Starbucks and find another one."

Susan nods. "In small towns, good men are hard to find. You have one, you better work hard to keep him. Haven't you noticed there seems to always be available women? Available men hide, and well, they don't stay available very long."

Maybe it's because I don't have a lot of women friends, but I don't remember any women talking like this. I kind of was thinking that if we were in love, we'd stay together, and if we fell out of love we would, well, fall apart. But I never thought of someone else having any impact on that. Never thought of it being like, you know, like a game. Like a contest. Jackson and I met, fell in love, got married, had kids, and...

Mid-sip, I realize I never pictured anything further. Never imagined just him and me again. Suddenly, I'm coughing and choking and grasping at my white cloth napkin to cover my mouth so I don't spit tomato juice all down my front.

"Carolina, what's wrong?" Susan pats me on the back, and Laney pulls my drink away from my flailing hands.

"Whew! I'm okay now." I take a deep breath and shudder. "You know what I just realized?" My heart pounds, and heat floods my face. "Bryan graduates four years from now!"

Confusion replaces concern on my friend's faces. "Yeah?" Susan agrees.

"In four years I could be all by myself."

Laney's smile looks almost sad, and she sighs as she tilts her head at her sister.

"Okay. Now, she gets it."

Chapter 40

"Does anything smell as bad as cabbage cooking?" I ask, nose wrinkled, as Jackson and I walk into the church's fellowship hall. The kids are already here as they had a youth work day cleaning up the playground.

"Collards smell pretty bad," he says.

"True. And at least the corned beef takes the edge off the cabbage smell. Hey, there."

Shaw grabs me and kisses my cheek, but doesn't let go of my arm and step away like usual. He folds my hand over his arm and leans closer. "Good to see you, Miss Carolina. You been off hiding at some beauty spa? You're looking very well tonight."

Laney's words from lunch earlier, about Shaw's nose for available women, come to me. "Thanks, Shaw, but I need to… uh…" My mind scurries to find something to take me away from my friend's husband, but it stumbles at the look on my husband's face. His blue eyes have gone dark, like Savannah's do when she's angry, and his jaw is actually clenched. Yep, clenched, just like in all my romance books in the basement.

Susan breaks everything up by coming in behind us with a crock pot in her hands. "Here, Shaw, can you put this with the other corned beef dishes?" She turns behind her. "Graham, the soda bread needs to be sliced, so take it to the kitchen. Thanks. And Jackson, sitting out beside my car is a gallon of tea. If you'd bring it in, I'd be so thankful."

She takes a deep breath as the men follow her instructions and disperse. "Look at you. Taking a page out of my sister's dressing book?"

"Well, it's green." I lift my chin and try to keep from looking down at the cleavage I brought to church for St. Patrick's Day dinner.

"Yes, it's green, but didn't you wear it over a turtleneck last year?"

"Hey, you're the one that told me about having to keep your man interested."

Susan laughs and steers me toward the kitchen. "Well, that should do it. Should keep most of the guys interested." She cocks an eyebrow at me. "Has Laney seen it?"

I pull away from her and dart into a hallway to the stairs. "I'm so embarrassed, and I didn't even bring my turtleneck to put on if I felt too naked. I'm going home."

Susan follows me and grabs my arm. "No, you're not. It's not vulgar or anything, it's just different for you." She steps back and looks me up and down. "You look cute. Now come on. I have to get to the kitchen. We were late getting here, poor Graham is just eaten up with this drug stuff. We'll be lucky if we don't all end up on the front page of the Atlanta papers."

"So when does he think it will all come out?"

A shrug is her only answer as Carter May comes rushing up to us. "Carolina, Susan, the dancers are already here. Should they do a quick number before we eat?"

Susan nods, but walks toward the kitchen. "Sure. Carolina, help her out."

All my hard work on my hair and makeup, aided by exposing scary amounts of breast, can't compete with Carter May's emerald green tunic over knit tights. Her ivory skin and red hair look like the day's color was selected just for her, and the high-heeled black boots remind us how young and lithe she is.

"Dancers?"

"Yes, my sister always did Irish dance, so I knew we could find a troupe to perform. They came from Cummings. Here, hold this."

She hands me the microphone and then bends down to plug it in. She takes the microphone from my hand and speaks into it. As I start to walk away, she grabs my arm, "Don't go away. I need someone to hold this when I'm done." She gestures to the microphone.

Great. Now I'm her microphone stand.

"Everyone? Welcome! The dancers from Startime Dance Studio in Cummings, Georgia have come to help us get in the mood for the annual St. Patrick's Day Corned Beef Dinner. Give them a hand as they make their way to the front."

Through the tables, young women and girls as well as a few boys make their way to where we stand. Their colorful outfits are covered with Celtic symbols and bright trim. When they are arranged in two lines, the leader nods to Carter May, who leans over to start the music. I fill my role and accept the handoff of the microphone.

The speakers switch on to a rollicking Irish ballad. The dancers' feet fly around the little makeshift stage. As they wind in and out of lines and patterns, for just a few minutes, we all forget that we're in a church fellowship hall.

A few swirls later, and with the finishing notes of a lilting song, Carter May takes the microphone from me amid hearty applause from the audience. "Wasn't that wonderful? Now, folks, the ladies in the kitchen are saying they are ready for us to line up. Our dancers will be back at the end of the meal."

She hands me the microphone without even looking at me and then bustles over to the dancers.

"You filled your roll admirably."

I turn to find Peter standing behind me. "Oh, thanks. Someone has to do it."

As he leans back, I can't help but notice his eyes take a quick look down. Then he mumbles, "Something's happening."

"I giggle a bit, but when I look up, his eyes are focused across the room.

His strides are long and take him to the other side of the hall quickly. All I can see is Graham and a tight knot of people, but the faces look heated and Peter isn't the only man rushing to the scene. However, the group quickly hustles out a side door. Peter is one of the few that slide outside before the door is slammed. Susan stands in front of it pointing to the food lines. "Folks, everything is under control. Just a little business to deal with. Let's eat so the dancers can get back up onstage."

Carter May turns on the CD the dance troupe brought, and as conversations pick back up around the large room, the mood lightens. I wander into the kitchen and find my husband wearing a white apron and holding a carving knife and fork. Beside the ice machine, he can't see me. His laughter and talking tells me he's happy. Really happy. We're only here tonight because he signed up to carve the corned beef. I didn't sign up to help or even bring anything. This really isn't my church, it's more Jackson's and the kids' and my friends'. Not mine.

Bryan is in line behind the Senior Citizens, with all his friends. They love church potlucks. Will is still at a table talking with Anna and meeting her friends from work. Carter May is standing behind Anna, participating in the conversation. Savannah isn't here. She went to Marietta as soon as play practice ended this morning. She'll be home tomorrow night.

I leave the kitchen and wander around until I'm against the wall beside the side door the arguing men escaped out of earlier. Leaning against the cold, pale green concrete block wall, my vantage point for Bill Weatherman's arrival proves perfect. His emerald green turtleneck acts to set off both his mane (yes it's clichéd for an author of a certain age, but it's truly a mane) of white hair and his creamy knit sweater. Lord, I believe that is THE sweater. The one from the back of his books. His old jeans and worn hiking boots complete the picture, and with his fingers pushed only a bit into the front pockets of his jeans he sways and surveys the room, even as several people talk to, really at, him. When his eyes hit me, he lifts his hands from his pockets and walks away from the group gathering around him.

"Carolina."

Only when his smile grows as he looks me up and down do I realize leaning on my hands has pushed my sweater out to greet him. Jumping away from the wall, I stand straight and fold my arms. Well, looky there, that pushes things up in an interesting way, doesn't it? I drop my arms and look anything but natural. "Hi Bill. Where's Claire?"

"They are in Roswell. I believe Aston and Savannah have a date tonight at an Irish pub on Marietta Square. Right?"

My shoulders fall. Of course, again, someone else who knows more about my family than me. I shrug. "Sure."

He lean toward me, "I'd like to see your house."

"What? *My* house?"

"Your house, tomorrow, at 11 a.m. Yes?"

"Why?"

He steps back and smiles wide. "But you've seen my home, shouldn't I see yours?" He checks behind him and sees a group headed in his direction. "Eleven. Right?

No words leave my mouth before he turns and greets his newest admirers.

He wants to see my house? On a Sunday morning? What if I was going to church?

As I lean back against the wall again, I examine how it makes my chest look. Fascinating how just a bit of movement can make things look so different. My fascination downward keeps me from seeing Jackson until he's right on top of me.

"We need to go home now." Jackson's blond head is dipped next to mine, and my sweater's maneuvers do not appear to have gone unnoticed.

Maybe I didn't exactly bat my eyelashes, but I did look up through my lashes like I've watched Laney do. "Now? We need to go home now?" This cleavage thing *does* work. I allow my husband to pull me away from the wall, and we are halfway across the floor when Peter catches us from behind. The side door is slowly closing in his wake.

"Jackson, that's not right. It's not like that. Wait."

Jackson doesn't let go of my arm, and doesn't slow down.

Peter grabs my other arm and tries to talk to my ear not closest to Jackson. "The woods, you know, what we were looking at?"

"So you *were* in the woods with him?" Jackson drops my arm.

"No, not really with him. We were…"

Jackson stops and looks at me. "We? There's a 'we'?"

Peter throws his hands up. "You're a fool," he says in disgust as he turns back toward the side door and stalks off.

Jackson shakes his head at me, then storms off in the opposite direction from Peter.

Laney sidles up to me and puts her arm around my shoulders, and we watch until the door has closed behind Jackson.

Laney pulls away from me and pointedly looks down at my cleavage. "Sweetie, you really shouldn't use those things unless you understand the consequences. Let's go have some corned beef and let Peter and Jackson cool off." She pushes me towards the kitchen and adds, "And they *will* cool off. The power of boobs wanes with distance."

CHAPTER 41

The front door slams, serving as my Sunday morning alarm clock. Although, as usual, I'm lying here awake listening for it. Now that Jackson is in his own room, I don't even have to pretend to still be asleep. I just stay in bed and am quiet, and no one disturbs me with questions about going to church.

Stretching my arms, legs, and smile, I turn on my side. Peter never came back into the fellowship hall, but when Jackson returned, he never left my side. Back at the house, he kept trying to work around Bryan and his friends who descended here to get me alone. My smile can't help but keep stretching remembering how he kept managing to do just that—get me alone. Carter May learned that teenage boys and girls will take advantage of everything you offer so she was kept busy cooking in the kitchen. She was fit to be tied as she tried to upstage me with the kids, because I let her. Jackson was supposed to be helping her, but, well, he was preoccupied with something else. I'm not sure what's going on with me and Jackson, but it was good to see he might still be interested in me.

When the mess and the noise was at critical mass, I excused myself. Thanked Carter May— CM, I guess I should say—and Jackson for providing the boys such a *fun* night. I took myself and my green sweater upstairs. And I might've said something about a bubble bath that caused Jackson's mouth to droop open and Carter May to press hers so tight her lips all but disappeared.

Laney would've been proud.

Wonder what Jackson would think if he knew Bill Weatherman, *the* Bill Weatherman, was coming to see me this morning. I kick the sheets away. "Wonder what I should wear?" I ask as I open the closet door. Laney definitely has a more seductive wardrobe to work with, but I'm sure I can find something Bill, I mean Jackson, will like.

Or Peter could stop by.

Maybe being the belle of the ball *is* all it's cracked up to be.

Bill Weatherman walking up my sidewalk feels like a dream. His cherry red ski jacket reminds me of the jacket he wore in an interview on *60 minutes*, or maybe *Good Morning America*. His smile when I open the screen door is just like the one he gave Diane Sawyer. Or maybe Katie Couric.

"Bill! Welcome to my home. So glad you get to see where we live. It's nowhere near as impressive as your beautiful house. That is truly an architectural masterpiece hanging on the side of the mountain like that." *Architectural Masterpiece?* Maybe putting on eyeliner and lip gloss has affected my brain.

"Carolina, just as beautiful as ever." He leans in to kiss each of my cheeks. My golden corduroy shirt doesn't reveal much, but I did leave a button or two more than normal undone. The risqué part of my outfit is the black leggings beneath the long tail of the shirt. I'd never wear this outfit in public, but it's just the two of us in my home. Perfect for a casual Sunday morning. "Here, let me hang your jacket up." When I step up to the landing, I reach high to hang his jacket knowing my shirt will inch up in back, just a bit. I'm practically giddy, channeling Laney.

"Your home is lovely. Just lovely, Carolina."

"Sit there and I'll get you a cup of coffee, okay?" In the kitchen I realize I forgot to grind the hazelnut beans. Struggling with opening the bag, I call out. "Make yourself comfortable, it'll be a minute."

The grinder fills the kitchen with noise, but also a delightful smell of fresh coffee. I scurry around unloading the dishwasher Jackson and the kids left full this morning, as usual. I put cream in a small white pitcher pulled from the shelf above the stove, and of course, it has to be washed first. Add a couple Splenda packets to the tray to go alongside the sugar bowl. By the time the tray is ready, the coffee's through perking. I pour it in the waiting thermos.

Guess I see why the sister that is a good hostess, Susan, is not the sister who wears makeup and dresses so stylishly. Doing both is impossible. I'm sweating, but trying to remember to not wipe my face or I'll mess up my makeup. Looking at my reflection in the microwave door, I blot my face with a paper napkin. Then before picking up the tray I jerk on the back of my leggings. They've started creeping on me.

"Here we are." Where is he? No wonder he's been so quiet, he's not in the living room. Oh no, could he be waiting for me upstairs? In my bedroom? Like in a book? Like in one of *his* books? I don't need a microwave door to know my face is really shiny now. Perspiration is running down every part of my body as my leggings are creeping up. "Bill?"

"Here I am." The cool breeze he lets in with the open door feels wonderful, but then I see what else he's letting in.

"Carolina Jessup! Where are your pants?" Missus leads a contingent of folks from the front porch into my living room. "FM, take that tray from her so she can finish getting dressed, and I'll go find some more coffee cups."

"Hey, Carolina." FM lifts the tray from me and swallows. "Guess Bill didn't tell you we'd be along coming?" As he tries to take the tray from me, he swallows again. "Yeah, well, you know we can't let folks know what we're thinking about quite yet, right?"

"FM, *I* have no idea what you're talking about."

"Oh, the club! The river club. Big things happening in Chancey. Big things. Now, scoot and put on some pants. You don't want people thinking we don't know how to do things, do you?" He pulls the tray out of my hands. "Now, shoo."

At the bottom of the stairs, I realize I'll be walking up them with a roomful of people watching. The fact that my leggings will only creep higher with each stair step forces me to grab one of Bryan's jackets from the coat rack and wrap it around my behind.

I hate these people. All these people.

"There you are." Missus looks me up and down. So much for making a quiet entrance. She pats my back as I step off the last step. "Much better. We're just headed outside to look around. Glad I didn't have to call you down to join us."

Holding the door, the people passing by me don't look familiar. Maybe one of the women, but no one else. Bill bounds out of the kitchen just as the last person lets the screen door slam. "Sweetheart, I'm so sorry I didn't tell you they were all coming. If I'd known you were planning such a nice treat for just the two of us, I would've come earlier and we'd have had plenty of time to chat. Grab your coat, Missus is waiting."

My head falls against the back of the door, and with Bill

outside the house falls still. I am such a fool. What is wrong with me? How do I get out of this? Whatever *this* is. Why did I ever think he was interested in me? I am such a fool.

A fool being summoned by the big-mouthed old lady in my front yard.

"Coming, Missus. Just had to get my coat." Straggling toward the walking bridge across the river, the group looks as if it knows its destination. I jog a bit to catch up and then edge closer to the man pointing and talking the most.

"Fascinating. I never even knew this was up here. The realtors for Laurel Cove never mentioned it to us. Did they mention it to any of you?"

All the responses were to the negative and must mean they are all from Laurel Cove. Explains why I don't know any of them. Maneuvering towards FM I catch bits of conversation. "Plenty of parking," someone says. "Great view," "membership," chime in others.

"FM, what's going on?" He shuffles his feet a bit, and then I realize he's shuffling away from the others. And Missus. Once we have a little space, he turns and points away from the others, towards the ridge above town. "See, they want a private club."

"Up there where you're pointing?" Even squinting I don't see anywhere to build a club.

"No, I'm just pointing to hide what we're talking about."

"Oh, okay." So I point, too.

"Now it looks silly, quit pointing. Just let me point."

"You don't have to get huffy. So where do they want this club?"

"On the other side of your driveway."

"What?" I turn, but he jerks me back around with a tug on my coat sleeve.

"Shhh. All that land on that side of the tracks, all the way down to the river is owned by the railroad. We're figuring they'll probably be glad to get rid of it."

"But we'd have no privacy!"

"But you'd have a great clientele. Missus is thinking y'all would be like the club inn, you know for the members' guests. Quaint, but with some remodeling, modern and elegant."

"Don't these people have a club up at Laurel Cove?"

A woman's voice from right behind us startles both of us. "Yes, we do. However, it's for anyone, anyone who buys a house there. Not exactly private, if you know what I mean. Mrs. Jessup, I'm Addison Palmer. I met your lovely daughter at Bill and Claire's Super Bowl party."

This is the lady who looked familiar earlier. "Wait, aren't you on the news or something?"

When she smiles and pushes her black hair behind her left ear, it hits me that I've seen her on one of the gardening and homes show.

"Yes, I host the Georgia Homes Show." Her dark skin and hair are set off with a coral sweater and her light gray coat.

"You live in Laurel Cove?"

"Exactly. You can see why people like Bill and I feel we need a private club." Her eyes open wide, and she lays a hand on my arm. "We left Atlanta because we didn't like always being treated like celebrities. We just want a place we can call our own." Her eyes are green and brown, clear, and looking straight into me. "You understand, don't you? We would love to be your neighbors up here on this divine mountain, Mrs. Jessup. And we are sure other celebrities from the metro area will also."

"Oh, call me, Carolina. Please."

When I step back a bit, the one thing that catches me is the smile on Missus' face. Wait, that smile never denotes good for me. Never. "Missus, how are you involved in all this?"

"Oh, dear, just as a go-between. You know FM and I are always looking for ways to improve Chancey. Let us all move down to the actual site for the club." Folks begin moving as Missus comes up to wrap an arm around my arm. "Carolina, this could be the answer to your prayers. No more groups of men wanting to look at trains and, oh, you will have such high-caliber guests. It will require a bit of updating on your and Jackson's part, but you can easily see how this would be a win-win for all of us. Right?" She pats my hand and then pauses her words and her steps. "Now, dear, you do realize Bill Weatherman is not good for you, correct? You need to work on your marriage, not entertain a fantasy about your favorite author. For all our dreams to come true, you and Jackson need to straighten up and settle down. His argument with Peter last night at the church dinner was unacceptable. You'll tell him, won't you?" One more pat of my hand, and she moves along to join the others walking across my driveway.

Unacceptable? Straighten up and settle down? I never got called to the principal's office in school, but I imagine this is how it feels.

CHAPTER 42

Car doors slamming in the front yard make me jump out of my chair on the back deck. Finally they're all home from church. I rush in to greet them.

"Hey, Mom," Will says as he comes in the front door, but it doesn't cause him to pause as he lopes up the stairs. "Going out with Anna for lunch. Gotta change."

Next through the open door is Bryan, but he doesn't acknowledge me as his head is bent over his phone and his thumbs are tapping out a message. Without looking up, or decreasing his tapping, or stopping his progress through the living room, he informs me of his plans. "Mom, I'm going to Brittani's this afternoon. What's for dinner?"

Rolling my eyes is wasted, but I do it anyway. "Why don't you just eat at Brittani's?"

"Okay. Sounds good. I'll get a snack to hold me over."

Waste of sarcasm, too, apparently.

When I hear Jackson crossing the porch, I whirl. "So, guess our boys have plans for the day?"

And I whirl just in time to see Carter May smile, and it's a smile that reaches deep into her eyes. "Oh, yes, guess they have things to do. We tried to talk them into lunch with us, but they wouldn't."

She emphasizes the "us" and reaches back to pat Jackson's arm. "*We* are going over to dinner at the marina with Susan and Graham."

Head tilted, I look past her to my husband, "We?"

"Yeah, you and Carter May and me and anyone else. Susan has a coupon for fifteen percent off the total ticket, so the more the merrier. She said she was going to call you."

"Oh, I think I have my ringer turned down. I'll check. Besides, Savannah called and wants us to come down to Marietta for lunch."

"Savannah wants to have lunch with us?" Carter May laughs.

Try as I might, elbowing Carter May out of the conversation just isn't happening. Cutting between me and Jackson as she heads to the coat rack, she asks, "Sure Savannah doesn't just want someone to pay?"

Adopting a matriarchal tone which would make Missus proud, I pounce. "Isn't that a bit rude?"

Jackson laughs his dismissal. "I've heard you say the same thing. So, Marietta with Savannah or the marina with Susan and Graham?"

Not above using shame, I shake my head. "Really? You have to think when choosing between friends and your own daughter?"

He drops onto the couch. "Yes, because the chances are high that our daughter will have changed her mind by the time we get there."

Carter May does one of those things only skinny tall women can do. She sits on the arm of the chair, crosses her legs and arms...and looks comfortable. She says to Jackson, "We were going to look over the last set of plans after lunch. Will you still have time if you go all the way to Marietta?"

"Why does Savannah want us to come all the way down there? We can eat with her any day of the week up here. I really don't feel like driving all the way down there." He reaches into the side pocket of his sport coat and pulls out his phone. "Let me call her and see what's up."

"Fine! Don't go. I'll go have dinner with our daughter." Jerking my coat off the newel post, I fling it wide. The front door is the next thing flung, and I storm down the porch steps before the screen door has even had time to close. It takes some work, but my angry face stays in place until I'm in the car. Jackson at least got up from the couch and now watches me from behind the glass of the screen door as I maneuver out of the driveway. Good to see he's got both hands on his hips, no phone in sight. With my phone on the car console, I dial Savannah's phone. I've seen her risk life and limb to answer her phone, but when I call, she never answers. I also highly doubt she listens to my messages, but what else can I do?

"Savannah, tell your dad…um…well, that you invited us to lunch in Marietta. Okay? I mean, if he calls. If he doesn't then, well, just forget this message." Why did I lie about having lunch with Savannah? I am not a good liar.

At the stop sign at the bottom of the hill, I text for her to either call me or listen to her voicemail. I go straight and let Chancey fall behind me in the rearview mirror as I take the long curve out of town. Big knobs of grass liven the brown stubble of the fields with their new green. Ditches along the road run clear, cold water, sparkling in the spring sunshine. The sky is a blue that winter never sees, and the birds dart from budding bush to budding tree. The light gray road is empty and quiet.

Of course I'm not going to Marietta. Embarrassment causes my face to get hot. Embarrassment that I not only tried to use my daughter, but that I failed. Now I get all the shame with none of the hoped-for results. When I get to the highway, I'll decide north or south and just go away. Running away from home never appealed to me before. I've always been the one too comfortable to leave, to run away. Now I've made my home untenable.

Yes, *I've* made it that way. Might as well admit it.

Jackson's words from earlier in the week pound in my head. It's not Chancey, it's my reaction to Chancey. Honestly, until he said that about his parents forcing themselves to stay together, I had forgotten they are getting a divorce. He said he can't think, and that's *all* I seem to do.

Yep, running away from home is the only option. However, nearing the highway another option comes into view.

Applebee's.

Chapter 43

Oh my Lord. I'm a woman alone at the bar on a Sunday afternoon at an Applebee's out by the highway.

Families, sometimes more than two generations of families, fill every table. Noisy children, Sunday clothes, grandparents saying the prayer. Norman Rockwell overload. But don't forget the poor, poor person hunched over their lonely bowl of soup, desperately gazing at the television above their head. He, or she in this case, completes the scene. Completes the happy family prayer, "And no matter our troubles, we have each other and are not alone like that poor creature there."

Arrgghh.

"Can I join you?" My face doesn't move a bit and remains glued on the TV soccer highlights above my head to my right, but I do close my eyes. Now I'm getting picked up on a Sunday afternoon?

"Carolina? You alone?"

My eyes pop open, and my head swivels. "Peter? What are you doing here?"

He sets down his salad and then his still-wrapped utensils. "Hiding. Imagine you're doing the same. Can I sit down?"

"Sure." I push back the high bar chair and think about denying his assertion, but can't come up with anything. Especially since my last lie worked out so well…not.

"Saw you sitting here, staring at the TV. Didn't realize you were so into soccer," he smirks. "Mother and Dad wanted me to join them up at the Laurel Cove Clubhouse with the Weathermans for lunch. Susan and Graham were inviting everyone out to the marina 'cause they had some coupon. The kids were all going to the Chinese buffet either in groups or couples, like Will and Anna, so I didn't want to go there because Anna would feel obligated to ask her poor, lonely uncle to eat with them. Yep, that about covers why I'm here. You?"

As he talks, he unwraps his silverware and spears a big piece of lettuce covered in Thousand Island dressing. Now, he pushes it in his mouth and stares at me while he chews. So we're doing honesty? Okay.

"I lied to Jackson that Savannah wanted him and me to come have lunch in Marietta so he wouldn't go to the marina with Carter May and my friends. And you might get sympathy from the kids at the Chinese buffet, but my children would die if their mother showed up there alone. Just up and die, chopsticks in hand. I was running away from home, but couldn't decide whether to go north or south, so like I always do, I chose neither and here I am."

The waiter sets a small oval plate in front of me. "Here's your Spinach-Artichoke dip. Careful, it's hot Do you want to order now?"

One thing about sitting at the bar, the food is so close to your face. "Oh, that smells wonderful. I'm not really ready to order." Chip in hand, angling for a scoop of the melting cheese, I stop the waiter before he leaves. "Wine. I want a glass of wine. White, house, I don't care."

The waiter nods and then slides his eyes to Peter. His eyes shift back to me, and you can tell he's not sure if he should act like we are together. "Um, sir?"

Peter plays with a miniature tomato in his bowl, and as he spears it, nods. "Sure. A glass of whatever you bring her."

The waiter steps away, and I bite into the loaded chip I'm holding. "Thank God you didn't say, 'I'll have whatever the lady is having.'"

We laugh, and as he takes a chip off my plate, he says, "I almost did. It was almost too good to pass up."

"Did you know Missus and FM were up at Crossings earlier today with a bunch from Laurel Cove?"

"Yeah, Mother tried to cover them not being in church with some story about her having a cold and not wanting to spread it around. Like her considering other people wouldn't set off alarm bells in my head. Something about a private club?"

"Yeah, the Laurel Cove clubhouse isn't private enough for some of its more famous residents, apparently. That lady from the house and yard show and, of course, the Weathermans. Rest of them are probably people only famous in their own minds, but with enough money to keep up the illusion."

"It'd be weird y'all having company up there, wouldn't it?" He finishes off his salad, and a steady stream of chips to my mouth take up some space, but finally he realizes the silence isn't just about food. "Wait, you *want* company up there? Neighbors?"

A shrug and elevated eyebrows aren't enough of an answer, but I can't tell him that what I really want is to move. Can I? That we've had an offer on the Crossings?

"Are you folks ready to order?"

Gotta love a good waiter, saw the conversation was awkward and stepped in with our wine glasses. Or the sight of me double-fisting chips and dip into my mouth led him to believe I've not eaten in days. Weeks, maybe.

Peter speaks up. "I'll have the steak with a baked potato."

"Um, I've not really looked, but the fish and rice thing on the cover of the menu looks good. Yeah, that."

Peter hands our menus to the waiter and then leans his head toward mine. "We have to talk about our little excursion in the woods. I know folks are talking about it, and I want to straighten things out, but it's turned into a huge mess."

"Is it the meth thing?" My own problems had kept me from figuring things out until just this very moment. "The meth thing Graham told Susan about, is that what's going on?"

Peter leans back and shakes his head, looking at me through squinted eyes. "For someone who has holed themselves away in their basement reading old romance novels, you sure seem to keep track of things."

I nod. "It just makes sense. So what do you know?"

He sighs. "Nothing much more than that, but that's where everyone seems stumped. There's more to it all, more moving parts, but everyone is stuck because they don't know who they can trust. Even when someone comes forward wanting to share information, like a woman did last week to Charles at the newspaper, we're afraid to listen to it. It's dangerous and no one wants to get set up."

"But what does anyone know for sure?"

"That there's a big supplier in this area somewhere. Big enough that it's been going on a while without folks knowing. Big enough that folks have had to know. And that's where everyone gets stuck."

"But Graham trusts you, right?"

He takes a swig of his wine and grimaces. "Seems like the area drug problems took a big jump right about the same time I showed back up. First marijuana and then meth. And then the way I was kind of here, and kind of not here, because of Mother's harebrained ghost scheme doesn't help me look on the up-and-up either. Then on the other side, me owning the newspaper, the authorities are afraid of what I'll print. It's a mess. Not just a mess, a dangerous mess." His voice lowers even more. "You had any more contact with the Carrs? Heard anything more about the kids' situation? They still upset?"

"Oh, Peter. I've not even given them a second thought."

"Well the adults in the Carr family have gotten over any objections they had with the power plant. All of a sudden they stopped railing against it with everyone who would give them the time of day and are all for it."

"Here you go, folks."

We half turn and lean back as the bartender takes the empty dishes in front of us and a waitress behind us sets our dinners in front of us. Peter's steak is still sizzling and the peppers chopped up in my rice cause me to take an even deeper smell.

"Another glass of wine?" the bartender asks.

I say "Sure" just as Peter says "Nope."

"Okay, I'm fine with just water, too." Embarrassed, I quickly start eating. What do I think this is? A date? I'm day drinking with a man who is not my husband.

Peter attentively cuts his steak and says, "You should have another glass if you want. It's fine with me."

"No, it's good." Again I'm eating like someone's going to steal my plate any minute. Consciously, I lay my fork beside my plate and chew. "So, you were saying the Carrs are now okay with the power plant?"

"Yeah, turned on a dime. One minute they're screaming about their privacy and next minute it's all good."

"Reckon they got some kind of payout?"

Peter shrugs.

With my mouth full, I chew and think back to our trip out to Nine Mile. "But I thought you said you found something on our trip out to Nine Mile. Yeah, you did. Got all secretive and then we left. And you mentioned it again last night." By now I'm turned in my chair toward him.

Peter nods and chews. And keeps on nodding and chewing.

"What?" I ask. "What is it?"

He moves his mouth even less than when he was chewing

and says, "Sherriff's car. That's whose car was out there."

"Oh, that blue car that freaked you out. Ohhh."

"Eat, your food is getting cold. It was the sheriff's car but turns out his wife is related to the Carrs. She's the grandpa's sister-in-law from her first marriage. Her first husband was the grandpa's brother. Thought I had something, but that's all it turned out to be. Another dead-end."

"But if the Carrs were behind the drugs then they would still be against the power company."

"Yep, that's what everyone's thinking. And when the power company surveyors went back in there, the Carrs greeted 'em like long-lost relatives that they actually like. Which is totally out of character and very suspicious, but…" He shrugs again before popping a chunk of potato in his mouth.

I mumble around my bite of fish, "Another dead-end." After a swallow, I add, "But I'll check with Laney anyway. See if she's noticed anything new with the kids when she's been at the school. Speaking of which, I guess I'll be spending more time at the school in the next two weeks. Drama club final rehearsals, I understand, require more attention. Brownies, bottled water, costume repair, scenery touch-ups. The email from Mr. Cross went on and on with suggestions of things the board and I can do to make things better for the actors."

"So Savannah is in Marietta? Or was that part of your lie?"

Peter grins, and I'm reminded of how his is the first beard I've ever liked. He is such an attractive man, but not the type I usually like. My usual style is the blond, tan, all-American guy. Robert Redford, Brad Pitt, Jackson Jessup. Peter smooths back his hair, which no longer makes a pony tail, but is still longer than most men in Chancey keep theirs. My hand raises from the bar to touch it. Whoa! With hand clinched into a ball, I drop it to my side. Good call on no more wine.

He leans a bit closer. "Savannah? Marietta?"

"Oh, no, I mean, yes. She's in Marietta. Did you know, well

of course you know, everyone does, that she's moving back down there for her senior year?"

"Yeah." He pushes his plate away from him and folds his arms on the bar. "Will is apoplectic. And can't say I don't agree with him, but I haven't heard your side. You'd just let her move down there?"

"It's not just up to me. Shouldn't her father have something to say about it? Why doesn't he weigh in? Why is this all my fault?"

"Seems to everyone like you've already told her she can go by herself to live back there."

"Well, maybe things will work so she won't be there by herself."

"What? Carolina…" He drops his head to his arms, and this time I don't stop my hand as I reach up to keep his hair from touching his plate. Oh, yeah, real good call on no more wine.

He lifts his head, and I drag my hand away as the bartender collects our dishes. Peter slumps in his chair and watches as our area is cleared and then cleaned. Finally the bartender leaves with a promise to bring our bills.

"Carolina, are you trying to get out of Chancey again? I thought you kind of liked it here now. Thought you got over all that last fall."

"That was before we had an amazing offer on the B&B. Before Savannah humiliated our whole family. Before Bryan got involved with an older girl. A floozy and an older girl. Before I realized I could be trapped here forever."

"Who wants to buy Crossings?"

I cringe. "I shouldn't have said anything about that. Forget it. No one but me and Jackson know, and besides, we don't know who made the offer. Came from a law firm in Atlanta."

"So you'd just leave."

When I swallow, his eyes watch my throat and suddenly a table between us seems like it would've been a great idea.

Before I'd felt his agitation in his movements, the way he ate, the way he kept twisting on the seat of his bar chair, the way he spoke. Now the agitation melts like a fire soaked with a wave of water, and he becomes completely still.

His voice is still. "You'd just leave?"

And like on the road earlier, I choose neither. Neither "yes" nor "no." I don't meet his eyes, yet I don't look away. When my head starts to tilt, I find myself wondering which way it will go, up and down or sideways. However, just thinking that, stops the tilt before it actually occurs.

Peter stands, pulls out his wallet, then pulls a twenty from it. He lays the money on the bar. "This will cover mine." He stops with his hands on the back of his chair, and as he pushes it in he says, more to himself than me, "Good bye. Good riddance." And he leaves.

Of course, he wasn't saying it more to himself than me. Right?

Chapter 44

"You were going to let Savannah stay in Marietta without you next year!" Bryan's yelling fills the living room. "There's no difference in me staying in Chancey."

Maybe it wasn't so bad when he wasn't talking to me.

"It was totally different. It's her senior year. You are just starting high school. Perfect time to change schools." My fingernails dig into the pillow in my lap. Jackson sits across from me on the couch. He's got his elbows on his knees, his hands clenched, and he's staring at the floor.

"Where are we going to live? Do y'all already even have a house picked out?" Bryan asks from his seat on the landing where the stairs turn. He's started upstairs several times, but doesn't seem to get past the landing.

At his question, Jackson's head rises, and our eyes meet. We were forced into telling the kids about the offer on the B&B. The appraiser came out when only Savannah and Bryan were home and spilled the beans. However, Jackson's fool notion of not moving hasn't been broached, with the kids, with each other, with anyone. Hey, maybe it never even really happened? Maybe it won't ever be broached? That would be awe—

"Son," Jackson says, "There's something else your mother

and I—"

"No!" I shout as I stand up. "No, nothing. We'll talk later, honey, go on upstairs. We just didn't want you to worry about anything. It's all going to be fine."

Bryan stands up, but instead of escaping upstairs to his room, he dashes past us to the basement door. His father moves behind me and whispers, "Dammit, Carolina, I'm sick of playing your little purgatory games. Nothing ever moves forward or backward. Everything kind of just slides around hoping for a good outcome. I'm sick of it." When the basement door slams, Jackson's voice raises and he steps away from me. "Were you always like this? Did you always ignore reality?

"Yes, and usually things worked out just fine. Only since we came here has it been a problem."

"Oh, there you go again, blaming Chancey."

"Well, who or what should I blame? You used to be happy with whatever came about, now you have all these ideas about what life should be like. Whether you admit it or not, you've changed. I blame Chancey. I don't know what you blame."

"Growing up? Having dreams? No, wait, making my dreams come true. That's what changed. I always had dreams, dreams you said were wonderful, exciting. However, for you they ceased being wonderful and exciting when they actually began to come true." With a sigh, he turns to walk to the front window, open for the gentle weather.

Lengthening daylight strings out blue and purple clouds infused with a soft yellow glow. The air shifts through the house, bringing a chill alongside our harsh words. Out of sight a train approaches, and the deep rumble stirs my heart. The memory of the day we moved in plows into me. Of watching Jackson and the boys viewing a train passing in the front yard. How my love for him, for them, nearly caused my heart to burst. How I determined living out his dream would be enough, no not just enough, would be wonderful.

Wheels on the rails changes to a metallic, screeching sound as the train crosses the bridge. It will soon be in view from our front window.

And I turn and walk to the kitchen.

Two pans of brownies wait to be cut and bagged for the actors and crew of *Our Town*. Jackson can enjoy the train in solitude; I have things to do since there are only a couple more rehearsals until the opening Friday night.

The play is getting under my skin. Those dead people sitting in the cemetery talking about how they didn't really see their lives when they were actually living them. That one bit that Emily has—and Brittani is a perfect Emily, but don't tell Savannah you heard it from me. That one bit after she's died as a young bride in childbirth and is looking at life from her new seat with the other townsfolk in the cemetery. Emily asks, "Does anyone ever realize life while they live it... every, every minute?" And the Stage Manager guy who is like the narrator of the play tells her, "No. Saints and poets maybe... they do some."

Lately I work to not be around when that part comes up in rehearsal.

Also that part where she goes back to one day in her life, just an ordinary day—because a special day would be too, too painful, the Stage Manager tells her—and she sees just how people don't really see things. Even children at the breakfast table, and she cries for her mother to just look at her. Oh, that. Well, that's another part I avoid.

When Emily's staring into Jenna's face, who is playing her mother, and pleading with her mother to really look, I find myself flooded with gratitude that Savannah didn't get to play Emily. Savannah saying those things, playing a dead young woman looking back on her life, begging her mother to see her would tear me apart. All this surprises me. The play never really moved me in the past. Maybe I'm just tired.

The play is this weekend, and then we have one more week

before Spring Break. A break sure will be nice. Savannah and Bryan are driving over to stay with their Grandmother Etta in her new beach house. We've not seen her since Christmas when she acknowledged Jackson's father's affair, told us of a recent inheritance, and showed us on the internet the little house on the beach in South Carolina she'd purchased. She gladly let her husband Hank have the old farmhouse in Kentucky. I was supposed to go with the kids to the beach, but at the last minute, we had a group of railroaders make reservations for the week. Apparently their wives and kids are going to the beach for spring break and they aren't. It's too much money for us to pass up. And truly, a house full of guests is a cakewalk compared to herding teenagers every day at home and at play practice.

Crumbs coat my hands as I slide the brownies into Zip-Loc bags two at a time. For so many reasons I can't wait until this play is done.

"So, I'm guessing they need you at play practice again tonight," Jackson says as he finally comes into the kitchen. "Makes one wonder how they'll manage to do anything next year when you're gone."

I lick my fingers and agree. "It does, doesn't it?" I lower my voice. "Have you thought about where you want to live? If you'll stay here?"

He opens the refrigerator and stares into it. "No leftovers? You and the kids eating frozen pizza every night?"

"Savannah is home for only a few minutes in the afternoon, you know that, and Bryan says he'd just as soon eat early so he can work out. He's spending every night lifting weights in the basement since Brittani is in the play. He's truly serious about playing football, it seems."

Jackson opens the freezer and pulls out a box of corn dogs. He sticks his hand in the box to grab a couple. "Even when my folks were fighting and not speaking to each other, my mother managed to put a meal on the table every once in a while."

I turn to the sink to wash my hands, "Yeah? Well, it was a different time, and we see where all that cooking got their marriage."

He turns on the oven and then moves over to the microwave to defrost his dinner. "I'm thinking I'll rent a place here. Figure I'll talk to FM and see if he knows of any possibilities." When the timer on the microwave rings, he opens the door.

I bend down and grab a cookie sheet from the cabinet near the stove. "Here. There are frozen French fries in there if you want some."

"Nah, I'm good." He takes the pan. "Thanks. You know Bryan will never make the football team back at one of the huge schools in Marietta. Maybe he should stay up here with me."

As if on cue, the sound of weights being dropped on the concrete floor of the basement hits my ears. Warmth from the oven fills the kitchen when Jackson opens the oven door and then Savannah yells from the living room. "Mom, I'll see you at the play, right? You're bringing brownies?" She doesn't wait for an answer, but skips down the last few stairs and leaves out the front door.

A hole in my chest opens, and tears fill my eyes. "What is wrong with us? Why can't we fix this? We can't...we can't..."

Jackson lets the oven door shut and turns to look at me. His eyes are soft, not ice-blue, but the blue of warm ocean water. He opens his arms and hugs me. My fists, both gripping bags of brownies press against his back. "Carolina, I just want you to be happy."

I smile into his collar and nod. "Me too."

He pulls away. "And you're not happy here. I see that now. I believe it. We just want different things." He turns his back on me to get a plate and glass out of the cabinet, but continues talking. "And next week when the kids are gone, we'll get it all figured out. Make some decisions so we can move on. You can maybe even get some resumes sent out." He doesn't turn back around but continues getting his supper.

Well, I guess I should get to play practice.

As the kids work through the last of the play (where the dangerous lines are), I wander down the hall behind the stage, well out of hearing range. On each side of the hallway, kids I've come to know succumb to their nerves and either chatter or mutely lean against the walls running lines in their heads. "Carolina, can you come here a minute?"

I stick my head in the small classroom which serves as the costume area backstage. "Hey, Shari, what ya need?"

A woman with spritely features pops her head up. "A favor. Can you pick up two dresses at the dry cleaners tomorrow? I took them in last week because the girls didn't change before they ate and some of the boys' roughhousing knocked over a whole bowl of salsa in their laps." Shari shakes her head and huffs out a head of steam. She's a thin, energetic woman who does something with the county government. "Anyway, I was going to get the dresses tomorrow in time for dress rehearsal, but I have an all-day workshop up in Dalton."

"Don't worry about it. It's no problem."

"Great, here's the receipt." She pulls it out of her jeans pocket. "And I called them today and both dresses are definitely coming in first thing in the morning."

"Anything else you need help with?"

"No, think that's it. Sure will be glad when this is over. I love it, but love even more when it's done. Kids are ready for spring break."

"Y'all going anywhere?" I ask as I lean against the door jamb.

"No, I have to work, but I won't have to get the kids up and no late nights doing homework. You all doing anything?"

"Kids are going to see their grandmother's new house at the beach in South Carolina. We have a house full of railroaders at Crossings, so I'll be here. But you're right, kids being on break is a break." Waving the receipt, I say I'll have the dresses for tomorrow night's dress rehearsal and head back toward the stage area.

In Marietta, everyone left town for spring break. Everyone. Strange how here it's like when I was a kid. It's a break, not a vacation. "Back in Marietta I always felt poor if we didn't go out of town," I mumble as I peek around the doorway to see if it's safe to enter the stage area. To see if the parts that make me think, and feel, too much are done.

Wait. I felt poor in Marietta?

I felt poor in Marietta. Hmmm, hadn't thought about that in a while.

Poor. That's not a good thing to feel, is it?

Chapter 45

"Have I got a surprise for you!" Laney yells through the phone.

"What? What do you mean? What kind of surprise?" I hit the button to put her on speaker phone and lay my phone down on the counter. As I pour water into the coffeemaker, she continues to yell, so that I wonder if I really needed the speaker phone.

"No, no, no! I'm not telling you like this. Be at Ruby's in twenty, no thirty, minutes. Oh, you are going to be so excited!" She hangs up as I push both the button to end the call and the button to start the coffee. Oh, well. So much for my plan of sitting on the back deck and reading all morning. A huge sigh accompanies my thought, but there's no hiding the excitement curling in my stomach and it takes real work to not let my lips curve into a smile.

Coffee at Ruby's. Early morning, demanding call from Laney.

Thought I was over all this.

Instead of the whole pot and another paperback book, only a full cup of hot coffee joins me on the deck. Sure, Laney said thirty minutes, but she won't be at Ruby's in thirty minutes. She'll be there in more like an hour. Besides, the morning is too beautiful to miss.

It's like, overnight, fairies worked diligently with buckets of green paint and giant paint brushes. Leaves that were just tiny specks yesterday have flung themselves open and, in chorus, dance in the breeze which for the first time this year doesn't bring a bit of a shiver. Instead of a shiver, it brings a release as I let my guard down and accept its warmth. Other fairies must've had buckets of yellow paint because dandelions decorate the newly greened grass on the sloping hill behind our house. On the weeping willow tree, the branches no longer look like a beaded curtain you can see through. Now it's luxurious as it sways, as thick and opaque as the velvet curtain at the high school theater.

Clouds bounce across the sky, bumping into each other in their race to tell the other clouds that the sun is on its way. Streaks of sunlight touch the trees at the riverside, and the dandelions call for it to hurry and reach them.

Okay, maybe I've been reading a few too many romances. Whatever. It's a beautiful day. Leaning on the railing, I marvel at the shades of green on the hills on the other side of the river. In the fall the variation of leaves is expected, but this palette of greens is fascinating in its own way. Dark, almost black in some places, then the neon green of new leaves. The reds from the maple seeds and spots of white where dogwoods have planted themselves in the woods, accent the different greens, too. One more long sip of coffee, one more deep breath, and it's time to go.

Ruby's, dry cleaners, grocery store, oh, and florist to get a bouquet for Savannah's opening night tomorrow. Or maybe I should wait until tomorrow to get it? But I could order it and that way I'd be sure not to miss getting her something.

How did I raise a daughter who knows so well what she wants, asks for it, then expects to get it? This morning she stopped before she left through the front door. Her long khaki shorts, which would've looked like old lady shorts in my day, were belted with a thin gold belt that matched her ballet slippers. Messily tucked into the shorts, her pinstriped blue and white men's dress shirt had the sleeves rolled up and the collar unbuttoned. A shiny gold ribbon for a head band completed her outfit, and as I start to tell her how good it all looked, she put one hand on her hip and bends her head toward me. "Mom, you do remember today is dress rehearsal? Right? And tomorrow night is the opening?

"Yes, Savannah. I remember. How could I not know this? Haven't you seen me there every night the past two weeks? Aren't I the one picking up costumes at the dry cleaners today because you and Cory didn't change before you had chips and salsa?"

"Don't freak out. I'm just trying to be helpful."

A nod to her highness acknowledges her helpfulness. "Okay, sure. Thank you, but yes, I know about the play schedule."

"And do you know the tradition of the actresses receiving bouquets on opening night?"

"Yeah, but I thought that was just for the star." *Oops.* "Yes. Yes, I do." More nodding.

She turns, chin held higher than ever. "Okay. That's good. Bye."

Leaving out the same door the princess had closed an hour ago, I sling my purse over my shoulder. Maybe I should try it. Maybe I should just start telling people what I want.

Would this be an appropriate place for LOL?

Chapter 46

Parking on the railroad side of the square gives me a chance to walk through the middle to get to Ruby's. The leaf canopy has filled out and only bits of sunlight peek through. The dogwood trees steal the show from all the others. Short, squat trees with their branches in layers reminds me of lace on a bridal gown. Row upon row of white lace, one beginning just as another ends. Sunlight plays upon the flowers, and when a breeze moves the limbs, it looks like a swaying hoop skirt. A lively dance floor right in the midst of downtown Chancey.

Past the gazebo, I move on to the sidewalk and then cross the street. Ruby's flowerboxes are crammed full of weary pansies. The florist has the same flower boxes, and the pansies there look just as leggy and tired as Ruby's. An empty flower box might actually be better than one with struggling flowers for a florist. But it's not my business.

Pulling on the wood and glass door to Ruby's causes a smile to splay across my face. Sugar, strawberries, and coffee are the first scents to greet me. Before the door shuts behind me, Ruby hollers out, "Well, look what the cat drug in."

Libby rests one skinny hand on a skinny hip and pauses in her coffee pouring. "Hey, Carolina. Good to see you." She winks then finishes filling the cups at a table of young moms. Ruby waves a dishtowel toward the last booth. "Sit here and we can visit when I get a chance."

I slide into the booth with my back to the front windows and door so I can talk to Ruby over the counter. "I smell strawberries."

"Of course you do. Got a shipment in from down in Florida this morning. You want to try the muffins I'm getting out of the oven in about three minutes? Strawberry Cream Cheese."

My stomach growls, but probably not loud enough for Ruby to hear so I answer, "Yes."

"Coffee?" Libby asks as she turns over my coffee cup and fills before I can answer her. She glances over her shoulder before she perches on the edge of the booth seat across from me. "Did you hear? I'm going to be a grandma again!" Her face lights up as she closes her eyes, lifts her coffee-pot-free hand and says, "Thank you, Jesus." Her eyes pop open, and she lays her just-lifted hand on the table between us. "Honey, they are so happy. Cathy just glows, and you know I wasn't sure about Stephen, but he's treating her like a china doll. He didn't come around when she was pregnant before, with them being in high school and all. But he's going to be a wonderful daddy this time. I just know it." She pops out of the booth. "Heard the oven door bang, better get back there before Ruby just starts throwing those hot muffins up this way."

Glad she chattered on like a magpie because from what I've seen the past two weeks at play practice, Steven has looked like anything but a good husband and daddy. He loves any attention he gets from the teenage girls, but he seemed to behave with them. With some of the mothers, though… Well, maybe he's only flirting. Hope so, with a new baby on the way.

Ruby and Libby work like a well-oiled machine behind the counter. Making coffee, one taking muffins out of one tin while the other fills a new tin, answering the phone, lining baskets with gingham cloths, and before I know it a burnt orange fiesta plate has arrived on my table. Dead center is a piping hot muffin, topped with a dollop of creamy icing and a fresh strawberry. I lift off the strawberry and take a bite of the frosting-covered tip. Mm, cream cheese frosting, melting a bit from being put on a warm muffin, but it only adds to how delicious it all is.

When I break open the muffin, chunks of strawberry glisten. I pick up one half. It's almost to my mouth when a shout stops me.

"Surprise!"

I put down my muffin, as I turn at Laney's voice, then add my own exclamation, "Patty! Where did you come from?" I jump up and give the large girl a hug. "Here, let's move to that booth. Setting my plate and cup on the nearby table, I slide into the booth and Patty slides in beside me.

"Hey, Miss Carolina. It's so good to see you." We hug as a smug Laney slides in the other side of the booth.

"Didn't I tell you it was a good surprise?" Laney snags the other half of my muffin and licks the dollop of frosting from her side right away.

"Sure," I snark. "You can have half my muffin."

Laney then bites into the muffin and conveys through her facial expressions how good it is. "Oh, I know I say this every time, but this is my favorite one ever."

Ruby yells from behind the counter. "Carolina, did you let her have your warm muffin? You really think I went out of my way to hurry and get that to you for her big mouth to have?"

My flung-open eyes and mouth declaring my innocence don't matter because she's already turned her back to me.

Patty laughs. "Nothing ever changes here. Everyone at Ruby's, new muffins, Laney acting a fool, and you acting all innocent. Boy, I missed it."

And suddenly a certainty fills my chest. I'd miss it, too. Genuinely miss it. And Patty, I missed Patty. "How's your Mama? How long are you staying? Do you want to stay at the

B&B?" Questions shoot out of my mouth.

Patty rolls her eyes toward the ceiling. "Fine. Forever. No. Well, I don't think so, but maybe."

"Forever? You're moving to Chancey?"

Laney jumps in. "Yep, ran into her at the bank this morning. Wait'll you hear where."

"Where?" Ruby asks as she slides into the other side of the booth, shoving Laney towards the wall. Ruby's wearing a T-shirt with a screen print picture of a huge power plant on it and a red circle with a line through it on top of the picture.

I point to her shirt. "But I thought you changed your mind on the power plant?"

She looks down. "Yeah, I did, but not before I had fifty of these made up to sell." She wads the front of her shirt into her fist. "Usually I wear a bib apron when I have one of these on. Damn. Anyway, where you going to live?" She brought a basket of muffins when she joined us, so we all dig in.

Holding a blueberry bran muffin in her hand, Patty says, "Here. Well, not right here, but next door."

My mind works at the empty street on one side and the florist on the other. "The florist?"

Patty nods. "Yep. Mama owns the building, and there is an apartment upstairs. And I get to start a business."

"Not a restaurant, right?" Ruby scowls at Patty.

"No, I'm not real good with food. But the space is big, and Shannon at the florist isn't making enough to pay her rent every month, so I'm going to sell something in the other half of the florist area. Just not sure what yet."

Laney reaches for another strawberry muffin, this time without icing and the color is a deeper yellow. She pushes it toward Ruby when she pulls it from the basket. "What's this one?"

"Plain ol' strawberry, but, here, put this on it." Ruby hands her a little ramekin she pulls from the depths of the basket.

"Strawberry butter."

"Ooh, that does sound good." Laney tears the muffin in half and offers it to me and Patty.

Patty grabs it. "Thanks."

Laney licks the knife she just applied strawberry butter with and then drawls, "Well, that's not all you can thank me for. I know what you can sell."

All of us stop to look at Laney just as she puts a chunk of butter-spread muffin into her mouth. She holds her hand up to tell us to wait.

Ruby growls. "Like I got all day to sit around watching you feed your face." She stands up. "Swallow and tell us what that hairspray-saturated brain has come up with now."

Laney pouts. "No. I'm not telling until you leave." And she takes a rather malicious bite of muffin. Ruby's face turns a shade not unlike the strawberries in her muffins and then stomps off to the back.

Patty giggles, but I shake my head. "You don't even really have an idea, do you? You just like yanking Ruby's chain."

"I might. I might have an idea. Let's finish this, and then go look at the place."

"Good," I say. "I have to go to the florist anyway to order a bouquet for Savannah since opening night is tomorrow."

"Tomorrow?" Patty asks. "That's awesome! I can go."

"Sure thing. So, tell us. How were things after you and your mama went back home? We sure missed you at Christmas. But you didn't leave us an email, phone number, or anything."

Patty pulls her sleeves down over her hands and makes fists to hold the ends tight. "It all just happened so fast, and well, Mama was real disappointed that I'd let Stephen slip through my fingers. She kept saying he was my ticket." Her hair falls towards her face as she sways her head back and forth. "My ticket out of South Georgia. My ticket to my rightful place in Chancey. My ticket to having a family. My ticket to help her out. My ticket to be happy." A long sigh lifts her heavy chest, then lets it fall. The large hoodie makes her shapelessness even lumpier. "You know, Mama can sure have a one-track mind when things don't go her way."

I reach out and lay my hand on her arm. "You are too good for..." I lean forward and whisper, since his mother-in-law is just two tables away, "Stephen Cross."

She pulls a strand of light brown hair into her mouth and mumbles, "Not really. I mean, look at him..."

Laney pats the table with each of her words, and her eyes are fierce. "Yes, you are. Way too good for him."

Patty smiles and reaches out to lay her hand on top of Laney's. "You're funny. Of course. I mean, it's great he's back with Cathy and their baby."

"Oh!" I exclaim, then wonder if I should tell. Libby didn't say not to tell. "Cathy is pregnant. Not that that matters to you, or to us."

"See." Patty nods. "They are supposed to be together, and that's not what I was trying to say. I don't feel anything about Stephen, except he is the reason I ever came to Chancey. But what I finally realized is he can't be my ticket to anything, 'cause he don't belong to me. I'm the one who has to be my own ticket, and when I realized that, I suddenly knew what I wanted."

Laney tilts her head. "And what was it you decided you wanted?"

Patty pushes her hands out of her sleeves them pushes her sleeves up to her elbows. "This. I want this. I want Chancey."

My eyes lock on hers as she asks, "Who wouldn't?"

With my own shrug, looking away from her, I finish my muffin and fuss with cleaning up the crumbs in front of me. Then I ask, "Have you looked at your new apartment upstairs yet?"

Patty shakes her head. "Nope. I had to go the bank with some paperwork Mama sent and to pick up the key, and that's when I ran into Laney." She wipes her mouth and fingers with her napkin. "Muffins and coffee are on me. Lord knows y'all fed me enough in the past. When Mama saw I was serious about moving back here she actually gave me some money." Pushing out of the booth, she turns as she adjusts her hoodie and sweat pants. "I think Mama was proud of me speaking my mind. She said she's going to give me some time and money to get things settled here, to find me something to put my hand to here in Chancey. I'll go pay and then meet you out front."

"Hey, Cassandra. Hey, Wilma," I say to two ladies at one of the front tables, but when I try to stop to chat, Laney grabs my arm and pulls me to the door.

"C'mon," she says under her breath. On the sidewalk she lets go of my arm but leans in close to me. "What the hell is wrong with you? Letting Jackson and Carter May go out to lunch with all of us just like they are some kind of couple? Girl, you've got to stop messing around and put an end to this! She's moving right in like she belongs here. And she's making all these noises about being here permanently? When I pointed out her part in the power plant will be over once it and the water park are done, she smiled and acted all secretive and said, 'Well, this isn't the only job in Chancey I'm interested in.'"

Laney backs up a step. "Here comes Patty, and the fewer people that know about this the better because you are going to fix this, right? Kick her out today. She is not playing around." Laney shakes her head a bit, "Wait, she *is* playing around, and I think she wants it to be with your husband."

"Here's the key!" Patty holds up a small keyring with a circle tag and two keys on it, one nickel and one a shiny gold.

She's so happy, and my Southern upbringing can't help but think how much prettier she could be with a little makeup and at least a different hairstyle. She could be so pretty if…ugh, I'm channeling Missus, Mother, and Laney.

If the words "lip liner" come out of my mouth, someone please shoot me.

Shannon, the town's florist, smiles and welcomes us in. "I bet I know what you ladies are here for. Bouquets for the girls in the play tomorrow night, right?"

Laney's face drops. "You mean I have to get one for Jenna, too? And if I get one for Jenna with her little role, then I guess I have to get one for Angie, too, since she's working behind the scenes." She plops her big yellow leather purse, accented with lots of silver metal work on the counter. "I bet the high school putting on a play is about as good for your business as Mother's Day."

Shannon smiles. "Well, it's not bad. You want one for Savannah, too, right, Carolina?"

"Yes, I do. She loves yellow roses, if you have any. And, Shannon, do you remember Patty? She stayed with us in Chancey back around the holidays? Um, her mother was actually from here."

Shannon steps from behind the counter. "Yes. No. I mean, yes, I have some yellow roses and, no, I don't remember meeting you."

They shake hands, and Shannon asks, "Your mother is from here? I've lived here all my life. My folks live up near the railroad tracks out past the high school. Do I know your folks?" Shannon is in her mid-thirties and has medium-length dark hair. Her shaggy long bangs always look like she just took a pair of kid scissors to them. Mangled and straggling, they hang in her eyes, and while they don't seem to bother her, I can't talk to her for long without my hands itching to push them to the sides. Oh no, channeling the fixers again.

"Actually, you do know my mother. Gertie Samson."

Shannon's mouth falls open. "Mrs. Samson? The owner of the building?"

Patty shuffles a bit and tugs on the front of her hoodie as she nods. "Yeah, that's her."

"Did Mrs. Samson send you here? I honestly don't have any

more money. Up until last month I was able to pay my rent in full, but then the cooler had to be repaired and the cost of flowers just keeps going up. And with people being able to order flowers off the internet I'm just having trouble."

She jitters, and her words come out faster and faster. Patty just stands there, wide-eyed in the barrage. Unable to say anything. Laney finally claps her hands. "Girls, girls, there's nothing to worry about. Matter of fact, Shannon, Patty is really here to help you. Now, Patty, speak."

While I wince at how Laney sounds like she is talking to a dog; it works.

"I'm going to live in the apartment upstairs. I'm going to help you with the rent."

"Really? Why?"

"Well, I'm not sure. I think mostly my mama just wanted me to move out, and this is the first thing I've been interested in. I want to live in Chancey. I was thinking maybe…" Her voice ran out as she turned and looked around the large room.

"She's thinking she can sell something here, too," I say. "What do you think? Seems like there's an awful lot of empty space."

Shannon nods. "There is. I always thought I'd also open up a gift shop or something, but it costs so much to start up something like that. Just the display counters and shelving alone would send me to the poor house. What do you think you would sell?"

Patty shrugs and looks at Laney.

Laney, however, has missed the conversation. She is buried into whatever is on her phone.

"Laney? You had some ideas here?"

She looks up, but between her vacant eyes and chewed lip, she's still not with us. "Hey, I've got to go." She pulls her purse off the counter, but stops and looks at the flowers around her. "Order me two bouquets for the girls. I'll get them tomorrow, okay?"

I grab her arm. "Is everything okay?"

"Yeah, just something I forgot to do, and now Susan is freaking out." She reaches over and squeezes Patty's upper arm. "And it's just great to have you back. I'll talk to you later."

"So, yellow roses?" I ask Shannon.

"Yes, not a problem. Think Mrs. Shaw has any preference for her girls' bouquets?"

"Not really. Just make them equal in looks and price. Having twins has to be like walking a tightrope all the time. Especially when they're teenage girls."

Patty speaks up from the far side of the room. "Can we go up and look at the apartment now?" She looks at me and then Shannon, and we both nod.

Shannon asks, "You have the key? I've never seen it or been up there. Honestly, I kind of forget there's anything up there. The stairs are along the back wall, see?"

As she says that and points, a stairwell does seem to appear out of nowhere. The back wall is painted black and so is the stairwell. Really hard to see it. Matter of fact, I'd never even noticed it.

Patty just stands looking at the stairs, so I go to her and prod her toward the back of the store. "Let's go take a look. C'mon. Aren't you excited?"

She's walking but just barely, so I leave my hand on her back and encourage her along with words and gentle pushes.

At the foot of the stairs, she stops our progress by grasping the metal railing and holding on. "Carolina? All of a sudden I'm not sure this is what I want. It's too much, isn't it?"

I step back and lean against the door leading outside. "Too much what?"

"Too much of what I said I wanted. I don't think I want it now." She turns to look at me. "What if it's a trap?"

"A trap?" I gasp.

"Not a trap like a bear trap. But, like my mom proving I

don't know what I want by giving it to me." She leans toward me. "What makes me think I can make any money here if she can't?" She pushes her head in Shannon's direction. "She has a talent and something people want, what do I have? Seriously, can you see me selling pretty little knickknacks?" She steps back and holds her arms out. "Look at me."

"Well, maybe some of us, not me really, can help you learn to dress more for your…your…"

"Size? Right. I've heard of that whole bull in the china shop thing, and this here would be it."

I throw up my arms. "Patty, I don't know. I know I don't feel like I fit in here. Matter of fact, don't tell anyone, but I'm about to move back to Marietta. Maybe you're right and you'll be as miserable here in Chancey as I've been, but I'm too curious about this apartment to leave without seeing it. So give me the key."

She reaches in the pocket of her hoodie, retrieves her hand, and then lays the flimsy key ring onto my outstretched palm. When I step past her and then continue up the stairs, she sighs, turns, and follows me.

"Might as well see it, even if I don't stay. Besides, Chancey won't be Chancey with your family gone." She sighs again.

Family? Who said family?

This time I join her in a sigh.

CHAPTER 47

"It stunk to high heaven. Smelled like, like pee."

Laney whirls me around with a hand on my arm. "Patty's apartment?"

"No, no. But that's a whole other story. That smelled like mothballs. No, I'm talking about the dry cleaners. Here, do you smell it on the dresses?" It's the hour before dress rehearsal, and nothing feels ready.

Laney and Shari both lean over and bury their faces in the folds of fabric I hold up to them.

"Nope," Shari says then sits back down where she's working on a costume. "Whew, there's just no time to have them cleaned again, and those girls would have been fit to be tied if their dresses smelled like pee."

Laney agrees, "Yeah, I don't smell anything bad." She wrinkles her nose and shudders. "Creepy enough having to drive right in front of the funeral home to go to the dry cleaners, but I sure don't want to *smell* a funeral home."

"Absolutely. I just held my nose and got out of there as quick as I could. No way I was asking about it. Too afraid they might tell me what it was."

Shari stands, takes the dresses from me, and hangs them in

their places on the wardrobe wall. "And I thought the worst smell at a funeral was carnations. When I smell carnations, I go straight back to my grandmother's wake in her big front parlor where me and my sisters had to stand for hours in the middle of summer with no air conditioner. Mama kept saying, 'Stand there and be ladies. Show this town you were raised right.'"

Laney leans on the short rack of coats in front of her. "Smell of carnations takes me back to the prom my junior year. Phillip Monroe was a senior and senior boys could invite junior girls. He bought me a huge carnation corsage. Later in the back seat of his car when my dress was up over my head that corsage was pressed right into my face."

"Laney!"

She winks. "Well, it's the truth. Love the smell of carnations to this day, and isn't my story happier than Shari's?"

Shari just shakes her head. "Now you know you just made it impossible for me to meet with my son's orthodontist without thinking of carnations."

I laugh, then pause. "You mean he still lives here. You still see him? He's *that* Dr. Monroe?"

Laney pushes the rack toward me and stands up. "Can't have no shame in a small town. Everyone knows your secrets. As my Mama says, 'If you don't want people talking about it, then don't do it.' Guess I'll get back out front. We're not taking actual tickets, of course, but doing a run through for opening tomorrow night to see where we might have problems." She waves at the door. "Good luck, y'all."

"Were you raised here in Chancey, Shari?" I ask.

She's bent over a pair of pants with a threaded needle. One of the boys pulled the cuffed hem out when he tripped coming off stage last night, but of course didn't mention it until he went to put them on for tonight. She bites the thread to break it. "No, I'm from Dalton, but my husband wanted a farm so we moved out here. Lord knows I swore I'd never live in any town smaller than Dalton." She holds the pants up and shakes them. "But here I am."

"Dalton's pretty big, isn't it?"

"It's a right good size, but it's still a little town. I always wanted to live where things happen. Planned on going to college and then straight to Atlanta or D.C. My family has always been in politics, and I thought I'd end up doing something really fantastic." She folds the pants and lays them on her lap. "But in my senior year of college I got offered a job in the mayor's office and then married the mayor's son. Dalton power couple until the aforementioned mayor got caught embezzling and sleeping with his daughter-in-law." She shakes her head. "Not this daughter-in-law, a different daughter-in-law, but needless to say this one no longer had a promising political future. So, we bought the farm down here, had the kids, and just lived." Shari smiles. "And it's been good. I went back to work when the kids went to school and now I chair the county economic council. Actually ended up with the best of both worlds. Y'all came from Atlanta, didn't you? Living in a small town getting to you?"

"Not exactly Atlanta, but yeah, kind of is. Wish I could have Laney's attitude, but I feel like everyone is always watching me. Judging me."

"Well, they are. But we always tend to make judging out to be something bad. It's just reality." She looks around the room. "This play will be judged. Is it worth seeing? Were the costumes stupid? Did my kid do good? At a traffic light we judge based on the color of the light what we will do. We judge what we eat. Will I want it again? Imagine trying to live a life without judging anything."

"But I mean the kind of judging that tears things down. You know, like gossip."

"With my father-in-law doing all he did, I know all about gossip and tearing people down. But if it's the truth, what do you expect? This may not be the normal definition, but I believe people just talking about what has happened is not exactly gossip. Of course, it can be used to tear people down, but what if it's just the facts? The truth? We tend to worry way more about what people are saying about what we're doing, than paying attention to what we are actually doing. If I had worried too much about people thinking I was involved in my father-in-law's shenanigans, I wouldn't have the job I have now. Most important thing is knowing what you want and who you are, then let the people talk." She stands up. "Because they are going to talk anyway."

She grabs one end of the rack of coats for the winter scene near the beginning. "Here, let's take this on down toward the stage." As we maneuver out the doorway, Shari turns to me. "You know the poet Emily Dickinson?"

I nod.

Shari continues. "There's a line from her I just love. 'To live is so startling it leaves little time for anything else.' Reminds me of the lessons from this play. Life is too short to not really see it." She pulls on the rack. "Or at least open your eyes. Life is definitely too short to spend it worrying about what other people think or say."

Following along down the concrete block hallway, I push on the rack and try to think. Not care about what others think? Not care if people are talking about you? Really don't think I can do it.

However, it might actually make living in a small town doable.

Chapter 48

Make-believe teenage drama may actually be worse than real teenage drama. Backstage vibrates like a million bees are making honey in the walls. Last night I took comfort in the obvious fact that things couldn't get any more nerve-wracking than a disastrous dress rehearsal. Wow, was I wrong. Opening night has ratcheted up things, and last night's rehearsal going so badly is not helping one bit.

Every couple minutes someone gears up and yells at whomever is making their life miserable at that moment. Brittani is currently ready to snap the head off of Ricky, who is playing the lead, George, as he keeps bumping into her. I don't know why he keeps doing it, but she's hissed several times, "Stop bumping into me!" Savannah's makeup continually has to be redone because as soon as it's done, she walks away and wipes off the wrinkles. "I'll act old, but I'm not going to look old," she practically spits at the girl doing makeup.

That I can do something about, so I step over to the makeup corner and grab the flesh under my daughter's upper arm. "Young lady, you need to apologize and then behave. You are supposed to look like an old lady. Get over it." I shove her into the seat and nod at the girl with the makeup-covered hands and smock. "She'll leave it alone this time."

Laney storms through the backstage. "I need dollar bills. Whomever thought charging twelve dollars per ticket was a good idea is now my mortal enemy. Everyone give me your dollar bills, and I'll pay you back later."

At my head shake and shrug, indicating I don't have any, she just yells, "Argh!" and moves on down the hall. Buttoning a dress, finding a napkin to blow a nose, straightening out a pinned-on hairpiece fills my time until I notice things are quieter, and there's nothing left for me to do.

Stephen walks by and winks. "Almost show time. You can go find your seat."

Sure enough, no one needs anything from me. Everyone is in place, and in the quiet I can now hear the piano music from the stage. Entering the front hall where tickets are being sold, I search for Jackson. He's coming straight from work, and we arranged to meet here. We purchased reserved seats, so no worries about finding a place to sit.

"Carolina?" A beautiful woman with creamy skin reaches out her hand to me just as the door exiting the hallway behind me falls shut. "I'm Angel Bennett, Beau's sister and Brittani's mother."

Her jet black hair throws me for a minute. "Oh, hi. I didn't, ummm…"

She shakes her head and gathers her long hair in her hand. "Oh this. It's a wig. Everyone in my family has that trademark red hair, so sometimes I have to change it up."

I laugh. "Okay, I thought I'd waved to you when we've either been picking up or dropping off the kids, and I didn't remember you having dark hair."

She swings her fake hair again. "Just one of the perks of my mother owning a hair salon, wholesale wigs. And I do love how short you let Beau cut your hair."

"Well…" I pat my almost-existent hair. It is coming back,

after all.

"So, aren't you excited? Can't believe Brittani got this part as only a freshman. And now you get to see both your daughter and your almost-daughter up on the stage. Isn't that fun? I just hate it's taken so long to get to meet you. We must get together sometime since we're going to be seeing each other so much. Aren't Brittani and Bryan so cute together? They are really good for each other."

"He's kind of young—"

"Nonsense," she says as she slaps my arm and then grabs onto it. "Mike and I got married right out of high school. It didn't last, but we got two beautiful daughters out of it. Zoe! Zoe, come here and meet Bryan's mother." A young woman who must be Brittani's sister turns and comes over.

Pulling my arm, I beg off. "Sorry, but I have to go find my husband. The play is getting ready… Hi, Zoe, right?"

"Yes, ma'am. It's nice to meet you. Brittani loves coming up to your house. She sure loves your family."

Zoe is not as pretty as Brittani, but she's got height to make up for it. She has the tell-tale red hair pulled back in a sleek ponytail. Standing next to her mother speaks in favor of high school marriages, they truly look more like sisters than mother and daughter. Angel puts her arm around Zoe's waist and pulls both of us to herself. "Group hug. Zoe got engaged last night! Show her the ring."

Zoe holds out her hand, and I use the opportunity to pull completely away from her mother's grasp as I reach for the newly-ringed hand. "Oh, beautiful. Have you set a date?"

"As soon as I graduate."

Before I swallow to rehydrate my mouth, I get out, "High school?"

Angel swats my arm again, but this time I don't let her grab it. "Nope, cosmetology school. Zoe is going into the family business."

"Oh, good. Good." And I almost smile before Zoe adds, "I got my GED last year so I could get into cosmetology school and finish it. My fiancé Howie said I had to be working before we could get married. Lucky for me I'll have a job the day I graduate!"

The lights dim, and the small groups of talking people move towards the entrance.

Zoe looks around. "Guess that means they're getting ready to start. I better go find Howie. Nice to meet you, Ms. Jessup. You be looking for your wedding invitation in the mail!" She heads off, and Angel slaps and, this time, grabs my arm. You can help us with the wedding shower, if you want, seeing as you are practically family now. Talk to you later!" She squeezes my arm and lets me go as she turns on her high, high heels and walks toward the entrance to the auditorium.

Laney looks wrung-out, and as I make my way to her, she holds up two tickets. "Here are your and Jackson's tickets."

"Jackson hasn't picked his up yet?"

Laney shakes her head. "No, no sign of him. Saw you talking to Angel Johnson. Had you met Brittani's mother before?"

"No, and she introduced herself as Bennett. Is Johnson her married name?"

"Yeah, but never really called herself a Johnson. Bennetts are real name-proud. Feel like being a Bennett is a great honor. Even though the girls only have Bennett as a middle name, they don't go by Zoe or Brittani Johnson, they use Bennett."

"True, I never knew Bennett wasn't Brittani's last name. Does their dad live here?"

"No, he never wanted to stay in Chancey and hightailed it out of here when the girls were little. No man seems to last long in that nest of Bennett chicks. C'mon, let's get in our seats."

I hand Jackson's ticket to the girl left manning the ticket table and tell her to give it to him when he shows up. Laney and I quickly walk toward the closing doors. "I'm going to kill Jackson if he misses one minute of this play. I told him Savannah is on stage early. Guess you didn't see Carter May come in either?"

"No, neither one of them." Laney shrugs. "They're working late together. You're still making up your mind what you want, but Carter May knows what she wants and knows how to get it."

Laying my hand on the solid wood door, my eyes narrow, and I look into Laney's eyes. "I'm not sure yet what I want. But if Jackson misses his daughter's play because he's with that woman, he might just be making it easier to decide."

I pull open the heavy door, and as we enter the dark, quiet theater, Laney whispers, "If you wait too long, you won't get to make any decisions. They'll all be made *for* you."

We've only missed Stephen's welcome, and as we slide into our seats, the play begins with the Stage Manager, the narrator for the play and the actor with the most lines to memorize, walking onto the stage. We leave the seat on the end open for Jackson. Laney sits next to Shaw, and down from them, I watch Susan, Griffin, Missus, and FM all note that Jackson hasn't arrived. With a shrug to them, they now know that I don't know where my husband is. My mind won't stay on the stage where Savannah has entered, but it's a bit before the action focuses on her. The Stage Manager is setting the scene by telling the audience about the little town of Grover's Corner, New Hampshire. Concentrating on the play is difficult when I'm thinking about Jackson. Like a hot poker, Laney's words made a mark on my heart, and I know she's right. Decisions about me, about my life, about my kids' lives are being made while I dither about what I want.

Onstage it's a normal morning in Grover's Corner, a small town many years ago with a milkman and a doctor who makes house calls. Moms cooking breakfast and kids getting ready for school. I guess it's true, the more things change, the more things stay the same. Brittani looks adorable as Emily. The green dress we thought was perfect for Savannah is even more perfect for Brittani and her red hair. Her mother practically has Bryan and her married. Why does it seem those who have had the worst luck in marriage are so anxious for others to give it a try? Always thought mine and Jackson's marriage was one of those that lasted. Thought we were like a castle on the hill, providing cover and shelter for our kids, even our grandkids one day, and now... Now he wants our castle to be in Chancey and, well, I don't. At least I don't think I do. Do I?

"Oh!" I exclaim out loud as the lights come up, and I realize I worried right through the first act. I also missed Stage Manager character telling the audience this first intermission isn't for getting up and moving around as there will be refreshments at the later intermission, but it doesn't look like many of the audience paid attention to him anyway. Suddenly Susan is sitting in Jackson's seat.

"Have you heard from Jackson?"

"Not that I know of, but I turned my phone off when the play started. Why?" I ask as I pull my blank phone from my purse and slide it on.

Susan sits back in the seat, stares ahead, and rubs her lips together like she's trying to keep something in.

"What is it?" I glance at my phone. "Nope, nothing from Jackson. Susan?"

She takes a deep breath and then leans close to me. "Griffin left right after the play started. He got a call and said it was about, well, about the secret stuff we talked about."

I mouth, "Drugs?" and she nods.

"Oh, wow. I hate for him to miss Jenna, her part is coming up soon. But it would be great for them to figure out what's going on, right?"

She stares at me for a minute then agrees. "Right."

As the lights lower she takes my hand and doesn't look to be moving to back to her seat. "I'll just sit here until Jackson comes, okay?"

Settled back in my seat, I lean towards her. "You might just save his life. At this point if he shows up and plops down next to me, I may kill him."

Susan squeezes my hand real tight, and I laugh and say, "Hey, lighten up. I probably wouldn't kill him right here, too many witnesses."

A lady behind us shushes me, and I squeeze Susan's hand back and then drop it so I can at least silence my phone. Halfway through Act Two, when everyone is gearing up for the wedding, I realize Susan has her phone in her lap and is texting someone. The volume and light are turned down so it looks more like she's praying. But I can vaguely see the little talk boxes coming and going. Before I can lean over and ask her what's going on, one of Savannah's big scenes come on where she and her husband in the play are talking on the morning of their son's wedding. As they worry and talk about how young George and Emily are to be getting married, they also reminisce about how young and scared they were.

"I want that." The words barely slip out of my mouth, but at that moment, I know for sure I want to be able to talk with Jackson on the morning of our children's marriages about our wedding, our marriage. On the heels of that realization comes the shock that Will is the same age Jackson was when we got engaged. Oh my! Now my head spins. We are old enough to be the parents in this play.

Suddenly, the play is all new. The wise, steady parents in this play always seemed so boring. Even though Savannah is playing one of the mothers, my attention has been on the new romance, the young couple getting to know each other leading to their marrying. Then the sadness when she dies delivering their second child. But the parents! That's the real story. It's all a big circle: one minute you're the young girl falling in love, next the new bride, then mother, and then you are watching your daughter fall in love, get married, have children. Savannah will be the age she appears in all that makeup one day. She will be a grandmother, Lord willing. I want that. I want that, to be the old woman who no longer is center stage but knows to move to the side and watch.

The scene moves on, and at the wedding both kids have to have their nerves steadied by whom? Not their friends, not their teachers, but their parents. I want to be the steadier, the consoler, the person patting their back and sending them down the aisle, out into the world, into the delivery room.

And I want to do it with Jackson.

When the lights come up for the real intermission, tears stream down my face. Susan looks at me and does a double take. "Uh, guess I've seen that so many times it doesn't affect me much. Hadn't you seen the wedding act before?"

Wiping my eyes and face, I shake my head. "No, I hadn't really seen it. Let's go get something to drink. They have punch and cookies out in the entrance." We stand up, and suddenly the air in the room seems enflamed. Folks are talking loudly on their phones or to each other. A lady in the other aisle is shoving people aside as she runs to the entrance hall. The woman who earlier shushed me and Susan pushes her husband out of their aisle saying, "Hurry, Ed!" She looks up at Susan. "So, is Griffin already there? I heard they've had to call out a special team from Dalton and another one from down near Marietta. Ed missed the first call, but his gear is in the truck." She follows her heavyset, graying husband up the aisle patting his back and saying, "Don't worry about me. I'll find a ride home."

Coming up from my emotions and with the sudden lighting of the auditorium and all the uproar surrounding us, I simply look at Susan with eyes wide. She pulls me out of the stream of people rushing to leave the auditorium and into the emptied row of seats across from ours. She pushes me into the end seat. "Carolina, there's been an explosion. A meth lab apparently.

That's what Renee, the woman behind us, was talking about. Her husband is a volunteer fireman. Apparently it's real dangerous due to the chemicals they use, and the smoke and dust are really harmful. But it's even worse because this lab was in a place with lots of other chemicals."

"What? A meth lab? Where? Not here in Chancey." I feel a hand pat my back from the aisle and looking up, I see FM standing there. His eyes don't look alarmed or excited like everyone else's. They look sad, and they are looking at me. Oh. Before I turn back to Susan for confirmation I know where the lab was. "The funeral home. Jackson's office."

Susan nods and puts her hand on my knee. "But there's no evidence of either him or Carter May being hurt or even being there. No one can get close to the site at all until it's safer. We only have a couple of the special uniforms needed. Jackson's and Carter May's offices have been cleared that no one is in there, but no one knows where they are. You still haven't heard from him, have you?"

FM squats beside my seat. "Missus and Shaw are heading over there now to see what they can find out. Shaw is a volunteer fireman, and you know Missus can bully information out of the best of them."

I try to stand, but Susan's hand holds me down. "No, you need to stay here for Savannah and Bryan. Laney herded Bryan backstage to help, and she's making sure the kids don't know what's going on. None of them are allowed to have their phones back there so we're hoping we can let things settle down before it really gets crazy."

"But I can't just sit here. Wait, Jackson's car. Is it there?"

Susan shakes her head. "Griffin texted me that they can't tell. Things are pretty hectic out there, and they are having trouble figuring out cars because people showed up when they saw the fire and then had to be hustled out of the way, leaving their cars, when they found out it was a meth lab. It's a mess."

I dial Jackson. "Surely y'all have called him. Isn't he answering?" As I listen to the rings, my heart drops. "And I didn't call him before the play to see why he was late because I was mad and now he might be…"

"Now looky here," FM scolds me. "We're not doing that. We're not giving up on anything. You heard Susan, things are a mess over there. Missus just texted me that the roads are blocked so the out-of-town fire departments can get in there. I guess between the drug stuff and the funeral home chemicals, it's a pretty nasty mix." When the lights flicker, he stands up, and folks begin moving back into the auditorium. "I'll go get y'all a cup of punch."

Susan and I rise. "How can I just sit here watching a play? I can't do that."

"What choice do you have? You heard FM, you can't get near to the place. Griffin is on the scene and will let us know as soon as he knows anything. If Jackson shows up anywhere, it'll be here." We sit down, with Susan in Laney's seat, and the aisle seat once again left open. She wraps her arm around mine and then holds my hand. "Just sit here in the dark and pray. As soon as there is something else to be done, we'll know it. Okay?"

When I nod, the lights go down as if they were waiting on my permission. FM hands us each little cups of lemonade punch and then scooches past us to his seat. The auditorium seems much darker than before, and I notice most of the sconce lights on the side walls are out. The stage lights seem brighter, and then I realize they've done that so the kids on stage can't see how many folks have left the show. On our row of about twenty seats, not only are Griffin, Laney, Connor, and Missus' seats empty, the rest of the row now has a couple empty spots. Grim faces in the half-light are spooky, so with a little shudder, I turn to look at the stage as the Stage Manager sets the Act Three scene and I gasp.

It's the graveyard.

Savannah is seated on the front row of chairs, which represents the souls already departed. The play has moved ahead nine years, and Savannah as Mrs. Gibbs has died. This is the scene the kids thought was like *Twilight* because the dead people talk. But these are too much like real dead people. What I wouldn't give now for a bit of sparkly skin or zombie eyes. My tears are streaming again, and I close my eyes. I can sit here and cry, but I can't watch this part of the play. I couldn't watch it before, but not knowing where Jackson is makes it even more impossible. So I bow my head and block out the words from the stage with words in my head.

Strange, most every other word is God. But I don't pray, I don't know how to pray. Yet round and round the words go and the word God keeps coming up.

Strange.

CHAPTER 49

"And then he's there. Just sits down in his seat like nothing was wrong." The bright lights at Ruby's show strain on Jackson's face, and I realize I don't know if the strain is from tonight or has been there a while. There are no pieces of pie or muffins on the tables, just lots of coffee cups. Ruby opened mostly to make thermoses of coffee to send up to the firefighters, and people just naturally started filling the cafe as word spread of the explosion.

Jackson hasn't said much, but apparently he and Carter May had car trouble, and they went to see if any of the Carrs could give them a jump. Around at the back entrance of the funeral home they rang the doorbell, and shortly after that is when the first explosion happened. It knocked them down, and they started running away from the building, out into the woods. They stayed back there as more explosions followed and then trekked around the property until they could get back to the road safely. Carter May had lost her phone when she fell the first time, and Jackson's was dead so they couldn't let anyone know what was going on.

But two bodies had been found, and we all made our way to Ruby's to find out who had died.

Savannah sits tight against her father on his other side. "I can't believe y'all just let us go on with the play when all this was going on."

FM shrugs. "Nothing else to do. The people who could help were there. Besides, your play took the rest of our minds a little bit off what was happening."

Missus, sitting across from us and next to FM, jerks her head up. "Here they are."

We all turn to look and a weary, dirty Griffin enters, followed by Charles Young from the newspaper. Charles is as dirty as Griffin, but he has an energy that says he'll be writing this story all night, and we'll wake to a special edition of the *Chancey Vedette*.

Ruby sets coffees in front of them. "Figure y'all want leaded, right?"

Charles take a big swig. "Yes, ma'am. Been a long night, you know, and goin' get longer."

Griffin holds his cup but doesn't take a drink. He stares at the cup, and weariness rolls off him. Susan had greeted him with a hug and given him her chair, and now she moves behind him to rub his shoulders. She leans down to his ear and whispers. Griffin nods and then looks up.

"That's a great idea. Charles, you tell what you know because that's public record, and I'm just not sure what all I should say at this point." He lets a long breath out, takes a sip of coffee, and sits back in relief.

"Sure thing. We can't say nothing yet about who died as their kin has to be notified, and their kin doesn't live anywhere around here."

Some of the pent-up tension releases as that means it wasn't one of the Carrs or any of our other neighbors.

"However, police are in the process of making several arrests, you know, and quite a few arrest warrants have been issued for folks in this area. Looks like the power plant and waterfront park made growing fields of marijuana out near Nine Mile less attractive, and so some of our neighbors had decided the funeral home was a great cover for a meth lab."

"What?" a man sitting at the counter says. "With all the people coming and going over there?"

"You know, I think they thought that would be a good cover. And who complains about smells at a funeral home?"

My mouth drops open, and Laney stares at me and points. "That's just what Carolina said! She said it smelled awful, but who wants to know what bad smells are at a funeral home?" She covers her mouth with her hand.

Jackson practically wrenches his neck turning to me. "You were there? Oh my God, what if it had exploded earlier?" He lifts his arm to surround my shoulders and bends his head to rest on my neck. He struggles to talk, and then says, "Let's go home."

Savannah scoots out of the booth, and tears run down her face. Jackson and I aren't in much better shape as we hold on to each other; we can't control our shaking. Susan pats Griffin's shoulder and picks up her purse. "Hold on, I'll drive y'all home. Laney, can you follow and bring me back?"

At the door, Jackson and I unclench, and as I hold the door open for Laney and Susan I look back at the concerned faces. FM and Missus look like they've aged tonight. Griffin has his head bowed over his cup of coffee. Ruby stands behind the counter, waving one hand while the other is clutched over her heart. In not one face do I see judgment or disinterest. Not one.

How could I have ever thought of leaving here?

Chapter 50

Jackson slept in our bed last night.

And so did I.

Sleep is all we did, but leaving him lying there sound asleep this morning when the birds and sunshine woke me was pure heaven. My robe is heavy, but I still don't usually wear it downstairs when we have B&B guests. This morning, though, Jackson getting to sleep in is more important that propriety.

One of my business partners in the B&B, okay, one of my friends, has already been here as a basket of fresh baked muffins sits on the table when I come downstairs. Used to annoy me when they would just come in and out without letting me know. Wonder why that annoyed me? is all I can think this morning as I make coffee.

Sunshine streams in the sunflower yellow kitchen, and I see it like my mother saw it when she picked this color. It's perfect with the black linoleum countertops (which I used to pretend were granite like we had back in Marietta – how silly was that?). And the tall, old-fashioned pine cabinets, which I planned on painting white and substituting with open shelving, look anything but old-fashioned this morning. The kitchen is perfect. Just perfect.

When I step out onto the back deck, I hear the birds who woke me up more clearly. They are exalting in this spring morning. The air smells warmer, more real. Like the ground is waking up and taunting farmers with promises of bigger vegetables, brighter flowers, more of everything. I lean on the deck railing and keep inhaling. I can't get enough of the air.

"I want Jackson, and I want this," I say out loud, and peace fills my body with the new spring air. So I say it again, louder.

"Well…maybe it's just too late." Carter May walks out onto the deck and I turn.

"Too late for what?"

"You know, and it's just as well. You won't want this in a couple months, just like you've apparently always done. You'll change your mind." She pulls her mass of dark red hair back and then lets it fall. Her running shorts and long-sleeved runners pull-over are black and turquoise and make her hair and pale skin stand out. She looks so young and powerful as I try to appear dignified in my thick red robe with spiky hair and mascara I'm sure is still under my eyes.

"You don't know anything about me," and yet as I say that I can see that she does. She does know me. Jackson has told her about me. Her words are harsh, but her tone is not.

"You'll do better back in Marietta. You'll be able to find a job, and you won't be forced to make so many decisions. You know you hate making decisions."

"Maybe I used to hate making decisions, but now I don't. I've changed."

She smiles in such a pretty way, and she means it, "Carolina, why should you change? You are fine just the way you are. If this life doesn't suit you, why should you change for it?"

"Don't talk down to me. I'm not a child. I do know what I want. I do."

This time her smile isn't as warm as she lowers her voice. "And like I said, it's too late. I am buying this house."

"You? You're the buyer? No way." I turn back to look out toward the river and the weeping willow tree sways in the breeze. I have to stay here. "Okay then, the house is off the market. It's no longer for sale." My shoulders straighten as I'm filled with strength and certainty. "We would never have sold it if we'd known it was to you," I declare as I turn back around to face her.

However, when I turn I'm facing her and Jackson. Jackson stands in the open doorway, and he looks pained. First I think he was maybe hurt last night, and then I realize he's in pain because he did know. He did know Carter May was the buyer.

He holds out one hand. "Carolina, I didn't know at first, but when I found out, would it really have made a difference if you'd known it was Carter May? You've hated Chancey and this house from the minute we got here. Remember?"

I can't look at them, so I turn back to the river and the weeping willow. Too late. I'm too late. I finally know what I want, and I'm too late. Just like Laney said.

"Well, I'm going on a run," Carter May says as she walks past me and then down the deck stairs to the backyard. I watch her stretch as I wait for Jackson to explain. Finally I decide he must be waiting for me to say something, so as I turn around, I ask, "My coffee is cold. Can I get you a cup?" But there's no one there. Stepping across the threshold, the kitchen is empty too. He's gone.

Along with my peace.

Sunday morning, and things are back to normal. I'm lying in bed alone listening to everyone else get ready for church. Last night's performance of the play was uninterrupted by explosions or tears or frantic text messages. It was also uninterrupted by flights of fancy by me. The parents in the play went back to being boring and old. The graveyard scene was just a bunch of made-up people sitting in chairs brought in from the classrooms, and I found myself dozing on and off through it.

The kids packed for their spring break trip to see their meemaw at the beach yesterday and are going to leave after they come home from church. I washed and cleaned the B&B rooms all day yesterday. Staying away from Carter May and Jackson was easy as they were cleaning up their offices. At least that's what they said they were doing. The picture of the two of them yesterday morning, united on the deck, won't leave my head, and as it pops up again I bury my head deeper beneath the covers. When the front door slams shut, it's safe for me to go downstairs, but moving is beyond me.

My bedroom door opens, and before I can dig my head out to see who it is, the bed bounces.

"Hey! Figured I'd find you here. Get up. I brought you a sausage biscuit from Susan. She can't be here since she has to go to church, so she sent food." Laney pushes me toward the edge of the bed. "Get up."

"Why?" I yank the covers away from my head.

"I told you. I brought sausage biscuits. House is empty so come on down." She gets off the bed and goes to the door. "Come on. We have a plan. You're going to love it."

"What is going on up there?" is yelled from downstairs.

"Wait, that was Missus. You brought Missus?"

Laney grins. "If we're going to stop the sale of this place, we need the big guns." She steps into the hall and then comes back to the doorway. "You do want to stop the sale to Carter May, right?"

And it's back. Peace moves over me, and with it a sense of knowing exactly what I want. I throw back the covers. "Absolutely. Get down there and save me a biscuit. There's champagne in the fridge if we want mimosas."

Laney gives a little wiggle. "Woohoo, mimosas. I'm in. Hurry up."

Waving to Savannah and Bryan Sunday afternoon as they pull out of the driveway headed to South Carolina, Jackson asks me what I'm planning on doing while the kids are gone.

"I was hoping you'd ask that." We turn towards each other, and I place one hand on his chest. "I plan on winning you back and proving to you we belong together and that we belong together here. In Chancey. In this house." My hand drops, and I continue up the sidewalk to the house.

"But what about when you change your mind and want to move back to Marietta?"

At the top step to the porch, I turn. "Not going to happen. We have a plan."

"Wait, who's 'we'? If you and I have a plan, I don't know anything about it, except I do need to clear something up." In two long strides, he's beneath me at the bottom step. "There is nothing, absolutely nothing between me and Carter May. I really hadn't thought what it looked like to you, since I wasn't interested in her, you know, like that."

"And seeing me jealous wasn't all bad, huh?"

He grins and shrugs. "Guess not. Sorry."

Stretching out my hand, I lay it on his cheek. "Thanks. Makes the first part of the plan easier." With a quick smile, I whirl around and enter the house.

Inside the house, the screen door falls shut, and I look out it at my puzzled and concerned husband. That peace I'm beginning to get used to fills my chest and causes a big smile. "We as in my friends and I. My friends and I have a plan, and you'll just have to wait to see what it is."

As I turn around, I pull the first piece of the plan out of my back pocket.

At Carter May's door, I knock and wait. She's stunning with her hair down and a tight wrap dress in bright yellow accenting her figure. She's stunning, but for the first time in my life someone being beautiful doesn't scare me.

"Here is your bill. You can stay here tonight, but your room is reserved for tomorrow night. We have no other openings."

She stares at the bill. "You can't do this. You can't just kick me out. Jackson won't allow it."

My right eyebrow creeps up all on its own. "Carter May, I don't know why you insist on this fantasy of taking over my life here, but it *is not* happening," I say as my eyebrow settles back into place and I walk away.

Crossing through the living room, I meet Jackson coming in the front door. "I just served notice on Carter May that her room is no longer available as of tomorrow."

Then I glide up the stairs—I have learned from Savannah that royalty is as royalty does, so I glide. At the top I pause to make a pronouncement, just as the royal family does in England from a balcony. Like Evita Peron spoke to her followers. Or as my daughter informs the family of her clothing and hair woes. "And Jackson?"

He steps into view with his face lifted up to me. Oh, this is good. I should get a tiara. "Jackson, I am now moving your things back into our bedroom. You don't have to sleep in there, but I warn you I don't plan on sleeping apart from you anymore. We are married. I have every right to sleep in the same bed as you, and I'm claiming that right, wherever you decide to sleep."

His mouth falls open, but that's all I see as I move on to the room he's been occupying and step inside. A survey of the room brings tears to my eyes. He truly has moved in here, and I just let it happen. It's going to take a while to get all this put back in our room, and while I do it I'm going to try that new thing I discovered Friday night. You know, where I talk and every so often throw in the word God.

Of course, it's not praying, because I don't pray.

Chapter 51

"Got 'em adjoining rooms," Laney says as she arrives to take her place in our booth at Ruby's. "Took some persuasion, but when the manager heard about the sales convention I could get moved to his place in the fall, he found himself persuaded."

Susan asks as she scoots over for her sister. "What sales convention?"

Laney fluffs her hair and bends her head while batting her eyes. "The one Shaw just agreed to sponsor for car salesmen next fall."

"Oh, wow, tell Shaw I said thanks. Here, have half my muffin. It's still warm." I hand her half a lemon muffin with a thin, sugary icing.

"Thank you, but Shaw didn't do it for you." She shrugs and licks her lips. "He did it for me. Believe me, he got a great deal."

Missus shakes her head. "Well I hope it works because getting out of that sales contract is proving to be might near impossible." Her gray hair is held back with a blue scarf, and around her thin shoulders is a kelly-green sweater with a gold chain connecting the top button and button hole. Her blouse is a bright spring print and her tailored slacks are navy. "I have another meeting with my lawyer, and this time he's bringing an associate who specializes in real estate law."

Susan pats the table top for emphasis. "We need her to back out. That's the answer. Griffin is working on the private club folks. They are right this minute having a breakfast meeting up at the Weathermans' home."

Libby comes by and pours us all coffee. She chats for a minute about her new grandbaby who's on the way. She doesn't stay long as we forget to ask the appropriate questions, and it's obvious we are preoccupied. I'm preoccupied with trying not to cry.

Choking a bit, I struggle to get my thoughts out. "Y'all are being so nice. All of you, even your husbands. Why?"

Missus stiffens at the emotion and holds herself a bit farther from my side, but Susan reaches across the table and covers my hand perched on my coffee cup. "Honey, we're your friends. Your business partners. You staying here is good for not only our town, but for us." Tears flood her eyes, and she grips my hand harder.

Laney exclaims, "Lord have mercy, you both are going to cry? Well, buck up. And Carolina, remember we said we need to know what Carter May has planned? Well, I figured out how to find that out. Jackson." She bites off a big piece of muffin and oohs a bit, but doesn't seem prepared to finish her statement.

"Okay," I jump in. "Jackson?"

She pops the last piece of muffin in her mouth, washes it down with coffee and then wipes her hands on her napkin. "Jackson knows what she's up to, and so we need to find out what Jackson knows. I know he told you there's nothing between them, but he may still feel loyal to her about work matters. "

"Okay. Yeah, I'll talk to him tonight." I reach for a pumpkin muffin on the saucer in front of me and get my hand slapped.

"Hey, what's that for?" I ask Laney as I pull my empty hand back.

"You will be talking to Jackson tonight, but we're going

to need to get him in a talkative mood. You and I are going shopping to get something for Jackson to get him talking. Something he can say everything but 'no' to. Something that will show every bite of muffin you eat this morning."

In disgust Missus throws her wadded-up napkin onto the table. "Goodness gracious, Laney, all you ever think about is sex."

"Correction, it's all men think about, and when their mind is on that, we can get their mouths to say whatever we want. Let's go."

Susan dips her head to hide her red face and laughs. "Go, I'll pay for this. You just go, I don't want to hear any more about it." She peeks up at me. "Well, until after it works. Then I want to hear everything."

Missus stands outside our booth and says to me, "Come on. I'm not finished, and I don't have all day for you to argue with this one. Besides, you know she'll win, and you'll be shopping at some sleazy storefront shop in the mall decorated with red neon and hearts sooner or later." She shoos me aside and sits back down. "Might as well make it sooner. Goodbye."

On the sidewalk, Laney digs in her purse. "I'll drive, you can get your car later. I'm over here."

As we begin to walk across the street, I motion towards the florist. "Wonder if Patty ever figured out what to sell."

Laney stops in the middle of the street. "Didn't I tell you? It's all figured out. You're going to love it, but right now we have more important things to think about." She buries her head back in her purse and continues across the street while I watch for cars.

"Darn it," she exclaims as we get to her big black SUV. "I know I have a coupon for Cupid's Palace for twenty percent off. It's got to be here somewhere."

"Wait, Cupid's Palace out beside the truck stop on the interstate?"

"Sure, those cute little places in the mall might be more tasteful, but honestly, who's going for tasteful? There it is. Twenty percent off." She pushes a button on her keys. "There, door's unlocked. Get in."

In the front seat I don't have to look at the mirror to know my face is as red as Susan's was. Laney hands me the coupon. "Here, hold on to this. Don't want to lose it again."

There's the red cursive script, the hearts, and hot lips, and then, in small print, lists of things we can use our coupon to buy. As they cover everything I can imagine and much I can't, I'm left with only one question.

"Do they serve alcohol? I think I'm going to need a drink."

Chapter 52

"Two mornings in a row? Nothing interesting up there on the hill to stay home for, Miss Carolina?" Ruby meets me at the door, holds it open, and then as I start to say "Good morning," she winks. I tuck my head and get to the booth where Missus, Susan, and Laney wait.

"Does Ruby know? Why would Ruby know? Can't believe you told Ruby." I run my hand over my fluffy hair. Since I didn't style it after my shower, my wispy bangs aren't so wispy.

Missus rolls her eyes. "Carolina, you do not have the sense God gave a goose. Sure the beautiful spring weather makes it possible to sleep with the windows open, but until you are actually ready to go to sleep you might want to keep them closed."

"Oh no. Are you saying…what are you saying?"

"Your guests were not out as late as you apparently thought they'd be since Peter closed the museum earlier than planned for them all to go out to the train bridge. Some special train was coming through. How could Jackson not know about that?"

Libby giggles as she pours me some coffee and then shuffles away with more giggling. "Well, he did mention something about the circus train coming through, but…" My face flames as I remembered what I said about being as entertaining as the circus.

Laney doesn't hesitate, though. "I bet you told him you had better entertainment than any old circus train, right? I've already told them how you found two perfect outfits at Cupid's Palace. Which one did you wear? The black lace one or the purple see-through thing? *That* was hot."

Susan is nibbling on her muffin and keeping her head tucked down, but I can hear her snickering. I lean across the table toward her. "So people, uh, heard us?"

She looks up and nods. "The railroad guys ran into the town council folks as it was just breaking up, and so they all went up to the bridge. Griffin says it was a real quiet night, and sound really travels over water, you know."

"Griffin? The town council?" My stomach is not reacting well to the coffee.

Missus purses her lips and then shakes her head a bit. "FM thought it was so very funny. Peter, however, was just embarrassed. FM has never had the decorum our son has."

Peter? Susan looks up at me and cocks her head and bites her lip as if to say, "Yeah, Peter, too."

Taking small glances around Ruby's I wonder at each small smile, each laugh. Maybe I *should* move back to Marietta. With a deep breath, I attempt to calm my stomach. "I can't live here now. Everyone knows, I can't do this."

Missus raises her chin, "Oh, wait a minute. What about at Christmas when Anna being from an illegitimate affair of mine came out, and you thought I should just roll with it? Quit being so uptight? No one cares, you said. Funny how your outlook has changed."

Laney laughs and says, a little too loud for my comfort, "Besides, what do they all *know*? That you and your husband are back to sleeping in the same bed?" She shrugs and grins. "Well, maybe not *sleeping...*" She laughs harder and holds her hand over the table for a high five. "Get over yourself."

Her hand hangs there in mid-air and I realize she's right. So what if people know Jackson and I made love last night, and so what if they know we really enjoyed it? I raise my hand and meet hers with a resounding smack. After a moment she grabs my hand. "So now, tell us what Carter May has planned?"

And my hand slips from hers. "Oh, that's right. I was supposed to ask about Carter May."

Missus closes her eyes and mutters, "Bless her heart. I'm going to strangle her."

CHAPTER 53

Standing at the kitchen sink, my hands under the stream of water, I have no defense when Jackson comes up behind me and puts his arms around my middle. He tries to slide them up from my middle, but by pressing my forearms tighter, I stop him. But I can't stop a little giggle from slipping out. "Jackson, cut it out. We have guests that could just walk in." I grab a dishtowel and turn around as I dry my hands.

Jackson leans against me. "They're already jealous of me, just like every guy in town. I'm not exactly sure how we got so off-track, but I'm so thankful you knew how to get us back on track."

With my head lying on his chest, I once again admit what I've said often this week. "Small towns are scary, especially if you've already survived one. I let my mind get so focused on hating Chancey, I forgot how much I love you."

"But what if we can't get Carter May to drop her purchase of this place? I've tried talking to her, but she's kind of desperate to hold on to it."

"We ladies have a plan, don't know if it will work, but we do have a plan. Carter May may have a weak spot. Keep your fingers crossed. Hey, when can you get back into your office, and what about the funeral home and dry cleaners? Not that I've minded you working from home, like today. But what's up with the Carrs?"

He backs away from me and leans on the kitchen table. "About half the family has been arrested. The ones that left Nine Mile apparently had done so because of the drugs, so I don't know if they'll get in trouble for not telling or what. Remember the kids Laney talked about at the high school that were living with their youth pastor?" When I nod, he continues, "Both their parents are going to jail. Funeral home and dry cleaners aren't either one opening back up anytime soon. State will sell off the property, but who knows how long that will take. Railroad's finding other office space, don't know what Carter May and the power plant people are doing."

While he was talking, I finished drying my hands and sauntered over to him. "Since the kids will be home tomorrow, today is our last day to go take a nap in the middle of the afternoon," I whisper close to his ear.

"Is this what it's going to be like when the kids are grown and all out of the house? I could get used to it."

Taking his hand, I lead him up the stairs. "Yeah, getting old isn't looking as bad as it used to. So, purple or black?"

He laughs, follows me into our bedroom and shuts the door behind him.

"Carolina! Where are you?" Laney shouts from downstairs.

"Get up!" I exclaim as I push Jackson out of the bed. "Get dressed. She'll come in here. Walk right in. Laney, I'll be down! Don't come upstairs."

"Too late, I'm coming up the stairs."

As she pounds her feet on the stairs so we can hear her progress, Jackson is laughing and running around the room finding his clothes. He throws himself into our bathroom just as Laney bangs on our door. "Jackson? You in there, too?"

I jerk on my old robe and pull open the door just a bit. "I said I'd be right down."

She grins and winks. "I know. I'm just rattling your chain." She turns back to the stairwell. "Come on down and see what Missus has done to us now."

By time I close the door, Jackson stands behind me. "I love this old red robe when I know what you have on underneath it."

I turn and let my robe fall open just to give him a quick thrill and then pull it tight. "Later, if you behave." In the mirror I see the way I look at my husband like I could just eat him with a spoon and I wonder when I became brazen as a hussy. When did I learn to flirt so outrageously with him? When did we get back the attraction we felt in college?

"Carolina, I'm waiting!" the answer yells from downstairs. Laney, I feel like Laney. Like sex should be fun and shouldn't be just another chore. We have more freedom than we had back in college. We have our own house, don't have to worry about getting pregnant, and have been married a million years, so why shouldn't we be screwing our brains out? Oops, now I'm beginning to even sound like Laney!

Jackson lays back on the bed. "Woman, you are wearing me out. I have a lawn mower blade to replace and you have to see what Laney wants, so get down there."

"Yes, sir. Anything you say," I giggle and slowly make my way to the bathroom to get changed.

On the landing to the stairs, I stop my descent to try and process what has happened in my living room.

Laney yells from the kitchen, "Two thousand!"

"Two thousand what?" I yell back.

"Plastic eggs from Mr. Reynolds at the power plant." She comes to the doorway into the kitchen. "Plus the candy and trinkets to fill all two thousand eggs. Again, compliments of Frank Reynolds."

Picking my way through bags and bags of Easter supplies, I get to the kitchen. "Why is it all here, though?"

"Missus is fit to be tied. She believes plastic eggs go against God. She says God gave us perfectly good real eggs to color and hide, and the plastic ones are obviously from Satan."

"Obviously, but what are they doing here?"

"Someone has to fill them and then hide them."

"We're going to fill all of these and hide them? Where are we going to hide them?"

"Out at the site of the waterfront park. Missus already has claim on the park downtown for the Easter Egg hunt the churches all put on tomorrow. The hunt with the real, God-approved eggs. So we're going to go out to the new park site and hide the heathen eggs." She tears open a bag of candies wrapped in pastel aluminum. "But first we're going to fill them. Chocolate?"

Jackson walks into the kitchen. "What's all this?"

"This is what happens all the time. For some reason there are two thousand eggs to be filled and everyone thinks our house is the place for it to be done." I can feel tears catching in the back of my throat. I wanted to spend this last night all alone with Jackson. Nothing ever goes right here. "It's Chancey. Stupid Chancey."

Jackson laughs. Just laughs. "Honey, I don't know how these things keep happening to you since we moved here, but I'm done fighting it. I think we should just embrace it. We'll get it all done."

Laney acts like she's swooning. "He's so charming, so pliable, so happy. Wonder, just wonder, how he came to be this way."

I smack her arm and grab a piece of the foil wrapped candy. "Shut up."

She steals the piece of candy from my hand once I get it unwrapped and pops it in her mouth, but manages to say around it, "Besides, we have to fill the eggs here because this is where the egg-filling party is. Didn't you see it on Facebook?"

CHAPTER 54

"Take a sip. It's blackberry." Laney hands me a flask. A genuine, silver flask with the cap screwed off. "It's too cold and too early to be out here in the woods without something to sustain us."

"Um, it is delicious. Blackberry what?"

"Liqueur. It's kind of sweet, but it makes hiding eggs out here in the boonies passable."

With a bit of a hip wiggle, my behind loses a little of its numbness from the old log Laney and I found to rest on. We're out of sight of the rest of the egg hiders, which are Shaw and Jackson. Everyone else we know is down in town helping at Missus' egg hunt. Some of the power plant people are supposed to be up here helping us, but Laney was in such a fizz to show up Missus (and get free chocolate) she signed us up before she realized we were the only ones on the actual list. "Give me another sip. That is pretty good."

Through breaks in the foliage, we watch our husbands hide (read: throw) the eggs around the uncleared land. As soon as the ground gets dry, they will break ground for the waterpark and amphitheater. Mr. Reynolds thought an egg hunt would be a good time to get folks out to see the site.

Laney stretches out her blue jean-covered legs and fur-lined wading boots. "So, you and Jackson are good? I'm proud of you. You two are good together."

I stretch my legs out, too. "You're right, we are, and I think we both knew that all the time, we just couldn't figure out how to get back together."

"Your kids are going to be ecstatic."

"Yeah, well, maybe not Savannah so much because now that I've come to my senses there's no way in God's green earth she's moving back to Marietta for her senior year. What was I thinking?"

"You were thinking her being there was halfway to you being there."

"Probably. She won't be happy, but I watched her at the end of *Our Town*. I think she'll be okay. Plus, I heard the Weathermans are giving a big chunk of money to the drama department at the high school so Aston can have the lead in next fall's play."

Laney stands suddenly. "Uh oh, do you hear cars?"

I stand and shout at the men to finish. "Our guests have arrived!"

Riding in the front car with Missus and FM are Mr. Reynolds and Carter May. As the cars park, sunlight comes over the ridge and illuminates the new green leaves surrounding us. The low angle of the sun causes the river to light up with millions of sparkles, and the warmth I ease into isn't due to the blackberry liqueur. At least, I don't think it is. However, when my sudden warmth chills, I know it's due to Carter May coming up to me and Jackson.

"So, you're back to square one, huh? You've got your family but nowhere to live. I hear the housing market in Marietta is on the upswing so you better hurry."

When I take a deep breath to really give her a piece of my mind, Jackson takes advantage of it and steps in. "Now, Carter

May, you don't really want to run a bed and breakfast. You're a businesswoman, you don't want to spend all your days cleaning sheets, talking to tourists, and restocking toilet tissue, do you? Especially since you now would be doing it all alone." As he says his last line, he puts his arm around me, and while it feels good, my heart sinks. I don't want to clean sheets, talk to tourists, and I hate replacing toilet tissue, too. However, just as Marietta starts to look good, I shut off that train of thought and think about Jackson.

And then my train of thought really jumps track when Carter May steps up to my husband and lays her wide open hand on his chest. Her palm covers the buttons on his dark blue flannel shirt. "Jackson, running a B&B was never in my *real* plans. That house will be gone soon, and the new private club will sit in its place. Right, Bill and Claire?"

The Weathermans come up at her bidding and each give her a hug. Bill has the decency to appear sorry for us. Claire just shudders and says, "I know you'll be so happy to get out of that old, drafty house. Find or build one not laid out so wrong, not so old. The club just wouldn't work up there unless it's on your piece of property, so we will put the storage facility down where we said we wanted the club. That was just all for show until we could get the contract on your home. Lucky you, you'll be able to buy something divine in Marietta, I'm sure."

The color has drained from Jackson's face, and when neither I nor Jackson can say anything, Carter May and the Weathermans wander off. Missus clears her throat behind us, and we turn enough to see her. "So, they told you?"

"Missus, you said you'd be able stop the sale," I beg as I grab her arm.

She pats my hand. "I know, I know. She won't budge. Not at all. She's even had paperwork drawn up to sue you if you try to pull out. I'm sorry, but when she got the private club people on her side, I realized she actually can make it work."

Kids begin spilling out of cars. In their baskets, there is evidence of the real eggs they'd already hunted for and found this morning. With the sunlight, laughing children, Easter frocks, and several long draws of blackberry liqueur, it's hard to be sad. Jackson and I hold tight to each other and smile and point when a little boy or girl reminds us of our own when they were the ages of these.

"Now they are in another state visiting Mom. Will is almost through college and will be off to law school in a few months," Jackson sighs and then guides me around the outside of the circle of fawning adults.

I marvel, "Do you realize he's the same age you were when we got married? And Savannah will be off to college in a year." With our backs to the sparkly river, we watch the kids as they show what they've found to their parents. I can't help shaking my head. "Who knew it would all go so fast?"

"And if we tried to tell these parents how fast it will go, they would laugh just like we did."

Tears threaten and then spill over, and Jackson pulls away from me to dig a napkin out of his pocket. "Here you go. Let's look at the water."

Our silence stretches for a moment. Then I wipe my nose and clear my throat. "Jackson, I need to apologize to you. This is all my fault. If I'd just let myself be happy, we wouldn't be losing our place in this community. I don't want to move back to Marietta, but I'm not sure we can find a house here that we'd want. Not exactly a booming housing market. I'm so sad thinking that Bryan won't go to high school here. I'm so sorry."

"Hush, hush. I jumped all over selling the house both before and even after I found out it was Carter May making the offer. I knew better than to force that on you, and yet I did. I'm sorry, too, but I do know wherever we end up, we'll be there together. I promise." He pulls me into a big hug, and I'm buried in his corduroy jacket, and I remember that first day in Chancey when

I watched him watching trains in front of the house. How I thought that wherever he was, that was where I belonged. How that thought, that feeling got so lost so fast, I don't know. But with my face buried in his chest, I vowed to never lose sight of it again.

Hands suddenly grab at us, and when I lift my head I see Susan with a finger held over her mouth. Laney is doing the same to Jackson, and they are pushing us toward the rest of the people. Frank Reynolds has stepped up onto a couple concrete blocks and is talking to the crowd.

"What's going—" I try to ask.

Susan shushes me. "Listen."

"So as to make best use of the additional land, we will be opening a living history center on the other side of the road there, across from the water park. It won't be as grand as some of the plans we've heard with amusement-style entertainment and shows, but all the crafts of the mountains will be taught here and on display and even for sale. From making jams and preserves to a fully operational blacksmith shop. Nine Mile will no longer be a place to remember the downfall and corruption of the mountains, but a place to hold onto our heritage."

As he pauses the crowd applauds, and Susan whispers, "The land from the Carrs is perfect, and Mountain Power had to move fast because the state was going to tear down their old buildings which can be used. Plus, between Bill Weatherman and Frank Reynolds and everything being done with private money, things move fast."

"Bill Weatherman?"

"Shhh," Susan says.

Mr. Reynolds has called Bill and Claire Weatherman up to where he stands, and then he holds his hands up for quiet. "Everyone here knows two of our newest and most famous residents of Laurel Cove, Bill and Claire Weatherman. This dynamic couple has just agreed to oversee the living history center, and once you hear just a few of their ideas, you'll see why this is going to be such a fantastic addition to all of North Georgia."

During the applause, Missus pops up from behind us and pushes her way up to my side. "Listen to what's next." She's practically giddy, and I wonder where the white-gloved lady who scared me has gone.

Bill Weatherman steps up onto the now-empty concrete blocks. "Several rumors, some with a lot of basis in fact and some not so much, have circulated in recent months. This agreement for the living history center and mine and Claire's involvement has led us to decide with the time we'll be putting in here there will not be time for the private club many of you might have heard us talk about." He looks over at me and Jackson, smiles, and shrugs.

"Missus? Not fifteen minutes ago they were telling us about their plans for the private club."

She smiles and shrugs mimicking Bill, and then FM steps forward. "Don't let her fool you. She developed the whole idea and then, when it all came together, she gave the Weathermans the chance to take her place if they gave up the idea of building the private club up where your home is. They just jumped at it a few minutes ago."

Carter May scowls at our group and whips around toward the parking area. However she's stopped by a young man grabbing her shoulder.

"Carter May! Did you hear?" He grabs her and kisses her, and I know why he's familiar. He's the man that kissed her in front of the funeral home. The man Mr. Carr told me is her husband. The man Laney had tracked down in her part of our plan.

"Todd, what are you doing? Why are you here?" She pushes him away, her face flushed.

The young man with the beard grins wide and pulls her back beside him. "Why should I stop? You're my wife, and I've got a job you'll finally approve of. Just signed the papers with Mr. Reynolds this morning."

"Mr. Reynolds, my boss, Mr. Reynolds?" Carter May looks up just in time to see her boss come through the crowd.

"There they are, my new favorite employee couple. Are you surprised, Carter May?"

"Completely. Um, what will Todd be doing?" She turns. "Todd, what will you be doing?"

"I'm overseeing the development of the riverfront here and at the other two sites the company is developing." Todd tightens his arm around his wife.

Mr. Reynolds adds, "When the Georgia Conservationist and Environmental Club told me of their objections with our river site developments and threatened to stop all our projects, I was elated to have their president recommend Todd for the job. It was his idea for me not to tell you until he accepted the job. "

Todd turns to Carter May and takes her hands in his. "Did you know we've been next-door neighbors all week at the hotel? What a crazy coincidence. I had to play hide and seek all week so you didn't see me."

Laney and Susan and I look at each other and roll our eyes. So much for that part of the plan. While we were trying to rekindle the fire between Carter May and her estranged husband, Mr. Reynolds was solving the real problem between them of his employment. Of course, the President of the Georgia Conservationist and Environmental Club might have happened to be at lunch at Missus' and FM's just this week. Coincidence, obviously.

Jackson and I turn our back on the couple as they talk with Mr. Reynolds. First we hug, then we join hands and walk toward our car. When I yawn, he reaches to lay my head on his shoulder and laughs. "It's been a long day and it's not even noon. How wonderful is it to know we get to go back to our home, and that it really is our home. Not. For. Sale."

"And the kids will be home today. I've enjoyed the week without them, but it will be good to have them home. Patty! Hey, I didn't see you earlier."

The shy young woman chews on her lip and nods. "I was kind of staying out of the way until everything got settled 'cause I got something important to ask you, Miss Carolina."

Laney is behind her and shoves her in the back when she starts stammering. Susan swats at her sister and puts her arm around Patty's waist. "Just ask her. It'll be okay, I promise."

Patty takes a deep breath. "Miss Carolina, I want to open a used bookstore in the shop. Will you help me start it and run it?" As the words tumble out, I know this is what I want, too. Books? Work with books again?

"Yes, absolutely yes. Oh my goodness, when can we start? Can we start now? Okay, not now, the kids will be home from the beach soon. But tomorrow, right? Tomorrow we'll start. Oh my."

I turn to look at my husband who had stopped a few feet back. Sunlight floods the woods from below off the river, and from above through the spring boughs of fresh green leaves. How very close I came to throwing all this away. How close I came to leaving this place, these people. The sparkles from above and below grow and blur together.

Patty suddenly cries, "Oh, no. We can't start tomorrow. Tomorrow is Easter."

Easter. My shoulders drop in release. What a good time for new things to begin. I take the two steps back to Jackson and reach for his hand. "Yes, you're right, Patty. We can't start tomorrow. Tomorrow is Sunday and on Sunday *we* go to church."

Don't miss...

Next Stop, Chancey
Book One in the Chancey Series

Looking in your teenage daughter's purse is never a good idea.

After all, it ended up with Carolina opening a B&B for railroad buffs in a tiny Georgia mountain town. Carolina knows all about, and hates, small towns. How did she end up leaving her wonderful Atlanta suburbs behind while making her husband's dreams come true?

Unlike back home in the suburbs with privacy fences and automatic garage doors, everybody in Chancey thinks your business is their business and they all love the newest Chancey business. The B&B hosts a senate candidate, a tea for the County Fair beauty contestants, and railroad nuts who sit out by the tracks and record the sound of a train going by. Yet, nobody believes Carolina prefers the 'burbs.

Oh, yeah, and if you just ignore a ghost, will it go away?

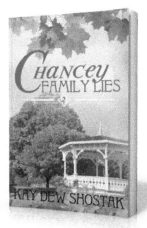

Chancey Family Lies
Book Two in the Chancey Series

Holidays are different in small towns. You're expected to cook.

Carolina is determined her first holiday season as a
stay-at-home mom will be perfect. However...

Twelve kids from college (and one nobody seems to know)
Eleven chili dinners (why do we always have to feed a crowd?)
Ten dozen fake birds (cardinals, no less)
Nine hours without power (but lots of stranded guests)
Eight angry council members (wait, where's the town's money?)
Seven trains a-blowin' (all the time. All. The. Time.)
Six weeks with relatives (six weeks?!?)
Five plotting teens (again, who is that girl?)
Four in-laws staying (and staying, and staying...)
Three dogs a-barking (who brought the dogs?)
Two big ol' secrets (and they ain't wrapped in ribbons
under the tree, either)
And the perfect season gone with the wind.

The Chancey books are available in both print and ebook on Amazon.com

You can find out more about Kay and her books
on her web-site, kaydewshostak.com

CPSIA information can be obtained
at www.ICGtesting.com
Printed in the USA
LVHW111523220119
604790LV00003B/307/P